T0312767

IF I DIDN'T CARE

GUERNICA WORLD EDITIONS 78

IF I DIDN'T CARE

Roger McKnight

GUERNICA
World
EDITIONS

TORONTO–CHICAGO–BUFFALO–LANCASTER (U.K.)
2024

Copyright © 2024, Roger McKnight and Guernica Editions Inc.
All rights reserved. The use of any part of this publication,
reproduced, transmitted in any form or by any means, electronic,
mechanical, photocopying, recording or otherwise stored
in a retrieval system, without the prior consent of the publisher
is an infringement of the copyright law.
Guernica Editions Founder: Antonio D'Alfonso

Michael Mirolla, general editor
Gary Clairman, editor
Cover design: Allen Jomoc, Jr.
Interior design: Jill Ronsley, suneditwrite.com

Guernica Editions Inc.
1241 Marble Rock Rd., Gananoque (ON), Canada K7G 2V4
2250 Military Road, Tonawanda, N.Y. 14150-6000 U.S.A.
www.guernicaeditions.com

Distributors:
Independent Publishers Group (IPG)
600 North Pulaski Road, Chicago IL 60624
University of Toronto Press Distribution (UTP)
5201 Dufferin Street, Toronto (ON), Canada M3H 5T8

First edition.
Printed in Canada.

Legal Deposit—Third Quarter
Library of Congress Catalog Card Number: 2024931042
Library and Archives Canada Cataloguing in Publication
Title: If I didn't care / Roger McKnight.
Names: McKnight, Roger, 1937- author.
Series: Guernica world editions (Series) ; 78.
Description: First edition. | Series statement: Guernica world editions ; 78
Identifiers: Canadiana (print) 20240289404 | Canadiana (ebook)
20240289730 | ISBN 9781771838962 (softcover) | ISBN 9781771838979
(EPUB)
Subjects: LCGFT: Historical fiction. | LCGFT: Novels.
Classification: LCC PS3613.C764 I3 2024 | DDC 813/.6—dc23

BOOK I

Kernels of Truth

1

Eddie Washington's mother figured family was everything, and she made it felt. "Share and share alike," MayBelle told her loved ones. "That's how we did in the Delta when pickins was slim. The sharin' spirit, you gotta have it, a special feeling from down home, brought straight to the Show-Me state. Open your heart, dear, so folks'll know where you's from."

MayBelle Washington's home wasn't really the Mississippi Delta, the chimerical River land of lore, and she didn't usually talk so strange either, except to folks that didn't know any other lingo. Riverboats and Civil War battles with gunboats and troops marching through snake-infested swamps? Sharecroppers or antebellum mansions anywhere you looked? Well, it was kinda true, that stuff. MayBelle's ancestors truly did live in the Delta once, but not her. And even if she had, she was too recent-born to remember anything from way back. Maybe she got her info second-hand from a book she picked up. Or out of stories from some aged wanderer, who remembered tales from chat-happy souls even older than the very oldest.

In short, MayBelle was a joyous soul, who knew life's hard knocks. Her talk often repeated stories about the Delta long ago, and she liked to pretend they happened to her. "They's salt of the earth, folks down there, and humane service they give, that's what comes from the humble at heart," MayBelle explained to those that would listen, which was mainly poor neighbors and her own kinfolk. "Why, once we were working outa Memphis but driving through the Delta, returning at four in the morning from Biloxi to this place that employed us in Tennessee and about to run outa gas. Fuel, you know? We pulled into a filling station on some lonely road in the pitch dark. We banged on the door. Finally we found this old gent, the manager, we had to go around to wake him from his shack out back. He's the friendliest fella rubbing sleep outa his eyes. He turned on the pumps and filled our vehicle all right, and we lucked out because white filling station owners didn't peddle gas to any folks like us, or they'd figure we stole the car and call a sheriff and we'd spend what's left of the night in a country hoosegow.

"When our boss took out travelers' vouchers for that old guy to sign on our purchase he looked at us and shook his head and we then knew he couldn't read nor write. So my boss let him make an X and we drove off into the sunrise, back to what city folks call civilized life, where they'd just as soon shoot a feller as look at him or take an X for his name."

MayBelle paused there to make sure folks were listening, like she was thinking of the kindness and violence afoot in the land, the two coexisting and never ceasing like a lesson in life.

"It's not all dirt poor down there, some are free gents givin' the best of service. There's indentured servitude, too, can't deny it," she said. "The man indentures us, and we indenture others ourself, for our self-interest, taking advantage of our fellows, if and when we can, some of us."

Anyone with a grain of sense had to guess that was only MayBelle's talk. Ancient stuff she'd maybe heard from her grand folks. Those were happenings MayBelle herself was too young ever to have experienced, like Eddie, her second son, verified from hearing her stories in different tellings and then citing much himself, verbatim like he heard it all, retold in the same wandering and repetitious way this narrative began. MayBelle surely knew a lot was made up by whoever told it first, but she wouldn't say so. A good story was always worth telling again.

2

Sure enough, MayBelle's people, the Washingtons, worked somewhere *around* the rural Delta long ago, but not as share-croppers or farm managers. They were town folk, city slickers from Natchez and Vicksburg. Eventually they worked their way up to running grocery stores in towns where real Civil War battles once happened. "Without a question," as MayBelle assured her innocent listeners, who, if they were naïve enough, could believe MayBelle herself was there a hundred years ago, if not earlier. Her kin weren't at the bottom of the social barrel, so why they eventually left home nobody in the family remembered except that social class seemed more important than race and they dreamed of climbing in the social pecking order. They became part of a flood of souls moving around back in time, like part of an endless, gigantic trek, the kind Moses or someone else in the Good Book told about. Wandering from their home and looking for a new and better one.

Restless pilgrims, black and white, started moving as soon as the Emancipation Proclamation happened. That was so long ago most folks MayBelle talked to couldn't've said what those words meant or even what year it happened.

"1836," somebody guessed, but MayBelle shook her head no.

"1863," she pronounced.

For sure, that year was intended to end their hard struggles and set some souls free, so streams of them came North, sometimes whites at the same time as all others, though it was a mystery why or how they'd come at the same time. MayBelle couldn't answer for certain. Simplest would've been to say she wasn't even a thought in anybody's mind that many ages ago, not even a sparkle in her great-grandsire's eye for that matter. Put straightforward, MayBelle made it to age 45 in '41, the year of Pearl Harbor and the Second World War.

Her ancestors had lived in St. Louis, what was called up North, for a while by the time MayBelle came on the scene, born, that is, to Ebenezer and JuneBelle Washington. It wasn't true her parents followed the River straight up from the state of Mississippi, like a casual glance at the map would lead anybody with an ounce of sense to imagine. Instead MayBelle's kin ventured to St. Louis by Greyhound Bus some time before The Great War, and that wasn't the Civil War, but the one to End All Wars, and that was "in the present century," MayBelle said, 1900-sometime or other. First early wanderers from the Delta country hit Memphis and then Sikeston, Parma, and St.-something-or-other, godforsaken holes to beat all, before at last stopping at the Gateway to the West, a direction not a soul of them followed onward to glamorous California, but they never said exactly why not.

"They were too dagblasted worn out's my best guess," MayBelle proclaimed. They felt done-in after fighting to shake off the label of unanchored traipsers, like tribes in the Old Testament. So before St. Louis they stopped in a succession of tiny burghs, one of which folks called St. Ben's. Some wanderers were Catholics but not icon worshipers, like the French that traversed those parts eons ago and gave settlements strange monikers, all named after sacred followers. Holy men and women of a strange and restless order, like Saint Benjamin and Sainte Genevieve and Saint Boniface. "Our people prospered in those weird places, when others couldn't, but we later moved on before finally reaching St. Louis," MayBelle explained. "We've been Jacks and Janes of all trades, planted gardens summertime and the men built schools and put up the wood churches over the ones the French left behind when they moved on before us. We worshipped in the churches forever and ever. But the white folk practiced benign neglect. That's what they called it. You can find it in books, if you care to read." Or can, meaning whether you ever learned how to, she thought to herself.

"Benign … whatever," some confused listener was bound to try saying.

"Benign, meaning nice and gentle-like," MayBelle repeated for them. "Killing us with kindness, so to say. It was like wrecking our hopes on purpose. You know, the white landowners, they bought cheap property and sold it for a few pennies to poor folks. They were people that moved to place after place, from areas all over the South and along the River, some from as far gone as Biloxi and the Gulf Shores, and everywhere they landed they set up thriving communities, but with some tenements, it's true, till the big shots, all white, come back and became slumlords and promoters of crowded private housing, sometimes 10 or 25 homes to a block that then fell into shacks when way too many newcomers crowded in them.

"It was communities built on sand and the investors knew it, that being their intention pure and simple. Whole settlements doomed to collapse on a dime. Like I said, all according to white folks' gentle, scheming plans. They built whole new towns then neglected them till they fell apart and then used the land for something new like bridges and high rise."

MayBelle knew that story since she heard it as a girl and never grew tired of reminding family or community about it, or letting Eddie learn it, too, and Eddie knew his kin remembered it like he did. Yet they never took MayBelle's story as preaching. They rolled their eyes as she told it time and again and her folks only half listening or labelling her as their Fabulator Supreme. Eddie being the exception. Even as a boy, he recognized the truth whenever he heard it. Like MayBelle told the family, Eddie judged men for their deeds above all else. He never went by what they said. With ladies it was different in his mind. MayBelle swore to that quality about him. The boy listened to women not for dull facts and figures, real or invented, but kernels of truth. The older he got, the more truth he found in what his mother said.

"Ever the more believable she becomes," he told others like himself.

3

"Like I tell you," MayBelle boasted with verve and enthusiasm because she believed in her folks' mission to gain equality. "Mothers of the past took pride in schools their menfolk constructed, and we had no kids that couldn't read nor write. But then the white slumlords that replaced the real estate dealers that got the land for nothing, or next to it, straight from land sharks, then they, the slumlords, overpopulated communities with our colored people and overused land areas that after a couple decades was said to be needed by City leaders for a new bridge or a ball stadium that only whites attended games at, and they tore down the neighborhood and people like us got run out of their homes. And the schools crumbled. Whole communities. Dispossessed and sent off to wander. Like in the Exodus. Forty years in Sinai or some back channel, you know?"

Oh, yes, Eddie knew. Whole communities, gone with wrecking balls. He'd seen it develop that way in his lifetime, or heard tell about it. Slave owners became landowners, whose descendants became slumlords and along the way they turned into real estate land grubbers, or even shady politicians and statesmen whose children devolved into robbers that gave land away or sold it for next-to-nothing to folks from the South, who got to occupy the formerly so empty land until the powers-that-be in City Hall wanted it back again. Then it was only a matter of City leaders flouting rules and taking back what they'd only loaned out to begin with, in a vicious circle, never telling the poor souls that got to live there a while how they were fated to be used as chattel in a newer form. Slaves to the urban dollar. Urban being St. Louis, the place MayBelle talked about and her forebears moved to.

"Racism makes it easy to bury a community," MayBelle preached to whoever listened. "Sure, rich men's kingdoms like Clayton and University City had some of us folks, tokens of tolerance, they're called, but if you read the histories Whitey writes you'd never know any of us lived there. We're invisible in their texts."

So it was, Eddie concluded from experience. He knew how the Mississippi Riverfront in St. Louis once bustled with commerce. It became a neighborhood for all creeds and colors, that is, until the powers-that-be, the very people that brainstormed and planned the project, decided to move those successful integrated folks out for a parkway and a new bridge, all for greater riches. That rigamarole started long before Eddie's day, but he was smart enough to see how things were done in his own time, the 1940s. He put two and two together and it added up to zero for his community.

Eddie also knew about attempts at mixing diverse groups in public housing. Apartment buildings sprang up, but failed. Greedy private contractors skimped on utilities, so the social funding infrastructure fell apart. When heating and lighting failed or elevators malfunctioned, hallways grew dark. Petty crime and muggings increased and families, first drawn by the attraction of affordable housing, moved out. Fewer incoming rent payments then made it necessary for the projects' managers to pay upkeep by draining reserve funds. In the end, intruders from outside crowded the formerly so quiet passageways and sex crimes and robbery grew commonplace.

As a youth, Eddie saw deterioration accentuate when the races, who were intended to live in harmony and share citizen management, began retreating to separate living areas in the buildings, thereby choosing segregation rather having it thrust on them. With failed fiscal control and poor facility management, the blocks of new housing fell into collapse. As Eddie made the rounds of the neighborhoods while still in school, he heard of people with some means blaming needy residents for housing failures. You had to feel pride in good things, as the saying went.

"That's how it is with those people, give them an inch and they'll take a mile. They destroy everything we give 'em," was the common complaint Eddie heard echoing in city neighborhoods of his youth. He carried anger inside him and felt his brother and other youngsters do the same. They needed a voice crying out on their behalf.

4

"What happens now must've gone on before, in the old days," Eddie told his mother. He'd heard talk of old Sportsman's Park baseball stadium being torn down someday and the way made for a new ball park for the Browns and Cardinals. Not a done deal, but soon, so he'd heard. "And where will that stadium go up, if not by the Riverfront, where folks like us have a lively neighborhood." They needed that space to prosper, but they'd have to leave and take to the aging ramshackle leftover buildings from the 1904 St. Louis World's Fair.

Folks of color prospered in many places, not unlike the Riverfront, until local government ran them out and built shopping empires where their homes once had stood. Left behind were only the tiny church buildings occupied from French times, which withstood the ravages of progress but lost their congregations, down to the very last soul. Eddie could imagine a time long after his own, when those temples to Christ would stand as forlorn testaments to MayBelle's older kin, the only sign of their ever existing.

"Sure there was anger about that," Eddie remembered MayBelle explaining. "Why there was one fellow in St. Louis. Thornton by name. He had a hauling truck but the authorities wouldn't allow him to park by the alleyway behind his own house, because they wanted to crowd something new in there. He took his anger all the way to the City courthouse but lost his case. He come back a second time arguing it was his own property and even produced his bill of sale, that he had purchased it and he could park there if he so chose, but the City and their judge said no dice. That Thornton gent lost every cent, even his wife and family, who just walked out on him 'cause the City foreclosed and put up cheap tenements where his house'd been. So Thornton got hisself a shotgun and went back to the courthouse and shot it up, pockmarks all over the walls. Mowed down everything in sight. Some bystanders died, and so that gent, Thornton, lost everything. Like I said, including his freedom. Life in the pen with no parole. There he may languish still, serving time for others' greed."

Eddie heard Thornton's story from other folks, too, without deciding whether to believe it, at least not all of it. True, something like that probably happened once, but whether the gent's name was really Thornton, or if he was just a thorn in the City Fathers' side, as per his name, well, that was up for debate, just like the question of whether this real-life Thornton, not the man of myth, had a family or a job and a personal history. Maybe that didn't matter, he was just an invisible colored man, except that the surname Thornton got to be part of lore. No one ever claimed they knew him or his kin in real life. But he stood for something, and that was human dignity. Folks talked about him and his memory lived on.

Eddie wondered if a colored man pulled the trigger in the courthouse at all. Coulda been any loafer hanging out on a street corner with only a bottle to nurture, or the fuzz theirself maybe they did the deed. As some street folk reasoned, the police planned the fireworks and lied about Thornton or invented that name to cover up details and hide the horror of their own deeds and what it could cost the lying cops if their actions came out in public. *It* being to see their name disgracefully appear in the newspaper and community tabloids. They'd risk losing what the establishment called carrying a good rep and pretending that having a good name was their greatest prize, when money was all they cared a lick about.

"The horrors were legion," MayBelle let everybody know. "More of our people kept comin' up from the South and settled in rinky-dink places nobody ever heard of, like Tulsa in Okie land, before the oil boom, which was nothin' then but ramshackle huts and tents ready to sink in the mud. Add to that the south end of Chicago that'd been most wetland and festering with swamp fever before it became farm fields. It all kinda skyrocketed after War World I. Folks from the Delta told of riding in the back of rickety buses the whole way to St. Louis, or on the trains, where conductors put coloreds in smoky compartments. Jim Crow coaches, they called them. Dirty windows and filthy floors, right behind the puffing locomotive, so they got covered with black soot that ruined their clothes and made it hard to breathe. Once up North, our people lived in horrible places with no running water or toilets. Here in St. Louis, that was in buildings left over from the gala World's Fair of 1904, like I keep telling folks about but nobody believes.

"But souls came this far North and wouldn't stop. They started campaigns for jobs, like *Don't buy where you can't work.* That was used against white businesses, and it worked. More men got employed. Then some of these folks started businesses themselves. In Chicago, I heard, it was in a neighborhood called Bronzeville. Ordinary people owned and ran everything from hotels and restaurants to sanitariums and funeral homes for their own kind. I never heard of any neighborhood like that in St. Louis, but I bet some existed on The Hill.

"After 1918, white fellows started comin' home from the front in Europe. They found colored gents, that stayed home from the war because the Army didn't want 'em in the trenches next to white troops, had got a foothold in the job market. While the white guys's'd been living through hell in World War I, some of our people even started businesses at home and talked about making big investments and getting ahead in life.

"It fueled white guyses' hatred to see fellows that were the sons of sharecroppers wearing fancy suits and ties and driving new autos while guys been on the front in France givin' their best for freedom, or the white guys themselves had even been next to making the final sacrifice in the trenches or surviving with trench mouth, and now they came back home and couldn't afford a cup a' joe. Or couldn't even find a job that'd start them on the road to having dough after they'd been slogging around and freezing as the Germans fired cannon balls at them from every angle."

5

MayBelle knew stories from far and wide, but her audience became more and more her own family members, near or distant. There was no end to the man's lies about how he suffered at the hands of those below him, she continued. How men blamed their own ills on colored folk or the poor Georgia crackers down South.

Added to MayBelle's storytelling quality was how she yearned and learned to be in one place and stay put. "Planting your roots," as she put it. Of course, that stay-at-home mindset wasn't true of everyone in her circle or of what they did in reality either, and she hadn't always been that way herself. Nothing was etched in stone for MayBelle, "as unchangeable granite." Things were either shifting like sand or "fast and focused," the way she liked to talk. She had "moving-about" present in her blood, but that changed a little. Way back in time, as she also repeated till kingdom come, which it never seemed to do, MayBelle Washington's ancestors had settled in St. Louis. And MayBelle was born right on The Hill, one of the city's best-known areas, but not its richest. She grew to be "at home with it," and seemed destined never to stray. But be and seem were not always the same.

No, no sense in moving to swanky white folks' towns like Ladue or Clayton or even across Eads Bridge and live among poor folks from East St. Louis, who were slipping backwards on the job market super-fast. MayBelle swore one of those places was just as detestable as another. The rich folk in Clayton, where she'd never yet set foot but could guess at from a distance, remained trapped in their greed on one hand and surrounded by the grinding ways of the poor on all other hands. The secret to good living, MayBelle knew, was settling down but not getting hemmed in, which was a danger easily avoided on The Hill long as good folks mixed with others just as purehearted as them.

That's how it was till some of MayBelle's people worked up a smidgin of social standing and got uppity. They spread across the metro searching for racial equality, or some ill-defined, dreamed-of social and financial fulfillment, which didn't exist yet and maybe never would. Just a phantom longing. Being privileged like Whitey was a miraculous utopian dream that always went dys—. Dysfunctional. Dystopian.

Integration wasn't about to work, but lucky for them that found surprisingly good jobs in the face of disappointment, like Postal clerking or bus driving, with paychecks and a municipal pension, which made life bearable for those content to hobnob with Mammon alone. A few souls were enterprising enough to start small businesses, like MayBelle's uncle Saul, a mechanic so light-skinned white men trusted their car motors to him and a great job he did, too. Or you could consider Aunt Jessie, who opened a salon where she colored black hair blonde and tried combing it straight. She did it great, maybe, you could decide yourself, but she raked in dough either way, and legal tender every cent.

Then there was Uncle Abner. He became the personal chauffeur for old Herr Hudkolf, the head honcho at Bock Beer brewery. For Abner, driving the main man around in his limousine was a sign of both privilege and subservience. Abner learned to keep his chauffeur's cap near at hand when driving his own fine car as well. If the cops stopped him, Abner showed the cap and claimed the car belonged to his boss, an honorable white gentleman. The cops respected that explanation, bowing and scraping without ever suspecting they were being taken for a ride, in a manner of speaking, by a humble colored gent.

New housing developments sprang up, with churches and high schools to serve them. Prosperous described the folks living there, but prosperity wasn't enough. No, not even in good times did it stop city builders from manipulating residential land and property for a new entertainment palace or some such nonsense.

So common folk packed up, yet again! Even those who seemed least hemmed in left, and the exodus continued. Some folks struck out on their own while others stuck together in spirit but sank materially into a despair that filtered down from old to young.

MayBelle herself finally abandoned the stay-at-home status she'd stood as a flag waver for. After her husband, an immigrant Santo Domingo hombre named Carlos, rode off into the sunset or died, whichever his fate might've been, MayBelle moved to Richmond Heights, a newer inner-ring community, with an ethnic and racial mix, and from there she rode the city buses back and forth, sometimes to Forest Park Amusement Circus and its Zoo or to an amusement area like Chain of Rocks or Delmar Gardens.

In all those places she peddled gimcracks and Gateway-to-the-West mementos and made a killing on them, which some claimed no colored lady could do, or anybody at all for that matter. No white folk, it was whispered, would even think of stooping down to the black people's level and taking a chance on losing out where MayBelle succeeded. Or, heaven forbid, what white man or woman would be so foolish as to risk falling off the high cliff at Chain of Rocks and landing in the Mississippi to drown? Or getting thrown off the precipice by a stray mugger? It could happen, as everybody knew, but MayBelle braved the dangers and made a go of it.

MayBelle took a risk, in short, and her new-found affluence, driven by memento sales, gave her the incentive to spread her energy to poor communities and congregations she passed by or sometimes visited. With her gift for gab, she started self-help groups for the unemployed of her race and a few humble white folk, who had a lot in common and once in a blue moon could band together against the super-rich, that MayBelle saw as their true exploiters.

Vicksburg in Mississippi hadn't been pure country. Folks there had some city savvy a century earlier, and the Washington family learned to follow the wise way with a dollar. They carried those smarts with them to the North and the Free State of Missouri, so purported. In St. Louis, MayBelle showed how to make something out of nothing. She turned the mementos and doodads into cash, which she never bothered to stash under any mattress at home. Each month she strode into the People's Finance Corporation, which in the 1920s started loaning mortgage money to Negroes and opening accounts for them. She carried cold cash with her on every visit and watched her poverty turn, one deposit at a time, into Croesus-like mounds of worldly security. That happened as People's Finance spread to cities like Detroit and Cleveland, so she became an ever so humble stockholder in a nationwide banking enterprise. At the same time, as a community volunteer she helped those less energetic than her get a humble start at buying and selling.

"Stickin' together as one," MayBelle repeated. "That be us, the Washingtons, a proud tribe special that way. Open your heart, dear, and show what you's made of. Family first."

6

Exactly when this migrating to north of the Mason Dixon Line and then from place to place really started among the relatives, meaning MayBelle Washington's family, and where all the stops were along the way, that was something Eddie couldn't say, but placing the beginning at sometime around the Great War, like his mother MayBelle argued, sounded sure enough like the early 1920s or before. Eddie coulda been alive then, but he'd have needed to be a kid in those days. Even as a young man, he thought those times sounded like remembrances from a far earlier universe.

Yet his ma was a clever lady. She had a couple years' study at teacher's college. Some place or other. No matter where. At least MayBelle had more book learning than her neighbors in Richmond Heights. In his youth Eddie couldn't have pinpointed the college she attended any more than he could describe with exactitude the elapsed decades in their family history. Asked to say where she studied, Eddie only answered "some place down South." That was his stab in the dark. Not the Mississippi Delta, he knew that much. The school was in truth Peabody, as he learned later, but neither Eddie nor his kinfolk had an inkling where that could be until they learned about it, also later in life. MayBelle said little about the place, which surely indicated she didn't like it much when she was there. She'd never been that quiet about anything else in her life, that was for sure.

Whatever the case, in order to get some education MayBelle had turned South from St. Louis in her younger days, for reasons nobody knew but her, and she never talked about it one way or another to folks in her family. When her parents Ebenezer and JuneBelle passed on, the nearest and dearest next-of-kin weren't on the spot any more to boast of MayBelle's serious study or lament their own sacrifices to pay for it

After Peabody, MayBelle taught school kids in Nashville. Looking back on her life as Eddie understood it, he reckoned that was before she married Carlos, who was from some town in the Dominican Republic, a colored gent of slave ancestry. Eddie's dad spoke Spanish and claimed he arrived in Nashville to study engineering, or was it Law? Finally, MayBelle brought Carlos to St. Louis with her. It wasn't really The Hill in St. Louis, a well-known ethnic neighborhood, that her hubby later "lit out for the territories" from and abandoned the family, as MayBelle described Carlos's flight to California or wherever he went. Eddie had a lot to learn about his mysterious father, and it wasn't until he himself went to college that he discovered his mother borrowed "lit out for the territories" from Mark Twain when he himself ran off West to escape fighting in the Civil War. Twain was known as Samuel Clemens, another privileged guy looking out for his own skin, or so Eddie learned from his college texts.

Or was it back to Santo Domingo in the Caribbean, whatever place that was, which Carlos headed for? If so, strange he'd head west to go east. Anyhow, Carlos eventually lit out for somewhere and left MayBelle alone, after they'd struggled to make ends meet, and she had their two sons, Charles and Eddie, to support and care for.

Now, back to speaking of The Hill, by the time Carlos flew the coop MayBelle had moved from there lock, stock, and barrel and settled in Richmond Heights. There she became a settled home-owner in her own right.

Way back when, MayBelle Washington's folks had lived in a St. Louis of mixed creeds and colors. In fact, some nosey neighbors spread rumors galore, and MayBelle's people were the subjects of some of them. There was this tale that said a n'er-do-well carpet-bagger roamed the Deep South after the War Between the States and around the time of The Great War and snuck into a haystack with MayBelle's granny or great granny Alice, not just once, it was claimed, but once too often. Maybe the gossipers' chronology was fuzzy, but they swore the truth was that Alice, who bore a baby as brown as all the others in the former Vicksburg family, had been head over heels in love with that wanderer and shyster and him being white as a slab of chalk but probably had Negro blood, too, only that he wouldn't talk about it, he just showed his true colors, so to speak, by the kind of flimflam fellows he ran with or the unsuspecting ladies he took advantage of and laid down to rest by in the dark of night, if a fellow got down to the nitty gritty of it. There were strange happenings all around. To her credit, MayBelle talked about them all and did her best to sort out the various folks, one from another, and their goings-on as well. MayBelle brought new bits of info out in broad daylight, some for the better, others for the worst.

7

Anyway, despite her tales about growing up "down home" in Mississippi and knowing that area like the back of her hand, MayBelle was born to a restless clan right in St. Louis. As folks said, she was "at home with it," meaning belonging in St. Louis not Mississippi, and she seemed destined never to stray. No, not to swanky white folks' hideouts like the suburbs. Over and over MayBelle swore how one of those glitzy places was just as desecrated a dungeon as another. The rich people in Clayton, where she'd never yet set foot but could "guess about from a distance," were folks trapped in greed, while the starving poor on the Illinois side were pinned in by the River to the west and endless scrublands to the east. As she also repeated again and again, the secret to good living was not getting backed in any corner, which didn't happen as long as gentle folks mixed together and understood each other.

Taking her time, MayBelle further improved her lot in Richmond Heights, an emerging community and not too big. Getting the longed-for home loan from People's Finance was a big break. From then on she continued riding city buses, peddling doodads, and making a killing. She had a notion about how to make something out of nothing, so she set about doing it alone. A husband could come and go, until at last he packed up and sauntered off for good one fine day. The last MayBelle and her two boys saw of Carlos, her man and their father, was at a train stop, where he spoke of going back to Santo Domingo, but pointed off into the far undefined distance. Those words sounded strange to MayBelle and the boys, but she kept them tucked away thinking Carlos merely was a failure at geography.

After Carlos left, joy lessened in the Washingtons' household. First to fade was the spontaneous glee MayBelle found in life. True, her laughter still reverberated through the house and she talked a loud stream to all who liked listening to her tales. Yet her words about their forebears' great migration northwards from Mississippi came to sound programmed, and her usual trust-me-I-was-there attitude faded. She complained more of endless injustices than she championed her people's march toward equal social standing.

"Sounds like a lament," the youthful Eddie said to his brother as she belabored them with new stories of discrimination.

"Or a rant," big brother Charles replied. "She harps on new themes with an old refrain. Your average yokel can only stand so much doomsday talk." Harp as MayBelle might, nobody claimed her themes were wrong-minded, but sometimes unbearably sobering after Carlos left.

Then arose a second lessening, that is, her hope for financial help from a hubby. Without Carlos, MayBelle experienced a reversal in her life roles. Suddenly she was the family's sole breadwinner. Being a single mom turned her into a decisive, manly figure of sorts. From home, she paid for herself and her sons without fail, like what folks normally expected from a responsible man of the family, and in public her years at college made her the most talkative person in bargaining souvenir prices with customers and also the best educated individual in any such crowd. Though a lowly peddler woman wasn't expected to use big words and keep abreast of current events, MayBelle followed the news and seldom failed to better tourists in analyzing the latest world events. She became an oracle to many who presumed themselves her social superior.

Yet in conversations with those closest to her heart, MayBelle preferred talking about Carlos and why he disappeared. "By the time my man left, the honeymoon was long over," she declared to kin but vowed to tell them no more, "except that he did bother to marry me, honest-like before a real preacher."

Slowly the news leaked out. As she gradually broke her vow about secrecy and told lady friends about her doings in Nashville, the truth appeared that she and her man had met while they lived in the same boarding house near Peabody while she tried her hand at practice teaching in a small Tennessee town nearby.

They were an unlikely pair. Neither fully understood the other's language, and so they communicated "on other levels," as MayBelle put it with a wink at her lady friends. Added to that, the absence of warm Caribbean breezes frustrated Carlos, and MayBelle complained when he confused her words about the Mississippi Delta with the Delta Queen, a floating gambling casino trafficking the Mississippi. Carlos came all the way from his island world and studied engineering after abandoning Law, or the other way around. MayBelle didn't rightly recall how his studies developed and never tried too hard to figure them out. What she never forgot and couldn't forgive was, he found no steady job after graduation because of faulty English.

"If he did ever graduate?" one lady in the family asked carefully.

"You can be great at calculating distances and constructions, but it's no good if you can't pinpoint your needs," MayBelle explained to listening ladies. "My man found that out the hard way. I hope he remembered."

MayBelle had tried her darndest to help Carlos with the new language, first through a tutoring job she had outside school classes in Tennessee and later in private lessons at their boarding house. In the process she discovered his dashing good looks. Long black hair and a full beard accentuated his casual stride and tall, muscular frame. A toothy smile appeared when he was sober. To MayBelle, Carlos seemed a statuesque Zeus of olden times.

Despite their hardship, a powerful passion bound MayBelle and Carlos. During various delicious intervals they appeared perfectly matched. If only he'd shared her dutiful habits, hard work might've paved their conjugal journey with gold and "blessed us with bliss," like MayBelle liked to say.

"Carlos talked nice and was good to me and I got in a family way," she explained to neighbor ladies. "But once here in St. Louis and we were hitched legal-like no technical job popped up for him. Bosses understood little of what he said. He only got to clerking in a grocery store and money became our issue. Big time. Low salary and there we were, me with my belly growing and wanting nutrition for the baby. I said we had to have more food and stuff and we argued. Big time. Sometimes all day, then we loved after dark."

She interspersed that spiel with occasional relapses into silence, waiting for the effect to take hold on her listeners, who were waiting for the truth to settle in. Their experiences varied but weren't always so terribly different from MayBelle's own.

A starving baby in its mother's womb was heavy stuff, which made ladies squirm when MayBelle told about those days. Sometimes she told the story more than once, but nobody tried voicing her over. They only waited in silence, imagining the baby's distress and wondering what would happen next, till MayBelle began fabulating—or speaking—again. As a boy, Eddie sneaked in on those coteries and listened to them discussing topics his Sex Ed teachers in school never dared touch on.

"My man was a player, as a habit. Sometimes I think as an addiction. Large, whatever the cause. At horses, I mean. The more we argued about dough the more of it he threw away at gambling. Always on fillies. So everything he made at the store disappeared. On ponies. Nags. Stallions. Mares. That was one bunch of terms he knew in English perfect, he mastered every word possible for a lousy equine. Perfect diction. And then when the baby came we didn't have money for food, but he helped me name him, our firstborn, a boy baby, I mean, not any stupid stallion. Sometimes I asked if he wanted a foal or a son. No, ma'am, he never answered me or maybe didn't understand the word.

"Carlos. That's what he wanted the boy to be named, Carlos, a good Spanish name, just like his, but I stuck with Charles and that's what I mainly got from him, a first chile with a real Christian name, meaning Carlos in English, but no help with anything else, that man never changed a single diaper. And then when I was nursing he hurt me in bed, or started chasin' after other ladies when I said no to that form of horse play. Lord knows, there's plenty of that loose kind, floozies, gigolos, men and women alike. Ridin' those fillies, that was Carlos's big deal.

"That's when I asked him to leave, which he did, but he came back now and again, each time enveloped in a cloud of booze and difficulty talking, but able to give me Eddie on one stopover. Child number two, and no fuss about a name now. Edward. Named after Eduardo, a distant great, great something or other, a patriarch from down home."

8

L eft with two sons to raise, MayBelle did her best. Her older
boy Charles was a mystery, but maybe he caused that himself
or got it from his dad in the umbilical cord. Big brother was
smart and perceptive enough to see that his mom raving—or was
she ranting?—about his dad Carlos made both Ma and Pa seem a
bit nuts to the world around them. Clearly nothing Charles saw or
heard at home made any good sense to him, but he never let on in
any tactile way, he just never touched in talk on what he didn't have
to. Not a boy to waste words.

To her younger son Eddie, MayBelle's actions could appear a
contradiction in terms, but he studied his mother and brother and
gave them both the benefit of the doubt, though he never figured
out what benefit there was to a doubt. Eddie did let on about things
he saw by speaking up more often at home than his brother. How
MayBelle felt about that tendency of his, Eddie never fully understood, mother of his though she was. MayBelle observed people
and talked. Charles studied the world around him but kept his own
counsel. Eddie himself talked much, if he must. He thought even
more and had a special flair for fancy cars.

Well, no matter. Theirs was a world in motion. What Charles
thought about most things that came his way was a mystery to
Eddie, partly because Charles was a few years older than his brother,
which caused some discussion on the sly among the relatives about
the paternity of MayBelle's sons. No matter in which direction
Carlos headed on this or that train outa town, hadn't MayBelle's
man been gone a precious long time before MayBelle showed she

was pregnant with Eddie, like some ladies in the family couldn't help whispering? Strange things happened, the women said they knew for a fact, when a young woman at MayBelle's fertile age was left too long living by her lonesome and her man off on his jaunts, following the fillies.

MayBelle herself limited her talk, or you could say expanded it, to broader topics than speculating about who fathered who. "We's family, yes," she said, but she meant more than the core group of ma, pa, and offspring. She included the whole grouping of brothers and sisters of their race around the States and the world as well. Good colored folk spread out across the continents to find peace, but wherever they went they met the same devilish demons in white Sunday-go-to-meetin' duds and even paler skin. So MayBelle forbade relatives to cast about with naughty talk about her two brown-skinned sons and her choice of where they went off to school or, for that matter, where Carlos, her browner-skinned Santo Domingo man, hightailed it off to in the end. Or was it the end? He'd gone off more than once but always came back. Wait and see, was the word she spread to wagging tongues. Like it was a tale to hear, then wait and see how it ended. Another life lesson.

"The way I said." MayBelle could continue any conversation, no matter where it began. And that habit, as Eddie discovered, was his mother's way of not only changing to a new topic but also switching it to something essential. "After the Great War, folks came flooding up from the South. To places that weren't anything. In 1921 Tulsa was just an oily hole in Oklahoma and black folks came there and started building it into a real city, but it was the old story. Folks couldn't bear to think how others they felt weren't as good as them could get ahead in life. It was petroleum, you see, and the saying was the black stuff rushed to black folks and stuck to 'em and like mad was making them rich beyond anybody's, meaning any white body's, wildest dreams, something the man couldn't stand to see.

"So Whitey staged a massacre and called it an uprising *against* them not *by* them. Folks burned the whole town of Tulsa down.

Flames roared sky high. They slaughtered coloreds by the hundreds and left their bodies laying in the street. Festering in the sun."

If MayBelle's listeners stopped to figure that *f-* word out, wondering if it was what they thought, *fester,* which was bad, or maybe *fiesta,* which was good? Just how did she mean it about human folk? "*Fester, fiesta,* or could it be *faster?*" somebody might ask while scratching their head in puzzlement.

"I mean rot, in the heat of midday, plain old die and get putrid on the hard road, like a dead deer, and ate up by maggots worse than road kill," MayBelle could answer. "Baked like in an oven. Humans dying in plain sight. Murdered by men, without conscience!"

Unable to fathom such scenes, though they may have witnessed similar or worse happenings themselves on streets of their own towns, which Whitey's lips afterwards remained sealed about, silent, in other words, about misdeeds they themselves committed, MayBelle's poor puzzled listeners could then ask, "Dead? Like vermin, you say? You mean people like us treated like animals on the highway? Or the rampaging men brought in airplanes from the oilfields and bombarded our people, then dumped dead folks in mass graves in the middle of the city? A blood curdling scene."

Silence set in at the same bewilderingly slow pace as the bleak acceptance of human brutality. Only slowly did bitter reality take form in listeners' minds. Hearing no man speak words of truth, MayBelle did so herself.

"Four hundred years since the first slave ships reached these shores. Four hundred! Only we can stop it!" she insisted. "Wake up! They took the chains off our legs and wrapped them around our minds." She hoped someone was listening.

9

MayBelle paused to let her message settle in and floor listeners with the truth, but Eddie understood there was more to it. His ma wanted listeners to understand she got stories straight from the horse's mouth. Her knowing about the rampage in Tulsa, now over 20 years past, meant she'd heard older white guys brag about their deeds back in Oklahoma as she worked the touristy streets of St. Louis. Also, colored folks that lived through a massacre one place told others in distant places about it, so the news spread through black communities, not to the beat of jungle drums or voodoo chants from witch doctors, like white folks imagined, but to the beat of the tellers' and listeners' own hearts. As MayBelle knew and Eddie began to understand, the Tulsa horror of 1921 avoided mainstream consciousness but etched out its own private primeval space in his people's memory. As a kid, Eddie figured Charles grasped the truth, too, but he kept his outrage to himself, where it simmered and grew by slow degrees.

MayBelle imagined the horror of it so intensely she had to stop now and again to gather herself and image forth again the awful sight of dead and dying human souls, maltreated and dispensed of like beasts of the field, now littering the pavement, or the screams of those burning alive in ramshackle huts set aflame by rampaging men, sleeping people unsafe in their own homes. The brutality of the 1921 Tulsa Riot, as white people called it if they named it anything at all, never came out in public because city newspapers and the mayor's office pretended it never happened and the Caucasian public went along with the silent sham, content to live in convoluted harmony with their twisted dream life.

"But I been among folks that seen it," MayBelle explained. "One old lady, still alive and staying here, not in Oklahoma anymore, she says she was in Tulsa then and saw black bodies rolling on the ground and dumped in the streets from trucks like loads of trash or dead fish dumped back in the sea. Men shot down. And Whitey pulling the trigger with a smile on his face or dancing in glee. Their mission fulfilled, like they told it to others."

MayBelle paused for effect again, then said, "Got me one! Whoopee!"

"And nobody knows about that?"

Such were the half-disbelieving questions from folks of all backgrounds, not the least being white men and women, who heard MayBelle and could co-exist with such evil and never think of it as real. Maybe some even committed the crimes in question but lived to deny them.

"If you can't touch it, you'll never feel it. That's right, brothers and sisters, but someday it'll come and be exposed, the cruelty and hate. And what was to come in other places, too, like Chicago and East St. Louis? Yes, that's right. Just across the River in our own backyard. I heard about that rampage there. W. E. B. DuBois spoke out about it way back in New York City, and he spread the word. Shameful things happen and we're invisible spectators, but there are those like him that knows and won't stay quiet. My hero. W. E. B."

10

MayBelle recounted tales she'd heard from East St. Louis, where City employees stuck weapons in the hands of hordes and hooligans to roam the streets and murder men and leave their bodies to smolder in the burning houses of the dead men's neighbors, as a lesson for those still alive to stay back, or toss the corpses out to packs of scavenging wild dogs, that were slowly taking over areas evicted poor people abandoned but desperate whites of the stubbornest stamp had not yet filtered into.

Those MayBelle stories came from so close to home Eddie saw the truth in them, and on drives by East St. Louis he'd glimpsed the charred remains of buildings from more than twenty years before. Poor folks viewed the ruins and remembered the killings, but talked about them with friends and neighbors behind closed doors or within secretive groups whose talk seldom trickled out to the world-at-large.

MayBelle had other stories that ended with question marks. They were wild, like the one about strange ladies of immense power, that escaped from slave areas and went to live in societies of their own, isolated from the world, and only keeping men for studs. And the women warriors of times past who held men captive, so one giant fellow fathered 280 babies for a single ladies' commune.

"Like a lone stallion out at stud," MayBelle explained. "Sly Jezebels and temptresses may have existed in Old Testament or Mythic times, but in the here-and-now it's gents causing all the ruckus we see in the world. The powers-that-be are men enslaving other men."

Some folks thought MayBelle hated men, but she told Eddie when he was growing up how she didn't hate anyone for the balls he had or was missing, not that she used those very words, but every soul had a special use in life. Some guys' usage was limited to one or two things, she argued, and those were waging war and making babies, even if they never bothered to scratch their heads in wonderment over why or how they did either one. Of course, Eddie figured that stud farm idea never really happened in any modern era, if at all, except as a theory in some ladies' lovely dreams or during their equally horrible nightmares, perhaps even as part of some inflamed male author's phantasmagoria.

"It's just me," MayBelle said. "I make a point with every tale, like a moral if you know what I mean, and it's pretty much always the same, about ladies keeping peace and controlling lawless gents."

Eddie remembered every bit of what he heard, including stuff he didn't like, and what he remembered best was her goriest tales, like killings in broad daylight and whole townships in Chicago and East St. Louis set alight by the criminals elected by voters to protect them all. In her wildest stories volunteer fire departments loved seeing flames grow higher and sometimes there were hoodlums paid to take the volunteers' place and set buildings to the torch. When at college later on, Eddie came to learn the intricacies of joining theory with practice, such as in tales that illustrated how to plan a genocidal act and then develop the workaday skills to put it into practice. Maybe, he guessed, Machiavelli was the archetype for that manner of evil, scheming man?

"Someday," MayBelle told him, "you'll need to read *The Prince* and find out if that's what Machiavelli really argued."

"I write it off as urban legends, pure and simple," Eddie responded. "I trust what I see men do, not squalid stories to rile folks up believing the worst. And without evidence."

Most suspicious in MayBelle's tales was what she said about white responses to the problems in Tulsa. Eddie knew about guys of all colors that headed for Oklahoma to work in the oil fields.

And there they saw a clean, tidy town growing like mad and getting rich on black gold. Those that had a few smarts returned with greenbacks galore and stashed their earnings away or spent them on spiffy clothes, to prove their worth as real men, equal among all others, surviving the Depression and civil conflicts and feeling they were coming out ahead in life over the long haul, if they were lucky enough to survive prejudice afoot in the land.

About young Negro men's foolishness and pride MayBelle was never silent. They were big brother Charles's age and loved tasting the sweet sap of "arriving" in modern America, but the arm of Establishment law would catch up to every last one if they tried making themselves look big in Whitey's world. Best for colored folks to stick close to friends and family and take care of their own, she argued. Self-pride would lead them to equality.

"Tuck your coins away safe n' sound, and stick with your friends at home," MayBelle advised anyone within hearing distance. "My yes, from down home don't I know all about distant places and to suspect or trust people from experience. Runnin' with strangers gets a gent nowhere. A gal neither."

Eddie listened and remembered his mother's words, but he hardly got further in the process of figuring his place in the community than wondering about her expression "from down home." If home wasn't where they were, where could it be? And what did it mean to be there? Or away from there? He'd heard that Whitey once put up a segregation fence for Negroes in nearby Ferguson, Missouri, which they locked every night at seven to keep colored people, who worked there as domestics by day, from staying in town overnight. And in Detroit, he'd heard, the city fathers erected an eight-foot high wall to separate Negroes from the city's white neighborhood.

Eddie wondered how it felt, to be locked out of a neighborhood you were specifically paid to keep clean or should have access to as a citizen? Surely the whites in a racially mixed city said something ambiguous if they chose to close themselves off through long dark urban nights from a race of detested people they still trusted enough to offer employment to by day. In Richmond Heights, he felt free to come and go as he pleased, at least within the realm of white men's reasoning.

11

When Charles was 15, MayBelle sent him to Sumner High School, which meant he had a nine-mile daily commute by City bus. Sumner was the oldest Negro high school in the city, founded back in the previous century. In his classes Charles proved to be "sharp as a double-edged dagger," to use MayBelle's term. He knew about the world around him and was keeping track of dangers from Hitler and Nazi Germany way before grown-ups in MayBelle's circle of friends caught on to that form of evil, though they knew of plenty other kinds closer to home and were constantly on the run from them, like KKK and that feller Jim Crow that they heard all about like they'd met him in person. He stayed invisible and untouchable though ever-present and very possible to meet up with when least expected.

Charles was a gifted athlete, who took to any sport as if born to it. Yet he had a way of staying out late at night as a teen and ignoring what his ma said. He was never lacking in respect toward her, but she wondered what he was up to. Nothing criminal, she knew, but dangers of many sorts were there when a colored youth thought faster and knew more than his jealous elders. Luckily, he seldom acted on impulse.

"He's darn swift upstairs," MayBelle liked to say of her Charles and he proved just as lightning fast on the track when he won Mizzou State titles in the 100-yard and 220 sprints and relay races for Sumner High in the Missouri Negro Interscholastic Association. Coaches of both races agreed he'd surely have won against white runners as well, but black and white never mixed at the school level in track and field. Comparing times of colored and white runners met with conflict when influential white coaches claimed Negro schools kept inaccurate records. Or their athletes and coaches cheated by clocking boys running with the wind, as it was argued.

Charles and Eddie's mother could be firm in giving support for individuals that needed it, or were victims of coaches fudging on track times. She was especially vocal in supporting her sons or their compatriots, but she had to know who the persons were before she opened her heart to them. She demanded youngsters learn to recognize and steer clear of whatever harebrained schemes the world threw their way.

"Like we're doctoring our stop watches?" Charles asked with a chuckle. "You think we do it or it's done to us? Which, Ma?"

"You watch your mouth, boy," his mother answered, with a disguised smile to temper her unfeigned seriousness. She winked her younger son's way at the same moment.

And so, as Eddie came to realize, MayBelle set out to do the best by her boys. Not the least was seeing Charles and Eddie got some serious academic credits to their name. With the fervent intent of realizing that dream, she sent Charles off to Tougaloo College in Mississippi when he was just short of 19. For his part, Eddie loved the idea of educating himself through self-study or in class, either way, but he never knew about Charles and whether he'd like Tougaloo or not. Choosing that school or singing its praises, as MayBelle did, when nobody in Richmond Heights or Sumner High had heard of it, felt wrongheaded to Eddie, geographically as academically. Was this Charles's college of choice or his mother's?

In other words, MayBelle sent her older boy back South to Mississippi, the very state her family early on left by heading Northward. She apparently expected Charles to learn what he needed from taking courses at the college his mother sent him to and paid for. Tougaloo wasn't necessarily in accordance with the young man's wishes or in a geographical direction he thought made any sense, but she didn't seem to ask his view on the topic, at least as far as Eddie could tell. And Charles never volunteered what his aims or ambitions were.

Tougaloo College was MayBelle's proving ground with Charles, and she broke her own rule about sticking close to home when she sent him so far away. There was no Federal aid for Negro colleges that she could find, so she decided to foot the tuition bill herself with withdrawals from People's Finance. Eddie stood by his mother at the bus station in St. Louis one late summer day when she sent Charles off toward the South. The youngster slouched at the back of a crowded bus while his mother and brother waved him off. The bus left St. Louis's Trailways terminal in a great cloud of exhaust. Eddie wondered if his brother's unsmiling expression spoke so eloquently of bravery or bewilderment.

"Maybe both?" he asked MayBelle when the bus was out of sight. He assumed she understood what he meant.

"That boy'll always get along," she replied.

"Why's that?"

"He's got the tools."

Tougaloo was small and Christian. It offered counseling for youth undecided on their direction in life. About the college's noble mission MayBelle was certain. How could an institution founded by brothers from the Church of Christ not provide the kind guidance needed in a Middle America wearing blinders? She sent Charles there to find his own answers, certain they'd be part of a lasting and positive heritage.

A lack of direction was what MayBelle feared most. Nobody in her family had gone astray yet, meaning the male waywardness mothers feared. That type of wandering was absent until Carlos came along and Charles showed tendencies to remain self-contained and reserved unless a topic interested him. MayBelle wondered if his ways ran in the blood from his father or were learned by observing Carlos's habits. In truth, the boy didn't have many years to observe his parents together. After Carlos left, MayBelle hardly spoke his name in full, Carlos Enrique it was, and the relatives soon conveniently forgot it.

They, the two, MayBelle and Carlos, came to St. Louis after she gave up teaching in Nashville and was four months pregnant.

"My parents drifted apart after I saw the light of day, hooch and horses at the root of it," Eddie told a buddy after Charles left for college.

He got it right. MayBelle and Carlos didn't bother to argue anymore. Finally, Carlos left, more than once, in fact, and finally for good, never saying where to with any exactness. Traces of him faded, except for a distant gaze Charles gave off and on, remindful of his father's. It spoke of something missing, the gaze a teenage track star might have about the time he won his town the race and all cheered him on, except for a beloved but absent father.

"And so my Charles grew up wondering about his dad, long gone. Out of sight, out of mind never was true for Charles, he remembered what happened and never forgot the sorrow of parting," MayBelle said. "And there was Eddie, too, but different. He studied his big brother like a book, because Charles was old enough to really know his dad. He grew up puzzled why the old man disappeared. To Eddie, Carlos was but a shadow coming in night-time dreams but leaving by morning light as apparitions dissolved. That figure from the dream world never expressed a thought about who he'd meet up with or what he'd come to in the end. My boys grew up with two fathers in one. For the older boy he remained a mysterious man of flesh and blood, for the younger a fleeting phantom."

Even while Carlos was home, Eddie wondered most about Charles, his substitute father figure in bodily form. Charles was mysterious of mind but physically there, giving off only hints about what could become of him. He dissolved into the morning light on the way to school but returned home at evening-time as a real live big brother. Eddie remembered that sight from the time when he was still of pre-school age.

When the boys grew up, MayBelle got Charles admitted to the college of her choice and paid tuition, which came with a modest scholarship. Tougaloo was only 900 students, which to her thinking seemed a family in its own way. She assumed it would nurture

Charles's soul and reward his study habits while letting him bask in glory on the track, outrunning everybody else. Sure enough, Charles made the college track and field team trouble-free, but why MayBelle chose a school back down in Mississippi remained a mystery to all who knew her. As the relatives repeated, that's where her kin left from so long ago not wanting the New Slavery of Reconstruction.

MayBelle's misguided intention, folks whispered, was that the young man would find a true personal direction in life down South, distanced from footloose and fancy-free living up North. By traveling back to where others like him had been before, he'd gain a new perspective and stick ever closer to those that mattered most.

Yet when generations of colored folks' own course in life has been taken from them, why inflict that deprivation on Charles anew? That was what several asked but nobody understood, maybe MayBelle least of all, or if she did, she never said. In short, she sent Charles to the distant South where others'd been shot or lynched from tree limbs, just for speaking up against the area's ways or trying to flee from them. What was worse, Charles had never been to the South before, not to mention it was a Negro college he hadn't even heard of. At Tougaloo the boy grew surly, contrary to his mother's expectations, and languished on campus for a couple of years without declaring a major or progressing toward graduation.

12

"My boy thought coloreds in those parts acted meek, they accepted what white folks wished upon them, with never a voice of their own," MayBelle lamented. "He was at odds with both races there, you might say."

Charles longed instead for "something different or somewhere else," as his mother put it. At college he ran almost as swiftly in confused mental circles as he had in the 220 meter races or the relays of his school days, the difference being that the 220 path had a goal marked out in clear terms, no mysterious Shangri Las or Brigadoons promised to his deprived people behind the fog of obscure valleys and loud talk bearing illusions of freedom and enchantment.

MayBelle couldn't coax from Charles any info about where she might find the magical power to motivate him, and Eddie stood bewildered before his big brother's spindrift gaze into a vague future, which could turn to a crestfallen look if Eddie suggested the existence of long-term fulfillment. Eddie's brother looked like their father, tall, gangly, and loose jointed, of superior athletic skills. He also possessed the logic and writing skills to pass any curriculum higher education offered. Yet Charles returned home after two short and futile years at a college acknowledged for making others like him responsible contributors to the future of their people. Once returned he worked at day labor and helped his mother with her paid job as a community organizer in Richmond Heights.

Time passed while Charles hung out. He made friends but clung more or less to his mother's apron strings. Sometimes it felt to Eddie like MayBelle's energies were for pumping up his brother's spirits, as menial jobs got scarce or went to whites who once would've sneered at them. Other times abundance seemed to reign down, as when Charles caught on part-time as a downtown hotel porter and later found work driving city buses, the one job emphasizing a role as kindly and respectful colored subordinate and the other testing athletic reflexes weaving in and out of rush-hour traffic.

Having something to do enticed Charles, but neither job met with MayBelle's approval, given her son's two years at Tougaloo. MayBelle talked of Charles assuming a pathfinder's mantel. Just as Moses led the Israelites through desert sands and Jesus gave sermons on the Mount, so Charles could echo men's needs and express their dreams aloud in glowing rhetoric. Yet Charles cast off the track man's spikes he wore with pride and turned his back on Tougaloo's lofty promise of commencement robes. No one knew why or understood how to ask him for an explanation.

13

Little brother Eddie sensed he was different. He rose to MayBelle's challenges and looked for new ways to understand the world. Yet he understood his role as number two. He was the second son, who got sent to Vashon High, the second all-Negro high school. Second, that is, historically and academically.

Attending Vashon meant a three-mile longer bus ride than Charles had. In the public's eye Vashon *was* its athletic department. It gave the school a lasting good rep. It was Charles who would've fit Vashon's athletic model, not his little brother. While Charles reaped in untold plaudits at Sumner for his track and field medals, he would have been one among many outstanding champions at Vashon. Charles also had the smarts to pass through any curriculum with flying colors.

Eddie didn't mind being a klutz regardless of the sports arena, so he did as MayBelle decided and commuted long miles to school, while resting atop the school's honor list with regularity. As with much else, neither Charles nor Eddie figured out why their mother failed to recognize she might've sent each to a different school. They obeyed their mother's wishes and went where she chose.

"Ma, really, we'd've been better off at the same school," Eddie pleaded while Charles kept his thoughts to himself. "There you have it, I spoke my mind."

As an 18-year-old, Eddie did as his mother wanted again and went off to Mississippi like Charles, but not Tougaloo. For him MayBelle decided on Alcorn State, an early land grant college, historically black. Unlike Charles, he found and got enthusiastic about eye-opening classes that offered insights on how society worked, or didn't work, and he loved them. Foremost was an increasingly vocal and general unrest with the color lines and discrimination common in middle America. No one forgot to mention race riots in Detroit or lynchings across the South. That mode of protest had much in common with Eddie's mother and brother's work in close-in St. Louis suburbs, but Eddie's college profs approached the issues with an academic focus on theories about the causes and effects of discrimination and their quieter yet persistent existence outside the South.

What Eddie learned was structure. How to understand and attack lynching as an injury to American society as a whole. First came the consideration of costs, meaning how much it cost in terms of lost manpower and human resources to exclude significant numbers of citizens from meaningful work. Next was the need to lobby Congress and build a consensus against lynching as genocide and a hindrance to citizens' civil rights. The argument for dismantling segregated education joined a drive to get Negroes who worked in trades to start up or join labor unions. Eddie liked the theoretical approach more than club meetings or door knocking at folks' homes during election campaigns.

At Alcorn he earned degrees in Social Science and English and progressed toward a teaching certificate. Along the way, he met Charlene Norse, in a Political Science course. The lissome daughter of a Baptist minister in Memphis, she introduced herself as "only a Music major" but told him of demonstrations in her hometown neighborhoods against white groups attempting to keep Charlene's folks from voting and preventing colored school kids from entering public swimming pools. Charlene herself had joined attempts at entering one such public pool and been tossed in jail until her father bailed her out in the wee hours of a weekday morning.

14

To MayBelle's surprise, Eddie and Charlene got married before her senior year began. Until she finished undergraduate studies and he earned a Master's, they lived in married student housing. Just before New Year's Eve 1941, they locked the door to their campus apartment and left Alcorn State. After a few days hanging with campus friends, Charlene hit on the idea they visit MayBelle in Richmond Heights, but Eddie decided they'd go there to live. He wasted no time explaining how they'd go there and arrive unscathed.

"I'm the car buff. I'll drive," he said.

"But we have no vehicle, my dear."

"Okay, car or no car," Eddie insisted while packing a lone suitcase with their meager belongings.

Gently, Charlene showed she'd let him have his way, this once. She stepped back in his shadow.

"But I'll never lose my voice," she explained. "I make you promise me. I visit my folks back home at least once a year, rain or shine." She smiled his way and looked determined. She wouldn't give up her own family.

Eddie smiled as well, answered yes, and shuffled his wife onto a city bus. It rode smoothly along an endless avenue of car dealers. Finally, they got off and gazed around before deciding they were exactly where Eddie wanted them to be, in front of Black Ben's, which advertised itself as "the fanciest Chevy shop" in Jackson, Miss.

Fancy anyway for a place run, not surprisingly, by Black Ben, a slick roustabout with a complexion to match his name, who peddled used autos to colored gents lacking transport and desperate for it. The cars had to show some flash, either in pick-up, body design, or color, while being unflashy enough they wouldn't catch a cop's eye off the bat. Not too rundown either; the police watched out for no-go as closely as go-go, for the give-away to Whitey was a black motorist or open bottles of booze, the one spied out as quickly as the other.

To stay on the safe side, Black Ben specialized in clanky wrecks run into the ground by white rookies, but with good paint jobs and no noxious fumes.

15

"Which is just what my last paycheck from on-campus work will pay for," Eddie explained to Charlene as they got off the bus and strode to the car dealer's desk, which featured loan applications from People's Finance, clearly a bank that knew its clientele.

"Just imagine, your ma's a co-owner," Charlene joshed her husband, who found no humor in her words. Impatiently Eddie looked for the firm's principal owner.

"Good day, Black Boy," Black Ben said in a loquacious greeting. His smile hinted at impatience, like he wanted to say other buyers are on the lot, too, you're not the first. In-again, out-again. Yet he needed to keep everyone interested as long as it took to earn a buck.

Eddie thought of the irony of the two calling each other by vile monikers about their skin color. They did so to lessen the sting of constant reminders they were trading in broken-down junkers on a former owner's s abandoned lot, which he had left for a new owner like Black Ben to clean up as well as possible. He was the Man, as folks called the white fellow who'd made a fortune here on shiny new Chevies and then taken the cash and run with it, leaving a covey of colored guys, also like Black Ben himself, holding the bag on the lot and telling their colored brothers, customers, that is, any half-believable tale about this or that vehicle, all to eke out a living.

The two men, buyer and seller, black boy and Black Ben, as Eddie reminded himself with a sardonic smile, stood in the middle of the parking lot, with cracks showing in the asphalt after many hard winters of freezing and thawing. They eyed each other. Eddie felt comforted knowing the salesman was of his race in a city loaded with racial distrust, if not hatred, but doubtful about used car salesmen of any stripe. Eddie looked in at the smoke-filled waiting room, which had once, under Whitey's ownership, been a showroom for the dealership's spiffiest autos. Charlene sat along the wall with a demure, thin-lipped stare and a steadfast forbearance. Her long, straight, coal-black hair hung over her shoulders while the whites of her eyes shone as she glanced out at Eddie. On the walls above her were rows of calendar photos and pinups of blonde bathing beauties, their radiant smiles beaming down on Charlene's ebony features.

Black Ben noticed Eddie checking out the auto scene, as well as the Hollywood-style photo reproductions, and patted him on the shoulder.

"We're making changes here," he told Eddie. "You know your little lady wouldn't have been allowed in a show room like that under the previous guy."

Eddie glanced again at the blonde pinups. "Them, though?"

"Yeah, they were ok then," Black Ben agreed. "We're new on this block. Haven't gotten around to removing old stuff yet. New furniture's coming. You want different pics, go over to our other place across town. We rearranged things there big-time."

Eddie shook his head. "Not what we're here for."

Nearest them stood a small green auto Black Ben had carefully maneuvered Eddie up to. "A real beaut," Ben said enthusiastically.

"Just my price, too, like what I told you, huh?" Eddie asked. "Or you guessed at? Which was it? I forgot."

Eddie recognized the model of car.

Black Ben started to say something, but Eddie interrupted him. "Yeah, I know. 1937 Ford, sure enough."

The auto featured white wall tires with a two-person coupe and a sharply sloping trunk lid on the back.

"Here's what I got," Eddie answered Ben. He flashed a small wad of bills. "Not much, but it's legal tender."

"Two folks'll fit real nice," Black Ben continued. "Added leg room for your little lady. A feller can't miss what that means. No streamlining, but fast as a deer. Can't go wrong." He pointed at the coup that rose straight from the chassis. "Perfect for lovers snuggling."

Eddie shrugged and glanced out across the lot. He spotted a 1938 Chevy Street Rod. He knew Black Ben expected him to respond to the joke about snuggling, but Eddie fastened his gaze on the Chevy, which the sales guy couldn't miss, Eddie's interest, that is, not necessarily the Chevy, which Ben hadn't placed there for Eddie's benefit.

Black Ben blinked to rid himself of his surprise at Eddie's interest in the Street Rod, but also to say, yes, you have an eye for curves, I see, the ladies and others, too. Eddie frowned in pretended disapproval but didn't bother to contradict the knowing wink. The car was to his liking.

"They're talking about Muscle cars coming up in a few years, that true?" Eddie asked.

"Muscle?"

"Yeah, tons of power, super lightweight, blazing acceleration," Eddie assured him. "Zero to 60 in five to ten seconds. That possible?"

"Don't know but the Street Rod's red, and super to drive," Black Ben assured him, with no attempt to hide his surprise about Eddie's love of speed. "Pardon me, you seemed such a studious gent."

Black Ben stepped back and offered Eddie the keys.

16

Not a few minutes and Eddie was behind the wheel. He inched up to the doorway. Charlene came out and rode along. The Street Rod ran smooth as silk, but it left an oil slick beneath the pan. When Eddie questioned Black Ben about it, he got no response but a steady stare.

"Ok, I'll ask again," Eddie said. "Does it use any oil? I'm always told to ask that off the bat."

"Hardly a drop," Black Ben assured him.

"Really? What's that black stuff I see on the tar surface?"

"Well, a feller can never be sure, maybe a quart to a thousand. I'll allow that. It's all. Maybe another auto stood here before. Yeah, that's it, for sure. A Ford, it stood right on that spot you saw. Was there for days on end."

When Eddie turned his gaze on Black Ben, Charlene bent down and touched the asphalt. On her finger, an oil imprint appeared.

"No, no, I swear, nary a drop," Black Ben repeated. Then like a gentleman he led Eddie into the sales room and began penning a purchase.

"A real beaut this baby. Drove all its life by the same feller, ol' Harry Hahn, a German feller from the river bottoms, never been to town but once or twice a year, the ex-owner at my lot bragged about him and his light foot. A legend in his own time, danged sod buster."

Eddie felt himself sinking irresistibly in Black Ben's b.s., at the same time as his paltry cash wad felt thinner. He looked long and hard at the Street Rod.

"Quart to a thousand, huh?"

Eddie watched Black Ben, who stood his ground and looked straight back at customers, which Eddie could tell he did by habit. Sweat began forming on the dealer's forehead, so he loosened his belt and breathed out.

"Nary a drop, I swear."

"A deal then?" Eddie asked as he made a round of the car. It was only four years old but already showed rust on the fenders, and coulda become unsure for long road runs. A worn-out jalopy maybe?

"A deal," Black Ben answered, which made Eddie wonder if their roles were reversed. Shouldn't the sales guy be suggesting a deal?

Black Ben showed his tacit agreement by slumping his shoulders and sighing. "Eye to eye, man," he said like a fella relieved to make a deal on a dull weekday when lots of customers milled around but few, if any, had the money or moxie for a deal. Eddie imagined hungry mouths waiting for Black Ben at home.

"How long have you had the dealership?" Eddie asked. He imagined the lousy transaction Black Ben had suffered through buying the car lot from the retiring boss, who likely up and sold it for whatever reason and retreated lickety-split to south Florida.

Ben shook his head. Silence replaced words as the two men shook hands, then exchanged a bundle of bucks for a car key.

"So you're in business," Black Ben congratulated him.

"Yeah, you, too," Eddie answered, his irony gone.

17

"Back to your northland, huh? St. Louie?" Charlene asked with a smile as they cruised out of Jackson. "But that Ben guy, he made no arrangement for your payments. Not a word."

"No need, this crate won't last."

"And he knows it?" she said in surprise. "You, too? So that's how it works. You're screwing him and he's screwing you, and you both know it? Where'd you learn that?"

"On the street, in the city. We're brothers. Pattern's set."

"And you believe that? The color of your skin is all that needs to match? Yours and his?"

"This crate uses more oil than gas, we both know it, but it'll get us to St. Louis. I hope. And he hopes I'm gone for good."

"And that's all we need?"

"That's all there is."

"To make a go of it?"

"College filled us with cause and effect. They taught us that."

"And you and me?"

"To get us where we wanna go and Black Ben to feed his brood. Gotta be wise to the street. The cause is we're poor. The effect is we make it home however we can. With maybe some ounce of pride."

"How d'you learn that?"

"It's written, on our faces."

"What is, Mr. Eddie Washington? Tell me, if you know so much. What did I not see that the two of you just did?"

Eddie drove on, feeling the Street Rod shift smoothly from low to high as he maneuvered out of town along Highway 51 toward

Memphis, then soon to be in Missouri. Breezes blew in through the open windows and the powerful, even if fading, V-8 engine gave him a jolt of freedom, yet the feeling mixed with uncertainties he knew were not his alone.

"C'mon, tell me, Eddie," Charlene insisted. "What's written on our faces? You're mine now, I'm yours, no secrets."

"What I see, in others? And feel, myself?"

"Yes, what I mean."

"Entrapment. Bondage. Living in this world we didn't make. Looking around at things. Whadda you see? Think we could live here in this state?"

"Well, I have or in one like it, all my life, I guess, one way or another. And us? We made it for four years, here."

"Well, give us four more then. What'll we be doin'? Pickin' cotton for the boss man. Like my ma says, we been pickin' cotton in this land for 400 years."

"So, Black Ben. He works hard. What's he, slave or boss man?" Charlene asked.

"Good guy, all right, part pimp," Eddie answered, but he hesitated afterward. He wondered if he knew enough to act so cocksure. Maybe being behind the steering wheel created illusions?

Charlene jerked back in her seat, looking ready to object, but she slumped down after considering the wealthy neighborhood Eddie was driving past. Clearly they'd never have access to a ritzy area like this. They'd left that part of the Mississippi capital behind and were out in open farmland when she spoke again. "True, but you never know. Life's full of surprises."

"Yeah, sure. Like me driving this white man's car when it was like new? Never in your dreams, till Whitey's used it up and junked it for a poor slob like Black Ben. Sure enough, some kid will pop up desperate for a ride."

"Like us? Going someplace? Or no place?"

"Yeah, like us," Eddie agreed.

"Somewhere real? Meaning back to your ma? Or is that imagined?"

"You mean, is MayBelle for real?"

Eddie studied his wife's features. The car swerved when his attention to the road failed. He righted it. Careful, Eddie thought. Imagine, me buying a first car and the fuzz stops me half a mile down the road, fines me for looking at my wife?

"Almost like if you're driving and are colored and a cop sees you, then you're done for. On the spot," Eddie said.

"So you mean it's different where your ma lives, kinda South, but better than way down Dixie?" Charlene asked.

"Honey, like I say, if we stay here with a sheepskin, we'll be picking cotton in the fields, like our grand folks before us. They'll call it something else, give us a fancy job title maybe, but the same servitude. I keep telling you."

"Real or imagined, you mean?"

"Sure, sweetie, the man can call anything any ol' stuff he likes, just don't you object to it."

"And so here we are," Charlene countered. "Desperate for a ride? Are there no buses going our way, honey? How'd you get from St. Louis to Jackson all these four years, my man? Shuffling back and forth all that time? By what means?"

"You forget, this is the other way around, Jackson to St. Louis, and I wanna go home a man, with a wife on my arm and under my own acceleration. Besides, you never knew how wild I am about a car. Any ol' jalopy's seventh heaven."

18

Feeling in seventh heaven, they drove on. Route 51 pointed straight ahead, ever northwards. Only three stops for gas, which included an uneasy oil check each time. Eddie added a quart to every hundred and motored on.

Easy going followed in western Tennessee and Kentucky. Only in Illinois did the bright red car stand out to state troopers. After crossing a rickety bridge at Metropolis, he found himself the focus of an Illinois State trooper's attention. Nobody called Eddie "Boy" but he got a citation for "driving while talking," as he explained to Charlene, who, like him, failed at first to decipher the trooper's handwriting.

"Driving while talking to his wife?" she asked.

"Probably, but are you sure he wrote 'wife'?" Eddie asked.

Only in Missouri, where Southern sympathy still held sway, did Eddie incur a fine. After crossing the Mississippi at Chester in Illinois and entering Ste. Genevieve, he swung a hard left without a turn signal, which brought flashing lights from a police car that had started following him at city limits.

The officer was short on words and politeness but long on forms. Eddie got a ten dollar fine for not signaling and another ten for "reckless driving," even though there was no other traffic on the block. When the cop gave him the choice of a night in jail or paying the officer on the spot, Eddie coughed up the last of his student dough and wondered if he had enough gas to reach Richmond Heights.

Drive on he did and before long Eddie was explaining he had no money. "I guess my ma does."

"And so we head North," as Charlene summarized their experiences with an ironic flair. "Never a rise from any cops south of the Ohio, but drive across a couple rivers up North and they crawl out of the woodwork, huh?"

Eddie stole a glance at her and admitted that, yes, he'd been desperate for a souped-up ride and here he had it. At the same time he realized coming back to MayBelle's was a reality check. There was a life to get on with and here it was staring him and his bride in the face. Neither had a job or any idea where to find one. Did a college diploma do folks any good at all? Especially colored youth like them?

"We got hitched in a rush," he told Charlene. "No shotgun wedding, we were head-over-heels."

"I still am, and you?" she replied.

He smiled while wondering if something as simple as giving his wife a loving look really could get him arrested in those parts. No police showed up at that moment, so Eddie drove on feeling relaxed but careful despite his worries about the future. He guessed at how adult life was in these Border States, like southern Illinois and Missouri, where the whites largely came from the South or had their sympathies there. When it came to mixing socially and economically with others, the competition for status and jobs could be fierce. Not to mention the pressure of associating with true Yankees, who filtered down from Chicago and above.

Eddie knew Charlene, full of empathy as she could be, was as uninitiated in the rituals of love as him, but her smooth dark skin and thick black hair filled him with a desire that made him feel a school boy in love, hopelessly unready to look for a job offering a living wage. He knew Charlene relied on him to make a living for them.

"You're a sure bet to care for those you love," Charlene told Eddie.

One thing Charlene surely never knew about on campus was Eddie's love for any vehicle resembling a Street Rod or a hoped-for Muscle Car, especially if it was bright shiny red. He'd gone out purposefully looking for precisely the sort of vehicle they were now nearing St. Louis in. He knew MayBelle would view it as way too gaudy and describe the red color as a harbinger of woe if any uppity white guys spotted it, especially those wearing badges. His ma was sure to demand he find a proper car or junk the Street Rod before it fell apart.

With those foreboding thoughts, Eddie shifted up to high gear and sped on toward Richmond Heights, ready to brave his mother's wrath and get on with life, no matter where it led him. Or them. He reminded himself his life was defined in the plural from here on out.

He knew Charlene sensed his determination to do as he wished on arriving home, so he relaxed behind the wheel and watched the highway disappear under the flashy vehicle, which might be on its last legs but still felt eager to show its stuff. Far from going 0 to 60 in a flash, the Street Rod was sorely wanting in muscle power, but it managed, with some encouragement, to speed along on level ground. At midday on a lazy Tuesday in mid-winter, it bucked and kicked right up to MayBelle's front door before sputtering into a deep slumber.

As Eddie left the car to rest in a gravelly and mostly deserted driveway, he spotted MayBelle on her porch. A stern welcoming party of one, she dried her hands on a flowery apron and spoke their names loudly.

"Eddie! Charlene! Why, I never!"

Eddie thought more of Aunt Jemima of advertising fame than his own mother, but he recognized MayBelle's aura of ownership of the space she occupied. In this case, it was a one-and-a-half story bungalow in a quiet part of a modest suburb, partly black, mostly white. Standing on her threshold at home, MayBelle looked the contented soul she was before Carlos left.

19

Eddie and Charlene came to St. Louis without forebodings. Leaving Jackson had been a thoughtful farewell to college life, which gave them their start as clearheaded thinkers about the world they lived in and the surety that Jim Crow posed a danger to their wellbeing and allowed others to kill people with impunity, as they sometimes did. The traffic stops by police along the route back North did little to darken their lovebird spirit. Married less than a year, they were capable of assuming their bliss would continue encapsulated within the bubble of affection.

Upon seeing MayBelle and realizing he'd spent the last paltry payroll money he had on a once-ritzy crate that gave up its life delivering him and his bride to his mother and knowing he had no plans how to support the two of them and sooner or later most likely his mother too in her old age, well, such thoughts made little impression on Eddie. Nor did it hit him straight on like never before, as it should have, that college was over and he a husband for real, and life expected him to assume a serious face in tackling it.

To alter that attitude, it would take serious things of unthinkable moment, which could hang in the air like multiple swords of Damocles, and threaten him, his wife, and the world around them with inexpressible doom. The first portents of that ugly reality shone in MayBelle's loving but unsettled behavior.

"Been waitin' for you forever, if not days. Why you been dawdling so long? And where'd you latch onto that piece a' ugly auto, anyway? Does it even run?" she demanded to know.

"No, not now, it fizzled out," Eddie answered. "Been dodging fuzz since the Illinois line." He waved his tickets for reckless driving her way.

"The state line? Why, that's the Ohio River. You been drinkin' or what?" she hollered back in jest.

"They got bridges, Ma, or don't you remember? Been that long since you went down home? Meaning never ever?"

"And that be Charlene beside you? Just think, she stuck with you all the way here. How long now, Chile, six months you been with him, dear? Feels like eternity, I bet. Welcome anyway. You gonna need it, you stay wed to this family. Family of mine, I mean."

"Hello, Ma, that's what he says for me to call you now, my ma," Charlene answered with something like a bow or curtsey, certainly a show of respect.

"Like you don't have a ma already? Just think, you came all this way with him," MayBelle replied. "Did he make you get out and push that horrible contraption on the way, with him idling behind the steering wheel? I'm surprised you made it, but welcome again, new daughter a' mine. Because that's what you gonna be. But what about him? Let's see."

MayBelle waved in feigned indifference at her younger son and made it clear she intended to dismiss him from her sight, though not really.

Eddie tried ignoring his mother's tongue wagging, but succeeded only a little. Seeing MayBelle planted steadfastly on the front porch, Eddie imagined her staring a new era of unlimited bloodshed into their bones, like she was thinking, feel pity and pray for the young, made to suffer for their elders' transgressions.

"At my house," MayBelle let them know, "you'll have hospitality and feel at home. But the horrors of Pearl Harbor are only just behind us and worries hang over our heads. Or hasn't that news reached the lovebirds yet?"

20

Eddie and Charlene reminded themselves they came to St. Louis like vagabonds touching down at Mom's for a rest. True, in the last year they'd learned the give-and-take of marriage. Eddie's preference for string music clashed with Charlene's growing interest in choir, and her decision to look for a job teaching vocal music, while her lack of knowledge about Eddie's hometown and his mother's attachment to it made the beginning of their post-graduate life an adventure into the unknown for Charlene. She missed her parents and wrote or called them often. For Eddie being in St. Louis was only a return to MayBelle and her routines. Eddie believed his and Charlene's trust for each other would carry them through any barriers to come, though they hardly fathomed a war in Europe could get ever worse on every front and affect their civilian lives.

Recently they'd learned a lot about the perils of living in an environment unprotected from Jim Crow, as relatively safe as a college could seem. Eddie's ventures off campus in Jackson taught him that the opposing realities of college living and life on the streets grew in increments. He experienced tolerance and intolerance where they were least expected, as on the highways of Mississippi, or meeting up with aggressive policing in a state like Illinois. Added to that shock was the young married couple's emergence into a world on fire after Pearl Harbor. Talk spread that the US military would start using colored troops in combat alongside whites.

"If Uncle Sam calls, you'll be fighting on two fronts, in the streets at home and wherever he sends you overseas with your white brethren," MayBelle explained to her sons. "Struggling against whites at home but fighting with them abroad."

Though hardly unpacked, Eddie and Charlene listened and registered what they could. Their drive from Jackson started as an unthinking farewell to a socially aware HBCU campus. They had a start as clearheaded young adults prepared for the unequal society they lived in. In addition, the community surrounding them instilled a knowledge that Jim Crow posed a danger.

This vestige of hate culture allowed police to serve and protect the public or kill them with impunity. Still, the traffic stops along the route up North did little to darken the carefree lovebird spirit Eddie and Charlene had. They'd blissfully hit the road and made it to Missouri.

Despite the truths their college taught them about being watchful progeny over the spirit of former slaves in America, they'd had little opportunity to study systemic prejudice first-hand and recognize the proper times either to insist on their rights as native-born citizens or acquiesce in the obedient roles white America assigned them to. Eddie came to understand that his black face, regardless of socio-economic standing, gave a generic signal to the mainstream that here was an individual whose will could be bent. The privileged class missed few opportunities to apply pressure. They succeeded in subjugating minorities, and MayBelle's insistent stay-at-home teachings impressed on Eddie the need to be cautious but intense about his rights.

Each time Eddie went into MayBelle's home, he felt like a man in new guises, first as a youth turned college grad, and second as a family breadwinner with no visible means of supporting himself, let alone his and Charlene's future family. Added to that uncertainty was the rock hard reality of a war overseas and America joining it.

Waiting inside at MayBelle's was also Charles, who nodded at Eddie.

"Welcome home, little brother," Charles said, with a touch of irony. "You're not so little anymore."

"Yeah, I guess," Eddie replied with a self-effacing smirk. "Me, the one who finished college? You next."

Charles didn't reply but smiled, as though Eddie's words touched a raw nerve but were okay if uttered between brothers. Charles spoke more easily with Charlene. "Nice to have such a fine, smiling face in the old shack we humbly call home. Ma keeps it tidy," Charles explained. He spoke in a self-confident and welcoming tone. It struck Eddie that a man of so many talents was still living at home with his mother when any number of girls must've found him attractive. That none pursued him or he showed no interest seemed strange, but equally unusual was that Eddie knew next to nothing about his brother's social life.

Though Charles was never a go-getter in public, Eddie knew his brother as both a gentleman and a careful housekeeper, so he followed along as Charles showed his sister-in-law around the house, which MayBelle had rearranged to give herself Eddie's former bedroom and allow Eddie and Charlene to use MayBelle's larger space.

"Ma and I agreed, the newlyweds can furnish it, meaning you yourself, I presume, Charlene."

"And about you?" Charlene asked Charles. "No change in where you sleep?"

Eddie was startled his wife got no direct reply. Instead Charles spoke in a slightly slurred voice, which Eddie had never noticed before. "There are other plans."

"For who? You?" Charlene asked.

Eddie saw a glimmer of good will in Charles's eye. Much remained unspoken. Few words but ample evidence Charles was the true fastidious housekeeper, who'd made plans before Eddie came home again. Anyone wanting to learn about MayBelle and Charles' housekeeping practices needed patience and questions.

Instead Charles himself was in the questioning mood this day. He asked about Eddie and Charlene's future, short-term as well as long. "Staying with ma, for good or not?" he asked.

Eddie wondered why the urgency. As Charles talked, a twitch started in his hands, which like the occasional slur seemed to have appeared since the brothers last met. Eddie wondered if it was caused by a nebulous fear his brother had developed or nervousness about not finding a proper job and still be hoping to support himself without MayBelle's help. Or was there anxiety about the war?

"Staying. We'd like a place to settle," Charlene answered Charles.

Charlene left the bedroom and went on to explore the house. The sound of her voice echoed from another room and MayBelle answered her even more loudly, as Charles also began talking. Eddie realized his reply about future plans could wait. Good enough that his wife gave her thoughts. Eddie was grateful his wife spoke up because he had no idea what to tell his brother. Whatever was to come—steady work or war—felt to him like the last thing college prepared them to face.

21

Another day Charles began talking slowly, which his slur melded into. Eddie was with him leaving a bookstore in Webster Groves looking for a bus toward Richmond Heights. When none appeared, they walked on. "You know, I was on Market Street the other day," Charles said. "In St. Louis. And heard about the most gruesome deed."

"Deeds and deeds," Eddie replied. "There're good and bad parts of that street. Some rundown. Which part?"

"Which part what?"

"Where it happened? Or where you heard about it, whatever."

"Where? Like this, you know. I was in this café and took a seat by some fella. I was reading the *Globe-Democrat* and saw he's looking over my raised coffee cup and reading along with me."

"Reading what? C'mon get to the point," Eddie urged him on.

Their talk continued as light chatter during the walk home, but when they got to MayBelle's place and went in Eddie still wondered about Charles's point. "What were you reading?"

Charles was ready to reply, when a blast on a horn outside interrupted him. Eddie realized it was a tow truck MayBelle had called for. He rushed out to meet the driver, who secured the broken-down Street Rod, which had languished in the driveway for longer than Eddie intended. The driver was winching it up.

"Got here lickety-split!" he exclaimed. A teenage assistant took over the winch control while the driver, wearing a *Center City Salvage* overall, produced a voucher, which Eddie offered to take only to have the driver jerk it away. "No, it's for your ma. She promised to pay. She said don't bother with you. You got no dough. Give it to her an' say it's from me, Bobby Joe."

The driver hopped in the truck and bombed off to find a final resting place for the colorful Street Rod. As the truck disappeared, Eddie looked after it and thought how he started the day with a broken down car, no money, and a wife to care for. Now he was reduced to a wife and only MayBelle to rely on. As for Charles, he wasn't sure, only that they were brothers. That meant something in a time of troubles.

While Eddie fumbled with his thoughts and headed back inside, Charles kept talking. "The *Globe-Democrat* article," he said, "it told how this Yellow Cab driver pulled off on a side street, you know near Market, to take a break, he'd been driving all day."

"Yeah, I know, man. A quiet street," Eddie agreed. "The city's full of 'em."

"Well, he's there having a smoke and his girlfriend comes along. They arranged it that way. Anyhow, they're sitting in his cab, innocent like, but there's these two punks prowling round and then sneak up and crawl, no, I mean kinda burst in through the back door. They got this gun and start demanding money, which the cabbie doesn't have any of except maybe a charge for cash on his dashboard meter, somewhere like that."

His thoughts back on their household, Eddie went to MayBelle's kitchen and stuffed the bill from Center City Salvage in her cookie jar knowing she'd see it and pay, like always. "Where is Center City anyway?" he asked.

Charles shrugged but kept talking. "You're not listening." His tone asked for attention.

Eddie glanced up. His brother was two or three inches taller than him but he'd lost a wee bit of the muscle power in his legs and arms that stood out in his not-so-distant athletic days. Still, Charles walked like the relaxed, agile sprinter he'd once been. His tone of voice was modulated, almost, it seemed, by choice. He lifted his head slightly, and Eddie was reminded how alike they were in expression, with thin lips and straight black hair, features they inherited from their father, not MayBelle, whose cheeks were fleshy and her lips thick. By contrast, Eddie remembered how his mother's eyes sparkled, radiating light and warmth, while Charles's always seemed to look out at the world through the cool light of logic.

"There is no Center City," Charles said. "It's just what guys call this city we live in. Folks born here figure it's the center of the universe."

"And so the two punks?" Eddie asked to get Charles' story back on track, though he was at a loss about what any of the last few minutes had to do with his own situation.

"Well, like I said, they pull out this gun. Nobody knows why."

"Maybe no reason at all? A couple a' kids."

"The newspaper said they wanted dough. For drugs? Whatever, they used the gun and shot the cab driver and his girl, both dead."

"Happens all over."

"But this was different. They didn't take anything. They dragged the bodies outa their front seat and stuffed 'em in the trunk. Took a couple of days before some cops got suspicious. They opened the trunk and, well, you can guess."

Eddie studied his brother, like hoping to see a point etched in his features. Surely others around the metro area had read this maudlin tale but chose not to discuss it at length. Why Charles? Something about the story struck him as salient. To Eddie it was only shocking.

"Sounds so dumb," he said hoping to dismiss the topic. "They must have some smarts. Doing something like that, they gotta know they'll get caught then sent to the big house. All for what? A violent thrill? Then spend their life in hell?"

"But that's the point, stuff they don't teach at places like college. About life on the street."

"And I haven't seen it? The street?" Eddie asked. "Like maybe what our pa went through when he teetered on the edge a few times?"

"That's imagined, not experienced, we can only imagine what Pa went through in the Caribbean. We could try and find out."

"Starting where?" Eddie asked.

"I mean if the street is hell, how can being behind bars feel any worse? In the pen these boys get a bed of their own and three meals a day for the first time in life."

"So you figure every place is bad, but some less bad?"

"Could be, to some souls."

"Maybe, but c'mon, get off it. What's that got to do with us, you and me? I reckon Jim Crow is hell, but not affecting us," Eddie said.

"Not yet, but it could. You been in Mississippi. Close enough, I guess."

"Even here, they say. Not unknown here either. Jim Crow takes place anywhere."

"Can happen."

Eddie thought of replying but held off. Lots happens, he figured. Planned or by chance, the effects could be equally helpful. Or harmful. What if a lynch mob came our way … what would that feel like, Eddie wondered, what guy's ever survived a lynching and described it?

"War is hell," Charles said of a sudden.

"You mean this, what we experience."

"Yes, segregation."

"Or *benign neglect*, whatever they call it?"

"So they taught you that expression at college, huh?" Charles asked.

"From Ma first. But college, too."

"Four years at Alcorn not wasted. Yes, this is war. But that, too."

"That? You mean what's happening in Europe?"

"Yes, but not just there, it's coming here. War's declared, we declared it on Japan, then Germany on us, you know that, and soon they'll ship us there. To Asia and Europe both. The U. S. is in it, for real, hostilities have started. You have a Selective Service number yet, little brother?"

"So it's kill or be killed? That's what's eating you?" Eddie asked, finally understanding what bothered his brother about the *Globe-Democrat* article. Getting drafted and fighting abroad was the farthest thing from Eddie's mind. Being new to marriage and needing to earn a living on his own, that's what he wanted to concentrate on. Yet he read his own likely fate in Charles's thoughts. Getting called up by the military to defend a nation he had yet to decide if he fully believed in.

22

"So we'll be fighting on distant shores for a freedom we don't even have here?" Eddie asked aloud, mostly to himself. At the same time, he remembered Negroes weren't allowed to serve in the same units as white troops. So would men of color even be fighting at all in this war?

Eddie eyed his brother closely, speculating in silence about Charles's future. In a way he knew why Charles came back to Richmond Heights from Mississippi. College could feel like a hothouse exercise in dry theory. But where would being back home get him? Nowhere, as far as anyone figured. He didn't finish college and except for MayBelle he had no personal anchor, like Eddie had in Charlene, as MayBelle's lady friends all agreed.

Eddie and Charlene had no firm plans, but surely there'd be work for Eddie, who had some learning. The more he thought about the profs at Alcorn and their dedication to social reform and equal rights the more Eddie leaned toward seeking a teaching job. With Charlene heading for Music Education, he'd follow her lead and make for the classroom, too.

"You know," Charles answered and interrupted Eddie's thoughts. "I had you pegged as one of those twerps that come back with a diploma but still act like students, exactly the way Ma figured. These guys discover home's not like home anymore or it's changed. They feel above it, too big for it. I don't think that's you now."

"We're different, you and me," Eddie answered. "You go by outward signs and latch on or turn away, but you make your decisions in private, so not even Ma reads you right all the time. Or maybe she reads you, then can't explain what she knows is there, what makes you you."

Eddie wondered if he spoke out of turn but couldn't convince himself he said anything untrue. He and Charles had the same parents but gave off different messages. Charles willingly aligned himself with movements or groups he had no agreement with, if for no other reason than learning what they were about, whether they were as odious or genuine as they appeared.

Charles's easy athletic stride made his silence seem the more imposing, even arrogant to those who didn't know him. Eddie felt his brother could tussle with the world and win either by exerting main force or by debating a topic till his opponent gave in to his careful choice of words. Charles had two different tactics for winning, but it wasn't sure he was putting either to use.

"Ma knows what I believe because of the way I help with the poor in her district," Charles answered at last. He peered down at Eddie, whose slim torso, eager look, and quick glances contrasted to Charles's calm observance of him.

"But my reactions are my private matter," Charles added.

"You'll do as you wish, even if somebody else knows more than you," Eddie said. "I see that, but it's a slippery slope. There's always somebody else looking for the upper hand. You don't understand best every time. Or run fastest either."

"And some others do? Is that why you think I left school?"

"No, I have no theory," Eddie said. With that, he turned and went to check if MayBelle found the tow truck bill.

She had.

23

At other times, Eddie sensed something gnawing at Charles, like maybe some people's unspoken demands that he finish college, or if nothing else stay eligible for Track and Field, which he well could do if left to his own devices, like free choice about what courses to immerse himself in or how to discover on his own what he needed to know. But he chose a different route and quit Tougaloo, which left him in Richmond Heights earning a living at this and that odd job. Notably he hung around his mother's place, stuck in what other folks saw as an arrested state.

Those were things Eddie never dreamed of doing. With Charlene's encouragement, he was determined to make his way. A home of their own would come. He felt sure that Charles, by contrast, wavered as usual, not over what he thought about college life or Jim Crow or the war newly declared, but how to respond to pressure from others. Sometimes he craved action.

"I repeat," Charles spoke up unexpectedly.

"Repeat what?" Eddie asked.

"Whadda you intend? Wait around to get drafted? It won't be long and they *will* come. Even for guys like us."

It was true, Eddie felt a keen awareness of Selective Service glaring his way.

"It can't be long. Is that what you mean?" Eddie asked.

"It's the here and now, man. Do you wanna be like the cabbie, that waits for somebody to come along and club you silly and stuff your body in a trunk? It's what Nazis are doing in the Old World, snuffing out lives. You gotta take action against them."

"And what's the alternative?" Eddie asked. "War is war, whether here or overseas."

"And your plans? That's my question."

"No plans laid-out. Charlene and I figured to look for work. That's all. We thought war was someplace else. Now it's here?"

"Closer than you think."

"So you feel the Draft Board breathing down your neck?" Eddie asked.

"Don't you?"

"Never thought of it. Life is war enough. Like how many ways there are to get killed by mobs at home?"

"We could relive the white uprising in Tulsa? Whites think they can hide knowledge of that among us black folks, conceal it, the way they lie to other whites, and the good burghers believe it and think we do, too."

"So now they'll send us to do their dirty work in Europe?"

"Me? No, they'll not send me," Charles said with determination. "I'll sign up on my own. Fight my own battle, on my own terms."

"Which is? Your battle, I mean."

"Facing enemy fire on Whitey's orders is like being lynched twice. Blindly doing what I'm told? With both sides against me? Not for me. I'll chose my own poison."

"Which is? Tell me," Eddie asked.

"I'll enlist. Ordered to sign up is the same as sold into slavery."

Eddie scratched his head at his brother's eager capitulation to the local Selective Service. He wondered who were the heads of those boards and what motivation men had for serving on them. Money? Patriotism? Love of country, if there were such things?

"You know," Charles broke in on Eddie's thoughts. "I read about Ferguson. You remember that town, you who's been away four years at college?"

"Yeah, what about it?"

"In the old days, they put up chains around Ferguson and locked Negroes in at night to keep 'em from leaving the city limits."

"Yeah, I heard about that, from Ma, but never understood if I got it right. I wondered, in or out?"

"Whadda you mean?"

"They locked folks in town or outa town?"

"Why, it was the whites lockin' 'em in. You dumb or something?"

"Dumb maybe. I thought Ferguson was all-white way back. It's changed?"

"You bet. Like a prison. The Nazis in Germany jabber on and keep denying they have any concentration camps, but they got 'em same as Whitey does here."

"What people? Who's in 'em? In Germany, I mean?"

"Why Jews and Gypsies. Even North Africans, folks like us, Brother."

"And by enlisting you'll be doing what? Joining one police state to help end another?"

"I be, like Ma says, doin' something. Anything. Making my own decision."

"That's war in a nutshell, I guess. Nursing our illusions."

"Meaning?"

"Believing we'll rid the world of evil."

24

Eddie paused to consider his words. They sounded clever, but he wondered if they were only babble, like what he'd heard from speakers at school who believed in classless societies. Or said they dreamed of them, but was that dreaming an illusion? Did it ever come true?

"If Whitey don't kill us one way, he'll try another?" Eddie resumed, regretting his tendency to make thumbnail summations of what Charles was driving at. "I see what you mean. That's our history, I learned that much these four years. You'd not be capitulating to a lousy Draft Board. I get it."

"What you don't see is that's how we get a chance at a Double V," Charles protested. "Never before in history."

"V? Like in victory?"

"That's it. We got two wars to win. A victory over fascism overseas and racism at home." Charles looked long and hard at Eddie. "College never taught you anything like that? That's why I'll enlist."

"Victory assured?" Eddie asked.

"Never know if we don't try. Anything else?"

Lots, Eddie thought. How to be a thinking man. Socrates said it, about the unexamined life not being worth living, but a life spent in whose society? In any conflict winners write the history books. He wondered if the winners were examining life or merely repeating empty campaign slogans.

"Are we the losers?" Eddie asked and wondered if he was speaking to his big brother or out loud to himself.

Charles nodded in understanding, like he read his brother's mind, which made Eddie ask if they were brotherly soulmates. True maybe, Charles was more withdrawn, but they could converse in this way without rancor and arrive at the same conclusions.

"We're in the same boat," Charles remarked. His statement sounded like a question, but Eddie recognized it as a quiet way of provoking him to take a stand.

"They think we're not human because of our color," Eddie answered.

"Who thinks that?"

"I dunno. Hitler, Whitey, some evil demon, wherever he is at any moment," Eddie said.

"Everywhere. Look around. *They* write the histories."

Like I thought, ran through Eddie's mind.

Charles peered down at his brother, and Eddie felt a silent weight cover him. He thought about traits the two inherited from MayBelle and Carlos. Surely, Eddie decided on the spur of the moment, Charles received our father's name in translation along with his weighty presence. More strikingly, it seemed, Charles's difficulty sticking with whatever he started was also his father's. Just as Carlos was once with them, or at least together with their mother, he could disappear, reappear, and then apparently be gone forever, like turning on a dime.

By the same token, Charles could be conversant one day and clam up and stay speechless for days on end. Eddie felt his brother's physical prowess while also experiencing his mental side as a shifting cloud. Charles ran every 220 he entered but couldn't manage a four-year degree. Not so different was the two boys' father Carlos, who got an Engineering degree, or whatever he earned, but only worked as a shop clerk.

"Ok, the Draft Board, you'll show up and go out to fight, but only if they let you enlist and not wait to be called up?" Eddie asked at last. "Fighting for one great white father against another?"

"Jim Crow vs. Gerry, you mean?" Charles answered.

"Or Tojo. It's the Nipponese that attacked us."

Charles turned silent and so Eddie was left to watch him out of the corner of his eye. He felt tense vibes between them.

"So you learned some geography, too, huh?" Charles asked. He nodded in a magisterial way, which Eddie knew was Charles's stamp of approval, but could look like an aura of superiority, as when he sauntered off the track after yet another victory at a 220 sprint or relay race and showed appreciation for his opponent but even greater pride in his own victory.

"Like a creepy crawly?" Charles asked, once again reading Eddie's thoughts.

"Meaning?"

"How I make you feel. That's what folks tell me. About my attitude."

"You tell me. Is it real or imagined?"

"Mostly imagined. Some real. Depends on the competition."

"Eye of the beholder?"

"The Anglo Army officers'll think they're better than me, contempt's the word, I'd guess."

"Boot camp'll level the playing field," Eddie warned him, though a mere bachelor's degree hardly made him feel like an expert on anything. "The Army will, I mean."

"Yeah, I looked at the Marines, they don't want me," Charles explained.

"Whites only? How do you know?"

"I read up on it, in the Marine Corps' own manual."

"And what does it say there? We're animals? Or worse?"

"We're defined as cowards, no good under pressure, can't read and write, buckle when the going gets tough."

"And you want that?" Eddie asked in puzzlement. "Going into combat with them?" He was finding the motivations of the big brother he'd idolized as nebulous as ever. Eddie saw Charles as living behind a shield of secrets. Maybe he wasn't capitulating to the Draft Board, but to an unknown inner force?

"Okay, do it how you want," Eddie said to accept Charles's way. But he felt puzzled trying to understand where the acceptance came from. Was there some mystical jungle-drum strain from the cane fields of Santo Domingo that Carlos carried with him and it lay latent in Charles? Eddie wondered what dark visions of old slave days in Africa emerged in his brother, relayed via some unidentified genes in their father, which Eddie was innocent of, but Charles stayed susceptible to in moments of great stress. Like an x-ray vision it could enable him to see and fear evil at hand but be drawn to siding with it at times, despite himself. If for no other reason than to play the devil's advocate.

"But don't you see, in this conflict there's no good guy. Why should we sign up to support one white monster over another?" Eddie argued again. "I'll go, but only if I must."

"Ma'd want you to," Charles agreed.

"Charlene wouldn't," Eddie countered.

Charles got a dreamy look that Eddie recognized from childhood. It spoke of big sibling remembering and puzzling over a problem or trying to solve a riddle from the past, always something suggested in a Science book or an Ancient History text from the school library, like how to square a circle or where to look for Cleopatra's tomb in Alexandria. Those big problems Charles never solved, of course, but even lesser ones intrigued him, like the question he thought up all by himself about Hannibal attacking Rome. "How many elephants did he have with him crossing the Alps?" Eddie remembered Charles asking once. "No historians ever say."

His far-off gaze was a tipoff Charles had something in mind at least as weighty as being refused by the Marine Corps. Or even, heaven forbid, wading ashore on some enemy-occupied beachhead. Eddie guessed instead the Draft Board's pressure caused his brother's concern. One day they call and you're signed in under some officer's control, not far from being kidnapped off some African shore and sold as chattel. Not your own man. Ordered to go off and fight and where to do it. Or even told how to die breaching what unknown rampart in whatever distant place.

Enlisting on his own was a step in Charles's own direction, though it left Eddie to wonder where it would lead.

25

Of course, Carlos had acted as the moment dictated, but he was gone.

"Where to, do you think?" Charles asked suddenly, his question following the similar beat of Eddie's thinking.

"Our pa, you mean?"

"Yes, would he say that I'm giving in to the draft by enlisting in the Man's military?"

"No, not if you got in the right branch of Service."

"Like what?"

"Like his. Engineering or the like. Quartermaster Corps maybe?"

"Dad never built anything. He designed stuff, but let the loose ends flutter in the wind and blow away. Retrieving? No way."

"So you and me, what were we in his life?"

"Or only loose ends trailing in the breeze? Is that what you mean?" Charles asked.

"Yeah, or something. Thought you'd know."

"Someday maybe I'll find out. Not any day soon," Charles continued with a melancholy tone of voice

"Patience is a virtue?"

"Glory to them that wait, to them shall be given. Isn't that what it says somewhere?" Charles asked in turn.

"Beats me. Is it true, Brother? Ma and her folks've waited ages. For their rights."

All Eddie figured was what MayBelle's words said about her own household. When Eddie and Charlene arrived, the numbers swelled from two to four—200%. The only other thing increasing so fast was uncertainty.

Now news poured in about wartime frenzy. Even if he'd only just arrived back home, Eddie also bent with the mounting storm winds and feared for his and Charlene's future. Lucky thing they got married when they did. Others put off their plans in the same way Charles did in finding his father, someday maybe, but not now. This was the 1940s and Uncle Sam was calling.

Yes, Charles might well find Carlos some distant day, but when and what motivated him to consider searching? "You're rootless copies of your old man, my young men," MayBelle told her boys. "There was no reading your dad or his moods. You yourselves need to set down roots."

"And I'm a carbon copy of him?" Charles wondered out loud.

"Not exactly. But he woulda answered Uncle Sam, like you. No idea why. We're all different, no accounting sometimes for what makes us do stuff. Your father lived like this life was a prelude. He had to go out and seek its continuation."

"The real thing?" Eddie asked when he heard talk like that. Was life acted out on a stage, with time for retakes? If so, where was the playwright, who knew the ending before the beginning? And would Carlos recognize the real thing if he saw it?

"War's real. Men go out in it if they must," MayBelle said.

Smart lady, Eddie thought recognizing MayBelle's refrain, repeated in different ways. Men fill the stage with sound and fury, while their ladies keep the framework intact. It took a while but in protest MayBelle had the Chevy Street Rod, the reminder of Eddie's youthful antics, towed away and scrapped.

Eddie and Charlene settled in at MayBelle's. For a longer or shorter stay? No one knew.

26

Soon enough Charles took Eddie to Selective Service where he and Eddie were to register for the Draft. Charlene went along for support. Questioning looks abounded among the three.

"February, two months since FDR declared war," Charles explained.

"Doing what we must?" Eddie asked. He'd been content to sail with the new decade and let life lead them, but now Poland and Middle Europe were in German hands, England under threat, and Japan was waging war in China, not to mention Japanese takeovers in the oil-rich East. Then there was Charles, seeming so distant and yet connected to immediate social problems at home. He insisted on America giving armaments to Europeans, the very allies who to appearances remained unmoved by colored folks' drive for equality in the States. No lack of sympathy for the cause, Europe's powers explained, we just have more pressing concerns at home.

"But Eddie, he's so little a fighter, not cut out for it," Charlene protested on the way to the Draft Board office. "The Army can't want him?"

"A picture of health, if I ever saw one," Charles insisted. "Just you look." All three laughed as Charles stood incongruously taller and stronger beside his younger brother.

Nearing the Selective Service building, Eddie thought about himself, as others might view him. Five eleven and a bit bowlegged. "I'm barely 150 dripping wet," he responded to Charles. He felt as scrawny as his words made him sound, which was unsurprising given his growing up in the shadow of a muscular brother, whose shaggy trousers and loose fitting sweaters set off his sturdiness and supple movements.

Eddie himself dressed like a spiffy college grad. He was decked out in boots, a red shirt, and a sweater vest. He also had wide khaki trousers with creased legs and cuffs. The bottoms fit snugly around his ankles, a style intended to prevent tripping, though Eddie had no clue why he'd be in danger of that.

"Not my idea of a zoot suit," Charles jested. "But it'll do to get you inducted. Any ol' garb. What branch'll you have? Army or Navy?"

"It's not intended as either," Eddie replied. "Not a zoot suit, I mean. This is the duds we wore at Alcorn."

And so he stood with Charles in front of a drab Selective Service office in downtown St. Louis, and Charlene joined them so she could watch. She was decked out in a burgundy and white polka dot button-front dress. It had padded shoulders and flared out at knee level. Unlike Eddie's naturally curly hair, Charlene's black locks hung down to her shoulders and set off her long thin face and broad smile.

Charles appeared with them unshaven, looking at first glance like anything but the track star of his past. Still, his physical prowess showed. Standing six three and rocking on the balls of his feet, Charles looked as likely to be the father of Eddie and Charlene as their sibling and brother-in-law.

"Only your ma is missing today, she shoulda come with us," Charlene said to the brothers.

Charles nodded, while Eddie studied the scene around him. "To a white audience our whole family history would seem like a stereotype. Kidnapped then brought here by slavers ages ago and now offering ourselves to help rake in a profit on the war market. Granted that's something resembling freedom but we're still poor and struggle to attain what we get," Eddie said.

"And what next?" Charles asked with a wry smile. "We're moving on."

"Bend or break," Eddie said with a shrug, knowing Charles's mind was made up.

"Stupid men," Charlene said with a sigh. "Going off to war and doin' your keeper's dirty work. Reminds me of Black Ben." She took a step back to let them go in and register. "You'll go to the man's war. The man'll stay in D.C. and fight in absentia. No doubt raking in dough off your labor."

27

Eddie and Charles left Charlene at the door and went in. A kindly looking white female clerk waited at a desk covered with papers.

Judging from the scrawled handwriting on the forms before her, Eddie assumed inductees had scribbled their names and surrendered to Uncle Sam. The prospect of signing away his own fate left Eddie feeling helpless. He'd recently committed himself to another path than armed conflict. Maybe Charles had other ideas, but enjoying peace was still Eddie's.

"Welcome," the friendly lady said. She seemed more like a dime store sales clerk than a rep for a military machine on the march. Eddie guessed hers had been an idle and low-paying job before Pearl Harbor. The rush to reshuffle her office into a hectic enterprise had yet to take a visible toll on her. No recruiting officers were in sight. Clearly men weren't showing up in that office for purely patriotic reasons. Uncle Sam sent out the order. They came, signed, and skedaddled, left to wait at home for an induction letter determining their fate, for better or worse.

The office lady left off shuffling papers and took Charles and Eddie's names, while handing each man separate blank sheets.

"Welcome. Nice to see you gents today. I'm Edna," she said.

Eddie paid her little attention and filled out his own papers, until he noticed Charles hesitating when he came to the lines under *Education*, which Eddie realized was sure to be irrelevant in a foxhole in France or Germany or whatever hell hole the US Army had in mind for lowly privates. Eddie himself scribbled "Alcorn" and a few other barely legible words on his form, but he noted Charles treating those lines less cavalierly. He bit a couple of times on the pencil's eraser and left the space blank.

"Why didn't you complete it?" the lady wondered after asking for both men's papers.

Charles mumbled something Eddie struggled to hear. He knew Charles was embarrassed about not graduating, a failure Eddie had never fully understood before now as hanging so heavily over his brother's head. It marked him as a drop-out, if not from society at least from his peers in Jackson and Sumner High. Star athletes are to shine, not fade away, Eddie thought to himself.

"Stand out's an expectation only Ma placed on me," he stated nonchalantly.

"What's that?" Charles wondered.

"Being imposing. Like you. With books. And body. Both."

Before handing the last papers to the smiling lady, Eddie bent down and filled in the name of Charles's college and years of attendance for him. The Selective Service woman glanced at both men's forms.

"I see you took English, Eddie. What branch? Verse? Fiction?"

"A mix," he answered. "Most interesting was Modern Poetry."

"Who?" she asked.

"Meaning what poet?"

"Yes and where? What school?" she wondered.

As she spoke, Eddie felt surprised a white person would show an interest in his studies. She also asked about courses he might've taken. Standard poets occurred to him. Frost. Sandburg. Even Millay, Edna St. Vincent. A woman writer. Each name spoke of white people's world and the everyday experiences a Selective Service clerk might recognize.

"And your name?" Eddie asked instead, not having listened when she introduced herself before. "Ellen?"

She glanced at both brothers, not suspiciously but in delight that they seemed to care. It dawned on Eddie that registering men to train at arms, as she did, must be a position causing fear and perhaps even loathing in young men. Were some too inarticulate or nervous even to talk civilly with her? Or maybe young draftees were ill-equipped to overcome their anxiety? Eddie's simple question brought an unexpected chuckle and she responded by producing a dog-eared book from her desk drawer.

"I'm Edna, remember?" She held the book with both hands while Eddie and Charles introduced themselves.

"Edna and Eddie, interesting," Charles remarked softly, glancing at one then the other. "What else do you have in common?"

"Who knows, maybe wishing to avoid war," she replied. "I'm too old and you're only here to register. Nothing more dangerous than that, so far."

Where this spark of fellowship came from bamboozled Eddie. He fished for a poet Edna might know about. From being half attentive Charles perked up and looked from one of them to the other.

"There's lots," Eddie mumbled, searching to name a poet accessible enough to light a fire under the average reader, but what if Edna wasn't the average reader? "I mean, those poets distinctive enough ..." He paused when it struck him he never used words like *distinctive*, then why do so with this woman he'd never met before?

"My brother means a writer sure handed enough to show in everyday terms how folks like us are. We're of a different stamp, you see, how we think," Charles added. He held out the back of his hand to show his skin color.

Pretty fancy words my brother's showing off, too, Eddie thought, but he saw no grimaces from Edna.

"I see your hue, sir," she said in a neutral tone. "Yes, our races are different."

Eddie stepped forward, pretending to want to say something, but he only looked at Charles hoping for him to speak up again. He had the right vocab, like a literary scholar.

Her smile broadening, Edna also peered Charles's way. "You're different from me by choice or genes?" she jested.

Charles nodded to show he wanted to avoid quibbling. Neither did he bother explaining more.

"The Road Not Taken," Eddie blurted out, not certain if that was a title or the theme of a poem. "Robert Frost," he added. "About when we reach a place, in life ... there's no use saying too much or going too far, he means. Frost is standing in a woods where the road divides."

Our people can choose, Eddie thought, which way to turn, what path is ours, but making a decisive move at the right time is the secret. No, that's too simple, sounds like a recipe. You take some ingredients, throw 'em in an oven, and they come out a pie? Not so simple. Maybe Robert Frost needed to be a colored man for me to explain it right, Eddie decided. Such a decisive step in life, he's presenting.

"The road less taken?" Eddie continued. He felt even more confused when Edna showed no recognition.

"Langston Hughes," Charles said at last to break the silence Eddie's jumbled comments created. Charles's words hung in the air like an oracle's.

Edna looked up in astonishment, which left Eddie wondering if that was because she'd never heard of Hughes or was astounded to meet a guy like Charles. Or was it the dignity in Charles's voice that caught her attention. Charles, whose calm tones sounded so professorial, but came from the mouth of a college drop-out.

"Yes, the Harlem Renaissance!" Eddie burst out. "You got it! Great man! You know of him? We read his stuff at college."

Edna shook her head to show she was in the dark about both Harlem and Langston Hughes, but she smiled ever wider to show she was charmed by a gentleman like Charles paying close attention to her.

"Harlem?" she asked. "In New York?"

"Yes, he was a writer there, colored," Charles said pointing to himself and Eddie. "But he came from all over. Kansas City, California, Columbia, you name it, he was there. Finally settled in Harlem and wrote.

"He penned verse and books, even some for kids. Just like me and Eddie here, Langston had trouble with his pa, except our daddy ran off from us. We think he headed west but no idea where, and Langston up and did it the other way around. He left his father at 18. He ended up with folks in L.A., then went east to New York, later Harlem, like we said."

"And became famous, I bet," Edna guessed, showing she sorta followed their thinking. "As a poet, I mean?"

Eddie and Charles nodded yes together. While Eddie did his best to remember more about the Black Literary Renaissance of the 1920s and Langston Hughes's wild ride to championing the rights of minority folk, he also wondered how to explain to the Selective Service lady what the poet and dreamer stood for, deep down inside himself. "Following your dreams, I guess you'd say," he began. "Accommodating others in his world. Becoming someone in a society that doesn't want you."

"*Dreams.*"

Charles uttered that word softly like he supplied the missing ingredients in an empty pie pan, making the pie puff up perfect.

"Dreams, yes, that's what we need, not war, but peace," Edna blurted out, sounding suddenly like sabotaging her own Selective Service role. When Charles stepped forward, she paused to judge his intent. What's this, she seemed to be thinking, another angry colored man and I misjudged him?

At first Charles too seemed uncertain of his move. Then he strode even closer to her and Eddie before speaking. "*Hold fast to dreams/For if dreams die/Life is a broken-winged bird/That cannot fly.*"

His voice was so soft Eddie saw Edna hesitate even more since she was unaware Charles had come there to enlist, and not wait to be drafted. Maybe, Eddie reasoned with himself, maybe my brother's changed his mind? He'll let them call him up for Service?

"Dreams," Charles said, quoting another line. "*Hold fast to dreams/For when dreams go/Life is a barren field/Frozen with snow.*"

"Yes, Langston Hughes," Eddie said with a sigh when his brother finished.

"He wrote that when only 21, in 1922," Charles added.

"What was it, that Harlem Ren ... what'd you call it?" Edna asked.

"An awakening. Least that's what East Coast theorists called it. A renaissance. It was a band of brothers and sisters breaking their bonds and expressing desire," Charles explained.

"*Your* desire? What is it?" Edna asked looking at both brothers.

Eddie had an answer. He felt it internalized, but failed now to express it. That inability created a longing inside him, which he knew Charles found but never managed to express either. Eddie saw his taller brother locked in deep thought, which seemed to make him come up shorter in an existential struggle to determine his mission in life. It was minutes before Charles straightened up and began to speak, this time in harsher terms.

"Trapped, you could say, we all are metaphorically, but in New York they built a concrete wall, seven miles long. It separated white and black neighborhoods around a place called Wyoming. That's part of the city with a large hotel. The wall was erected on purpose to keep Negroes from being free to come and go in their home city," Charles explained. "Our desire? To exercise our rights, that's what."

Hearing his brother speak so fervently, Eddie realized why Charles chose to join the War effort and not be called up like a sweating sharecropper from the cotton fields, unable to write his own name or tell what state he lived in. Act on your dream, that was Charles's argument and the poet Hughes's, too.

"*A dream deferred,*" Charles said more to Edna than Eddie. "*Does it dry up like a raisin in the sun? Or does it explode?*"

"Understood, quite well," Edna said. "That comes from your writer, too?"

She spoke while looking through a drawer in her desk. While she did so, an assistant took Eddie and Charles's papers and sent them on to another office.

"Hughes was his name," Eddie added to answer Edna clearly. He wished her to remember.

28

"A few minutes and you'll be up for a physical," Edna said after receiving a report on how examination lines were moving.

"What about me?" Charles asked. "Wait among the masses? I'm here to enlist, not be drafted."

"Pass the exam and we'll induct you separate," she said.

"Some other coloreds? Or mixed company?"

Edna smiled faintly and coveted her book some more. "Mr. Washington, you surely know Army makes the rules, not me."

"And the Marines?"

"All-white, so far," she said with a sympathetic nod.

Eddie watched his brother hold his temper until Edna held out her thin volume. She handed it to Eddie, who studied the title page. *Spring Book of Garden Verse.* As the Registration room fell silent and the call for physical exams waited, Eddie began reading. He expected nothing above what the title said, poems of a garden variety. He guessed it was to be sentimental versifying published in the 1930s to lift Americans' low spirits during the Depression, but the calmness that crept over him deepened the longer he read. Most of the verses described nature's vernal rebirth, but some touched him as sincere attempts at serious art. Eddie lingered on one titled simply *November*, misplaced, of course, among the titles about spring, but the poem had somehow snuck in. Eddie felt it not altogether out of place, maybe because the title matched his own flagging mood at the drab Selective Service office.

"Hey, listen to this!" he exclaimed, knowing Edna'd be pleased that he acted pleased, which he was, to his own surprise. "No schmaltz this one!"

"What?" Charles asked.

"Sixteen lines, about the death of the old year. The eleventh month. I like it. Sure you wanna hear?" he asked Edna.

"Yes, it's very good but I always look on the cheery side," she said. "Like in May. Sunny and flowery."

"Go on," Charles insisted. Eddie knew his brother was growing weary of him cajoling a Selective Service clerk hoping to get a break in the call-up lists, meaning to be drafted last or not at all, which was probably a fruitless wish when the Military Service took anybody able to stand upright.

"Here goes," Eddie said offering the book to Edna so she could read the verse aloud, but she declined. "Sixteen lines, twice as long as *Dreams*."

Charles waited impatiently. Edna smiled in encouragement on hearing someone so enthusiastic about a tiny book she cherished.

Night fell heavy and early/A distant siren blared/The neighbor's dog barked for attention/A cat stared wide-eyed in the dark.

Eddie paused for a signal they wished more. Seeing them nod yes, he read on.

He slumbered under a leaden blanket/And dreamed of books he'd read/One about death and an old guy/who babbled a' green fields.

"Who's the *he* in the poem?" Charles asked.

Eddie was surprised his own brother could hear a scene narrated straightforward and miss that the third-person could be Everyman.

"He's any of us, right?" Edna asked more to herself than her new companions. "Coming to terms with thoughts of death."

"Yes," Eddie added. "The old year dying, and only a lonely dog to lament it?"

"Not to mention his own mortality. Life fading away," Charles added, suddenly rejoining the conversation. "What's next?"

Eddie tried to decide if Charles was bewailing his own humanity or asking if there was more to the poem. Figuring the latter, he continued. *Day dawned slow and weary/Siren silent/Dog downcast/ Cat clawing witchery from her eyes.*

"Yes, and go on." Edna encouraged him.

By now Eddie was sure she knew the poem by heart. Maybe she wrote it? He looked again at the title page but saw only a single byline and publisher.

"Rev. Gene McElroy and Three Square Church," Eddie said out loud. The volume gave no other authors' names or place of publication. Its only illustration showed a church spire towering over a densely wooded valley. So Edna's treasured book had to be a collection of this pastor McElroy's verse, whoever he was. Eddie imagined the poet laboring mightily and at last putting down a few lines of consolation, to make an unfathomable world in an explosive era feel less futile.

The poet's reward was surely relative anonymity, which made Eddie remember slaves of old, who toiled in the cotton fields of the Mississippi Delta only to die dusty deaths, as some other poet had described humans' last breath, and MayBelle spent so much of her mental energy reminding families about.

"Wretches like us go unmentioned in schoolbooks and fail to record our feelings," Eddie muttered. He paused to reflect but realized his words sounded overused or lamely borrowed from some college text he pored over but was now unable to cite. Hearing no response from Charles or Edna, he turned again to Rev. McElroy's last stanza.

He studied an ash tree across the alley/In the night it tired of its dead leaves/They lay and glowed, like a gay scarlet wreath/Around the thin, dark trunk.

Eddie watched Edna, who surely had beheld the scarlet circle of dying leaves around the wet, dark tree trunk in her visions, but found no soul to share her thoughts of it with. Now here was a humble kinsman of a different skin color reading it aloud to her, with feeling.

"Don't you love that imagery?" Edna asked. "Reverend McElroy, my favorite."

"Who is he anyway?" Charles wondered, clearly touched by the lines but not so visibly as Edna, or even Eddie, who acted stiffly surprised at finding a touch of poetic feeling in a U.S. Draft Board office.

"Your poet, I mean," Charles repeated when Edna failed to respond.

"No clue," she said with a shrug. "I'm told he's a pastor, out in the sticks somewhere, across the River beyond here."

"God forsaken place?"

"Small town, most like," Edna added. "Anyway, I like these lines, though sad. I've seen ash leaves in the fall. They glow in the soggy air."

"Yes, something glorious about it," Charles said.

"Like they have an inner light. They die and summer's a faded memory," Edna said dreamily.

29

Once again, Eddie thought of a road not taken, or if taken, was it the right one? He wondered about a woman like Edna inviting two guys into her confidence and clutching a book of verse tight to her bosom before sharing it with them. Then asking them for opinions like they were men of authority. Did she think before acting?

"It's like Pastor McElroy speaks with the same voice you do," she said at last to Eddie, but nodded more knowingly toward Charles. "In his lines."

"It requires courage, you know, for a guy to write by name. To keep doing it even if your name means nothing to readers, if there are any. It's a choice," Charles said.

In his brother's voice, Eddie heard echoes of MayBelle's pronouncements, sometimes self-promoting but containing a truth. To Eddie there was something glorious about carrying on despite the odds. It felt as it must've for their folks, who struggled nameless and forgotten in generations past, for a cause, though they were unsure of life's outcome or their cause's success.

"You know what Langston Hughes wrote?" Eddie asked. He felt as unsure of what to quote from Hughes as his forebears could've been about the outcome of their causes.

"*Beautiful is the sun. Beautiful, also, are the souls of my people,*" Charles spoke up and stole the line from Eddie. "Langston was 22 when he wrote that line."

The three fell silent and Eddie imagined them wondering how it could feel to be an acclaimed author and barely twenty. Before

Eddie could describe his wonderment at such a miracle, a call came for the men to report for their physicals. Edna showed them to the door, where lines of raw youth in civvies were gathering.

"I can tell both of you studied English. You act and talk different than those out there in line. Good luck," she said. She pointed at her copy of *Spring Book of Garden Verse* and held it high up. "Remember, you belong."

Eddie heard her. And then he and Charles marched out, hardly in step with each other, but brothers, together. At 6 3" and 170, Charles rocked on the balls of his feet showing all his athletic prowess. Only a bag of bones by comparison, and bowlegged besides, Eddie felt like a lamb being led to the slaughter. Yet he was educated and fast becoming a proud family man. Deciding at last that war and domesticity didn't mix, he gritted his teeth, waved at Charlene in a crowd of well-wishers, and went along to be judged as fit or unfit to defend a country that demanded their help but remained divided about what role to give them in the struggle.

The line for whites was long and noisy. Some sounded jubilant to go out and fight. The line of colored guys remained short and silent. With Edna's words in his ears, Eddie waited to have his value measured.

"Whites here. Coloreds there," a sergeant hollered.

"Like a slave auction, huh, man?" Eddie said.

From there the line led straight to the examining room. Eddie waved again at Charlene.

"We'll be out in the blink of an eye," he said.

Charles didn't speak until he stepped up to the exam line. Even then he barely moved his lips in a quiet word.

"Tulsa."

30

With the Street Rod useless and long gone besides, Charles, Eddie, and Charlene waited outside Selective Service for a ride. Eddie made a mental note they'd reached the Ides of March, the date Caesar was killed. That happened hundreds of years ago, as he remembered from reading Shakespeare, who was certainly just another old white guy, as some of his college classmates liked to remind him, but a guy that cast a suspicious eye at tyrants when he felt like it. No matter that, Eddie thought now. They'd agreed to meet MayBelle for a taxi home.

"Here we are in 1942," he said to Charles and Charlene. "Four o'clock and still no sign of Ma. She agreed to meet us now. On the dot."

"Her making it on the dot? Dream on," Charles answered.

Charlene smiled at her husband's impatience and her brother-in-law's calmness. "Sometime before dark, surely," she said.

The three whiled away their time together, as the growing afternoon traffic whizzed by. From a pack of Lucky Strikes they'd received from a tobacco company for registering with the draft, Eddie shared cigarettes with Charles but Charlene shook her head no. Soon Eddie flipped his smoke away and ground it out on the pavement. He noticed Charles stuck his behind one ear, unlit.

"Cool dude," Charlene said to Charles teasingly. He looked away in embarrassment, which Eddie took to mean Charles was as inexperienced with nicotine and accepting compliments as him. With no words and props, like a cigarette stub or pop bottles to fiddle with, they stood idly watching traffic. The Army physical passed through Eddie's mind.

"It was like an orderly nothingness," he told Charlene. The medical men tested what any M.D. would. His heart, lungs, and vision proved normal.

"Your feet are a bio-mechanical nightmare," the orthopedist said, on the other hand. He and another medical guy asked Eddie to run on a makeshift track, so he hobbled a couple laps and that was it. "We'll get back to you," the second medic said, who seemed to know his podiatry.

"You're sure you guys have the same father?" Charlene joked when Eddie told her about the experience. She nodded toward Charles, who was striding ahead of them toward the taxi stand. "How tall was he? Your dad?"

"Same father, different feet and body," Eddie replied. "Don't remember Pa's height. His physical self must've changed between when he made Charles and then me," he joked.

"His arches fell? You don't remember? Or don't want to?"

"I was too little. He and Ma had me then he was off to the races."

"The races? Truly?"

Eddie didn't answer, but watching the cars passing by made him imagine thunderous horses' hooves and his father beating it for greener pastures far away. Hialeah, probably, if only Carlos knew where it was.

"Strange. Can horses have flat hooves?" he asked as MayBelle's cab pulled up. Charles and Charlene didn't understand his humor, but they saw the taxi and piled in. Charles took a seat up front while Eddie let MayBelle sit between him and Charlene.

"Yeah, flat feet, that's you, boy," MayBelle chimed in when they told her of the conversation. "No, not really, I don't think so," she added growing serious. "Not horses."

Otherwise MayBelle sat in silence when the cabbie, who was older, said he'd been in World War I and got injured by a cannon that misfired at the Battle of Chateau Thierry. He talked on until the news on his taxi's radio interrupted him.

"The latest is Nazis crossing north Africa," the driver announced. "They've got General Rommel leading the way and aim to take Tobruk."

"Tobruk?" Charlene asked in confusion.

Eddie shook his head and turned to Charles, who also drew a blank. MayBelle quickly picked up the slack. "The Battle of Chat ... whatever you said," she uttered in a try at the French words. The cab driver understood her.

"Yes, 1918. Chateau Thierry and I was there, quarter century ago."

"But what's Tobruk?" Charlene insisted.

"That's in this war, now," Charles explained. "They're calling this World War II."

The cabbie thanked Charles for the explanation and continued. "A sergeant I was and we were trying to take a muddy hillside where there'd been snow. I led my men and we slid in to a battery of artillery. Trying for Hill 204, they called it. One a' the blasted cannons on a ledge above us, manned by our own troops, misfired right over my head. A shell casing hit me on the leg. I charged up that danged hill anyway, with barrages over our heads. We aimed to cross a river near the town, but my leg collapsed. That was the end of war for me. Happened quick, didn't even hurt till they got me back to the infirmary. A makeshift tent, it was. Then the pain came. They gave me something for it. I laid there in agony and nausea."

"Until?"

"An eternity till some medic came around and dressed it. Gangrene precaution, he said."

"So you made it through to the end? That same year?" Eddie wondered.

"Yes, but limpin' ever since. That's why I'm driving this crate, don't need to get out and walk if I'm driving."

"Still bothers you, huh?" Eddie asked.

The cabbie grew quiet, like he didn't tolerate dumb comments and expected words of substance. When none came, he turned to

Charles and said simply, "One thing I'll tell you."

Eddie had been expecting more description of combat after the comments on Tobruk and Hill 204, but he waited for what was next.

"Why, the French countryside. Sure is pretty over there. I'll never forget. Rolling hills and green everywhere. There's a quiet to it."

"Even in war?" Charlene asked.

"Horrible guns firing over our heads and it's like people and farm animals just get on as best they can, but of course you don't know what fears they have inside them. And the boat ride over the pond, I only got seasick once the whole way."

"Bad leg and all?" Eddie asked. "Which way? Going or coming back?"

The cabbie shook his head and changed the topic to refresh his memory on where he was driving them.

"Okie Joe's, the barbecue joint. That where youse is heading, right?"

"We can need refreshments," Eddie joked. "After this afternoon's Army physical."

The cabbie nodded at Eddie's comment, but clearly found it innocuous. He draped one hand over the steering wheel and drove on. They were nearly at Oklahoma Joe's when he spoke again. "Yes, never doubt it. War's hell."

"Because you never know from day to day?" Charles asked, finally breaking his silence.

"No, not quite. There's down time. Even long periods when there's no combat, just sit and wait like the Gerries're as bored as you. All in the same damned mess. You know it can be a lull for a month or two and nothing happens. Hill 204, or whatever it happens to be, can lay and wait with the forces on either side piddling around. Rations but little appetite and a bit of cash, nowhere to spend it. Spring comes with poppies red as blazes, then summer, and fall. Maybe the first snow falls before the generals finally decide to get a move on. We had an officer, Pershing. Black Jack they called him. He got things going."

"So what happens, the hell?" Charles asked.

"Yeah, not like you think. There's guys'll tell you it comes in stages. You go out there and it hits you after a while, like this is dangerous stuff, but it's the others that get hit. Can't happen to me, you feel sure. Then you see your pals slumping down in the ooze dead as hell and you realize it's damned dangerous and you need to be careful so it can't happen to you, but at last you see what's really going on and guys dying like flies so you accept the truth. It not only can happen to you but it's going to any moment and there's not a thing you can do to stop it."

"You're doomed?" Eddie asked incredulously. "You experienced that?"

"Hell, yeah, the feelings, for sure, but I was lucky. I came home alive."

"Like we can see?" Charles said with an understanding smile.

The cabbie grew quiet as he pulled up to Oklahoma Joe's. He turned and peered at the back seat since Eddie's voice was the clearest one from there. When neither Eddie nor the ladies said anything, the driver turned to Charles as though suddenly realizing who among his customers was likeliest to see combat. The two looked calmly at each other. Words had become needless in expressing what everybody thought but didn't say.

"Others took the hits, I mean. Not me," the driver said. "Least nothing that killed me."

Charles nodded and reached for his wallet as Eddie and Charlene got out to give MayBelle room to stretch her legs.

"No charge, on me," the driver said to Charles, who offered him a fiver.

Charles said nothing. Charlene and MayBelle thanked the cabbie for their free ride. Like Charles, the driver grew quiet before driving away. Eddie thought the smile on his face made it seem he was saying, "Good luck. You'll need it, Soldier Boys."

Looking out over the rushing traffic and bustling crowds, Eddie felt he'd reached a point where the world was doubly dangerous, at home and abroad. Either that or events had sneaked up and caught him unawares as he reached what people called manhood. He needed to take extra care now and see nothing happened to him. Or to Charlene. MayBelle, he already knew, was a survivor.

31

"Okie Joe's, so this is it?" Eddie asked and peered up at a stucco barbecue joint with shaded windows and a dull neon sign. In contrast to the outer shabbiness, the restaurant had a sparkling interior. The Washingtons, party of four, came to dine in peace, meaning they were among the earliest guests and the locale cradled them in a sweet mid-afternoon aura.

Charles and Eddie ordered a bottle of California red wine. Each took a polite sip before dinner. Eddie described his physical exam to Charlene and MayBelle, who took nothing to drink. The physical itself was routine, Eddie said. He came away with the feeling a guy needed to be on his last leg to fail it, or have a rich patron who'd pay the docs to label him 4-F, which meant a deferment. From the white guys' line he heard a few loudmouths so cocksure Eddie guessed they had powerful fathers or unimaginable pedigrees that made them above the law.

"None a' that nonsense among us," he added. "We acted patient."

"And you?" MayBelle asked. "Your awkward stride, if that's the word for your gait?"

"They got a foot doc," Charles answered for his bother. "He took Eddie aside." Charles spoke like he wanted to deflect interest from his own exam, which no one doubted went well.

As the others took their meal, Eddie looked on. For breakfast they had only nibbled at tidbits, so Okie's ribs hit the spot. MayBelle and Charlene let Charles fill their glasses at last. Eddie saw satisfaction settle over the table. When everybody finished, he raised a glass.

"To the war effort," MayBelle proposed, though her unaccustomed weak tone made it unsure what she thought of military efforts in general or how the war would affect people in her neighborhood.

"I tried to find a Marine Corps booth or officer in charge," Eddie explained. "Something for you, Charles."

"None. Army takes us, but not Marines."

Like their wine, the afternoon began slipping away. Eddie wondered about his immediate family. Once four in number, they were then reduced to three when Carlos disappeared. Now upped again to four with Charlene, they seemed poised for a new era, but one shrouded in unknowables. He considered his mother, a neighborhood mover and shaker, now in middle age. His brother, of enormous athletic skill and intelligence but limited ambition, his one desire being a Marine Corps enlistment, denied by the white world's refusal to share blood, sweat, and tears with him, or even death, on whatever bloodstained beaches. Charlene and Eddie himself, ready to start a life together and have children, while facing a future of new-found freedoms or continued bondage.

As they studied the tab and talked about whether to hail another cab or "hoof it on home," as MayBelle put it, Charlene stepped forward.

"The ride's on me," she said showing her purse.

"Oh, no," her mother-in-law protested. "The gentlemen here ..."

They hesitated. It was clear Eddie was broke and Charles seemed reluctant, though he'd earlier offered the cabbie a fiver. Behind them two white couples waited patiently to pay their tab. Eddie eyed them apologetically until he remembered Oklahoma Joe's welcomed people of all sorts. Even so, it seemed MayBelle needed to step up and rescue her grown sons from their penniless dilemma.

Unwilling to be stopped, Charlene insisted. "It's the last of my college money, too," she explained. "Let's splurge and move on."

Charlene fished a few crumpled bills from her purse and handed them to the cashier. When she received her change, she strolled over to their table, where a colored busboy was clearing dishes. She handed him a couple of quarters and turned to their white waitress and gave her the same amount.

Eddie brought up the rear behind Charles and their mother while Charlene led the way out. Her pride at paying settled when she found the few coins left over didn't make cab fare. They turned to MayBelle, who talked again of hoofing it on home.

"For real this time," Eddie mumbled.

"Never thought you'd see the day, huh, this son of mine Eddie and no car?" MayBelle said with a laugh. "If only you'd seen what I saw in my day."

"Here it is, 1942," Eddie stated with a combined sigh and chortle. "There's plenty enough to see now."

"Worse to come?" MayBelle asked.

All four sauntered along with the goal of getting back to MayBelle's place, but in no particular hurry.

"Strolling along, with no particular place to go," Eddie said.

"Sounds like a good line for a song," Charles suggested.

"Any casual motorist passing by would see that," Eddie continued.

"See what?" Charlene wondered.

"Like storied darkies of the Delta we are, no particular goal, trudgin' along anyway. Down there in Mississippi it'd be on a dusty road leading nowhere."

"I know, that's the picture you'd see in folk art," Charles added from out the silent shell he'd inhabited after the Exam Center experience. "Free to fight but lacking the freedom to decide who for, an ironical mess if ever I saw one. The desire and the liberty to choose where or how should be equal."

"Not in Whitey's world," Eddie cautioned.

"We're looking to the future," Charlene insisted. "I won't give up."

Eddie was surprised at his wife's outspoken determination, but he stayed quiet while the four walked on. He felt thankful for MayBelle's approval of Charlene.

"My advice to you all is this, youngsters," MayBelle said as they neared home. Mind you earn enough dough, turn it to cash, and stick together, that's what we got in the family."

Her words led Eddie to study the four of them again. They were indeed all they had. The only hope of more to come rested with himself and Charlene, unless Charles came back from the war and found a lady to wed.

"You got your aunts and uncles and cousins spread out, but us four is the kernel," MayBelle continued.

Eddie felt his mother still living with a pre-world war mindset, but he admired her steadfast plan. As for himself, he wondered what he thought of the new world emerging before their eyes. Impossible to tell where it'd take them. In another week or two Charles would march off to do battle, and he himself would be the man of the family, at least until Selective Service came calling for him as well.

"Us two," MayBelle said directly to Charlene, "not long now and us females be heading things up."

Not altogether displeased, both ladies chuckled at the suggestion they'd rule the roost. In turn, Charles increased his step knowing it was Army for him. Eddie lingered behind. In his struggle to imagine the future in any predictable form, he preferred staying home to waging war.

"That be your life," as his kinfolk said.

BOOK II

Outrunning the Ball

1

Only weeks after Eddie's physical he was scouring the newspaper for teaching jobs. He spread Classified Ads across the kitchen table as MayBelle regaled him with details of her first war-time call from Charles.

"You remember," she began. "He enlisted and got called up the next week."

Eddie nodded. "Remember, too, the school year's two-thirds kaput and my dough all the way so," he said. "War's my only way out."

He was folding the newspaper in despair when Charlene came in with a brown postage-paid envelope, which she quietly placed before him. "Speaking of which," she said.

He picked it up with a mighty effort as though the contents contained lead.

"Be brave," Charlene calmly encouraged him. "From the Gov, I bet."

"Selective Service? Imagine. Two sons of mine soon in uniform," MayBelle uttered with pride.

Eddie fumbled with the envelope. That it contained a draft notice was clear. Not a half-bad option for the unemployed, but maybe a death sentence. He wondered if the Army would send him to one of its remote Missouri training bases.

"Well, what'll it be?" MayBelle asked, reading his thoughts. "Your brother says it's hot as blazes at Fort Leonard Wood, this time of year."

"Late March? And how would he know after only a week there?"

"Better bet you gonna find out," she warned Eddie.

"So you figure the Army's dumb enough to send us to the same base and then to the same battles to get killed together in the same dumb assault?" Eddie answered. He eyed his mother and Charlene with unease as he pulled the slim single sheet from its envelope.

"Well?" Charlene asked eagerly. She moved closer.

Eddie unfolded the sheet and let out a sigh of relief mixed with a sheepish grin.

The paper hung loosely from his hand until Charlene took it from him. "4-F?" she asked.

Startled, MayBelle looked up and backed away, "Why, you got a deferment? Whatever for, boy?"

"That's right, they judged him flatfoot!" Charlene said, in sudden understanding. "I forgot."

"That's right, Ma," Eddie agreed. "They got no need for a guy that can't run and send him storming enemy beaches? Suicide, plain and simple."

MayBelle frowned.

"For someone wanting everybody at home, Ma, you sure look sad," Eddie ribbed her. "You wanna lose us both? What's Charles say anyway? About training?"

"Tough, but seventh heaven. Hundreds of guys, if not thousands, he says. Training's a cakewalk. Running and jumping. Like being on a track team. And excelling at it."

As the truth of how Army doctors viewed the brothers' physical capabilities sank in, Eddie, MayBelle, and Charlene settled into a silence during which Eddie read their thoughts. As vulnerable as the two women seemed, he understood their determination to take care of what they treasured. In him and Charles they saw a quiet bravado and manliness but found something in them that could falter under pressure. Courage needed to be wed with split-second thinking. Eddie reasoned slavery instilled that quality in generations of men and women alike.

Eddie gathered the classified section together and looked again under the column *Education*. The ads he found were for teachers in the fall of 1943, but his needs were more urgent.

"Now! I'm looking for something now, full-time," he burst out after a while. He finally wadded up the newspaper and prepared to toss it.

"We're not about to starve, Honey," Charlene reminded him as she picked up the paper and neatly flattened its crumpled pages. She urged him to pay attention.

"I showed you before, but you won't listen," she argued. "The Army's jerking working teachers out of classrooms in droves. Or they're joining the Service themselves. Look at columns on other pages. You'd find what I did, if you weren't so dang-blasted stubborn."

Charlene turned to MayBelle, who nodded in approval. Both women knew substitute teachers were in demand, especially at Sumner and Vashon, where men outnumbered ladies on the faculty. The youngest of those men were fast leaving for the military.

"You knew this all along," MayBelle reminded him, "but in your male mind you wanna be the big man at home for your little harem of wife and aged parent. You find out the hard way, we take what we get in life. And us ladies are strong."

Eddie smirked in self-derision before glancing at the newspaper again. Feeling his wife and mother's watchful presence, he followed down the page to *Education: Part Time*. He studied the listings alphabetically until a weary look from Charlene caused him to glance ahead faster.

"Lookee," he said at last to confirm her calm insistence. "Down at the bottom. *Sumner High.*" He picked up a pencil to mark whatever seemed interesting. Lord knew what.

"Great," MayBelle interrupted. "But nothing from Vashon? Where I sent you?"

"No, Sumner's looking for ..."

"But Vashon?" his mother insisted.

Eddie put down the pen. He looked up and saw MayBelle squarely in the eye. "Been there, Ma, done that."

"Yes, I suppose you done that, okay," MayBelle said with a sigh. "Outstripped 'em all in classwork." She returned his steady gaze and winked, which brought a brightening smile to his face.

"I'm kinda uppity, huh?"

"Yeah, maybe a little, now that he knows how to dump a car without paying," Charlene said. "Doubt they taught you that at Vashon."

"Yeah, you learn that elsewhere," Eddie replied, but his joke aroused no glee.

Feeling outnumbered, he looked down at the paper and read aloud. *Wanted: Substitute teachers. K-12. Apply by Mail.* "Did you hear? My stentorian voice overwhelmed you?"

"The same tone you used reading to Edna?" Charlene asked in a tease.

"Edna? Who she be?" MayBelle demanded affecting her semi-literate voice.

"Never you mind," Eddie replied to keep the conversation on track.

"That's the lady got him a 4-F for the bad feet he only sort of has," Charlene explained.

Eddie couldn't decide whether Charlene believed her own statement or was teasing him. Maybe a bit of both he guessed. So he wondered if his reluctance to join the military reflected a degree of cowardice or a firm conviction that he could do more good helping youth in the classroom. If schoolteachers in war-torn times were nearly always women, was his lagging behind the same as assuming a feminine role? If so, to what purpose? Was he to wait at home for his braver big brother to come home?

There seemed no choice. As badly as the military wanted troops, they wouldn't take him now. He'd be better off teaching.

That very evening the two young marrieds sat at MayBelle's kitchen table and typed letters to Sumner High. Eddie gave his educational background and suggested he'd be okay at Social Studies or English and History. He read Charlene's letter after his own . She had a firm notion of what she liked.

"So it's choir for you?" Eddie asked as they left the Post Office after mailing their letters.

She nodded. "Yes, you knew that."
"Nice school, don't know if they can sing, though," he kidded her.
"Guess, they'll have to learn," she needled him.

2

Fast and furious or so it felt. Dr. Leon Russell, the Sumner High principal, called a week after they applied. He explained that a teacher of U.S. Government up and enlisted in the Army. Not to be left behind, his wife joined the Women's Auxiliary Corps (WACs). Within days, Eddie and Charlene were interviewing for substitute positions at Sumner, full or part-time, as needs arose. A mixed bag for sure.

"War's good for the economy but bad for us," Dr. Russell said. "The couple that left shared an office. She taught typing and ran our secretarial pool. We need subs in a rush."

"Sorry, I don't type well," Charlene protested.

"Well, the typewriter's like a piano keyboard," Dr. Russell continued and ran his fingers along his desk top like playing a Grand. "The Duke, you know. Ellington, my man." He looked gently at Charlene so she understood the principal had a staff to fill. If you had a sheepskin, he'd find you a place with his school.

"Provided you can read, and write, too," Dr. Russell said. "I'm only partly joking, you'd be surprised."

"But I'm not a pianist either," Charlene announced. "I sing."

"You read notes, I see here. And Alcorn has taught your husband this or that about our founding fathers, if I'm not mistaken," Dr. Russell continued. He nodded to a framed photo of W. E. B. DuBois on the wall behind him. It showed DuBois in middle age with a sharp pointed chin and serious look. Principal Russell's visage was like DuBois's, including a receding hairline, but his manner struck Eddie as milder, less strident. Dr. Russell grew silent and waited, his last comment a clear invitation for Eddie to reply.

The young man hesitated.

"I read your letter," the principal added. "Courses you took. You learned this and that? In class and out?"

"Yes, I know some things," Eddie agreed while searching his memory for stray bits about DuBois. His thoughts drifted instead back and forth between the man who asked the question and the figure on the questioner's wall. Dr. Russell was an imposing figure with a gentle smile, while W. E. B. DuBois, as Eddie remembered reading about him, was a small man who spoke out, and could be frightening to some, no-nonsense to all.

"I know what I heard and saw," Eddie answered.

"Which is?"

"My ma. Her books. Our leaders went along with the wishes of politicians, who'd open schools for coloreds but keep Jim Crow in place. DuBois argued for full rights. No compromise."

Eddie glanced at Charlene for help. She smiled but nodded Dr. Russell's way meaning Eddie should look at him, not her. She said simply, "Yes, that's what DuBois believed in."

Eddie remembered stories MayBelle told him as a child.

"Yes, my ma," he began but stopped. "My mother, I mean. She talked about that. After The Great War she meant. East St. Louis and then …"

Dr. Russell smiled but the creases around his eyes showed sadness. "We call it the Massacre of East St. Louis," he interrupted solemnly.

"Yes, that's what she carried on about. Our people came home after that War, the one to end all wars, and went for better jobs, but whites massacred coloreds that replaced striking white workers. Two hundred and fifty black men, she said. Slaughtered. Like animals. In the streets."

Eddie was talking so fast he had trouble pausing. His mind churned with info but he struggled to bind his words to a sequence of events. Dr. Russell roused himself from his seat and leaned forward. He glanced from Eddie to Charlene. The principal fidgeted with an empty pipe he kept on the desktop but seemed never to have smoked.

"The Silent Parade," Charlene said to urge Eddie on.

"And, yes, we heard about that in a class. Or my wife did, she took the course and told me. About The Parade, I mean."

Dr. Russell looked at Charlene, as if inviting her to continue. Eddie seized the opportunity.

"DuBois organized a parade in New York City in 1917. The Silent Parade, newspapers called it. Nine thousand New Yorkers marched to protest killings in East St. Louis. It was DuBois, the organizer, in the picture behind you, he's the guy. He got things going after East St. Louis."

Dr. Russell looked once again at Charlene. "I understand you're not from here."

She nodded. "Yes, I mean no. Memphis."

"The East St. Louis Massacre happened across the River from here, in Illinois. Horrifying," he said with a shake of his head, "but people start to forget. In time our memories fail."

"Not my mother MayBelle's," Eddie shot in. "She can't stop talking about it. That and Tulsa."

"As we know, writers often ignore the truth and those that did it are silent," the principal said with a sigh. "Someday ..."

"My mother knows," Eddie assured him.

Dr. Russell looked down at his desk and the papers on it. He tapped the pipe at a bare spot on the desktop while fumbling with Eddie and Charlene's letters. Seeing no tobacco stains on the wood, Eddie wondered how long the principal had been sitting in his office with an empty pipe searching for new teachers to replace those gone off to war or tempted by higher paying jobs in the expanding Defense Industry. Eddie remembered MayBelle predicting a third of teachers would be gone after another year of war.

3

"Var's bad for us," Dr. Russell repeated. He shook his head but reserved a smile for Eddie and Charlene. "I have substituting for you in April and May. Full-time in the fall. Interested?"

The two youths said yes and realized that finding paying jobs was a predicament solved. As they got up to leave, the principal reached out to finalize the deal. While shaking hands, he showed a hint of joviality mixed with melancholy, understandable for a man embroiled in a struggle to hire a staff amidst a tide of departures.

"Your 4-F deferment? It's sure to stick, is it?" he asked Eddie.

"Yes, but not to my mother's delight. She likes to think of me wearing a uniform like my big brother."

"Let's hope not. Some are needed on this front," the principal responded and then hesitated. "You know, nothing to brag about, but I grew up in Tulsa and wrote my graduate paper on the race riot there, so-called. Ten thousand left homeless, thirty-nine people killed, whites and colored. Black Wall Street Riot, they called it. It was the wealthiest Negro neighborhood in the city, so the white hoodlums and some cops, paid off by the white crooks in Tulsa's City Hall, destroyed that part of town in revenge."

"For what?" Charlene asked in surprise.

"For being successful, it seems," Dr. Russell said.

"And getting ahead in life, ahead of white guys, my ma says," Eddie explained.

"Most likely, in the grand scheme of things, but the immediate cause was a 19-year-old bobby boy that was said to have assaulted a white girl in a hotel elevator he operated. Silence has prevailed, for all these years. Neither Negro nor white talk about it in public, so we may never know. I'm impressed you two heard of it."

"Thank my ma for that, too," Eddie commented as he opened the door for Charlene. "She's the one that knows."

"Impressive lady then, your mother."

"She says she's heard of you."

"We'll let you know when contracts are ready," the principal said. "You'll need a temporary teacher's certificate. We'll help you. You'll be paid by the hour as subs. And don't forget."

"What's that?" Eddie wondered.

"Your quiz for the day."

Eddie smiled as he spied an unopened pouch among a stack of books on Dr. Russell's desktop. *East Side Tobacconists* was imprinted on the leather.

"East St. Louis? When?"

"1917," Eddie and Charlene answered together.

"Tulsa?"

"1921."

"Welcome aboard," the principal said. "Any questions?"

"Yes, any tips, for beginners?"

Dr. Russell answered quickly, like a harried physician besieged by a multitude of hypochondriacs. "Only one rule," he began. "Never assume your students won't ever know more than you do."

Eddie joined his wife in exiting through the main door at Sumner High, in jubilation over landing a job. At home, they heard on the news that Tobruk was in Allied hands, Bataan in the Philippines suffered a Japanese siege, and a ferocious Battle in the Coral Sea, wherever that was, had only begun.

That afternoon MayBelle received her longest letter from Charles, postmarked March 28, 1942.

4

Eddie and Charlene returned to Sumner the first week of April. Eddie got his substitute assignment for Problems of American Government. Facing a seventh-hour class of high school juniors, he was shocked to discover they were not nearly as somnolent as he expected. In fact, they knew more about the Constitution and *habeas corpus* than he did. In truth, he'd barely ever heard of the latter concept, but refused to try bluffing his way through the class hour. Instead, he listened patiently to a group of impatient kids until one angry boy in working man's overalls patched at the knees, presumably by his mother, bravely stood up and explained, "Yesterday's teacher told us …"

"Just a minute," Eddie asked in astonishment. "Whadda you mean, yesterday's?"

"It was a sub like you. A lady, with white hair."

"What'd she tell you?"

"*Habeas corpus* means produce the body in Latin."

"And?"

"If you wanna arrest somebody, you can't punish them without taking them in person to a courthouse first."

"And explaining the charge to a judge," a second boy added. "And saying what they did wrong."

By then the class was all ears, which made Eddie aware most were hearing it for the first time, either because they weren't present the day before or had been off in another world as yesterday's substitute teacher spoke. This sub from yesterday, whoever she was, must've known what she was talking about. As for some kids not hearing her, Eddie guessed at the causes—hunger pangs, homes with missing parents, or an attention disorder from lack of sleep? The two boys who spoke wore shabby clothes, which Eddie guessed was a fashion statement, but they were clean, both the clothing and the boys themselves, so Eddie figured parental care varied from family to family.

Suddenly a tall, thin boy with coal black hair rose to his feet. His eyes shone as he blurted out a long line of utterances Eddie strained to understand. "The teach tell ..." were the only clear syllables.

A girl with light brown skin and a spotlessly clean white dress turned in her front-row seat and spoke without standing. "That's Alphonse. He means to say you can't put anybody in lockup if you don't charge him to his face in court," she explained and shifted in her seat so Eddie saw she wore braces on both legs. "He's from Haiti. Me, too, I understand him. My brother."

Eddie felt a wish to learn more, not about the court system, but the kids facing him. Before he had time to ask them, another rough-looking boy, with kinky hair, stood up against the far wall and spoke in a gravelly voice. He wasted no time. "Mister, *Habeas corpus* means the Klan can't lynch no stupid sucker without cops reading him his rights. No mind Whiteys pays to the law, though. They string us up in trees and ain't no judge stopping it. That's what Miss Crankpot told us."

"Miss?"

"Yesterday's sub. Not her real name, what we called her. A crusty old white dame, white hair too, but she told it like it is. The whole danged story. Ain't I right?" He looked around for backing, but only a few nodded yes.

"Mostly right. Who're you?" Eddie asked.

"Webster Russell. They call me Web. Wanna get me suspended?"

"From what? What for?"

"Swearing. Or close to it."

Eddie knew what *sucker* stood for. He felt a trap being set.

"Send me to the principal's office," Webster said. "See what he says."

Several girls giggled, other boys smiled cynically. Eddie caught on, by intuition or guesswork, to what was up. "Not a chance. Don't tell me you live in Webster Groves either," he said.

The boy's anger softened, but he didn't sit down. "Actually I do, live there, I mean, but like you say, not a chance."

"W. E. B., Web," Eddie replied. "Why don't you sit down."

"How you know me?" Webster asked with a smile.

"Your father," Eddie replied. "In the Principal's office. He gave me this job."

"And who you think he'd suspend first? Me, a smart ass? Or you, for not keeping discipline?"

"He needs somebody to ride herd. I'm that sucker, as you say. Besides, I figure nobody'd get the boot long as nothing happened," Eddie answered. "But probably you, it'd be you in a pinch," Eddie continued in a softer tone, so the mood in the classroom lightened. At the same time, he realized what much of his classroom work would be, calming angry kids or at least preventing them from rash acts. If Dr. Russell, the most thoughtful educator in his school district, faced an ongoing struggle with his own unruly son, troubles clearly loomed ahead for guys in Eddie's beginner role.

With some insight into Webster's life, Eddie felt he'd defused the rancor in a classroom where no students were of privilege. Eddie turned again to the girl in the white dress and braces on her legs.

"Your name?" he asked.

"Gloria, that's me," she answered.

Eddie expected her to follow with a kindly word. Sure enough she gave him an innocent look but wasted no words, "Police stopped my dad and sent him to court for a fine, he said it's because he's Haitian. We pay fines to cover the City's debt, not because we did anything wrong. You been arrested?"

"Yeah, have you?" another girl blurted out. "And did you pay a fine when your kids had no food? My dad stood on the street corner once holding a sign, begging help. He prayed nobody he knows'd see him.'"

Bombarded by questions and demands, ranging from scowling to gentle, Eddie thought back on his and Charlene's drive from Jackson. The State patrolman that stopped him for careless driving—or was it speeding? a trumped-up charge in any case—seemed only doing his duty, but his bare hand extended to Eddie for a direct and illegal payment, now seemed to him like Jim Crow corruption. Deciding whether to explain this insight to the adolescents, they being the ones who gave him the insight, Eddie glanced at each kid but said only, "Yes, I have, but I got no kids at home."

A rustling around the room let Eddie escape the feeling of being quizzed. He was likely a rarity to the youngsters, not a loud authoritarian like Miss Crankpot, despite her voice of social disobedience. Eddie was tempted to ask about that lady, but he had no business discussing other teachers with students.

Still, male teachers were disappearing from the classroom, as MayBelle and Charlene had told Eddie all along, and that's likely why Miss Crankpot was there. I may be their first teacher, who can speak to troubles their fathers encounter everyday or go to jail for. Or am I? Aren't the other teachers like me? All were, it seemed, but with different approaches to similar problems.

With a hint of irony, he said, "You see, the other day the cops stopped me. I paid a fine, but not in court. They got no *habeas corpus* in Illinois, huh?"

"No, not in a guy's life," Webster said with a knowing smile Eddie saw in the boy's father as well.

Eddie figured the class wondered about him. He wasn't much older than the youngsters he monitored for a day, or maybe a few days, but for what purpose? Glorified babysitting? Moral guidance? Academic progress? Deciding he didn't know, he struggled on through a humdrum wait for the final bell. Eddie's lingering uncertainty centered on what the day's lessons-learned actually amounted to.

When the final bell rang, the class filed out. Two or three kids nodded his way and Gloria, who was on crutches, smiled. Alphonse followed carrying her books. Eddie was alone until Charlene joined him.

"How was your day?" she asked.

"Learning they already know more than me," Eddie replied with a shake of his head. "You?"

"Taught a day of typing without knowing a thing," Charlene said. They walked to the bus stop in silence. Charlene spoke again when the bus arrived. "Wonder how often that happens?"

5

Lots happened after that first day. The week following Eddie's appearance in Problems of American Democracy, Dr. Russell offered him a position in Social Sciences. Or History. Or English. Whatever popped up. Russell promised Charlene a job as the school's next Music teacher. How those sudden teaching appointments came about remained a mystery. The truth only came out later. By that time Web Russell had graduated from Sumner High or just quit attending, nobody ever said, least of all his father. The boy up and joined the Army under a false birth date. Eddie bumped into him on one of the youth's visits back in uniform.

"We gave you a hard time that first day. Strange you stuck around. We coulda got busted big-time for giving you hell," Web said.

"So that's what it was? Hell?" Eddie asked. "I didn't catch on at first. It dawned on me when I remembered W. E. B. Dubois on the wall in your father's office."

"Yeah, his big hero. My dad sat me down at home and asked about you. How you were."

"And how was I?"

Web smiled but didn't answer. Instead they talked about Army Navy football playing that weekend and Web's future. He'd probably ship out one day. The Allies were advancing on southern Europe. Maybe that's where he'd head.

"If they take guys like me. They use us to unload ships or drive bulldozers. Doing the dirty work Whitey doesn't wanna do. Guess I'm less likely to get killed."

"Italy's the soft underbelly of Europe, they say," Eddie commented. ·

"I hear the Russians will get to Berlin first," Web added.

Eddie thought back, "I remember my brother talking about Tobruk and who'd win there, Aussies or Rommel?"

"Who?" Web asked in confusion.

"No matter. Another time, another place," Eddie philosophized. "I'm getting old, I guess."

"How old's that?"

"20-something. You?"

"18. Maybe. Doesn't matter," Web said with a sly smile.

Eddie saw Web dig the toe of one shoe in the gravel path they stood on. "I wonder what it's like?" he said. "You were never on the front?"

"No, they gave me medical deferments, but I could tell you what my brother says."

"He's there? In combat? Where? Doing what?"

"Hard to tell. Mainly lousy jobs. Loading and unloading like you say. Not allowed to fight next to white brethren."

"That'll be me next," Web replied.

"No, the war'll be over," Eddie assured him with no idea what he was talking about.

Web dug his toes in the gravel ever deeper, no longer the cocky and angry boy. More subdued, Eddie thought, but probably just as angry, only fitting, but a thinking man in the making. Intriguing, too, considering Eddie himself was becoming a man with a past.

Web stretched on his tiptoes and looked at Eddie, as if measuring his 6' 2" against his former teacher's 5'10" or 5'11", depending on what day a guy got measured at the doctor's office. "What I told my old man about you?" he began.

"Yes? I wondered. Your dad offered me a job pretty much off the bat. Mystified me."

"I just shrugged and said, 'Cool Cat.'"

"Thanks for that."

"Still are, cool cat. See ya, man." With that, Web sauntered off into a fading autumn day having given Eddie a rare glimpse of positive reinforcement.

"Troubled times," Eddie said.

6

Other surprises caught Eddie and Charlene unawares. Despite her title as Music teacher, Charlene had to earn her job. Make it happen, so to speak, which wasn't bad for a lady who loved singing. First Sumner kept her on as a substitute typing teacher. When the regular instructor returned from having a baby, Charlene went to the copy center, a job that entailed mimeographing tests and meaningless letters. As 1942-43 wore on, Dr. Russell found Federal funds to hire a music staff. Charlene's job was creating a choir.

"I dug up dough from the Lanham Act," the principal explained with a sly look. Lanham was enacted in 1941 to aid schools overburdened by the influx of children from families employed in Defense. Not many Sumner parents worked in defense plants. "However, our males are in Military Service. So I fudged the figures to show our need for educated staff to replace those gone off to war," Dr. Russell continued.

"And that includes both of you," MayBelle joked with Eddie and Charlene when they came home with the news. "You see what a pinch of learning will do for you. Going to college and finishing is paying off."

During the fall of 1942, news came of Britain in bitter combat with Germany to control Egypt. While that battle hung in the balance, Axis forces invaded southern Russia to gain oil reserves of the Caucasus. If Hitler also won Stalingrad, Europe would be in dire straits. It looked like Hitler truly could conquer all.

"Strange," Eddie said at Thanksgiving that year. "Who's ever heard of Stalingrad? And here it is about to decide our fate. This is a world war, in the true sense."

"Thank the Lord, our Charles isn't there," MayBelle said. "He's with his own kind now, even if we don't know where they're stationed. If only he'd write more often."

As the winter of 1942 set in and the New Year of 1943 came and went, the three of them gathered around MayBelle's large console radio every night as spring approached. Reports from the world conflict inflamed their desire for a clear picture of all that was afoot and, more important, what was bound to come. As one reporter said, 1943 could mark the conflict's turning point, for better or worse.

Eddie learned the art of teaching during that stressful time. By the middle of 1943, he gained the insight that he'd passed three phases of his *performances*, as he came to describe the level of self-awareness he experienced during class routines. Phase one happened at the start of having his own classes. While standing before his students and explaining material, he paused, even while speaking, and took a step back from himself. Then it seemed he was an outside observer of two Eddies. One was the real man of flesh and blood, who lived and breathed on the streets of his hometown. The other him was a false construct playing a role assigned by a distant entity called society.

As he progressed into a second year, he felt like a rote memorizer of lesson plans, which guided him through class periods, but it felt like he and the students' minds approached the work as novice dancers do the dance. Their steps were automatic, like stick figures needing a soul. He and his classes learned new material and even gained maturity, but they lacked any depth of feeling or empathy for their study partners or any inner sense of what increased knowledge might give them in the long run.

In time, Eddie liberated himself from lesson plans. He saw himself and his students as integral contributors to society. Eddie began teaching from his heart and spoke spontaneously about his classes' role in the America they were part of. Increasingly he talked *with* students not *to* them. By that means, he was in some intangible way joining the dancers with the dance. If a societal oneness was possible, could it translate into a general acceptance of people's differences? He felt determined to try.

Taking a baby step toward acceptance was what he unwittingly did on his first day as a sub, when he listened to students with a touch of humor and understanding. Was it that patient quality in Eddie that Dr. Russell read into his son's dinner table report?

Eddie decided he'd likely never know, and that first day of substitute teaching was slipping into the past, much as the great world war seemed to turn with the battle of El Alamein and the decisive defeat of Hitler's forces at Stalingrad in 1943. Those many experiences, local and international, reached Eddie and he heard talk of an Allied advance into western Europe.

There were one-time occurrences, too, that molded society. In Major League baseball, the lowly St. Louis Browns rose up to take the 1944 American League championship while the St. Louis Cardinals won the National League pennant. The two teams played a first-ever World Series in the same Sportsman's Park stadium they shared all summer long on alternate home stands. So-called Subway Series were nothing new in New York, which had three big league teams, but the '44 World Series was a big deal in St. Louis. It was celebrated in the white print media, whose reports Eddie's mother seldom took as nearing the truth. She read their columns but was disappointed when the lowly Browns lost to the mighty Cardinals.

"White men all of 'em," MayBelle lamented, "but a team named the Browns oughta reflect some of the players' skin color. Why no colored folk ever play Big League ball?"

"If we aren't wanted for cannon fodder in the Marines, why be welcome in the Majors?" Eddie answered. "Besides, big leaguers from the South'd never take the field with us."

That was Eddie's only stab at an answer. Nor were other replies expected. Personal happenings were even more disappointing. In the two years after moving to St. Louis, Eddie and Charlene put off trying for children. She was intent on getting a start in teaching and the school system provided no parental leave. In the not so distant past married women teachers were frowned on because pregnancies meant they'd leave the profession to care for a family. Charlene chose to put off motherhood while she developed her school choir.

Added to that cautionary approach was the uncertainty of war. If more Allied victories failed to materialize, American forces were sure to need greater manpower in Europe and the Pacific. Sooner or later Eddie's flat feet, which may actually have been Edna's invention, were sure to catch his draft board's renewed attention. Even the semi-lame might storm enemy beaches in dire need.

Or, as was more likely, a recruit with some learning was always fit to type out requisitions for the Quartermaster Corps. Colored men seldom, if ever, saw combat along with whites anyway because, as Charles had cited from an official 1920s government report on the military, colored men were "too dumb to fight, they cower in fear and panic under pressure, waiting for a white man to lead the way. That's the reason there were only 4,000 of them in uniform in 1940." Be that as it might, Eddie knew Charlene feared her husband would eventually join Charles in uniform. The longer the war carried on the more he saw that fear in his wife's eyes.

So Charlene and Eddie put off parenthood and thought twice about buying a house. Instead Eddie shared space with his mother and his wife. All three worked, saved for a rainy day, used rations for sugar and meat, and pooled their pennies for a secondhand 1940 Magnavox Regency radio. Each night they gathered around the large console and waited for news of the world, hoping in vain for the latest on Charles and his battalion, wherever it was and whatever they were up to. White media reported on white units.

7

Keeping track of Charles got harder. He reported for duty in early spring of 1942 and went for basic training at Jefferson Barracks southwards on the Mississippi. His letters said nothing of value except the training felt disorganized and ill-planned. The venerable site appeared rickety, and the Army couldn't decide whether *to switch it or ditch it*, as Charles wrote. *First they put us recruits in Basic and we lived in tents on the grounds.* Soon thereafter the government turned the camp into an Army Air Forces training site, only to remake it into a military hospital. That meant Charles moved a lot.

Judging by the confused tone of his letters and the lone call he placed from a pay phone, Eddie and MayBelle guessed he spent barely a couple weeks at the camp so close to St. Louis. The final ten weeks of his 13-week Basic Training found Charles at Fort Leonard Wood near Rolla in the Missouri Ozarks. Summer heat took a toll on recruits, Charles reported, him included, even if his speed afoot and endurance helped him through the daily grind unscathed.

Here where you'd least expect it, Jim Crow makes himself felt, he wrote in a letter to MayBelle, who read it aloud after a family dinner. *We're all gathered together in uniform to defend our democracy, whites and blacks, but us colored are packed off in dingy barracks at back edge of this dusty hell hole in daytime temps of a hundred or more. Battalions of Negro recruits in basic but the officers white. All from the South, who bark at us like dogs. They expect us to act jolly and tractable while cooped up in kennels.*

If I Didn't Care

In our time off, we go by bus to downtown Rolla and have to sit in the back, though dressed in the uniform of our country and ready to defend it. We buy clothes in stores but must go outdoors to try them on, or can attend the movie theater for a show, only to learn we can't occupy empty seats on the white side of the locale if our side is sold out.

Charles's early letters showed him as an ordinary recruit, one of the 70,000-plus Negroes the US Army called up when other branches rejected them. Even the Army had a skeptical view of their combat readiness. Most were in crews loading and unloading supplies or doing kitchen duty. Hard labor matching a sharecropper's lot befell others. Late in the summer of '42 Charles received different news than the majority of recruits. He got orders to report to Camp Tyson, a new and expanding citified base in the wilds of northwestern Tennessee, which featured all the modernities of civilian life, cafés, picture shows, social clubs, libraries, and a hospital. That much scuttlebutt had already reached Charles, but why he was sent to Tyson was a mystery until he left for his new posting.

A whole load of us colored men boarded a train from Missouri to Memphis, Eddie read in a long letter from his brother. *There was news in the papers about battles on the Eastern front in Europe between Gerries and Ruskies. We knew Hitler had the Ukraine and Stalingrad was next in line. At least I knew it, most of my buddies didn't have an inkling, I mean why they should care about places they'd never heard of before. Most had never left home and here we were hurtling through the night in an overcrowded, smokey train. 'One a' them Jim Crow cars,' a guy grunted, which meant we were breathing in coal dust from the engine ahead of us while the white guys sat farther back in fresh air.*

Once in Kentucky and heading still farther southward, we heard pings against the coach windows because white crackers outside were shooting at the coaches with Negro troops inside. Keeping the blinds pulled was the only way to keep outsiders from seeing in to where the white guys sat and where we were.

Charles's first sight the next morning was a formation of hydrogen barrage balloons above the green farm fields and forests outside Memphis. He'd been chosen as one of 8,000 troops, white and colored, to train and launch monstrous unmanned balloons over invasion sites. In Charles's case that meant western Europe. *Drawing closer, we wondered if the balloons were piloted from cockpits, but soon we saw they were anchored to the earth by long lines or cables. They'd hover over battlefields like floating minefields obscuring the scene below for enemy aircraft or entangling enemy planes in their lines.*

"A defensive line in the sky," Eddie explained to MayBelle and Charlene, who formed an image of Camp Tyson in their mind's eye. On the ground, the prevailing lineup of racist America ruled. The endless blocks with segregated troop barracks and mess halls emerged from Charles's letters. His quarters were, as elsewhere, located in back of white living areas.

"The story Charles is telling us about will never end," Charlene lamented. She looked MayBelle's way with a sigh.

Her mother-in-law understood but kept her spirits up. "He's doing his thing, my boy," she said. "You see the Army recognizes him as an educated man. Why, you know all those other poor souls, out cleaning latrines and mopping floors. Sharecropping supreme, dressed in a uniform. And there you see, Whitey respects Charles wearing his country's colors."

"But he's still my big brother?" Eddie teased her.

"Why he'll be in on something big, wait and see," MayBelle insisted.

"Well, Service is nothing like college days at Tougaloo," Eddie continued.

"Or Alcorn State either," Charlene kidded her husband. "So tough you had it there, Eddie my man. We were spoiled."

Despite the kidding, it was clear Charles was chosen for something big. Not only the camp grounds expanded at Camp Tyson but the military operations as well. It was September 4th of 1941, three months before Pearl Harbor, when the first barrage balloon had been raised in Tennessee. But the numbers exploded. Altogether 30 Army battalions were destined for the camp, as Charles wrote, and four of them were Negro. His own battalion was number 320.

Numbers 318 and 319 preceded his, and 321followed after. Each battalion consisted of 1,100 enlisted men with 54 barrage battalions per division.

Sounds terribly glamorous, but it's hard, Charles wrote from Tennessee during a long weekend leave in 1943. *I've already had Basic Training at Leonard Wood and thought that was tough. But Tyson gave us nine more weeks of special stuff, to make us able to hoist and maneuver balloons the size of boxcars. We got these white officers, all from the Deep South. They shout vile things at us and make training hell. Reveille at six a. m. followed by calisthenics and laps.*

We do the Infiltration Course and that means crawling through a mess of barriers with a rifle at our chest plus machine gun fire whining above. If guys panic, barbed wire is dropped on their heads to protect them. It's said the machine guns don't fire live ammo, but who's to know? We gotta understand if we get up and run in real battle that'll be the end of it. One mistake and no more to write home about after that.

8

Camp Tyson crawled with journalists wanting a glamorous story where it didn't always exist. Only reporters from the Negro press were allowed to cover Charles's battalion. Whatever stories they published never leaked out to the Negro newspapers that reached MayBelle's house. That included *The St. Louis Argus*. What Charles saw of those articles that appeared in nationwide news releases was stuff he found during his off-base leaves. Being a Negro on leave in rural Tennessee meant finding few public places open to colored troops. Charles wrote of buying some reading material in local stores and then embarking on searches for places to read and reflect in peace and quiet.

You have to be on your guard every step, he wrote in explaining the social climate surrounding Tyson.

Helpful in that way was *The Green Book*, a slender pamphlet published by a Negro man in New York City named Green. It advised colored travelers in Jim Crow's America where they could find welcoming hotels and dining places. Charles wrote about a guest house in Paris, Tennessee, between Camp Tyson and Memphis, run by Aunt Faye, a talkative and friendly lady, whose husband served in World War I. She offered overnight accommodations and a stack of newspapers and magazines from the Negro press.

Charles's letters told about the news he received at Aunt Faye's about his own Camp Tyson, stuff that was reported by Negro news reporters. In Charles's words, the Negro journalists observed activities of the four colored barrage balloon battalions, whose preparations for combat went unnoticed in the white press. The publications described how colored recruits learned to inflate the enormous barrage balloons without sparking dangerous hydrogen that kept the balloons airborne. They learned to launch the balloons by controlling cords anchoring them to the ground, all of which would be done in actual combat while braving enemy fire. Then came the task of taking the balloons back down to earth and cradling them, as in a bed, and camouflaging them under a netting to keep enemy aircraft from bombing them.

Charles's letters showed Eddie he was ever mindful of those he and his fellow troops loved and left behind, but it was war the recruits enlisted for, not guaranteed safety and security. *Here's the trouble,* he wrote once in 1943. *Every step reminds us we're in combat on two fronts, at home and abroad. It was never so noticeable down here in Tennessee or the Deep South when I was at Tougaloo, but the farther South we go now the harsher the treatment. The Army's no better or worse than society. The folks off base that will beat us for wearing the uniform of our country are no worse than the white officers that call us vile names, rouse us, and demand 25-mile nightlong hikes.*

MayBelle proved a better talker than writer. She read Charles's letters over and over, but left answering to Eddie, who found it hard writing back to Charles and making the daily classroom grind at Sumner, or dealing with government rations books, sound as stimulating as combat training. Eddie lamented that he, too, was not in Service. Charles replied, *We got one lieutenant demands we do 12-minute miles on fast march with 60-pound packs. Eddie, my boy, your feet would never manage that. Be happy for 4-F.*

Gradually, or "over a period of time," as MayBelle put it, the horrors of Jim Crow that surrounded Eddie at home faded. He felt separated from and invisible to the white majority, but experienced none of the extreme racial hatred Charles described on and around Camp Tyson. There it was a hostility the white population acted out with violence, and without remorse. Charles described how German POWs sent to Tyson straight from combat in Europe were allowed to use the base commissary with white Americans simply because they were Caucasians. At the same time, US Army

Negro troops were forbidden to enter the facility. Then there were local bus drivers who kicked colored troops off buses with the simple explanation that they were "dirty vermin" and lowly white recruits "needed seats."

Eddie read his brother's missives while he pondered the development of his own feelings. Dr. Russell bore with him as he learned to teach. After two years Eddie acquired a permanent teaching certificate and assumed the title of teacher of American History, a course required of high school juniors. He studied Charles's letters from the South and thought his brother should be the classroom instructor. Charles learned history by being part of it.

Nonetheless Eddie wondered how to incorporate teenagers in the discussion, so they learned to accept less of the apartheid-like injustices they'd grown up under. He decided to introduce texts by American Negro authors, starting with Langston Hughes. Charlene, in accordance, endeavored to insure a high school choir would exist.

Letters continued to arrive from Charles. They contained steady reminders that his troops were preparing for a battle of life against death. Charles and his battalion learned that barrage balloons were meant to fly at five thousand feet, which presented a problem in extreme wind. If any broke loose, they had to be chased down or shot and disabled. If that failed, a balloon might drift across vast stretches of the American continent. In one fierce electrical storm, lightning struck a balloon's mooring cable. A winch operator touched the line and was electrocuted. Charles knew little of events in the white battalions but understood dangers were the same for all troops alike.

9

Letters telling about mishaps, such as the electrocution Charles witnessed, reminded Eddie of school documents from various inner city schools near him. They were dry factual accounts of accidents on the school grounds but still shockingly full of brutal frankness, as though the accidents were part of an evil master plan of Fate, intended to prepare those who were innocent of mortal combat for a greater mass slaughter to come. He remembered his mother's tales of Tulsa and East St. Louis and Charles's words about some troops who ended up in combat but had no training with protective barbed wire to prevent them from panicking and placing themselves in the way of live bullets.

Other mailings from Charles read like a humanist growing to higher levels of understanding. *On weekend leaves we don't have much choice. Where to go? What to do?* he wrote at length near the end of his training at Camp Tyson. *Towns around here are all like Paris, Tennessee. There's a Negro church that welcomes us. Though sincere, its brotherhood, as they call it, is pretty boring. Mainly older folks who been here forever, nothing too exciting for us young guys. But better than lazing on base during our free time.*

Charles told of some wilder troops, who went off to Memphis on free weekends. They hung out on Beale Street, where jazz music and booze ruled and the on-base chatter about war felt distant. Or a few recruits ventured as far away as Paducah, Kentucky, to live it up. That was 70 miles from Paris, but being located near the Ohio River it was a portal to the North and offered less of Southern segregation. For the guys with little money there was the desire to escape ill-kept barracks in the semi-swamp lands surrounding their camp. They retreated out into the woods or visited the smallest villages, where jukebox joints abounded. Those were commonly tumbledown shacks in the darkest recesses of the countryside. What happened in them was often secret, but they offered night life and the obligatory jukebox, with tunes, sometimes raunchy, for a nickel a piece.

Charles's letters made one thing clear. He was still as averse to strong liquor as to cigarettes, a topic he touched on briefly in his longest letter from Tennessee. *The guys in camp head out for other places to drink because this county is dry. Sometimes we can buy home brew on the black market from local Negroes, if you trust it, but bootleggers're wary of us guys from the base, and I don't touch the stuff myself. You gotta go elsewhere to be sure of getting any that's not rotgut. They're what we call juke joints.*

The best known is run by a lady called Ma Hatchet and her son Junior. Ma lives in a room behind the bar and Junior bunks, they say, in a bordello out back. It's dark inside the juke joint, with almost no lights and the faces of us coloreds don't make it any easier to see who's hanging out with who. It looks for all the world like some hide-away in a deep dark gangster movie, but if you see it in daylight it's just a tar paper shack ready to fall in. Some old-timer said it keeps burning down and gets rebuilt over and over.

'Burned? How'd that happen?' one of my pals asked the old guy.

'Friction,' he said with a laugh.

'What's that mean, friction?' somebody else wondered.

The old guy chuckled at how dumb we were. 'You know, the ordinary kind. Friction from the owner's mortgage payments rubbing against the insurance premiums.'

He watched us as it sank in our thick skulls. Greed behind the arson he referred to, real or imagined, was rampant while we felt dumb for not catching on sooner, but those're things guys like us adjust to and make life possible here. Be cunning and keep your sense of humor. If the man don't set your house on fire, you may have to do it yourself.

'But what insurance man would be dumb enough to sell insurance on a place like Ma Hatchet's?' another trooper asked.

'If there's a way for society to screw a poor feller outa any dough or property, they'll do it. Sometimes even they'll take your life. Don't put nothin' past nobody.' That's what men of experience tell us.

Eddie was astonished at the length of Charles's letter. His others had seemed scratched out, like time was short and some urgent training maneuver awaited him. That surely was the case at the six-week camp, when British barrage balloon officers taught the 320th to fill balloons with hydrogen. The seriousness of that process was evident when Eddie read Charles's words aloud, and the three guessed at his stress level. More than one trainee had died from touching a sensitive mooring line or being in the wrong place while moving equipment. Heavy equipment could bowl a fellow over flat as a pancake.

10

In this most recent letter, Charles seemed more at ease describing his surroundings and fellow recruits. Nevertheless, his comments about racial tensions seemed a prelude to something dire. Like maybe the hate was imbedded deep. *One colored guy in battalion 318 turned and walked away from a white Military Police patrol and they shot him in the back three times,* Eddie's brother continued, *but the Army just took the MPs' word that he was a prowler, even though lots of guys protested, including white troopers, some from the North. They were slammed in the hoosegow. We have other examples. The civilian police in these cracker towns are brutal on any Negro in an Army uniform, even a rare one with sergeant's stripes. One fellow in our 320th was seen walking on the same side of a nearly empty street as a white woman, and the cops arrested him. He's charged with rape because he actually looked at her. Never spoke. Just glanced her way. Officials are deciding whether to try him in town or hold a military court martial.*

Eddie read to MayBelle, who shook her head in confusion at the contradictions she herself helped create. While she knew the threat of Nazism and applauded Charles for joining the Allies, his letters described horrors remindful of American violence. Eddie's mother had long contended her people should stay home and meet their fellows in peace, but now, Eddie realized, she saw Jim Crow rearing his desperate face in the midst of a holy fight by whites and coloreds to be rid of a worldwide evil. The dilemma was now at a two-sided impasse in which guys on the good side could be as full of harm as their enemy.

While Eddie considered how to ask a question he had at the ready, MayBelle beat him to the punch, "Oh, yes," she asked, "which is the greater evil? The bad we have at home or what's afoot in the world? Are they of the same parcel?"

Without considering an answer, Eddie remembered something Charles had written in an earlier letter. The worst insult to soldiers in his battalion wasn't random killings and racial indignities, but the influx of German POWs to America. They worked in labor camps or idly waited out the war. *Our commissioned officers at Tyson are banned from using the commissary or dining with white officers, but the German war prisoners are given full mess hall privileges and passes to camp facilities. And why? Because they're white! Our colored American troops and officers have to wait at the end of the mess hall line—behind our enemy!*

Only slowly did such descriptions creep into Charles's writings to the folks. Eventually Eddie detected in his brother's letters a note of fatalism, even as the Allies made inroads against the Axis in North Africa and approached Italy. *Will there ever be a clear winner?* Charles wondered.

11

*I see more and more guys losing hope and we're not even through
with training,* said one letter. *No drinking allowed in camp, so
guys relax with smokes. There's a mini-pack of Old Golds, Camels,
and Lucky Strikes wherever you look. They even pop up in our rations,
planted by tobacco companies. Everybody knows they're bad for us, but
there's the saying 'Smoke 'em if you get 'em.' Taking a few puffs relieves
the pressure on us. Besides, guys wanna do what their buddies do, so they
follow the crowd. We even get waterproof paper matches supplied by the
USO, to make sure we smoke 'em.*

*Like a few guys here say, who're back from the front in Europe, if
you're dug down in a foxhole, smokes are a solace for the wounded or sore at
heart. Cigs are a sure way to get addicted to nicotine. 'But what the heck,'
one fellow told me the other day when he lit up a Chesterfield, 'I won't
come out of this war anyway.' Could be he's right. Maybe none of us will.*

Charles was of a serious bent, but never downbeat. In his letters
Eddie could see him pull himself out of the doldrums by sheer willpower. Or was it some outer force that lifted his spirits then shoved
them down again?

"It sounds that way," Charlene suggested and MayBelle agreed.
"But be hard to stay yourself when everybody follows a deviant
path."

At first the ladies sensed a sudden upturn in the letter's conclusion, as Charles turned his attention to the genteel part of local
society he formerly described as too boring for young men like
himself. In the last weekend before barrage balloon training ended,
the men were due to ship out, but didn't know where to, though

guesswork spoke of England or Wales, where their British training officers hailed from. They were decent blokes, to borrow the Brits' own expression, and showed less of the prejudice common among white Southern officers. Charles's letter mentioned a last-weekend surprise.

I'm finishing this a whole week after I started it, Eddie read aloud from Charles's scribbly handwriting. His battalion had received orders to pack up. He wrote the last lines on paper resting atop his hastily readied gear.

Two things happened at once. One good, one bad. We finished training a week early and a Methodist church in Jackson, that's Tennessee, not Mississippi, invited troops from our battalion to visit one last time. Not many of us took them up on it, a small bus load only. I was one, though I'd never been to the church before. In truth, we weren't so interested in church, mostly something to do, so the pastor himself took us into his parsonage. You know, it was pretty darned sedate, those folks' version of tea and crumpets. We fellows sat politely till this spectacular, lovely gal waltzed in and introduced herself as the pastor's daughter. Sounded like in a Dorothy Dandridge movie.

'Hello, gentlemen,' she said. 'I'm Carina. Lovely to see you here at my father's church.'

She's about my age, tall and dark with a sparkling smile. It lit up my heart. She entertained us with small talk. Said she's a teacher, which I didn't pay much attention to, and the guys told where they're from and what their job in the battalion is. Or what they did back at home. I mean I didn't notice much except how beautiful she was 'til she said she went to Alcorn. That made me think of Eddie. So she and I fell into this conversation that pretty much shut the other fellows out, which didn't bother me a bit, she's such a beauty. Turns out she's an English instructor at a place called Lane College right there in Jackson, not a hop, skip, and a jump from Camp Tyson.

'If only I'd known,' I told her.

'Known what?'

'That you're so nearby, I'd've come here more often,' I said. She smiled and blushed a little. Funny how a girl that dark can show her blush.

'I'm a pretty busy girl,' she said, but I added that I studied English, too, which was only half true. I didn't major in it.

'Where?' she wanted to know, and I said Tougaloo, which she knew about, a little bit, and I felt really bad about not finishing there and then being her equal that way.

Eddie tried reading on but the writing grew squigglier. He slowed his pace as the contents heated up. He felt MayBelle and Charlene were growing more intrigued, like they were aroused by Charles at last showing an interest in a girl, who had something academic to give him.

"What more?" MayBelle urged Eddie on. "What's he say?"

Eddie skimmed a couple pages. "He says suddenly he remembered me, Eddie, how I brought up lots of writers when we met Edna, the friendly employee at Selective Service, all those months ago."

Eddie thought back on that time in St. Louis, which seemed eons gone.

"Charles says, *And it turned out Carina knew Langston Hughes's writing. So we chatted about his line that Eddie and me quoted to Edna.*

"What line?" Charlene wished to know. Both she and MayBelle acted disinterested, but they squirmed slightly in their chairs, to hear more good news from Charles in the South.

"Charles gives it here," Eddie replied. *Beautiful is the sun. Beautiful, also, are the souls of my people.* He stopped and thought back to that touching moment with the Draft Board lady. "My brother seems to find a soulmate lovely as Langston's verse."

Eddie read on from Charles's long letter and wondered how his brother found time and willpower to compose it leaning against his backpack while frantically breaking camp on the double. Eddie imagined a horrible rumble and a barrage of voices as Charles's battalion readied itself for the great venture into combat that weeks of training prepared it for. In that atmosphere, Charles continued a rhapsodic description of his talk with Carina. She'd once been an undergrad at Lane College and studied English. She originally applied at Vanderbilt University, but they didn't accept colored undergraduates. Their Negro students were enrolled in professional programs and grad school. So she put off Vanderbilt till grad school. *Just to prove I'd pass any courses other students could,* Charles recorded she told him. After that she spent two years teaching at a Methodist school in Tanzania, which was a sister institution to Lane College and her father's congregation.

'I thought it would be so different than here, but everybody looked like me. They were brown-skinned and tall, at least they were where I lived, but was different, too, the big game, lions and other cats. I remember elephants, but I noticed people, too. You know what? The biggest difference was the ocean, I never dreamed it could be so huge, never-ending expanses. So strange for a landlubber like me.'

Charles left off quoting her for a moment. Instead he summarized his fascination with her manner. *She sat with both hands clasped on her lap and looked straight at me with a kindly smile while also calmly weighing each word like a precious treasure. I felt that fear had no home with her,* Charles wrote. *She learned that from the Africans, you know, they were poor and lived in bad housing, near the school she taught in. Still, they were happy and knew none of the stress our people show, where intimidation rules. They went about their life without a care. They weren't afraid of anyone, only the lions filled them with fear. No one would go near those beasts, horrible killing machines.*

Carina learned to act that way, too. The Africans were our blood brothers and sisters, but grew up with a different view of the world. She learned from them to treat other Africans and white men with dignity and respect. She eventually discovered her own self-worth. 'In the end, I steered clear only of the big cats and the ocean, if I got near it,' Charles quoted her.

I've never been on an ocean, Charles said he told her. *But will soon.*

Charles told how Carina kept her steady look on him. *She leaned forward and touched the back of my hand while saying softly, 'You'll get seasick, but you'll make it. I did, you will.'*

Did? I asked her. She said it was before the war her mother got sick and died. She came back to Tennessee to be with her father.

He joined us in our conversation and knew of Tougaloo as well. A fine school, the pastor said and congratulated me for graduating. He was a fine man, but I never bothered him with the truth, Eddie quoted from Charles's letter, *to my shame, but I got Carina's mailing address. We'll write.*

"That means we'll get less news from him from now on?" MayBelle chortled, revealing what she most desired for her older son, a happy ending to his young manhood. Eddie guessed his mother formed a mental image of Carina. "Tennessee, not a fur piece from here," she concluded with a smile, but one that faded as Eddie read on.

12

*O*ur cloud burst in a hurry, Charles continued. *Not my Carina cloud, but the white cracker one. Not that crackers were ever on my Top 20 list. The Christian Methodist Church rented a bus to come to Tyson and get us and bring us back here. All that for a friendly visit to a pious congregation. They treated us nice. In a good mood we piled on the bus to get back to camp before curfew. It'd been ages since I had a real meal or pleasant conversation. Some of the guys hadn't seen anything off base but clapboard juke joints and who knows what kind of ladies.*

Then outa nowhere we heard, 'You got no right to be here!' This big burly cop comes charging on board, 'We takin' this bus NOW! We got a load a' folks needs a ride back to Paris. Their bus done broke down.' Everybody looks dumbstruck and nobody leaves their seat. We got bruisers big and tough as the fuzz, but it's Jim Crow down here, so we sit still, fuming but confused. Eddie read on about how the cops ran them off the bus like a load of school kids, calling them *'Boy!'*

Tension overwhelmed some of our guys and they froze in their steps in the parking lot, like they were locked to the asphalt. Meanwhile a crowd of whites marched ahead and boarded the bus. Those guys were all decked out in white shirts and ties, like they came from a Kiwanis Club meeting. When we saw that, one of our guys—Squaley, they called him, no idea why—that was smart and went to school and played blocking back for UCLA sprang right outa the crowd, huge muscular guy. He went after the Kiwanis clodhoppers and yelled, 'That's OUR bus, you! We're too dumb to fight, huh? You got another think comin'!'

That's when the fuzz went after him. He heaved a couple off of himself like midgets, but the others jumped him from behind so they pulled him to the driveway where you could hear his bones crunching. The cops beat him with night sticks, so each blow to his head rang in the night air like a rifle shot splitting the skull of a mighty ram in rutting season. While he writhed in pain, they tore off his uniform till he was sitting there butt naked freezing in all his dark brown glory and they were too dense to see what a giant they'd cravenly felled.

Some of our Army troops coulda run out to help, but were weaponless and the cops pointed service guns at us. That's when the first cop that entered the bus stepped to Squaley and pulled his revolver and shot him clean in the back of the head, so the poor black giant lay there with his face gone and blood running on the driveway under him. A murder, simple as that.

'This is white man's country!' the lead cop yelled at us and lotsa whiteys drove off, some of them in our bus, all of them in haste. Squaley remained on the asphalt with the pool of blood getting bigger and we waited for a hearse, because there was no help. Somebody yelled for an incinerator truck to come scoop up the body, but not even that happened. The remaining cops stood and grinned their murderous grins and any colored guy that's stepping forward woulda got what Squaley did but front on. This continued till the last cop was gone. Then we gathered around the mighty blocking back and patched together some rags of his tattered sergeant's uniform to make him look human, while the blood leaked from his head and we could see where they tried to crack his skull open and would've succeeded if they hadn't shot him first.

Eddie put down the letter and let out a shocked sigh. He knew about lynch mobs, some even carried out white on white, but why Whitey would hang Whitey defied their flimsy logic. Still, memories of photographs showing black men hanged by the neck across America's countryside coincided with Billy Holiday's harrowing song *Strange Fruit*, which Eddie first heard at Alcorn and felt horrified by. "Bulging eyes and twisted mouth," he uttered under his breath. "Men hanging from poplar trees, their lives snuffed out." Such evil as Charles described felt deeply disturbing. Eddie never dreamed the Law openly executed soldiers in uniform. Now his brother described it.

"A coward's way for sure, shooting from behind," MayBelle stated, as if she'd seen it before, which she in fact may never have done. "It takes courage to look a man in the face and pull a trigger." She swayed back and forth in a wooden rocker, whether to comfort herself or release her rage Eddie couldn't decide. He knew only from her acrid tone that she was aghast. It was bad enough that the policeman murdered a man. Even worse that he remained willing to dismiss the uniformed dead man as "a pail of cinders," like MayBelle said. Eddie guessed MayBelle was equally taken aback by her older son's matter-of-fact description of how his group's visit to Carina and family ended so monstrously.

"Almost like the pastor expected it," Charlene interjected, reading Eddie's thoughts. "Who knows what he's seen in his day, but keeps his humanity?"

MayBelle quit rocking, which Eddie read as a signal she needed a rest from war. Eddie saw his mother's reaction and thought of Charles, who wrote of uniformed combat at home, while he also wondered what was to come of the conflict he'd gone abroad to take part in, both struggles ungoverned by civilized articles of war or peace.

Not sure what his brother, or he himself, was up against in this new world of good vs. blatant evil, Eddie chose not to act philosophical. Instead he turned to the conclusion of Charles's letter and the sheets of paper rested heavily in his hands.

"A mighty missive," Eddie said to MayBelle and Charlene, who were still listening, even though both sagged in their chairs. "Not exactly a hi-Mom note home."

"He should be a foreign correspondent, sounds like he's in a strange enough land to make it seem overseas," Charlene added.

The ladies remained quiet while Eddie read on. Left was only a PS, which he first only glanced at but then read again. "Charles says on the bus ride back to camp, the only talk was like in whispers. They saw Squaley get killed by supposed friendly fire and everybody knew it could happen to them, too. Some guy gets a wild hair and fires at anybody that looks different.

"He says the guy next to him, Salazar, told about seeing Zoot Suit riots in San Antonio where he came from. Guys going after Latinos. Down there're mostly Mexicans and Catholics, so the Army guys went after *jovenes* with baggy pants and cuffs tucked in at the ankles. The gangs rode around in US Army trucks and clubbed Zoot Suiters, tore their clothes off, and left them laying naked on the streets, just like they had with Squaley. Mexicans that fought back they killed and dumped their bodies with a shrug."

13

"So evil," Charlene said with a groan, while Eddie folded Charles's letter and tried unsuccessfully to stuff it back in the envelope. He stared at the paper in confusion.

"Almost too big," he grumbled before finishing the text.

'Guess that's the war for Squaley?' somebody next to me says, and some other guy says, 'Depends on what war you mean,' and I think about town folk in Europe and what they're going through freezing in unheated houses or farmers starving in unplowed fields while the war goes on around them. So that's how we spend our time, with no bus but blasted thoughts and knowing we'll get back to camp late and be tossed around like tardy brats at school.

Finally a pack of MPs show up in a big truck and pitch Squaley on the flat bed, still naked. They toss his rags down by him and drive off, so somebody must of called them and that means the camp commanders, or somebody, knows we're here still, in their eyes lollygagging around, but to us we've glimpsed the empty spaces where some men's heart used to be.

I mean after Squaley's death, there's no life in us either. I try to conjure up Carina and how smart she is and lovely. I see her in my thoughts and try to think about her words. She's moving her lips, so a smile forms and her eyes sparkle, but no sounds come forth, which fits our mood. I see the other guys staring into the dark, shivering cold, though it's warm out.

Finally our rented school bus returns. The driver says the Kiwanis guys are back home. We clomp aboard, but are deaf to our own footsteps. The driver yells at us to sit down. He gets a few bold stares from us then shuts up. Afterward, we sit in more silence, thirty-odd of us in crowded seats for school kids and one jerk at the steering wheel, as the bus cleaves its way through the pitch dark world, where they murder you for wearing your country's uniform, like I said before. Since reporting late to camp, we've been on latrine duty. Now this."

"What's he mean, *this?*" MayBelle asked Eddie.

Having no answer, Eddie shook his head slowly, as sad as Charles said he and his fellow troops felt on the bus back to Camp Tyson, stunned at the insanity they witnessed.

MayBelle closed her eyes and tilted her head back. Seeing her like that, as though imagining Charles in such a schizophrenic setting or invoking higher powers to intercede on her older son's behalf, led Eddie to notice his mother had gained weight with age and worry. It dawned on him that MayBelle was beginning to rethink how proud she was of Charles bearing his country's uniform and defending what his nation stood for, or if in fact he, and they, belonged to any nation at all. Sobering how stricken she appears and speechless, too, Eddie thought to himself.

"Oh, those poor souls." Those were the only words Eddie heard. Eventually he realized it was Charlene speaking, not his mother. "Like going overseas won't be bad enough for them. Then that evil."

"Who knows, maybe better," MayBelle said sadly, momentarily breaking out of her mental absence. She leaned backward and closed her eyes again.

Eddie said nothing more. He fumbled clumsily with Charles's stationery until he figured out that the paper and the envelope didn't fit together. He read the last lines to himself.

Charles had written his letter at white hot speed, so much so that his handwriting was nearly illegible toward the end. The men arrived back at camp way late, he wrote, and were assigned cleanup jobs a few days, till suddenly they were told to pack up and ship out. *They meant it about shipping out,* Charles wrote. *Change uniforms without even time to shower. I tried to remember Carina, but couldn't bring myself to it in this reeking mess. Here we are, our bodies covered with stench. From the toilet to troop train, heading East and overseas! On the double!*

Eddie chose not to relay this distasteful info to MayBelle and Charlene. Instead he turned to puzzling again over the strangely folded 8 1/2 x 11 inch writing paper and its small, square envelope. He fumbled with them until he saw British stamps on the envelope and realized Charles carried the letter in his bag from Camp Tyson to the American East Coast and across the Atlantic. He'd mailed it weeks later in Great Britain. So the news was old. Where were they now?

"Overseas at last," Charlene said with a sigh.

"Wonder if he got a shower?" Eddie mused to himself before closing the envelope. Only then did he see scribbled on the back, under Charles's British return address, the words 'Seasick all the way.'

"I never doubted him," MayBelle finally said. "He made it. Praise the Lord."

She opened her eyes wide and sat up straight.

14

So it happened, Charles's last letter written Stateside made it to St. Louis from Wales. Then came silence. No news by mail but no telegram from the Army either declaring him missing or dead. Every evening Eddie, MayBelle, and Charlene gathered around their venerable console to hear news of the world. German blitzes over London stopped, and Allied air attacks against Germany began. There was talk of an all-out invasion, most likely against Hitler's fortified Norwegian coast. The gravelly voice of Edward R. Murrow, reporting by radio from bombed-out London, expressed doubts and mentioned beaches across the English Channel in France, where Hitler had fortifications but seemed preoccupied defending Scandinavia.

The world waited, even at Sumner High, which lost more male teachers. By year's end 1943 and early 1944 only instructors too old for the draft or unable to bear arms remained in classrooms. As the United States entered its third year at war, more boys disappeared from Eddie's classes, mostly 17-year-olds lying about their age. Charlene's school choir became all-female.

"Europe, something's bound to happen," Eddie was telling MayBelle one late afternoon when Charlene came in with the mail. She held out a square, brown envelope but acted undecided about who needed it most. Eddie saw a glint in his mother's eye and nodded her way. MayBelle squiggled nervously up from her cushioned wicker chair and reached out, only to fall short in her effort. Charlene stepped closer and placed the letter on her mother-in-law's lap.

MayBelle toyed a while with the envelope. She looked first at the back but found nothing. Then she dared turn it to the front, where she saw her own name and address typed out. She tried to decipher the postage, but recognized only a likeness of George VI and a few numerals. She let Eddie and Charlene glance at it, too, but they also failed to determine what was penny, shilling, or pound.

"No clue how much it cost, pretty clear, though," Eddie said. "He sent this from an English post office, not US Army mail. That's why it took forever. Strange postmark, too. Aberystwyth. Whatever that is, a city? Or how to pronounce it?"

The ladies shook their heads about the exotic sounding place as Eddie gently took the letter from his mother's hand. As usual, he marveled that she, the true teacher in the family, deferred to him as the letter reader. He guessed how dearly she held onto thoughts of Charles, the namesake of Carlos, and feared being first to get official word of his demise. Carefully Eddie opened the envelope, this one large and white, and studied it. No typing on the stationery. It was in Charles's hurried hand but lacked the excitement and fury of the last letter from Tyson.

Barracks bags galore, Charles wrote from abroad. *We filled our bags with everything we'd need and sometimes more. The clumsiest but most necessary was two pairs of boots for every guy. They stuffed us into train cars, packed as tight as our bags and blackened the coaches, so white guys outside couldn't see in through the windows. Only days after we watched the scum murder Squaley, a train brought us to Camp Shanks in New York. Six days later we were down at Pier 86 in the Big Apple. Then we knew, it'd be either Europe or Africa. The gut-wrenching feelings we had from watching our buddy get gunned down made everybody anxious.*

Eddie recited the letter. All 687 men of the 320th clambered aboard the Cunard liner *Aquitania* on a cold November day. Their bunk beds were cramped and the food horrible. Little of what they swallowed stayed down. *By then we figured it'd be Europe, and braced ourselves in the forty foot waves and threw up chow in our helmets.* The ship pitched and rolled despite its reputation as extremely reliable.

It'd been in service unscathed since The Great War, but Charles guessed it had more torpedo scares than troops learned about.

After seven days at sea, we saw land at a place called Gourock in Scotland. We got off and stepped aboard a British train. Super woozy after tossing at sea, we stumbled on board a train headed southwest across Britain to our camp in Wales. We rode in un-curtained coaches, and could luxuriate in the lovely countryside. The land lay under a covering of light snow. It felt like freedom.

What Charles and his battalion did militarily in southeast Wales in the following months wasn't clear. His letters came infrequently and a few gaps in the ongoing accounts indicated some of his letters were sent but never arrived. The battalions continued barrage balloon training in the hills of Wales. Exactly where those hills were or what that training consisted of Charles never explained. Eddie suspected his reticence was following orders. Surely there had to be an invasion sometime, somewhere. Why else turn thousands of Americans loose on Great Britain unless there was some use for them?

The "dark-complexioned" newcomers to the islands were easy to spot. Charles wrote that the local Welsh population of factory workers and coal miners had normally never seen a black man before and now they were facing hundreds of them. *Us dark men with white smiles and gracious manners are liberating the Wales people from their ignorance of the outside world,* Charles wrote after a visit to a larger Welsh village, *just as their openness is a breath of fresh air for us.* He quoted a Cardiff newspaper article praising colored men as the only American troops with polite manners.

During a long hiatus in his brother's letter writing, Eddie quit trying to understand everything. Following the long missive describing Squaley's murder and as the war carried on with news from all fronts about destruction and despair, Charles at last wrote about visiting a settlement near Pontypool. Even after looking up the community in a World Atlas, Eddie had only the vaguest knowledge what Pontypool was. He didn't need much explaining to understand its greatest attraction to Charles was a young woman named Clarys.

Believe it or not, we met in a graveyard. Every church has one next to it, Charles explained. *Hello, pretty lady, I greeted her.*

She was walking her bike home on a shortcut, and I was reading tombstones from way back. Some older than America, it seemed. People been here so long.

She invited him home to meet her parents. Over endless cups of tea, they compared their careers, or in Charles's case the lack of any. Straight out of university, Clarys went off to London to gain fame as a clothing designer, but found it hard to break the barriers of older, established fashion houses. Or even get a foothold. 'Like you perhaps?' she had asked Charles, showing an awareness of social barriers facing a colored man in America. 'Me,' she said, 'I can join the enemy, so to speak, the rival designers. We all look alike, pale skin and all, and I can go to work for them, if I choose, and be accepted. Maybe you don't have that option in America, of everybody being the same color, I mean?'

15

larys reminds me a little of Carina, from Tennessee, Eddie read aloud to MayBelle and Charlene. Though he was sparing with more info about the Welsh lady, the three at home in St. Louis understood Charles took a serious liking to Clarys and carried on an affair with her, played out against the uncertainties of war and made the more poignant by their knowledge that flames can burn brightest under threats of annihilation.

"What flares up hottest dies out fastest," MayBelle said. "Foolish boy, he had a girl of his kind in Paris, not the city in France either."

"Yes, in strange times like these," Charlene agreed, "love and death go hand-in-hand. He meets the girl of his dreams and sees his battalion mate killed the same day. And now this Clarys pops up with combat or invasion hanging over their heads."

"True," Eddie added. "The Army didn't send them across the pond to chase skirts at tea parties. Anyway his letter says Clarys is only living at home for now. She'll be back in London when war's over. What'll Charles have then?"

Eddie fidgeted with the letter and wondered what kind of paper it was written on. Was it, too, rationed and recycled war goods, useful for the moment like people's emotions and spontaneous, embattled love affairs? And would there be another letter like it?

No, nothing identical, but something else arrived at MayBelle's on the same kind of square British stationery as Charles used. It appeared weeks after Charles's most recent letter and came to MayBelle from Doris Corry, Clarys's mother. The British mom praised MayBelle's son as a "genteel gentleman." Charles sang in the church with Mrs. Corry and Clarys every Sunday. Clarys's mother said Mr. Corry and her would forever look on Charles as their son. MayBelle wondered out loud if that last statement was a figure of speech or a statement of hoped-for romance in Charles's relationship with their daughter.

Mrs. Corry's letter was written in a pleasing style, but Eddie recognized it as a weak antidote to the unrelenting determination the Allies showed about advancing on Hitler's Germany. There was no room in that advance for gentle sentiment. To no one's surprise, the Germans dug in and waited for the invasion to come. The question was, by what route?

What came as a surprise in St. Louis was the next letter Eddie opened from Charles. He wrote calmly of meeting Clarys and her parents and the placid months he spent in Wales. The Corrys were a touch of civilization amidst the chaos of preparing a vast military force whose great task drew near. The average GI learned little about that endeavor, except for the sometimes empty sounding admonishment: Be Prepared!

We wait now that spring is near and know we weren't sent across the Atlantic to sit and dawdle, which we do more and more and war feels like someplace else. Only an occasional Gerrie bomb falls in Wales. One landed at a factory north of here the other day when no one was at work. They pulled the plant manager and his dog out alive, Charles wrote. *We're headed for something. Something somewhere, as the talk goes, while we remain in the dark about what it is and ignorant of the outcome. It won't be pretty.*

Eddie came to a blank space in the paper, where Charles had left off writing, as though reckoning what he had left to say. *There's good people at home and here,* he concluded at the bottom. *In between, forces of Hell. Love you.*

We carry on as best ... Eddie wrote back to his brother from wartime St. Louis. *Keep it short. Keep it cheerful.* That was a motto the military provided for people sending letters to troops overseas, so Eddie told of his and Charlene's days at Sumner, and MayBelle added notes about her work in the community. In one letter Eddie described the Browns and Cardinals heading for American and National League championships, which would lead to the first ever all-St. Louis World Series of baseball, played in venerable Sportsman's Park on Grand Avenue. He addressed his letters to Charles by name and regiment or sent them by the later use of V-mail, which he explained meant Victory Mail, a quick and efficient way of getting millions of micro-filmed letters across the oceans without overloading the mails, especially in Great Britain, whose Postal Service forwarded mail to and from the frontlines in Europe.

Following his words about the forces of Hell, Charles failed to respond to mail. As the folks at home understood, he wrote that letter only days before his battalion embarked for the June 6, 1944, D-Day invasion at Normandy. After that date, MayBelle kept on dictating messages to Eddie, who continued writing full-fledged letters, but nothing came from Charles. It seemed the English Channel had swallowed him up, as it had with other troops as well. Yet no communiques from the Army mentioned his name and the daily newspapers' casualties lists failed to report on him.

All the while riveting accounts flowed across the Atlantic about the stupendous Allied invasion that weakened Germany evermore. First had come the conflict culminating at El Alamein in north Africa. Then followed attacks on the soft underbelly of Axis power around the Mediterranean, which especially struck fascist Italy. Following was the Russian victory at Leningrad in 1942. By 1944 the stage was set for northern and western Europe. While Hitler wavered between expecting a full-force attack against his forces in Norway or the coast of France, American news sources recorded how the British and American command bore in on what the Germans termed The Atlantic Wall that they created to stop attacks against them in mainland Europe.

Eddie read in St. Louis papers that Allied forces going against that bunkered defense system needed clear, dry weather for an air attack and calm winds for coordinated approaches by sea. After a day's delay on June 5, 1944, the Allies launched their D-day attack on the morning of June 6. With temps in the 50s, strong winds and rough seas brought the tide in more quickly than expected. Landing craft pitched and bobbed in the waves. Some had difficulty nearing the beach and let their troops off in deep water causing some to drown carrying heavy packs while others waded slowly and were easily picked off by German fire. As Eddie later read, given the combination of a large number of armed Germans, the encumbered Allied attackers, and the limited beach space for incoming allies, an individual invading trooper had about a one in four chance of surviving the combat.

However, German defenders were enough taken by surprise over the invasion taking place in chancy weather that they dropped into partial retreat, which allowed those Allied troops who hadn't fallen under gunfire to seize German bunkers and disarm other gunneries. Nevertheless, reports Eddie found but withheld from his mother indicated the enormous toll German guns and defense forces took on men wading ashore. Those who survived seemed only barely to outnumber those who drowned under the weight of their landing packs, died from German *Stuka* dive bombers attacking the sandy stretches beyond water's edge, or fell to enemy fire while storming the fortified banks farther inland.

"One in four doesn't sound half bad," Eddie fibbed to his mother. "There's a chance Charles made it, but it's his battalion's job to carry in those barrage balloons, assemble, and launch them. You know the Gerries got fighter planes and ground gunners doing everything to shoot holes in the balloons."

"But pictures in the paper show lots of balloons over Normandy," Charlene interrupted him. "So some of our guys must've survived to put them aloft. Right? And where else could Charles's battalion have headed, but to the invasion?"

"Yeah, we can hope he stays safe if he's in the thick of it," Eddie allowed. "He'll write sometime."

Charlene nodded when her husband spoke like that. When they were away from MayBelle, they tried to imagine the horrors of Atlantic Wall shores, only to realize the futility of reproducing in their own minds the shock and familiarity of violent death as it struck at the men wading from the frigid waters into a hail of bullets. Surely the carnage left corpses never to be identified or even found. Living with the dead couldn't help but create mental voids in men who survived bodily.

MayBelle remembered episodes Charles had described in his letters. "I recall one such," she remarked as the three watched a thunderstorm descend on Richmond Heights one afternoon in July of 1944. "My boy," she began as if speaking to strangers. Catching herself, she paused and readjusted her focus on Eddie and Charlene. "He wrote to us of lightning striking the line of a barrage balloon. That was during training in the States. It broke the heavy cable, which swept away one of the troops."

She shuffled her feet so they knew perfectly well what was on her mind, though she hesitated to say it.

"I wonder."

"What?" Eddie asked.

"If a German plane doesn't see a balloon cable and flies into it, will it electrocute any of our boys on the ground? How horrendous."

Eddie and Charlene gazed at MayBelle. The war changed lots of folks' attitudes. Not the least among them was Eddie's mother.

"Don't rightly know," MayBelle reasoned, "It seems after a bit a soldier knows what's on the way but chooses not to think about it." She hesitated, then added, "Not over much."

"We know you're worried sick about him," Eddie comforted her, "so are we, but we can't constantly invent scenes in our imagination."

"He's probably perfectly all right," Charlene said. "Well, maybe not perfectly, who is these days? Be calm."

16

Getting fewer letters from Charles had its impact on MayBelle. Her loneliness also grew noticeable when he wrote so enthusiastically of meeting Carina and Clarys. At first Eddie wondered if MayBelle and Charles's sharing of social work among the poor had created a deep bond between mother and son that MayBelle never developed with him. Or if Charles was the love child of MayBelle and Carlos and Eddie only an afterthought. At times Eddie could imagine that his older brother was conceived in the first blooming of a mad passion between MayBelle and Carlos and that Eddie, by contrast, came into the world while the parents were gliding apart, both spiritually and geographically.

Whatever the case, Eddie felt no rancor. Instead he became a patient spectator to MayBelle's mood swings and a careful proprietor of their household as his mother grew older, if not extremely so in years. As summer 1944 lengthened, the days following Normandy felt interminable without Charles sending a word. They longed for any first-hand description of what the landing had been like and how it touched Charles. The Army still sent no dreaded casualty notice either, so he must be alive. Only in what shape? And where?

Barrage balloon battalions were news media darlings only while their balloons hovered over embattled beaches. They looked imposing in aerial photos, but there was no practical use for them as the Allied invasion pushed inland. Eddie guessed those men of the 320th who survived the on-shore fighting were at work maintaining their balloons or dismantling them and preparing to move on. But where to? What was the next continent or island to wade ashore on?

By late summer, school teaching again demanded Eddie and Charlene's attention in St. Louis and the Browns and Cardinals' impending World Series took up increased column space in the sports pages. Imagining these were normal times would almost have been possible, but there was still no mail from Charles. Eddie saw the painful sense of loss, absence, or abandonment struck MayBelle hardest.

The shock subsided into a dull ache. MayBelle referred to Charles in roundabout terms like he was an object from the past. If death hadn't taken him, the horrors of Normandy had. In turn, accounts of the invasion that crept into the popular press left Eddie with an image of the beachfront as an enormous bomb crater that sucked everybody into it. While the beach was strewn with dead bodies, those who survived were left with psychological damage. The most objective reporters said seeing comrades blown to bits etched itself in men's brains and left many as speechless automatons, competent to carry on with the slaughter of others but unable to utter any lucid description of what they saw in battle or knew it to be about.

"Survivor's guilt, they call it," Charlene explained to MayBelle one evening after they'd bowed over the console radio and listened to accounts of troops facing combat. "We heard tell of it in the newsreels. It's inescapable. Why did that bullet hit him in the heart and another missed me by an inch? At Normandy it was worst. A mad onward thrust. No time to think."

"No rest, no retreat, no comfort. Storming a beach you can only go forward, no way back into the ocean," Eddie continued. "Imagine if that's what Charles went through or carries inside him. Memories of that. No escaping it."

17

"Looks like he found a retreat, all right," Charlene said cheerfully as she came in from the mail box on a springlike day. She handed Eddie a long white envelope. "Hawaii? My word! Who'd ever believe it? Is this a macabre joke?"

Eddie took the letter nonchalantly, but sat up as soon as he looked at it. It bore Charles's name, return address in Oahu, Hawaii, and ordinary U. S. postage. He turned the envelope around, as had been his custom during his brother's barrage balloon training, when Charles penned long and sobering letters, that arrived in jig time, with postscripts scribbled on the backside. This envelope was featherweight.

Charlene brought MayBelle to the kitchen, where Eddie was searching through the cabinets. MayBelle crowded him away to locate a letter opener. With it, he carefully opened the envelope and removed a single sheet. Through the neatly folded paper he recognized Charles's upright lettering.

European war's over, for us, MayBelle read aloud, after taking the letter from Eddie. The note began after Charles only briefly greeted MayBelle as Ma. Tense at hearing from Charles and aghast at his unaccustomed telegraph-like messaging style, she read on, hesitantly. *We took our balloons down in summer and unloaded cargo for the Army. November of '44, embarked for the States. Storms and seasick, those still alive. Straight through Panama. Seven months we been on Oahu. Late in the game. D-Day? Done.*

MayBelle refolded the letter and let it dangle between her thumb and forefinger. Eddie tried to figure if that was a gesture of relief or anger.

"An eternity, and now just this?" MayBelle asked. "He's all right?"

"Sailing down the U. S. East Coast and making it across the Pacific without a moment's furlough? Strange," Eddie said. "It's the military gone nuts."

He didn't deprive MayBelle of whatever thoughts she had, but talked the matter over with Charlene. They agreed to let it ride why Charles remained silent for so long. Charlene wondered when MayBelle's joy at Charles being still alive and in the Army's fold would overcome the despair she'd nursed.

In the days following, Eddie hung out at the public library's newspaper room. He snooped in enough national newspapers to see reporters suspected a buildup of American troops on the West Coast, in certain preparation for an invasion of the Japanese homeland. Barrage balloons were being manufactured in California. That Charles's 320th battalion would be landing on Japanese soil seemed certain. Plus an inhuman bloodletting to follow.

"Some hell that will be," Eddie reported to Charlene.

"Wading ashore under kamikaze maniacs? No sirree," she replied.

"You know what they're calling this one? V-J Day. V as in victory. Some bloodbath that'll be," Eddie moaned. "With both sides losing."

For the time being Hawaii served in Eddie's mind as a haven for the battle scarred. He read about the transport of allied wounded from the Pacific front to Oahu and from there to the Veteran's Hospital in Long Beach, California, where medical teams put GIs' broken bodies back together and mended their minds, if possible. Eddie and Charlene helped MayBelle build castles in the air for Charles, who surely had it better than his wounded fellows. They imagined him passing the months in languorous ease under swaying palm trees and dismissing combat from his mind. Yet why he hadn't written to them was a puzzle. Eddie felt uneasy about it, but failed to bring it up at home.

"Don't be hard," MayBelle warned Eddie. "That boy got a load on his mind. Your own brother. You and him. Remember?"

"Yeah, with one dad in two different guises, Charles shows us that by not responding," Eddie replied, only half in jest.

"He be in the shade now, takin' it the easy way, my Charles, like they say down home," she answered in a tone meant to calm herself, but also indicating what she wished for Charles. Rest and recuperation.

"A long trip to Hawaii," Charlene added. "At least he's free of enemy bombs."

The three made a friendly bet on when they'd see Charles again. Eddie figured it'd be a long battle defeating the Japanese on their home ground. An invasion far outstripping D-Day was sure to kill millions, military and civilian. Charlene opted for a general blockade of the Japanese homeland despite her realization it could be years before starvation caused a surrender. If the war dragged on, Charles would be in active service and launching barrage balloons in Japan for who knew how many years.

"The Emperor will surrender before long," was MayBelle's immediate bet. "We gotta believe in his humanity. Charles'll be here."

MayBelle was most right, but it wasn't *many* bombs that brought Charles back. One was enough. On August 6, 1945, the Enola Gay, an American bomber, dropped its atomic payload on Hiroshima, and the world stood still.

"I know," Charlene admitted later. "That's suffering decades of blockading and starving could never equal."

In turn, Eddie imagined he saw Charles on a high volcanic slope in Oahu gazing out over vast stretches of Pacific and watching a mushroom cloud rise skyward. Eddie wondered if war made the imagination run wild.

Not long after that, MayBelle received a telegram. Dated Oahu, September 15, 1945, it read quickly. *Hi, Folks. Expect a discharge. Home soon. All's well? Charles.*

Back to his senses, Eddie still wondered where reality lay. Would his brother be on another overcrowded troop ship bobbing on seasick swells and laden with crippled troops? Or would he leave Honolulu with leis and come home to a hero's welcome?

"Be prepared," Charlene cautioned Eddie. "I suspect him to write little about the war and speak even less. I read that about some colored souls in the good ol' United States. They escaped lynching, but never talked about it afterward."

"We'll see," MayBelle said. In a calmer mode than usual, she waited for the reward she'd get from winning her friendly wager. That came in the form of war's end combined with Charles's return. Both happened in fall, 1945.

"Not a moment too soon?" Eddie asked.

18

"Never too late for that."

Those were Charles's first words to Eddie since he left for induction. He'd just stepped off a West Coast Flier from Los Angeles. The express was two hours late, but that seemed to bother nobody in the euphoria of newborn peace. Hostilities were over, that's what mattered.

"Welcome home, Hero," Eddie greeted him after a brotherly hug. "You have to tell us about it, before long."

Charles smiled, maybe for the first time in eons. Eddie guessed as much anyhow after looking at the solemn lines on his brother's forehead, which had appeared during his absence. The slight twitch was there, too. Eddie would've continued studying Charles's countenance, but MayBelle found her older son at the railroad platform, tucked an arm under his, and allowed herself to be whisked away from the station as she gazed in admiration at his uniform. Eddie followed, basking in the afterglow of mother and older son. After all, Eddie had needed to tear Charles away from MayBelle to shake his hand and wonder, what manner of man is this returning from the great wide world. Without delay she stole back the returning hero to continue her longed-for reunion and lavish motherly affection.

"He's spoken only five or six words," Eddie reminded Charlene.

"I know. I heard," she replied. "Words from what world?"

Eddie didn't answer. He gazed ahead at his mother and sauntered after her and Charles. It seemed their pace was that of the

Mississippi cotton fields, but in an epoch without Jim Crow and barrage balloons, when men lived an easy life under languorous skies.

"Seven months in Hawaii and now returning to this happiness as well. Is that what Charles will know now? Like Life before the Fall?" Charlene asked.

MayBelle got Charles home to Richmond Heights, where the family planned a gala dinner, but they had to postpone it. Charles had been at sea on military transport from Hawaii. Once arrived in California he received an Army discharge, which left it up to him to arrange his transport. That meant two days and nights on the West Coast Flier from L. A. to St. Louis. He was exhausted and it showed. At home he found some of his civilian clothes ill-fitting. Other pieces seemed out of style and of a time now gone.

Like a prodigal returning to the home folks, he found an easy chair that first night and gazed around at photos and paintings, most of which Charlene had placed on the walls. There were familiar Rembrandt and Gauguin reproductions of Renaissance potentates and Polynesian *wahines*. Only an untitled black-and-white drawing, with a scribbled artist's name, caught Charles's eye. It showed a stand of leafless beech trees in a semi-alpine setting. On each tree trunk someone had carved the date of death for some unnamed person. From each inscription hung a small amulet commemorating the deceased.

To Eddie the drawing described a reign of windless and breathless silence. He wondered what caused Charles to fasten his attention on it. Eddie got up to study the drawing closer, but his brother motioned for him to sit back down.

"Listen," he said softly. "I was in a small town on Oahu the day the war ended. It was in this luscious green valley. They had some stores and a movie theater I remember. Then out of nowhere came this announcement how the Japanese Emperor surrendered.

"From the clear Hawaiian blue, it felt like, two boys burst out across the city park yelling *The war's over! The war's over!* They headed for a white church opposite the park on one side of the valley. One of the boys was a teenager, the other just a squirt. He had trouble keeping up with the big one and nearly stumbled. The church bells were in a tower outside the building. The boys clambered up a ladder to ring the bells. The bigger boy pulled for all he was worth so you could hear them clanging and echoing from one side of the valley to the other. The little squirt did his best, and each time he got a clang the rope lifted him halfway up the shaft toward the bells themselves.

"They kept shouting, *It's over! We're free! We're free!* They were Asian and probably Japanese but as American as me and came from a camp near town. The boys must've grown up in a Japanese internment camp, who knows for how long. Now they'd be out. I listened a while, then went back to camp. The bells cling inside my head still."

Eddie waited patiently in the silence that followed.

"It's strange," Charles continued after a while. "I thought then of the interned Japanese Americans and Rousseau, whose books we read at Tougaloo."

"What's that?" Eddie asked.

"*Man is born free and everywhere he is in chains*, Rousseau said. I guess that's true. Musta felt that way for those boys, anyway."

Along with MayBelle, Charlene, and a couple of MayBelle's cousins that she'd invited, Eddie waited for Charles to tell more. He seemed to be drifting to another world, only to snap out of that mood and converse calmly, accepting his mother's favorite dishes, mainly sweet potatoes and rabbit stew, for dinner. He told Eddie about endless hours aboard ship from Hawaii to California.

"What'd we do? Nothing much, lounged on the deck and played cards. An endless ocean. Nothing like life, which passes fast. The Pacific goes on forever. At least until you give up hope and then one day there's light on shore and there you are, back where you left off, more or less."

"Which is it?" MayBelle inquired. "More? Or less? More or less what?"

"They never tell you before."

"Before what?" his mother persisted.

"The bombing. But you find out—eagerness, anxiety, then dread," Charles answered. "You don't find out in those terms, it's a sensation."

"But after, though?" Eddie wondered.

"The words for it are stuff I read about, in Hawaii. And what's your meaning with after?" Charles asked imitating his mother and Eddie alike.

"After is back here," Eddie said.

"What's in me?"

Eddie nodded, playing the innocent observer of his brother's return, which was not yet either triumphal or dismal. "Judging by your months in Hawaii. No battleground there any longer."

"It was still on a war footing," Charles said with a subtle smile that seemed to say, you'll never know.

"We did our best here," MayBelle burst out pleadingly.

"It's not what you did or couldn't do, but them to us. Us to them. All to each other," Charles said with a broad but incongruous smile meant to soothe his mother's frazzled nerves as her joy at seeing him returned then wavered and gave way and finally shattered after months of tense waiting and hovering over the console radio for news that never said what she wished for, which was simply, where are you?

Eddie saw tears of confusion in his mother's eyes.

"No clue," Charles continued. "What I feel? Fatigue, confusion. Avoidance maybe?"

Eddie listened to this and others' conversation hoping to make sense of it. The end of a war must be like any death or leave taking. Weighing what was gained and lost.

"Sure, some GIs are too young to know what hit 'em, even though they survived, but us, we're mature and can reflect," Eddie suggested, in control of his words but wondering what he really wanted to say. Or if it made sense.

"It's called re-experiencing," Charlene explained. "Bad things revisit us till we work them out."

MayBelle, Eddie, Charlene, and the cousins sat as though trying to recollect horrors they'd never experienced. Charles was the first to stir. Sensing Charlene's words were soundest, he rose to his feet. He thanked them, gave his mother another hug, and went to the porch for his rucksack.

"My boy, like he's never been away," MayBelle said with gratitude.

"The more you think about it, re-experiencing leads to arousal, sooner or later," Charlene said in reply, trying not to sound a know-it-all. "It's sure to come, Psych 101."

Eddie, for one, sat still while Charles hoisted his gear and went upstairs. The sound of him carefully making his bed and rearranging furniture, untouched since induction, floated down to Eddie, who figured this is how it'll be for Charles. Quiet, reasoned reactions mixed with wild whims. Avoidance followed by arousal, both of which could try MayBelle's patience.

Eddie agreed with Charlene, but hoped she got it wrong.

19

Charlene almost got it right. About Charles, that is. He came home but talked little. For the first weeks he lounged around the house and then the neighborhood. He used his last Government pay as a GI to buy new clothes and a winter jacket. Nobody expected him to do more, so he did no more. Eddie wondered if he was waiting for orders, like in the military, so he had MayBelle take charge. Once in a while she hauled him along on her rounds in poor neighborhoods to help with clothing for children and food for families.

Eddie never knew what Charles did during the daytime. School was in full swing at Sumner. He and Charlene were in class but also working, at what Charlene called "Guard duty" for basketball games and student clubs. They often came home to find Charles with no tasks except for his habit of assiduously washing dishes, scrubbing plates spotless, and redoing them.

"Only that," Eddie told Charlene, "until one day I came home before you. I stopped in the doorway and watched him pick up some melting ice cubes. He washed them with soap and water and put them back in the fridge clean as a whistle, to freeze again."

Charlene smiled at Eddie's story. "Not his mother's son for nothing," she said mildly. "Waste not, want not, you know."

"Like life in the Delta? Ancestral traits?"

She nodded yes. "Who knows what horrors are spooking in his mind. Could be a gentle touch is needed after …"

"What?"

Charlene didn't answer, but looked inquiringly at her husband.

"But never a word when he saw me watching him with the ice cubes," Eddie added to defer her silence. "Just a smile, gentle as yours."

"That's what war does?" she asked. "Maybe? Make the broken whole again?"

20

And so Charles's lack of participation in others' routines became a routine. He neither shared his family's comings and goings nor stood outside them. He stayed home and mixed with them alone until MayBelle took Charles out socially. Her first idea was to reintroduce him to their community the way they helped him say goodbye to it. So she nixed dinner at home one day near Christmas and treated Charles, Eddie, Charlene, and two of her older brothers to fancy dining at Okie Joe's, the barbecue place, which had actually abandoned the Okie stamp and now went for the more sedate *Chez Joseph*. In truth people still called it Okie Joe's, but the owner emphasized the finer tone by buying a real neon sign with the name spelled out in italics.

MayBelle's bunch skipped the taxi ride, unlike on their last visit to Okie's. As they neared the restaurant, the thick barbecue aroma felt familiar, and entering the locale made it clear a few years of world war did nothing to affect the homey interiors. Statues of enormous steers lined the bar top and the far wall featured murals of oil derricks with electric beams to resemble gushers. Eddie quickly noted the same racial equality. The cook was colored but more like from India than Africa. Their waitress was white and approached the party quickly. She showed them a flicker of recognition.

"Back from the Army?" she asked with a glance at Eddie and Charles.

Eddie remembered his family ordering a simple dish in the past and Charlene footed the bill. They ordered the same barbecue beef again and ate sedately. Strangely, only Lemuel and Ezekiel,

MayBelle's brothers, spoke. The opposites of their sister, they were short and thin and talked slowly.

"Tell 'em where you served, Zeke," Lemuel said to his elder brother.

"In the Canal Zone, like you," Ezekiel replied. "As a scullery mate."

It was family lore that Charles and Eddie knew about since boyhood, how their uncles signed on with the merchant marine between the world wars and saw the globe from cargo ships. It remained a secret how two black men had gotten themselves enrolled in that line of work dominated in the U. S. by whites, but their time in Panama left the brothers content with their racial status.

"There everybody was colored, so no black this and white that, right?" MayBelle encouraged them to explain, but she had little success. The brothers bent over like starting silent prayers before tackling the barbecue. In the past Eddie had heard his uncles hint at voodoo sounds from jungles in the Zone, but he didn't ask.

"Nuff said," Lemuel noted afterward. "Brown people every-where. Different beliefs."

"Liked it there, but hot as blazes," Ezekiel added.

Eddie saw MayBelle relax. "Kith and kin?" he said to her.

His mother nodded in assent.

It was still early for other diners. Only a mellow oldie played on the juke box. *I'll never smile again* came the lyrics.

Until I smile at you, Eddie sang along as though serenading Charlene.

I'll never laugh again, what good would it do? Charles said of a sudden.

"Good tunes," Zeke added.

"Yes, The Ink Spots," Charles said. His voice surprised the oth-ers, who looked his way and expected more, but he didn't sing.

"In Tennessee we had juke boxes like this out in the country. One guy, Lewis, Lew we called him, which was a big joke once we got to Wales because there that name means the john. Anyway,

Lew loved the Ink Spots, knew every song by heart. That one, about smiling again and *I Don't Want to Set the World on Fire.*"

"Oh, yes," Charlene burst out. "Love it!"

Eddie looked up. Not surprising his wife knew pop stuff too, after all she taught choral music, but *I'll Never Smile Again* was all he'd heard of the Ink Spots. "You? You know it?" he asked Charlene kiddingly.

"*I just want to start a flame in your heart,*" Charlene sang even softer than Eddie's uncles spoke. She tenderly placed a hand on Eddie's.

"Once we got to Britain," Charles continued. He appeared oblivious to the others finishing off their barbecue or Eddie and Charlene's love bird shenanigans. "Lew kept singing Ink Spots tunes, which was a novelty to the Brits. Lots of people in Wales had never seen a Negro and here was Lew black as coal and didn't need to imitate blackface darkies, like in the movies the Brits saw."

It seemed everybody had forgotten Charles could even converse, but he could and did. Yeah, talk was one thing. Charles had been saying things ever since he got there from Honolulu, or wherever he'd been. Oahu? Was that the place? But carrying on a conversation, engaging others, was something else. Now here he was and had everyone hanging on every word. His eyes brightened.

"You mean a real live colored guy like us?" Ezekiel asked with a smile. He looked around the table at the others.

"No, sir, I mean this fella Lew was dark as the night, I'm telling you," Charles continued.

"Anything else, folks?" came a voice. It was the waitress, who popped up from behind and spoke as if to say, yes, just like you, real people.

"Yeah, this guy Lew," Charles went on while glancing at the others to keep them in the story. "And, certainly, ma'am," he said to the waitress in the meantime and took the check from her like a confident head of the family. "Lew was a hit in Wales. I mean a real attraction in town, which had one of those absurd Welsh names nobody but them can pronounce."

"Like Aberystwyth?" Eddie asked.

"Yes, something like. Anyway, this Lew was out launching a balloon and it failed, nobody knew why, except there was talk our American balloons let in air that fouled the hydrogen. The balloon launched in a lightning strike with Lew getting caught in the cable line. It pulled him aloft with it. Guys stood and looked as it drifted higher and higher and him entangled in the line. Nobody knew if he was electrocuted or still alive. At last we saw this body fall loose and come to the ground from high up. It was a soundless spectacle, but guys close in swore Lew was singing Ink Spots as he plummeted down. *If I Didn't Care* ... Not even a plop when he hit the ground. Like in a silent film."

Charles leaned to the side like he imagined a body smashing down. Eddie watched as the others fingered whatever glass or cup they had. They took a swallow of water or cold coffee to still their jitters at the thought of a guy so calm he sang love songs in death. A somber mood hung over the group until Charles described MPs arriving and clearing the field of GIs talking about the sudden accident.

"MPs, that's Military Police," Charles explained.

The others nodded yes, they figured that. Eddie started to say something, but he stopped when Lemuel and Ezekiel hrmpphed about the bill on the table. Eddie politely signaled to his brother.

"We'll get it?" Charles asked.

Charles and Eddie covered the bill. Lemuel and Ezekiel said thanks and footed it home. Eddie hailed a taxi to Richmond Heights. Charles sat up front, but said little. Eddie watched him gazing out the window while the ladies chatted about the evening meal. That day set the tone for Charles's post-war years, Eddie suddenly realized. He was sometimes morose, other times full of talk.

21

1945 gave way to a new year.

Eddie and Charlene taught now for the first time in a post-war era. Their salaries rose. At last they had some cash. Eddie bought a rundown Ford but kept it in MayBelle's garage. He and Charlene rode the city buses to work and on shopping jaunts.

During the day, Charles often stayed in his room tinkering with a few mementos he brought back from the war, or writing letters, to a list of persons, whoever they were, no one knew.

"Most likely battalion buddies," Charlene guessed.

"A lot of months to spend on pen pals," Eddie joked. Otherwise he went easy on his big brother. "I give him the benefit of the doubt, which I never believed in before, he's been through a lot."

Each evening Charles came downstairs light-footed like nothing was out of order. It was his time for a walk, usually with a handful of letters to drop off at the post office. Once Eddie tore himself away from after-school homework and followed along. Charles talked about what he'd written. Surprisingly he held up an envelope addressed to Langston Hughes in New York. He wrote to the poet every week, but never got any reply, he lamented. Hughes was still writing but maybe wasn't the super young ball of fire anymore.

"D'you ever think he'll give it up?" Eddie asked.

"No, I like his stuff," Charles said. "You know me, if I like something, I like it a lot, but there's not so much I like. It has to be special."

He stopped in the middle of a cross walk and looked long and hard at Eddie. "I even write to a couple dead guys. Fellas I knew."

"Dead? For real?"

"Yeah, for sure. Really dead, some of us didn't come through it all. You see lots. I miss 'em."

Charles's hands trembled a bit and Eddie saw the trait had begun to indicate his brother was nervous but in a mood to talk.

"We had this guy from Las Vegas in a white battalion. Kinda tan complected but with a Gerrie name. Gustav. They called him Gust. He was smart as all git out and talked to everybody. Him and me were buddies. He was originally from Minnesota and told me how he went out to UCLA but was gonna go back to the Midwest once to visit, so he latched onto some jalopy with some black college brothers in a second-hand lot and started out across the Mojave desert. It got hot so the sun burned right through the windshield and was baking 'em inside the car. Gust pulls over at a rundown *taverna* out there in the sands and orders a beer."

Eddie guessed at the next part and nodded. "Refused service I bet."

"Yes, and here his buddies were in ROTC jackets the bartender thought were regular Army issue.

"Boys, you musta stole them somewhere," this bartender guy says.

"Gust says, 'Here I am white and them colored, all of us Americans and in Army officer's training besides.' One geezer behind the bar aims a shotgun his way and fires it off at the ceiling and says, 'The next one's at your head, darkies.' Gust repeats he's studying for the Officers Corps and starts to climb over the bar top and take him with his bare hands, but the guy calls him a wetback and they don't allow no night fighters or greasers on their premises no how."

"And so what?" Eddie wondered.

"So Gust's already over the bar and got the geezer pinned to the floor when the cops arrive and pound him silly with Billy clubs. Then they slap him in the Needles clinker, where he slept on mud floors and had no running water, to 'rot with the other illegals,' they say, which is where Gust languishes till his buddies, who're made to sleep in the car or on the ground every night, find somebody at UCLA on the phone who'll get him sprung from that damned hole."

"But this can't have been your battalion buddy?" Eddie asked, stunned at hearing Charles swear. He'd always been too calm for vulgar words.

"No, you're right. But I knew him. Gust always said, 'Look at you colored guys. You fight for this country and get clubbed half to death?'"

Charles grew animated telling the barroom story, like he meant, well, that's what you could expect from Gust, everybody's buddy less you did him wrong.

"After that Gust quit UCLA or got dismissed from ROTC, never clear which came first. Shunned for buddying with Negroes, even in sunny California. No good reason. Two months later Gust was in Tennessee launching barrage balloons with the rest of us slobs, just another buck private, but in a white battalion. Beat that if you can."

"You say you write to dead guys. Gust's gone?"

Charles looked away from Eddie and stared at the lazy clouds of early evening. His mind was some place far away until he remembered they were in a crosswalk. He motioned Eddie onward.

"Normandy," Charles announced with a sudden jerk of his head toward Eddie. "Gust and I landed on the same day. A shell exploded in the sea behind us and sent spray over our crafts. The fronts opened and we jumped out. My rucksack weighted me down. I sank."

"You couldn't swim to begin with," Eddie reminded him.

"Lots couldn't. The Service gave us swim lessons, but we …"

He left off, which Eddie took to mean they never learned.

"Petrified of deep water, memories of white guys drowning sharecroppers in creeks and streams," Charles said. "Guys drowned like flies at Normandy. Me, too. I was sinking like a rock when Gust dived under and yanked me up again. That guy could swim like a fish. Said he learned as a kid in some Minnesota lakes. I was gulping sea water as he pulled me to the shallows. Bullets hitting around us."

"And?"

"Like I said, you know."

"No, tell me."

"We ran like mad, no thought of living or dying, or what color our skin was. The krauts didn't either, they'd shoot any of us. We had to set up and launch the balloons while the Gerries were making things tough on us. *Ratta tatt tatt* and *thump thump* as the machine gun bullets and shells hit the sand. Gust was helping me one second. I turn to him another and his head splits open and his brains blast out. There he is or what's left of him and my buddy's a hump of dead dough, whatever you'd call it, and pretty soon the flies'll descend on him. Maybe other bullets'll riddle the spot, too, or a *Stuka*'s sure to drop something from the air. Then all we'll have is a mass of flesh from thousands of GIs rotting in the sun, though it's only 50 degrees out there, but hot as hell in the fighting."

Charles paused and stared at Eddie some more. Sweat formed on his upper lip while his one hand still trembled, as Eddie couldn't help noticing, like a little icon of what war had done to ruin a world-class sprinter and make him a recluse, who only went out anymore when folks were less likely to see him in his new guise of a recovering war vet.

"All that's left for me was, well, nothing really, just run for cover with that image of Gust, a falling man, printing itself in me, along with scads of other sights, not to mention the awful sounds of clashing metal and dying and wounded crying for help that didn't exist or would arrive too late or couldn't do a blasted thing even if it got there real fast. Some guys already dead, others crying out not to die, but gonna anyway. One fella trying to hold his guts in while they splurge out despite him."

Eddie looked at the ground as Charles talked. Both realized there wasn't anything more to say that made any sense to someone that hadn't been there, but it made even less sense never to tell it to anyone and someday die with it unuttered and your mind warped beyond the saying of it.

Eddie was speechless, except to apologize. "I remember that day at Selective Service. I chickened out," he said.

"Nobody belonged at Normandy," Charles explained. He hesitated some more. "You needed to be where you are. It's your place."

My brother, ever the thinker, Eddie thought, ready with the right word, like when he quoted Langston Hughes to Edna at Selective Service and won her sympathy for giving Eddie's 4-F, not his own. Yes, or like their mother ready with the right word, too, but not everybody had her outspoken social conscience. Great that MayBelle remained at work in the projects of St. Louis. She found her place in the sun and stuck with it.

"Trudged on," Charles resumed. "We got the balloons in the air, despite it all. I kept hearing this other guy in the battalion singing Ink Spots. *Would it be the same?* Lew had sung the same lines both before and while he fell through the sky. *Would my every prayer begin and end with just your name?*"

"Yeah, I know that one," Eddie said. "*If I Didn't Care.* But he was already dead, that guy? In training camp? In Tennessee? Died in the air?"

"Lew. Yes."

"And you write to him still?"

Charles dropped his envelopes in a mailbox. "Can't help it. I write others, too. Can't lay off."

22

1946 was the next time the Cardinals won a World Series. It was a bitter struggle before St. Louis's beloved Red Birds beat the Dodgers in a playoff for the National League pennant. They finally banished the Red Sox, too, when Enos "Country" Slaughter scored from first on a single to right field in the Series' decisive seventh game. This was one time Eddie worked up some enthusiasm in Charles. Even while MayBelle chided the boys for "worshipping a white man's game," Eddie and Charles sat before the console radio and listened pitch by pitch.

"Yet there's little joy in Mudville, meaning where we are," MayBelle razzed them. "All the St. Louis World Series celebrations are in Whitey's hangouts and they sure as shootin' don't welcome us there. They'd just as soon shoot you as look at you," a trite saying she often came back to, mainly because history proved it was true. Lotsa white folks needed some poor souls to take their anger out on. The most fervent racial hate consistently came from poor trampled-on souls, she argued.

That's how the '40s went on, in a slump in St. Louis. After 1946, the Cardinals quit winning, and civil rights for MayBelle's poor colored folk lagged behind. Of course, there was Jackie Robinson breaking the color line in Major League Baseball, but he was in far-off Brooklyn and a constant pain in the Red Birds' butt.

MayBelle, Eddie, and Charlene continued to work in their neighborhoods and at Sumner. Charles eventually got a job as a beat reporter for a Negro newspaper syndicate in St. Louis and Kansas City. The Hoover Concern was its name, so called, silly rumors went, because it covered the Negro neighborhoods and gathering places like a vacuum cleaner. The papers used Charles mostly as an observer of folks' comings and goings. Trivial stuff but it gave him a foot in the door. He got the job after sending in his letters to fallen comrades to the St. Louis *Rainbow*, which published them and gave him an evaluation.

The *Rainbow* eventually made him a job offer. His comments on street life in areas of St. Louis were now published in the syndicate tabloids, so he quit mailing them to the often-forgotten addresses of men now out of touch with him or dead for a few years. He also was forced to go out in the streets to meet with the folks he wrote about. In his case that meant mixing with them.

"Walk to the post office with me and you'll become a true *flaneur* like me, if you know that word," he told Eddie on one of their strolls. Charles mailed in his articles on local customs and hidden horrors when he didn't report to the newspaper office.

Only Charlene probed at uncovering Charles's themes. "I've read about survivor's guilt," she repeated to Eddie and MayBelle. "He's hinting at the eternal question. Them and not me? Why am I still alive and my buddy's not? Like that guy Gust. I read that you can hear it echo a lot from vets, if you examine what's going on in their heads."

"I know what my boy feels, better than anyone," MayBelle explained. "War's like life on the streets. It turns a man's heart to steel. Don't you see that?"

23

After hearing Charlene, Eddie read and reread his brother's articles and also some in the *St. Louis Argus*. Charles's pieces gained readers for the press. One raised a scandal in the community, as it came on the heels of a police officer shooting an unarmed purported burglar to death in a St. Louis suburb. Charles failed to mention that incident directly. Instead he recounted what he himself witnessed at Normandy.

Unprovoked, an officer shot one of his own men, a barrage balloon private, in the back while they were braving German gunfire. The soldier died on the spot while helping launch a balloon. Ignoring the fact that the dead man lay facing German bunkers, Army commanders accepted the officer's tale that the dead man had deserted fleeing *from* combat with Germans and toward Allied lines.

"You can't shoot someone in the back who's running toward you," Eddie declared after reading Charles's piece.

In the aftermath of the killing of the burglar near St. Louis, if indeed he was a burglar, repeated calls from civil rights leaders across the Midwest, both colored and white, fell on deaf ears in the local city council. In the end, it was the word of the white cops, the only eye witnesses still alive, against circumstantial evidence gathered by civil rights leaders, who came on the scene days later. In the same way, Charles lived with the knowledge his writings never reached the mainstream reading public or were not easily grasped by anyone who'd never seen combat.

And so in the late 1940s Charles began behaving as Charlene once predicted. He wrote more but talked less. Only at home was he his occasional engaging self.

24

We'll meet again, don't know where, don't know when …

    Eddie listened distractedly while Charles hummed a melody and sang a few lines of the song. They were walking to the post office again. Charles was in a good mood, which was a sign he felt pleased with the column he was about to mail in. A year had passed since he started with Hoover Syndicate, and 1947 brought good things, principally in the form of a column he penned once a week. Readers asked for more from him, but the publishers were reluctant to flood the market with too much good stuff at once. "Better to spread it out, so the public doesn't get spoiled," his *Rainbow* editor argued.

"That's by the Ink Spots, too?" Eddie asked about the tune Charles hummed.

"No, not really. They recorded it. During the war. But they didn't write it."

"And Lew sang it as well?"

"Probably. Don't remember really. Just that I think of her."

"Clarys? The girl in Wales?"

"No, Vera Lynn. She recorded it first. 1939."

"Just as the war started in Europe?"

Charles nodded yes. "I heard it in Wales. On BBC. When the world felt about to end. Always wondered if she was as beautiful as her voice. A sound you wouldn't mind to die for."

"And some did? Kinda?"

Charles nodded again and glanced at Eddie knowingly, as if to say you'd never guess. They stopped and each waited for the other to speak. Eddie was patient knowing only Charles had anything to say. He saw his brother's hand tremble again, the one carrying the envelope. Eddie had gone through a lot, too, especially since 1946. He and Charlene took on special duties at Sumner and had their first child, a girl, with a second on the way. Bonnie Jo they called their daughter and hoped for a son soon enough. Yet he gave way and figured it was best to listen because it wasn't everyday Charles spoke.

"You got the floor," Eddie joked and watched Charles grow relieved at the chance to say it, whatever he had on his mind, and that was surely not Vera Lynn. Not really.

"Carina and Clarys."

"Yes, I remember, you wrote about them."

"It runs together in my head. Sometimes I'm in hell. The war and guys blasted to Hades and then Lew. Him falling from the sky singing The Ink Spots, knowing Clarys, feeling her love, then hearing Vera Lynn, not remembering a hundred percent who recorded it first, and thinking of Carina and how she woulda liked Gust if some cop, enemy or friend, hadn't shot him in the back of the head, all for being black in skin color and obeying orders and running the right way, then the officer avoiding a court martial, because of his victim's race. Colored boy's too dumb to fight, the commander claimed about Gust."

Eddie looked on in confusion, while Charles stopped to think. A worried wrinkle formed on his forehead. "Wait. Or am I getting my stories and men mixed up?" he asked. "Wasn't Gust a white guy? Or was that Squaley? Sometimes I start forgetting who was who or what color they were or who shot them and who that commander was that said so about Gust and why and where I was when the War ended. Or if it will. Black and white blend together, guys and their fate. War's fair or is it not?"

Eddie realized Charles lived with restless impressions that refused to let him be, despite the passing years or maybe because of them, as the import of the slaughter and violence he'd seen imprinted itself on his brain.

"It's like a mad kaleidoscope, flickers on and off," Charles complained. "First there was Carina. Her beauty haunted me. She had curly hair like on women you see photos of from Africa. Calm but with a flashing glance. It spoke of concern for others, but anger as well that demanded someone talk reason with her. Or the passion that could've been awakened in her, by the right guy. 'What women feel in war,' she told me. 'The panicky need to have some fellow to love when he's away, and avoid the sentimental side. It's our crazy way of seeking meaning.' A mad era. We met people we'd never meet in peace time."

"And fell in love with them?" Eddie asked.

"Yes, some, all right. Not Carina. We would've made each other miserable. She needed a guy with humor to lighten her serious side. I loved her anyway, like a soulmate. That came out in our letters."

"Clarys, then?"

Charles slouched a bit and looked down only to jerk his head slightly upward so he caught sight of Eddie anew out from under his raised eyebrows. Eddie smiled and waited.

"Mad and glorious," Charles said softly. He smiled mischievously.

"You and her? For real?"

"People in Wales saw us as ordinary folks. Clarys had kinky hair as well but light-colored and a kind look that never betrayed anger. 'The passions of the moment can overwhelm us,' she said the first time I was at her and her folks' home. 'White Americans are new to this jumbled world, they're used to being in control and so behave badly when they're in Wales. Rudely. Only the Negroes have manners. They're used to dealing with chaos.'"

"My foot! That's you speaking!" Eddie raised his voice. "For chrissake, fella, get off it."

With his big brother too shy to say the truth, Eddie inched his way forward and gave Charles a soft nudge.

"Tell me."

"We made love wherever the urge hit us, in public parks and jeeps my buddies requisitioned. If her folks were gone on weekends, she served me breakfast in bed. She stuffed love notes in my pockets and gloried in my sprinter's body. She was taller than the coal mining guys in their area. She treated me like 'equal mates,' in her words."

Eddie laughed. Passersby looked his way, but he paid no mind and felt he had his old brother back again. Eddie listened for more.

"I fondled her and admired her pale sun-free hue, so she asked if I'd ever touched a naked white woman, and I said, no, not even a clothed one. Then we joked and kidded and she said this could get serious if we weren't careful. Yes, maybe it's love, I suggested. I said that in the soapiest poetic style. She laughed with me, not at me."

Eddie listened in delight, only to see his brother fall silent. The evening light faded around them. The post office was closed, so Charles dropped the envelope with his latest column in the outdoor box.

"You see me, I smile," he said to Eddie. "In bemused surrender, I give in."

"At what?"

Charles shrugged. "Impending nightfall, maybe."

As the two meandered back toward MayBelle's, Eddie thought it strange he, Charlene, and Charles were still living with their mother. He and Charlene had looked into buying a place of their own, and were close to closing a deal on a house nearby. Charles stayed in limbo, except for the work with MayBelle and his newspaper articles about the war. Those were bound to lose their impact as the world moved on, but there were other possibilities. Lately the *St. Louis American*, another Negro paper, had made Charles overtures about a possible better-paying reporter's job. Eddie and MayBelle got Charles signed up for GI Bill benefits, which would've paved his way to completing a college degree and helped him buy a house. He hesitated.

Eddie discussed Charles's inaction with MayBelle, who remained puzzled but not wholly uncomfortable since it kept Charles "close to hearth and home," as she put it. In contrast, Charlene read about post-combat shell shock and fear conditioning, a confusing bundle of possible outcomes. She was struck most by psychologists' descriptions telling how returned GIs had periods of confusion, nightmares, or impaired sight and hearing. None of those seemed Charles's problems, but she wondered about a final set of symptoms. Those were avoidance and arousal, which she felt Charles exhibited in refusing to apply for full-time work or college re-entry, which so many other ex-GIs took advantage of.

"The Army felt like being a child," Charles continued to Eddie. "No responsibility. If they tell you to go dig a ditch or launch a balloon, you do it. Make camp one week, move on the next. Take nothing with you, leave nothing behind. We were all those months at this camp in Wales like Army slaves, housed and fed in barracks, but I lived like a civilian, married man on weekends, coulda been the same in Hawaii but for the loneliness."

"Couldn't she join you?" Eddie wondered.

"Things changed."

"Things?"

"Being an Army child doesn't last forever."

25

Eddie studied Charles's long, lanky build, the jingle-jangle body movements seemingly impervious to shock. He'd always assumed Charles's mind was made the same way. The possibility that anything could change his brother's psyche and render him unable to rejoin the love of his life would have seemed impossible before the war.

Now it was only dawning on Eddie how often distressing memories flashed through Charles's mind. He wasn't alone in that regard. First came Web Russell, the Sumner principal's son, who defied his father's wishes and joined the Seabees while still a teenager. He came home from service in the Marianas with a limp, both bodily and mental. In fact, Eddie saw many of Sumner's students, who'd begun the 1940s at classroom desks, return from the great conflict inhabiting two worlds, one in a violent battle for world supremacy, the other in a homeland struggle between citizens separate and unequal.

"We changed in a big hurry," Charles said. "One day they told us to pack up and re-deploy, like getting jerked out of bed, no time to rub sleep out of your eyes," Charles replied. "I never saw Clarys again. Just remembered her accent and her way of looking at me like I was her love, any man's equal and better than most."

"But you wrote her," Eddie said making it seem he *knew* and wasn't guessing.

"Yes, but Normandy got in the way. Death and destruction had its way with us. We were launching barrage balloons while *Stukas*, or whatever the kraut planes were, kept strafing us. Then the front moved inland and the Army had us unloading transport ships and hauling. Before long we were heading for Hawaii. It was in those days Carina's words came back, about chaos overwhelming us."

"Carina, you wrote to her, too?"

"I wrote to everybody. There and here. You included."

"I mean them. Not Ma and me."

"Yes, I wrote them two ladies," Charles answered with a friendly smirk showing he was aware of the faulty grammar.

"And they answered? Faithfully? Them two?"

"Yes and no." Charles's words came after a return of his smirk, which Eddie saw was meant to hide a touch of self-doubt. "Carina wrote me once or twice a month, for a while," he continued. "A worldly lady. She saw the surroundings for what they are, our—I mean America's—form of apartheid. Maybe I attracted her stateside because I endured prejudice and had some learning, though she said it in fancier terms."

"And?"

"My letters after Normandy disquieted her. What I said about it was rawer than folks wanted to believe."

"So she ditched you?"

"Something like that."

"Or maybe she sensed Clarys in the picture?"

"Could be, lots of ocean separated us."

"And Clarys?"

"She wrote until the war ended. I was gone from Hawaii the last time. She was back in London. She had that way, being at home with both, bumpkins like me and big city hobnobbers."

"Those with some style?"

"An affair here and there. In unsettled times you never knew who'd come along tomorrow, or if there'd be one. A tomorrow I mean. Sometimes there wasn't any. She had both sides to her. Have and have not. A good lady."

"I see."

"I guess."

"Bumpkin *and* hobnobber?"

"Yeah, that's what they said about her in London, too, or so she said. Or maybe that's what she thought about herself and projected it on to others' opinion of her. I don't know."

"You miss her? Dumb question?"

Simple as Eddie's question seemed, it stopped Charles in his tracks. His hand trembled, in a way Eddie had decided came not from any physical defect to his brother's still athletic physique but a tic, which thoughts of change brought on him.

"I long for the touch we had."

"So why wouldn't you stick it out, both of you? The world's shrunk."

"Differences. Over the long haul. Why I came back and stay here. Why she left Wales and sticks it out in London."

Eddie shrugged. The lack of restlessness he and Charlene had settled into surely seemed unusual to those who'd been jerked from home, sent to do battle, and exposed to sights and experiences they never dreamed of.

"So where you heading now?" Eddie asked. "If not back to her? Strange, you went to launch barrage balloons and fell in love."

Oh, dumb joke, Eddie told himself. Charles's expression reflected none of the humor his brother so clumsily intended. Instead conflicting realities were etched in him. Foremost were the racial conflicts among American troops fighting together against a common enemy, as well as the deaths of comrades in arms. Deep in Charles's soul, his voluptuous interval in Wales with Clarys must've felt to him like betraying those souls who suffered at the hands of Nazis and racists and paid what politicians so tritely called the ultimate price. This bitter irony had to strike home with men whose skin color made them the object of subjugation by men on either side, who enlisted them to fight in defense of systems that caused their own enslavement.

That insight into the workings of Charles's mind spread from the one brother to the other and further concreted them as siblings.

At the same time the differences between them emphasized their separateness, Eddie remaining his usual talkative self, while Charles retreated into his shell.

"I've learned to still the mind," Charles said at last. "I long greatly for something, but don't know what."

"Keep searching," Eddie encouraged him as they returned to MayBelle's.

Wrapped in his own contradictions, Charles went upstairs without replying.

26

MayBelle had been in a stew for two years. Well, not exactly a hundred percent so. She took Charlene to her heart when grandchildren became a reality and insisted Eddie keep his budding family in her home. Like always, family was everything. "Share and share alike, I say," she repeated. Charlene listened and smiled, often while holding a child or writing to her own parents about their new role as grandma and grandpa.

A happy post-War family it was. Or would have been but for the puzzlement surrounding Charles.

"Your brother lives alone among others," Charlene told Eddie. "If I may put it that way."

"He needs to kick his heels up," MayBelle said. "He's not like his brother, meeting and greeting."

"In World War I they called it shell shock," Charlene said. "Men withdrew from everyday life. Avoidance, it's called. Guys get stuff stuck in 'em, but can't let it out."

"Why, my boy, he needs something more than following me around. Something to pep him up," MayBelle decided, "and I know the thing." She looked at Eddie, who guessed he'd be the implement for whatever she had in mind.

Charles had tired of track and field, but he followed baseball in the hometown Cardinals' '46 Series win over the Red Sox. Loyalties in the Washington household shifted dramatically to the Brooklyn Dodgers in 1947 when Jackie Robinson broke the color line in Big League Baseball. MayBelle didn't need to drag her sons to Sportsman's Park for the Brooks' first trip to St. Louis that season. Whether in running the base paths with abandon or standing up for his rights in public, Robinson awakened pride in his race. Seeing Robinson fly from first to third on a Texas League single caused Charles to stand and cheer.

Richmond Heights also sponsored a Rec League in men's fast-pitch softball. So MayBelle's idea was for Eddie to join a team and take Charles along. Eddie tried out for the Heights Homers, sponsored by Richmond Heights Realtors, which surprisingly had a Negro employee or two. That Eddie made the team spoke to the League's varying levels of competitiveness. As it turned out, he could throw all right and had decent reflexes, but his flat feet caused the team manager to put him at third, where he had some decent moves but didn't need to run. He seldom got to first base, because he swung the bat as poorly as he ran.

Charles presented the opposite problem. He ran like the wind. Charles also packed a punch when he hit the ball square on. He ended up playing centerfield and seemed in his element, while his frequent home runs lived up to the realty team's corny motto, *Bringing 'em home, one at a time.*

In the outfield, Charles loped after hard-hit liners or potential homers and snagged them with ease. "That guy coulda played pro ball, if not for the war, or Jim Crow," astonished spectators allowed.

Jackie Robinson's rookie summer with Brooklyn carried on as the Dodgers neared the National League pennant. Meanwhile Eddie and Charles's first season with the Homers continued. It brought hope that Charles was loosening up socially. The ladies sat through every game and knitted or chatted while Eddie flubbed his way to an understanding of how to play infield grounders and Charles excelled in the field.

The expectation that Charles could catch or hit any ball coming his way built up among local people. Charles laughed off any suggestion that he was great by reminding fans this was bush league stuff.

"You can't outrun the ball no matter what kinda wheels you got," Eddie heard his brother repeating to guys on the bench.

"What the devil's Chuck blabbering about?" Eddie heard from puzzled teammates.

27

On August 15, 1947, the league title was on the line. In the last inning the Homers were behind to ace pitcher Cliff Benefield and his team called Bald Pate, who despite their team name were a squad of shaggy male hairdressers specializing in perms for women. Males running a females beauty parlor made the team a joke among other men's squads. None of that stopped Bald Pate from having great good fun and taunting their own teammates for errors on the field and failing to comb their scraggly beards. Opponents knew only one thing with certainty. Bald Pate understood what to do with a bat and glove.

"Pretty danged good, them fellers" came praise from an older gent in the crowd and nobody disagreed as Bald Pate took the field with a 5-1 lead only three outs from taking a league title from the Homers. Pate's side let out a cheer when Eddie led off the final half frame by striking out on three pitches. He sat and watched while the next batter went out, too. Then the miracle started, as Bald Pate let up and decided they had this one in the bag. Two walks and a single brought in a run. Next came the Homers' number three hitter. He drove a triple down the left field line, scoring two. At 5-4, Bald Pate's rooters fell quiet and their pitcher grew grim.

"Casey at the bat," someone on the Homers' bench yelled and the crowd laughed nervously.

Yes, Eddie realized, it's Charles in the batter's box! Just like in the famous poem! A shiver ran down Eddie's spine, a grand chance for his brother to snag victory from defeat, this time with his bat!

Bleachers ran along each foul line. They were full of players' families. The cheering was friendly but tension mounted. A four-bagger and Homers would be champs, 6-5!

The imposing Baldie's hurler Cliff Benefield was an Army vet like Charles but unlike him given to boasting about it, though where he served and in what capacity no one rightly knew. Locals listened in awe to his loud war stories. It was the same about fast-pitch. Cliff claimed he'd faced legendary touring pitcher Eddie Feigner once and beat him 1-0, but at what Podunk road stop that happened was as vague as Cliff's military service. What folks knew for sure about Cliff was how he once ran the car wash at Miller's Chevrolet Dealership before becoming "a plain old barber," as he called his job at a spa in nearby Lakeside. Another thing everybody knew 100% sure had to be that Bald Pate's star hurler was tall and barrel chested and struck out yokels in their dozens, in addition to featuring a vicious beanball.

Eddie looked up in the bleachers to check his mother and Charlene's enjoyment of the spectacle. Two opponents so different in body build, personality, and team allegiance faced off against each other when, it occurred to Eddie, they were treading the same path in life, that of working-class slobs in a social order purposed to exclude them.

Cliff held the ball loosely and Charles focused on its seams. Cliff's first pitch was a rise ball. High. *Ball one!* Charles stepped out of the box and spat on his hands. He stared out toward the pitcher's rubber, not so much at Cliff, but his grip on the ball. Untroubled by the first-pitch call, Cliff threw his rise ball again, this time at the letters. Charles took it, too. *Strike one!*

Loud razzing came from both benches.

"C'mon, Ump, move around, yer gathering dust, way high!" Eddie shouted.

"C'mon, Washington, get the bat off your shoulder!" came the Pates' reply.

Time stretched out between pitches. *Ball two!* Low and inside. It bounced in the dust, but the runner on third couldn't score.

Strike two was a vicious line drive that Charles drove over the left field fence. It would've ended the game but hooked foul and disappeared into a gathering shroud of late-summer mist. Cliff shrugged and waited for a new ball from the ump, Karl Keller.

"Just a long strike," someone yelled.

Ball three was a fast ball, again in the dirt, which the catcher made a nifty pickup on. Eddie realized the second errant pitch showed Charles's previous foul-ball liner shook Cliff more than he let on.

Beads of sweat popped out on Cliff's forehead. Or was that the first sprinkle of rain? Eddie couldn't decide. He saw only Charles's calm, patient practice swings.

Cliff looked in at the ump. "Karl. Count?"

"Three and two!" Karl bellowed out. The ump was a muscular railroad engineer, who loved his sport with a passion but took no nonsense. He strode out in front of home plate, looked intently at Cliff, and held up three fingers on his left hand and two on his right. He dusted off the plate. "Three and two, play ball!"

Locked at three-two Cliff threw riser after riser, which Eddie guessed was the only pitch Cliff could control in a true pinch. It never missed the strike zone, and Charles fouled off a long line of soft rollers, long drives into the night, and one looping fly wide of the right field foul line, which the outfielder made a heroic dive for but couldn't hold.

Eddie glanced up into the light standards and saw a mild sprinkle filtering through the lights. Frustrated that none of his rise balls did the trick, Cliff went powder puff. He let go a soft change-up that floated temptingly toward home. Charles eyed it greedily, reared his left leg, and cocked the bat back, but he was fooled by the softness of it and off balance with body weight on his left leg. He took a weak swing and sent a slow roller past Cliff.

The second baseman swooped in, trapped the grounder, and underhanded a swift peg to first. Charles lunged for first and crossed the bag with a powerful exhalation.

No call …

The first-base umpire, Trigger Kirby, got his nickname from a habit of greeting everyone by pointing his trigger finger at the newcomer and firing off a make-believe shot while saying a hearty *Hey!* Trigger wore eyeglasses with goggle-thick cataract correction lenses, which made him quite nearly the blind ump of diamond lore. Locked in indecision and astraddle the first-base line, Trigger looked for Karl, who'd followed Charles down the first-base line. In suspended animation, pitcher, batter, first baseman, second baseman, catcher, and home plate umpire waited until Trigger pointed a finger and pulled the trigger at Karl, who immediately raised his fist aloft.

Out!

5-4!

Bald Pate's kids and wives rattled the bleachers in jubilation.

28

Oh well, just another Rec game, Eddie thought, we did our best. Cliff and his teammates ran off the field, or at least to the third-base line, where they halted at the sound of MayBelle's voice and looked back at first-base. Charles sank to his knees and his face turned ashen gray.

"Out? I beat the throw! I'm safe!" he screamed.

Trigger pointed a finger Charles's way and clicked with his tongue, shooting him dead in fun. Charles rose to his feet, rushed Trigger, and knocked his glasses off. Realizing what he'd done but still in anger, Charles backed off to the bag itself and touched it.

"I'm safe, I'm safe, I tell you! I beat the throw. See my shoe print? Here!"

He beseeched Karl, who stepped to the bag and stood on it, his arms folded across his chest. He formed a shield to protect Trigger.

"Out! Game over!"

"But," Charles said. "I'm … I'm safe. At first. You saw it."

Charles crumbled on the infield holding both hands over his head sobbing.

"I did it. Lew. Gust. For you."

With that, MayBelle rushed across the infield. Unable to stop his tirade, Charles again rose and approached the umpires.

"Blind as bats. I was safe. *Safe!*"

He sprang from Karl to Trigger, screaming that he outran the ball. "I did. You saw it," Charles beseeched the few spectators remaining.

Charles kneeled in the dust until the bleachers emptied fully. Groundskeepers smoothed the infield while the evening precip settled, creating a gentle sheen on the outfield grass. When Charles got up, Eddie carried his hat and glove. Karl gave him a hand.

The flood lights dimmed. Eddie wondered when Charles would be all right. Since the war, he'd only been so off and on. Two years had passed.

29

"It's arousal," Charlene told Eddie a couple weeks later. "I told you. A guy can hide things, avoid them, but they seep to the surface, explode."

Eddie considered Charles's varying moods and habits since he arrived from Hawaii. His wry humor mixed with empty stares and silent reflection. He told Eddie, MayBelle, and Charlene some of the unimaginable happenings from Tyson and France, but he surely kept others locked away.

"What's he's got inside him?" Eddie asked. "Stuff he saw and heard?"

"We'll probably never know, in concrete form," Charlene answered.

"He looked so calm at the plate. I thought he'd come through."

Charlene glanced at Eddie, as if to say that's a man's world you're in now.

Eddie read her expression but persisted. "If only that one long line drive had stayed fair," he said with a shake of his head.

"Someday, some way, this episode still would've happened," she said.

"But ..."

"No buts, and no, dear, it wouldn't've happened to you. You two have the same father, but ..."

"But?"

"Your dad was different when you were born," Charlene said and squeezed Eddie's hand. "Makes no sense, I know, but there's a real but to it all, I know there has to be."

With that, Eddie and Charlene went back to their everyday affairs. Those included child care, returning to teaching, and living with MayBelle and Charles, who had needed only a couple days to put the softball game behind them.

"My boy? He be his old self," MayBelle told relatives in her made-up Delta accent. "We be just so happy to have him home."

"Indeed Charles carries on as usual, seemingly," Eddie told Charlene.

"Indeed and seeming, aren't they contradictions?" she asked.

For a while, *indeed* appeared more true than *seeming*. Charles played with Eddie and Charlene's daughter Bonnie and helped with meals. As fall drifted toward winter, he went in to the newspaper office daily and came home with a series of opinion pieces he'd written on what he termed "soldier's heart." Syndicated under the pseudonym *Carlos*, the soldier's heart theme was a distressed description of whites on the home front rejecting Negro heroes decorated for valor in World War II. Most cases involved restaurants and businesses refusing service to Negro veterans. Authorities gave jail time to customers who protested ill treatment.

Beanball Ban, the series' lead text, told of a fictional black man named Dominic Bankman. The hero in Charles's tale returns from war and signs to play minor league baseball, thus breaking the color ban. From a barrage balloon accident at Normandy, Dom develops nervous tics and jabbers while leading off from bases. During an at-bat, he hits the dirt when the pitcher tries beaning him. Dom charges the mound. For that infraction, he's banned from Organized Ball, while the opposing pitcher goes unpunished.

Jackie Robinson's rookie season with the Dodgers caused a serious backlash in conservative white quarters, and some readers believed Dom Bankman was a real person and *Beanball Ban* a true story. Readers in colored quarters praised the tale even more when Charles's Chicago editor wrote an Introduction describing the short story as "a believable tale with real-life parallels." Charles seemed to be in seventh heaven, even though he had to explain to relatives he himself was the true author, not the mysterious Carlos.

After his series ended, Charles wrote no more. That hesitancy confused even Charlene, who possessed the readiest insights into Charles's post-War mindset. To her, he was an emissary for his people. Yet Charles grew even more silent, both in print and in person.

As Eddie and Charlene started a family, MayBelle's distress deepened. She knew her older son was doing right by sticking close to hearth and home. Yet she rued his mysterious decision to quit writing. He grew more silent. In the sunnier, milder late winter weather, MayBelle hoped his moods might improve, but she wasn't sure they would.

Eddie doubted it even more. "You know, being out at first, that was only a game," he said to Charles. "Means nothing, Man. Forget it."

Charles heard him.

"He goes off every morning for coffee or walks around the block," MayBelle complained to Eddie and Charlene. In the late afternoon, Charles was on time to help prepare the evening meal. Attention to detail cheered him. He wondered at times how Clarys's life worked out in London or whether she met a guy.

"Why don't you go there?" Charlene asked one evening as the four stirred their tea.

"I will," he replied with a distant smile. "Maybe." He gazed past MayBelle, Eddie, and Charlene, like at a receding storm.

30

World War II faded from MayBelle's thoughts. Through the Berlin Airlift in the late 1940s, she kept busy helping local charity. "Poor's poor," she lamented.

Charles carried goods to humble folk and looked for full-time work. His moods could be somber or loosey goosey. He stayed close to his mother, like Eddie and Charlene planned to do a while longer. They still had a realtor on the lookout.

The war was three years past when Eddie and Charlene came home one spring evening to find Charles leafing through mail orders.

"Hi, what's up, Man?" Eddie asked.

"Looking."

Charles bent over the catalogue, folded back a page, and tore it out. "Hiking boots," he explained.

"GI issue!" Charlene said in surprise while sneaking a look at Eddie.

"Signing up again?" Eddie asked. "Enlisting, I mean?"

Charles shook his head, so Eddie dropped the topic, as MayBelle burst in from a day of selling mementos. Surely at a profit, Eddie thought. Her happiest moods hinted at good luck selling.

MayBelle peeked over Charles's shoulder. "I been thinking," she said. "That trip to Clarys?"

MayBelle beamed at the idea, like it was her own, so Eddie and Charlene brightened up as well, though Eddie had no clue what Army hiking boots had to do with Clarys.

The next day Eddie and Charlene stopped in downtown Richmond Heights at Bonnie's day care center, then they picked up MayBelle after work. Waiting at home was a simple note from Charles. *Off on a hike. Eastwards. Shall return.*

Eddie read the note twice before crumpling it in his hands.

"Didn't your dad go off west?" Charlene asked.

"Yes, he was a dope. And so my brother heads east? To find a guy that went west?"

In distraction, MayBelle picked up Charles's note. She flattened it out on the table.

"Spring now," she said. "A soul tells her folks to stay home."

"They leave anyway," Eddie said.

"They do. Always for a reason."

Eddie searched for any kernel of truth in her words until Charlene called them in to dinner.

"A family man dines with his folks," MayBelle said.

She led Eddie in to another of his wife's amazing meals.

BOOK III

Patients and Prisoners

1

Newcomers to Illinois could agree with Flo Maxwell. Her Salina looked pretty darned idyllic for a simple prairie town, except, that is, for its ill-named Pan Pacific railroad station, which—easy to see—was going to hell in a hand basket. Cracks appeared in the ceiling, the lights outside grew dim, and creepy characters lurked in dark corners.

The West Coast Flier stopped there four times a day anyhow, impatiently taking on travelers in its westward rush to St. Louis. Along the last legs of that stretch appeared other dull Illinois depots and fields of winter wheat. Yet in such unimposing tracts MayBelle Washington's wish for racial fairness started moving toward its fulfillment when Flo, a blonde Salina homemaker and mother of two, set off to visit the big city's Barnes Hospital and learn if she'd won or lost her two-year battle with breast cancer.

It was a chilly April morning in 1954 and Flo shivered on the Salina platform for an hour with her son Ronny until the Flier glided to a stop before them. Once aboard, she warmed herself in a sofa seat. Looking out her Pullman window, Flo spied the Starr Hotel, whose massive wall sign boastfully offered travelers a night in Salina's classiest digs, *European Style*. Those words appeared in red italics against the hotel's somber brick. A glimmer of sunlight helped Flo imagine tuxedo-clad lords and polished ladies in Old World salons. That was a world of high culture Flo might never attain, but she could dream about it. Her fantasy lasted while the Flier slowed for incoming eastbound traffic. Flo jerked to attention as it gained speed, moving in tact with the fast rising sun.

After two hours, the train made its way onto mighty Eads Bridge at East St. Louis and crossed the Mississippi. Flo gazed at the River below. Afraid of heights, she felt a neural urge to plunge into its depths, even from inside her coach, but she steadied herself and watched as sunlight glanced off *Huckleberry,* a tugboat maneuvering between chunks of driftwood and blocks of ice left after a long, stormy winter. After repeated visits at St. Louis' most prominent oncology ward, Flo knew about battling the odds and cheered for the tiny vessel. It was struggling to within a stone's throw of docking when tall buildings blocked her sight. By the time the view cleared, Union Station popped into sight and she realized the River's foreboding current robbed her of patience and courage, but the tug's persistence offered hope.

2

Looking toward downtown St. Louis, Flo thought about the afternoon's final exam of her left breast. Despite the hospital's thorough treatments, she feared the winter-weary moment of truth with Dr. Corale, the surgeon she chose to believe in.

To avoid more anxiety, she glanced at Ronny, who stirred drowsily beside her. She wondered that a teenager was going along and not her husband, Merrit. It wasn't fair, Flo reasoned, that her spouse had to head off to work that morning and send their teen-age son to sit alone in a hospital waiting room while she discussed cancer with her medical team, but she decided not to worry. Her Merrit needed to guard his job security. Besides, it was Easter week, which meant school was out in Salina, so why shouldn't a youngster like Ronny catch a glimpse of the big city? Weren't there scads of sights to see? People to meet?

Despite herself, Flo focused on the chilly weather and the uncertain medical news to come.

"Don't overestimate the risk," Merrit had told her. "Your doc knows his stuff."

True, Flo trusted Dr. Anthony Corale, but felt unsure of herself. In early morning optimism, she'd put on a flowery sundress and a light jacket purchased two years earlier to cover the big hole under her arm in case the doc opted for a radical mastectomy. That hadn't happened, so she was able to lift one arm to take her hat from the overhead rack while gently tapping Ronny with her free hand. He rubbed sleep from his eyes, then stood up.

"You missed it again, the River," Flo berated him with a pretended sneer while pulling on a warm sweater she had the foresight to bring along. "I swear, you gripe about never seeing anything stupendous, then you're asleep when the Mississippi River pops up."

"You know I'm never awake in the morning," he replied. "And the train's so danged bumpy. Even for a so-called Express. When's a guy gonna sleep anyhow? An *S* at every darned depot all the way from here to …" He hesitated to remember other towns on the route and in the order the train passed them. "Salem, Sandoval, Shiloh, and Sardis. Stupid names."

"You left out Salina, that's us," Flo reminded him.

"Just as dumb," Ronny said.

"The last *S* is St. Louie," she said.

The train stopped but he showed no desire to move. He glanced at the bustle of passengers getting on and off.

"Salem's short for Jerusalem, the earthly paradise," Flo said to change topics, at least partly, "but Salem in Illinois has a ratty train stop just like ours." Realizing she was blocking the Pullman aisle, Flo moved to the side and let others pass. She was torn between leaving the Flier coach and staying where they were in order to talk. What better time for corralling an adolescent boy for a chat, she thought, but Dr. Corale was waiting.

So she herded her son out of the Pullman, knowing he'd always be by her side, even if he considered it way too old-fashioned to discuss the terrifying illness that took his mother to the city every few months. Or maybe it scared him to think about her problem. Whatever, Flo knew he understood her fear about seeing Dr. Corale. The boy was quick on the uptake, more than most grownups, and lost patience with their slow thinking. He never tore them to shreds, though, like some teenagers, at least not directly or in his mother's presence.

"We go everywhere in this City like when we're here now. Forest Park. Amusement rides. Mississippi River excursions on the Admiral Paddle Boat. But nothing's enough for you. Whadda you want?" Flo asked him, though her question answered itself.

He's a typical teenage boy, she reminded herself. It was baseball he had in mind, a game played in a real Big League stadium, like Sportsman's Park, but that was miles from where they were now. Not to mention it'd been blustery cold lately. The Cardinals lingered back East playing ball on the road.

They were a summer treat, the Big League games he revered, so Ronny didn't push it. Instead Flo thought she'd treat him to a blockbuster movie show at the Fox Theater if the doc gave her any reason for hope. Ronny adored some Hollywood starlet named Natalie Wood. He put her pic on his bedroom wall, but a peek at the *St. Louis Globe-Democrat* gave no glimpse of any movies with her. Besides, Hollywood starlets were a far cry from Major League Baseball, though the girls were close enough to real excitement in a pinch. What else was there? Ronny had mentioned the Zoo, so, well, could be there's hope, Flo thought, maybe we'll make it there. Everything depended on Barnes Oncology.

Thinking about hope for herself, or the lack of it, gave Flo added worries, one being the new concepts medical experts threw her way. She'd always known about folks short of breath, or bad off with high BP and weak joints, but hearing modern docs talk of *COPD* and *Hypertension* left her wondering if these were trendy new terms bantered about to frighten unwitting patients. Or were they true everyday threats to middle-aged folks, and were their fancy labels used to make the maladies sound even worse? For sure none of those high falutin' terms hit home like *metastasize.* That word taught her cancer had no conscience. Surgeons could find The Lump and even remove it, but would it come back? Worse yet, in Flo's mind, was the fear it could be silent and sly like a thief on the darkest night.

Studying Ronny, she realized a thing less troubling to think about was the outside chance of finding Fatso's, the Italian confection stand by the Forest Park tennis courts. They sold the cotton candy her son couldn't resist, even this early in the season. It lured the boy back to his childhood ways. Her most immediate concern about her son, though, was where to leave him at Barnes. Minors weren't allowed in consultation rooms during adult appointments or left to wander the hallways, where passages wound in and out or spiraled ever upwards and then turned back on themselves until mysteriously emerging on the ground floor again. She'd need to make a quiet fuss over leaving him in some hospital coffee shop and finding a friendly cashier to keep an eye on him in case any bored office girl tried whisking him away on a tease or a tempting flirt.

Flo imagined her body as a labyrinth like Barnes stairways, with a cancer slithering around her rib cage and creeping up towards her chest till it left her as an unrecognizable bag with only hollow bones intact, some sticking out through a weakening epidermis. She tried to avoid such unholy images but failed and further thoughts of Oncology did little to cheer her. She'd squirmed in her seat most of the way to St. Louis.

3

When Flo finally dismissed the frightening images of cancer from her thoughts, for now anyway, she and her son entered the vast passenger hall of Union Station. She spoke to Ronny again, but fumbled for words.

"So splendid!" she exclaimed while admiring the station's shining marble floors and high gilded ceilings, which pointed to the heavens themselves, like the First Christian spire back home, even if that building was only stucco. She marveled too at the bright light the ceiling let in. She felt even more astounded at a glorious glow the electric chandeliers let escape through domed glass. She imagined the glow extending far into the late morning sky.

Equally impressed but little inclined to consider the hall's celestial aspects, Ronny gazed around the lobby. He strolled to the Info desk to run a finger along its shiny top. Turning his mother's way, he asked, "What's this! Polished rock? Or fake gemstone? Who're they kidding? It's nuts trying to fool folks."

"Shame on you, questioning your elders," she admonished him, but found it hard to calm her nerves. She had tons of questions for the doc, but she wouldn't dare ask them brashly like her son questioning the station's decor. Most likely, she'd think of her questions too late, when she was on the way home again and well on her path to death. "A teenager like you that can't stay awake," she continued chiding Ronny in order to avoid plaguing him with worries about herself.

Ronny spoke like he read her mind, "Worry wart, that's you."

Flo nodded and kept talking. "They made these coast-to-coast liners like the Zephyrs and Fliers near war's end, in the forties. Now here we are marveling at things in the slick, shiny trains' own show-case, gigantic Union Station itself."

"Like you said, we get fancy coaches when they're fading from use?"

"Feels that way, but Pullmans've been around for ages," she explained. "Railroad big shots in England called 'em Lounge Coaches. Pretty soon and there won't be any passenger trains left. Just automobiles crowding our roads. No mercy for folks that can't afford autos."

"Yeah, Dad said the Army transported troops in Fliers during the War, fast and slick. Then the fighting in the Pacific ended because Truman dropped the bomb," Ronny explained. "It woulda been tough invading Japan. Thousands dead. They're people, like us. The enemy, I mean, they're real people. That's what my teacher, Miss Jordan, says."

Ronny talked with an adult air like lecturing children. Flo thought how often Miss Jordan, this young teacher the boy had for different classes, popped up in his conversation. A schoolboy crush? Maybe. Miss Jordan's mind worked like his, Flo could tell.

"Yes, by invading we'd've been fighting on Japanese soil for-ever," Flo said. "So here *we* are, us two, not American troops or wealthy snobs. We ride these luxury coaches. Pretty good, huh? But how'd you know all that? I mean about Hiroshima? They teach that in school? At Salina High?"

"And Nagasaki? I saw 'em in news reels. At the Roxy. How insane. Miss Jordan, too, she said the same."

"I suppose. Now here we are a new decade after those bombs. What I've faced in life feels nuclear, too. My world torn apart. Like with a surgeon's knife."

"A decade? That's half my life," Ronny said. "Or more. First I put you through a lot, a breach birth? Now you're riding Fliers with me that pass for luxury but are getting old and creaky. Or is it cranky? How I feel when you make me get up every morning. Cranky as all git out."

"No, cranky's me, your own ma. Me and my achy bones," Flo answered and boxed him gently on the ear again, a habit that showed they were pals, but mother and son as well. "I know what you're thinking. Me scared about Barnes. Why go to a hospital when we coulda had a fun time in the city?"

Ronny glanced up at her knowingly like he saw through people and understood their motives by instinct. Like zoos and ball parks weren't really places his mom would enjoy deep down. "There's the Fox Theater, too, but what'll the doc at Barnes tell you? First things first." He intoned his question like a statement.

With Ronny, Flo shared a tendency to cast quick incisive glances, but she lacked his rapid decision-making. It seemed people revealed their inner selves to him with quick jerks and tiny tics or impulses visible to all but decipherable only by him or someone that knew him inside out. She'd realized eons ago there were no secrets between the two of them or, better put, she might read little in his glances but understand his intentions anyway. He read meanings in the blink of a stranger's eye or understood the tender touch of someone's hand on his, interpreting wordlessly what he saw or heard and sharing it with his mother by ellipsis, a strange word she'd heard some place, she forgot where, and felt what it meant. Short-cut communication.

As she thought about all Ronny intuited from gestures and expressions, Flo also remembered the day two years before when she found The Lump. The First Lump, that is, there could've been more, or so she suspected, but The Lump's what she came to call it and in time the moment of discovery took on mythic proportions for her, to be told and retold to those who'd listen. At its ugly core, the cancer seemed a reprehensible giant emerging with barbaric intent from a bottomless black hole. It allowed her no time for invoking reliance on prayer. Why did cancer land on her while bypassing other women? What grand and Providential or devilish master plan was afoot and Flo its unwitting tool? Or did the disease invade my cells by blind chance never to leave me in peace, she wondered?

For the rest of the day, Flo's thoughts leap-frogged each other, as they had for the past two years since her diagnosis, until they wove an intricate quilt of past and present happenings, and she seemed to be living in multiple years melded together to contain one and the same occurrence. And today a culminating pronouncement was coming from Dr. Corale, that this was the end, nothing more to hope for, a shock to her nervous system reverberating throughout her torso. Stage 4 cancer or whatever they called it. She tried to banish such imagining, but her medical history and the repeated visits to what proved a house of death for so many poor souls haunted her.

To begin with, she kept going back to her doc and expressing fears of yet another bump or lump, when nobody, not even the experts, could do more than speculate on such matters or, as she realized later, make guesses about what our genes have in store for us. Yet nothing matched the jolt of first finding The Lump. She couldn't remember which was worse, the shock of feeling it or the medical men's decision to remove it.

First she'd gone to Dr. Radebach in Salina, an old ex-Army sawbones, who delivered babies with the finesse of a Civil War battlefield surgeon, smoking a stogie above his operating room patients and blowing smoke on their open wounds and his hands dripping red with someone else's blood. Rumor said he amputated newborns from their mothers rather than delivering them and, sure enough, Flo hated going to this doctor because he'd attended her at Ronny's difficult delivery. Radebach paid little attention to his discovery of "a thing" in Flo's breast that would've disturbed even the most battle-hardened warrior. Or was it Flo's discovery? Even the doctor's reports, such as they were, left that issue in doubt.

"Just a bulbous blob under your armpit," Radebach announced gruffly after a hurried exam of Flo's breasts. "No trouble. It's due to the overgrowth of cells. Often found in the obese. Hard to locate when it's buried among mountains of blubber."

Radebach eyed Flo but seemed unaware she was trimmer and taller than him. Or was he straining to remember that, yes, indeed, he *was* the one who brought Ronny into the world during Flo's horrendous 12-hour breach birth. Her appointment with Surgeon

Sawbones to have The Lump examined was on a busy weekday in a flu-ridden season, so Radebach shooed her out of his office after an indifferent examination and barked to the nurses to usher in yet more coughing and wheezing sufferers.

"Next victims!" Flo remembered him commanding.

"Folks get sick, things happen." Merrit consoled Flo as she wept out her frustration and horror on his shoulder. Only when Flo insisted on "doing right" and threw a fit filled with anguish and bile, driven by her gnawing fear of pain and death, and added a dose of stronger vitriol to it, did her hubby give in. The next day he spoke to the doc in a determined tone. He immediately hustled along to keep Flo company on a no-nonsense second visit to Radebach. The couple appeared at his office as unexpected by the clinic secretary as the doc was flabbergasted to see them.

Merrit was slow on the uptake in social settings, but he acted invincible in other ways. Foremost among them was having the muscular build of a railroad section boss, which he was, and the love of biographies about history's great personalities. "My friends, and you are my friends," Merrit loved quoting his hero Franklin Delano Roosevelt. Merrit had memorized FDR's Fireside radio chats during the Depression. "We have nothing to fear but fear itself," Merrit told Ronny any time the boy showed uncertainty, especially about his fear of dental visits. Even if the social context of FDR's high-sounding words went over Ronny's head, Flo realized her husband and son shared a love for high drama and great men's singleness of purpose.

The weird and devilish also drew Merrit's attention, especially Rasputin, Machiavelli, and Swedenborg. Flo heard him talk about those weirdos with a mixture of admiration for their dubious successes and a clear dislike of them for doubting humankind. In that regard Merrit showed his true colors after a heated confrontation with good doctor Sawbones, whose brusqueness caused Flo's husband to flex his muscles and exhibit his imposing stature.

"You, damned Sadebach!" Merrit roared alluding to Marquis de Sade, his most hated of history's eccentrics. "I'll throw you through this damned wall and call Barnes Surgery myself!" echoed his bass tones, which was Merrit's way of politely requesting a doctor's referral from Radebach to Barnes in St. Louis for a second opinion.

Radebach puffed ceremoniously on a saliva sodden stogie. Flo wondered if he even heard her husband. Maybe a random World War II cannon shot at Salerno, where he served, robbed him of his hearing and nipped his senses in the bud?

"Get at the facts about this damned lump!" Merrit intoned mightily.

"But we're talking about the inner half of the breast," Sawbones protested and wrung his hands at an amputational procedure he'd surely never imagined himself performing, though had he attempted it his failing at the operation doubtless would have left him unfazed.

Merrit became red in the face, but rose even higher in Flo's love when he demanded help, obviously after regaining his speech. Half a week later Radebach called in the referral to Barnes Hospital, and Flo stewed for days in dread of their first-ever Flier ride to St. Louis. Merrit decided to treat the family to first-class, never dreaming how many more such rides might follow and how the costs could mount up, as they eventually did.

4

As Flo stood in Union Station and thought back to the troublesome Mississippi and the tugboat battling it, she remembered her family's fateful first-class jaunt two years earlier. With late spring of 1952 easing into glorious summer, Flo, Merrit, and Ronny ventured off to Barnes. Ronny, who was fifteen plus, made the most of it by observing people and places. The flat, verdant land eventually gave way to high banks above the River. As they crossed over to St. Louis, the boy wisecracked about this Missouri trip being a trip to "the State of Misery." Deep down, Flo agreed. The specter of death or physical mutilation in the Show-Me State gnawed at her. Still, she thought in a moment of selfish escapism, the luxury of a soft Pullman coach might compensate for her demise, should it come.

That 1952 visit gave them time for a quick lunch, which Flo in her nervous state barely kept down. On the street outside the tiny diner, which they found more by accident than plan, came blaring sounds of a police car with a fire engine on its heels. The ruckus reminded Flo she'd once learned *siren* was the word for lilac in some obscure immigrant tongue. She reflected on how her mind wandered from impression to impression. Given the chance, most folks in Salina willingly and facilely took an *is* for an *ought-to-be* and felt content with that bit of received opinion. She saw that tendency in her own Merrit, who argued that his sensitive son Ronny should try out for football, because "that's what boys do, not sissy stuff," when Flo wanted their boy to study piano. Likewise, she'd championed the rights of migrant Mexican workers, who the Salina City Council limited to seasonal labor and sent them to bunk out in a barracks of renovated chicken coops. "Right shall be right," as Salina folk reminded her, often with a wagging finger, Puritan schoolmarm-like. At times like that, she felt acutely her lack of higher education. She'd done well in high school and reasoned well and thought clearly. Still, she lacked the deeper insights college classrooms might've given her.

Once oriented in the big city on that 1952 visit, the three of them went to find Barnes Cancer Ward by taxi. Their cabbie explained that the ride from station to hospital had to be on a route chosen by Yellow Cab. "Out of necessity, not plan," he insisted.

The way was roundabout, all right, but it gave them a view of rundown Market Street, which had been redone beginning in the 1930s but with only questionable visible improvement. There was a resultant economic nosedive and a housing problem for what once was a respectable Negro residential neighborhood. The driver stood outside his vehicle and explained that homes there had been demolished, none of which actions stemmed the flow of African Americans into the city or stopped the influx of poor Missouri whites. The two groups were more or less equal in earnings and social status but seldom saw eye to eye.

"Average folk prospered when others couldn't. Even on the Hill, Italians and Negroes lived in the same neighborhood, shared it even," the driver explained. "But benign neglect ruled, and racism makes it easy to buy the land cheap, way down to the Riverfront. You move poor folks in, give 'em a place to live and work, but when the big shots need space to develop, they dump the poor folk."

"Right down to the River?" Merrit asked. "Looks empty there now."

"Used to be a bustling commercial area with homes and immigrants," the driver responded. "Slumlords came in and bought up the land but ignored city ordinances. They moved folks in till we got the overcrowding you see now. Landowners overcrowded the tenements, then took the money and ran. Bulldozed the homes under. Plain and simple."

5

"I see, the browner the poorer, is that it?" Flo asked.

She'd put her best foot forward and taken the front passenger seat, so the driver turned to her and told how the area once served as a showcase for St. Louis, the Gateway to the West, after city fathers opted to build it up as a hype for the World's Fair. It was "much talked about, much raved about," the driver assured them. In fact, this city looking into the setting sun had been the grandest Westward-looking expansion town in its time. Flo understood this, against the dictates of what she saw around her now. It was where wealth outmuscled all else and cared for little but itself.

"The great World's Fair. It ushered in a new century, for the Universe to see!" the taxi man emphasized. "I mean with a capital U! But even that was a dream. The Fair ended and the rich residents made a killing by joining the outside developers. Then both groups hightailed it out of town."

He paused and waved his hand out at an indistinct place or places he'd yet to show them.

"And where'd you get all this info?" Flo asked. The unexpected tour came to her as a surprise, but it opened her eyes.

"I seen lots of it, born and raised hereabouts. Downtown's decayed, been 50 years in the making."

"When was that? I mean since when, these 50 years?" Flo asked, doubting that any spectacle so grand or regrettable could've happened in her lifetime and for all the world to see, with The World's Fair pretty much in her own backyard to boot. Despite the sobering reality the neighborhood displayed, she marveled that a ritzy building site might fall into such decay, like humans wasting away from famine or dread disease. "Folks drift in, drift out, leaving the remains behind? Like that, easy as pie?"

"Beats me when," came the driver's puzzled reply, as he seemed to reflect on Flo's words. "Stuff behind the scenes maybe, before The Fair started, I guess?"

"In 1904 maybe?" Merrit asked. "So even the rich can be deserted, stranded high and dry?"

"You bet, Mister, left in the lurch. Here today, gone tomorrow. Money and people both."

"Fame, too. It came and went. Wasn't there a Judy Garland movie about the World's Fair?" Flo insisted on hearing about. "*Gilded Age*. Something like that?"

"Yeah, I think so. *Meet Me in St. Louie*? Or was that the show's theme song?"

"Trolley cars and all, they seemed a miracle in that film," Merrit chimed in. "Yeah, I remember. The movie, I mean. A hymn to the golden past."

"It pointed to a riper future, greater than what went before, none a' that's left," the driver responded. "The stuff of dreams. They built a fantasy city with canals and Gondolas on them, like in Venice. And a Palace of Fine Arts. Fifty million visitors invaded the city. Some guys even put up solar panels, a long way before their time. Visionaries, those gents."

The driver hung a sharp right down a broad but lightly trafficked street. It featured a manor house with grated fences. Exotic birds flew about but even more sat on tree branches, keeping idle company with a keeper. Otherwise no one was in sight. An extensive lawn stretched up a hillside.

"Just for the birds," Ronny chimed in and the adults chuckled.

"That's the amusement-park-that-was," the taxi driver continued. "The Pike, was its name."

"That's what they called it?" Flo asked incredulously. "My sister sent me pics of The Pike in Long Beach, California. Near Hollywood. She lives there. A long pier, stretching out into the ocean. They have amusements."

"Yeah, some big shot promoters from our World's Fair moved out West and took the Pike name with 'em," the driver assured her. "They created a California Coney Island."

"With a Ferris wheel?" Ronny asked.

"Sure thing, still exists," the driver answered. "Right here, where we're driving, this is ground the Ferris wheel stood on in the glory days. They buried throw-away parts right under us. Afterward, I mean, when the Fair was kaput and everybody moved on. They scrapped lots a' stuff. We call this Forest Park now. Not much forest left."

"So then, this is what's left from 1904? Or was it '05?" Merrit once more insisted on knowing.

"You mean the good stuff? Sure, some's left. The Palace's now our Art Museum. There's a clock tower standing from 1904. Their bird house you just saw expanded into our Zoo."

"But the other fancy buildings? What happened to them?" Flo insisted.

"Weren't intended to last. Tore down within a year."

"The Greatest Show on Earth, now Gone with the Wind? Nothing left?" Merrit asked.

"Like I said, the clock tower 'n other stuff," the driver added with a shrug. "What lasted best was the eats."

"Meaning food?" Ronny asked.

"Chow, we called it," Merrit added.

"Folks claim the St. Louis World's Fair left us with iced tea and clubhouse sandwiches. Nothing else lasted. And Judy Garland. She was still a girl then, in the movie anyway. *Clang, clang, clang went the trolley.*"

"I grew up with that song," Flo reminisced, smiling at Ronny, who drew a blank at her sudden sentimentality.

"In the Stone Age?" he kidded her.

The cabbie scratched his balding head and rambled on about growing up Italian on the Hill, he called it, where other eats reigned, like ravioli, but the Hill had more than Italians to boast about. "Like a Negro population till the landlords forced 'em out.

That's where Yogi and Garagiola come from, too. No glamor and without schooling but know their stuff, baseball."

"Like you know yours, too, huh? History?" Merrit complimented him.

The driver smiled wanly at the simple comment, which could've been taken as Merrit chiding him, but Flo recognized it as her husband's way of patting a guy on the back. Even in middle age, Merrit was youngish and robust. He had a full shock of brown hair and could carry on with guys' locker room needling or railroad chatter, much of it acerbic but in the spirit of fun, even if the comments sometimes hit on guys' weak points or known shortcomings. Unaware of the put-down tone of his merriment, Merrit thought of the chatter as a note of compassion for the taxi driver and his fading hair locks. Flo understood as much but also knew how insensitive Merrit's words could sound. She would've changed the topic, but the men were wound up in their own thoughts.

"Yogi and Joe, both Big Leaguers, aren't they? Yogi's for the Yanks and Joe catches for the Pirates," Ronny broke in. The boy's words didn't totally change anything, like his mother wished to do, but turned the attention away from his dad.

"Yeah, thata boy, you got it!" the driver exclaimed. "Except Garagiola plays with the Cards now. A funny guy, real comic, but he can't catch worth a darn. I saw him throw a ball once from home to second on two bounces on a steal attempt. Runner made it all the way to third."

"But what's so hilarious about him?" Ronny insisted on hearing.

"Why, he tells these crazy stories. On the air. Like you know he's training to go to broadcasting after he quits playing, but doesn't always know what he's saying. On the Hill we all got along, no matter your color, but still, ya know, a smart guy's gotta think before he speaks, no matter what."

"Yes," Flo agreed. "Any little word can get you in big trouble these days."

"Yeah, especially in the work place. And, wow, don't I know it in my business. Never know who the next jerk can be that flags a taxi cab."

He stopped talking and glanced back to see if Merrit was listening. He did so much in the style, Flo figured, of an experienced storyteller gauging his listeners. When Merrit showed he was following, the cabbie carried on.

"During one boring game Garagiola was guest announcer and told the fans over the radio, there's this guy and his girl in the stands, and the guy says, 'He kisses her on the strikes and she kisses him on the balls.' He says this right out, over the airwaves."

"Hush, you've got a child here," Flo hushed the cabbie, who nevertheless let out a loud guffaw at his own joke and sought a response from Merrit, who smiled before ruffling his son's shock of thick dark hair. The boy responded neither to the off-color joke nor his father's attempt to brush it off. Meanwhile Flo told both men to think before opening their traps.

"No disrespect to you, Ma'am," the cabbie apologized.

"Some men are like kids," she joked, "better seen than heard."

6

While the men jabbered on about their favorite sport, Flo studied the street scene and saw block after grimy block of decaying multi-storied buildings. Most were of crumbling brick, Depression Era siding, or falling planks. In other places masonry revealed cracks where mortar had crumbled and crashed to the sidewalk. It lay in smashed-up pieces after being crunched underfoot by pedestrians. Egress windows in the lower floors were either cracked or boarded up. All of it seemed former state-of-the-art glasswork for businesses or showcase studios. Once-elegant hotels, now deteriorated to flophouses, were home to single men or squatters, while onetime residences of the wealthy had slowly decayed into tenements. Some empty buildings had window panes broken.

Sensing Flo's flagging attention to baseball, the cabbie turned her way and nodded toward a couple of the most ramshackle rentals. "They were the center of a universe, or so it's said, during the Fair's heyday. It was the Gilded Age, like you meant, Ma'am."

"Days of yore?" Flo ventured to ask.

"Yeah, faded luster."

Lining the sidewalk were rows of wooden benches and dilapidated sofas. Despite the chill, men of different races, brown, black, and white, lounged on them while others leaned against brick walls in the background. Flo saw how decades of men's backsides had worn off the paint or polished the bricks a shiny brown. It appeared another world from the obsessive cleanliness of her Salina, where housewives and shop owners swept sidewalks and alleyways with the same devotion they gave to their living rooms, an extreme attention to duty, she guessed, that outdid what they gave to their monotonous personal lives or dastardly and sometimes philandering hubbies.

The driver slowed for a group of middle-aged men crossing the street in mid-block. They showed no fear of the slow-moving traffic but seemed to have no special destination in mind either. They were empty-handed, except for one who slung a small back pack over his shoulder and another with a lightly-clad child in his arms. They said nothing that Flo could hear, but smiled at each other's words.

"Why aren't these men working?" Merrit had asked.

The taxi driver scratched his head and gestured in frustration.

"Half a century of neglect and this area fell to ruin. The rich moved on. Leaving a penniless gap, so only the poorest remain. They come here from even poorer places where no one wants them, except maybe as sharecroppers. They move in where nobody wants to be, including them." He glanced back at Merrit. "Think you'd find a job in this hood?"

"Drive a streetcar maybe, great transport, but they're mostly gone, I see," Merrit answered.

"I notice lots of Negroes and whites? Nobody looks prosperous," Flo added.

" 'Cause storekeepers live somewhere else," the cabbie explained. "You got dough, you leave."

"I feel bad for people," Flo said. "Why are you taking us the long way around? For the reason you gave us earlier?"

"Maybe you feel bad for yourself, too, by extension?" the cabbie asked.

Flo wondered.

The cabbie spoke while looking straight ahead at traffic. "There's road repair uptown. This way's longer as the crow flies but faster in minutes. You don't wanna be late. I sense it."

Studying crowded streets and the mixture of faces outside, Flo had wondered then if the driver was telling the whole truth about his taxi routes. Did he take her family for yokels new to the city, which in fact he wouldn't have been wrong about, and then grab the opportunity of enlightening them on the realities of urban life? If so, for what reason? Or could the down-and-out ways of living so obvious on this street be an everyday illustration of how too many people suffered during the present era, no matter where they lived? Or a portent of the future for all alike? Flo imagined what it was like fifty years before, then she wondered how her surroundings in Salina would appear in half a century.

The South Midlands where her family lived offered a mix of lifestyle improvements in recent times. Other parts of the country? Yes, maybe things were great. World War II produced penicillin, modern conveniences, and ready cash. Yet it was less than a generation after the Great Depression, and for common folk, white or black, many towns and neighborhoods remained stagnant. In Flo and Merrit's area, there could be untold want for the masses. Riches and property existed for those that lived where jobs existed, but they remained the luckiest ones. With her own eyes, Flo saw an unavoidable truth. In this urban area, the twentieth century left much of downtown in its lurch. Who was to say if a place like her Salina could avoid the same fate? In 1952 her town tottered on a brink between feast and famine.

7

Flo's questions remained unanswered after the Maxwell family's first trip to Barnes Hospital. While moving about in the city with Ronny on this present April day of 1954, Flo felt the same questions still flittering in and out of her mind. On the way to her hopeful but edgy post-op exam two years following the fateful taxi ride down Market Street with the Yogi Berra-friendly cabbie, she and Ronny stood outside Union Station and studied a steady parade of pedestrians. Unlike the unhurried folks of every race she remembered from two years before, these crowds rushed from the terminal to the business district or hurried to catch commuter trains for home. They brushed Flo's shoulders or jostled one another.

In that moment Flo felt a bump. She turned and realized she'd collided with a black lady, who stumbled in high heels and dropped her purse, which Flo snatched out of the air. The other woman was Flo's height with a narrow face and sharp features, unlike Flo sensibly wearing a coat for the day's chilly weather. They flashed expressions of cheer and empathy as Flo handed back the purse. Like long-lost soulmates, they studied each other frozen in the moment, until the stranger smiled then turned and walked on.

"What was that about?" Ronny asked.

"Nothing. Another lady," Flo answered, though she realized touching the other woman and exchanging smiles sent a jolt of undefined joy through her.

"She's in a hurry, like me," she told Ronny with a shrug that belied her flash of emotion.

"Who bumped into who?"

Flo didn't reply but looked back over her shoulder. She felt sad seeing the other woman go but calmer for meeting her. Getting to her doctor's remained an effort only because she feared arriving late.

The other woman's spontaneous smile and look of recognition failed to disappear from Flo's mind when she returned to looking for the right street toward Barnes. So she made herself think again of her surgeon Dr. Corale and the bits and pieces she'd learned about him during their consultations on cancer from 1952 to the present. Dr. Corale wasn't overly friendly or approachable, though he had a human side and showed it at times, as when he talked of his Italian descent. "Our family name was Corallo in the old country, but ended up as Corale here, don't ask me why," he said.

In ways, he remained as scarred by World War II as many combat veterans. With time there were obliquely sentimental sides to his personality that crept out. He was a transplanted New Yorker, from Brooklyn actually, which to Flo's Midwestern mind seemed exotic beyond the speaking of it. Dr. Corale made his mark while a Navy surgeon doing follow-up operations for GIs at Veterans' Hospital in Long Beach, California.

The mentioning of that hospital and the city it was in rang a bell for Flo because her older sister Margarite had moved to the West Coast in her late teens, as Flo told the doctor. The sister did volunteer work for that very hospital's long-term care unit during World War II. Wounded GI's and Navy men brought in on hospital ships from the Battle of the Coral Sea gave Dr. Corale his introduction to war, as he candidly told Flo and Merrit. That Coral Sea experience brought out the meaningless correlation between his own name and the fateful ocean that did its best to claim the lives of battle-scarred men he treated. In many cases, the surgeon's skillful scalpel was all that stood between them and permanent disfigurement or death.

In post-war times, Anthony Corale approached the public sternly and seldom smiled. In private with patients, he spoke clearly, sometimes a bit philosophically, but seldom at great length.

Flo felt a touch of humanity behind his business-like mask and an ability to judge people's character by intuition, as she calculated his reactions to her and Merrit at any rate. Corale never suffered fools in the form of incompetent doctors who sent the sickly to him under wrong diagnoses. Unlike the sadistic Radebach in Salina, a buffoon to be tolerated even less than others, Dr. Corale showed an understanding side that he mixed with a thorough analysis of the patients' ills and an awareness of their shock and fear, which was often abject. His humanity shone through the more Flo learned of his methods. He realized Merrit's interests, for example, and said he rooted for his Dodgers against the Yankees' Bronx Bombers. On every Barnes visit, the two men chatted baseball a moment, but the chatter took a serious turn when Dr. Corale mentioned surgery. He spoke of success and never doubted himself.

"I'm not supposed to say so," the doctor announced on Flo and Merrit's last pre-op visit, "but it scared me to death operating on the Navy guys from the Coral Sea. I was young and spent long sleepless nights. Surgery was new to me and I came to fear it like the patients themselves. Maybe more so. I was their only hope, which gave me some hope. Exceptions were many of the severely wounded, who'd been through so much combat and endured half-successful surgical procedures so often that they took surgery in stride. Operation tables became a part of their lives, which it is for me, too, now. Us medicos learned our trade during war."

Flo said nothing then, but Merrit asked in a meek tone unusual for him, "What?"

"What did we learn? A company of colored guys came in. News to us, didn't know there even were any coloreds in uniform, not in combat companies anyway. Don't know where they fought, in the front line somewhere. Most got shot up bad. Others built military roads in Alaska, I heard."

Flo and Merrit waited patiently, in surprise.

"Oh, yes, I see. My point, what is it?" Dr. Corale continued noting their uncertainty. "Others' pain is the same as ours."

He fingered his slight mustache and winced at eye-opening

moments he'd had. Flo guessed that from studying his wrinkled brow. "We have our methods here, based on science. We see people and the world through our lens."

"It never fails us, science?" Merrit asked.

"Our resolve, yes. The facts never."

"My sister worked there," Flo added. She saw the doctor wrinkle his brow but refrain from asking where.

"I mean at Veterans in Long Beach. Who woulda thunk it. My big sister an aide at your hospital."

The surgeon looked away, like thinking back on the wounds he'd treated in his Long Beach days.

"You wondered, who ever talked to the wounded, especially colored guys," he said.

Meanwhile Flo had questions about tests on her own ailment. The doctor could've marched in and spelled out the verdict, which was probably normal among surgeons. Certainly patients were nervous, some even near collapse, Flo guessed. Being on the spot was torture enough, so why keep patients in suspense?

Her papers lay on Dr. Corale's desk, seemingly untouched. She wondered if he'd read them briefly or ignored them altogether, and whether his clinic charged patients by the minute or at a flat appointment rate. If it was by the minute, Barnes was sure to rake in a considerable wad from her visit about The Lump. She read the same thoughts in Merrit, who shifted impatiently in his seat.

For Flo suspense reached a breaking point, when Dr. Corale picked up the report about her examination, which he himself had ordered but declined to discuss with Flo and Merrit unless in person. A long distance call had set up this appointment. Two days of tense waiting built to its peak. Now they sat before him awaiting the word.

Dr. Corale paused only to nod. From that gesture, Flo gathered he recognized her symptoms. Nothing surprising, but, she asked herself, what does he know? Has he ever performed routine morning ablutions and found a strange lump in his chest? Lumps like hers weren't the sole domain of women, she knew, but Dr. Corale appeared in perfect health. What could he know about the anguish of eminent illness and the nodules and swellings that presaged them? Did he only perfunctorily remove those growths from a long line of poor souls, inevitable victims of their own mortality made worse by unhealthful lifestyles like smoking or exposure to wartime radiation and chemical additives to their daily fare? Did he routinely perform surgery before moving on to a round of nine-hole golf at his suburban country club?

The doctor glanced up from the papers with a mixture of sympathy for Flo and contempt for what life could do to her, or anybody. Surely, she realized of a sudden, he'd stood or sat stolidly in this very room countless times and chucked the official medical reports, just as he did literally while seeing Flo. Her diagnosis slid across his desk to rest there. Instead of barking out an indecipherable protocol, like Dr. Radebach, he turned his back to the shiny steel-top desk and not only faced Flo and Merrit but sat down opposite them. He peered steadily at her most of the time, glancing now and then at Merrit.

"So, Mrs. Maxwell, you were washing up one day and felt something in your left breast?"

"Yes, which I'd never felt before," she answered.

"Or you noticed it before, like a mass, but thought it wasn't there?"

"Maybe. Hoped it'd go away."

Dr. Corale smiled slightly while also fighting a slight twitch in his upper lip. His questioning glance went from Flo to Merrit. He could have hastened to the point, wanting to get the truth out, good or bad, and move on, but Flo saw his approach as an attempt to judge how much anxiety, or fortitude, she and Merrit possessed. It was exactly Dr. Corale's recognition that Flo and her husband were what she called *real people* that caused her to turn away from other oncologists. She chose him because he was the exception on a staff of driven perfectionists.

"Feenoms, pure and simple!" Merrit had said with a sigh. Flo's husband used a term common in the sports pages to describe high-performing but callow baseball stars when he referred to the previous oncologists the two of them first consulted at the hospital. By contrast Dr. Corale didn't pull any punches in presenting the facts, but he was patient in waiting for a response. Are they brave enough to expect the worst and not fear it, she assumed Dr. Corale was wondering? Surely that's the question he inherited from his early days with combat veterans, studying guys in pre-shock, shock, or near-death, who either learned to hide their apprehensions behind hard words and unrepeatable sounds or quietly accepted what came their way. Life or death? Maybe the two experiences seemed the same on savage South Seas beachheads where men grew numb and were reduced to having little to win or lose?

As she searched within herself for a way to face her own possible doom, Flo realized that maybe the feeling of nothing-to-win-or-lose was what poor Negroes or new immigrants also endured in America, land of the future and social success, as it was called.

Nothing changes. That must be the mindset of folks hard-pressed beyond their means. Both after the World's Fair of 1904 and now, she felt sure, they saw their living spaces labeled for demolition and they themselves shunted off to live on the street, or worse.

8

"It's cancer?" Flo dared ask at last, her feelings as fragile as her words were few.

"Yes," Dr. Corale replied with no hesitancy or emotion.

"What stage?"

"Cancer, yes," he repeated. "We're getting it early."

Flo glanced at Merrit, who seemed more stunned than her. She moved her purse from one knee to the other, and wished for inner strength. Finally, she swallowed deeply and came up strong of voice. Though with no idea what to say, she realized an inner ability to face the truth, when the doctor stopped her with a gentle wag of a finger.

"This isn't the old days," he stated. "We're getting a handle on it."

Flo understood. She'd read about breast cancer in medical books, especially those from the Mayo Clinic, where she knew Dr. Corale did his internship. For cancer of the inner half of the breast, surgeries had once been a highly disfiguring operation and still were in some hospitals. It seemed to depend on the surgeon, though that info seldom, if ever, emerged directly. In medical books, radical mastectomy was the term she found to describe it and wondered what was so extreme. Radical came from the word for root, and the surgery goes all the way to the origin of the cancer. That's what Merrit figured from the description she gave him. "The operation pretty well digs the illness out so nothing's left. Parts of the body go along," he'd read somewhere once Flo's finding lit a fire under him.

Dr. Corale backed up Merrit's layman's talk. "Before the War, I was taught that if you have this lump, you remove the breast," he explained. "That meant removing the whole breast, the breast bone and ribs, and even chest wall muscles, to get all the cancer cells." Now, in the 1950s, he added, other philosophies prevailed, in some circles. If Flo preferred to play it safe and use another method, she was welcome to try, according to Dr. Corale. "You want another surgeon? I won't mind," he told Flo and Merrit.

Flo imagined with horror the huge hole in her left side like radical mastectomies created. It would leave her left side limp and weak as well, she was sure. She got a shudder considering the demurely stated catalogue descriptions showing clothes for victims of such surgeries. They featured bras with specialized inserts and jackets that covered the disfigured body parts. The garments had a baggy fit. She looked questioningly at her husband and the surgeon and wondered how to discuss a woman's feelings about body types with male listeners, including those who had a right to know. She was pleased to listen and not talk when Dr. Corale broke the silence.

"As early as the 1930s a new wave sprang up among surgeons, who slowly started changing the paradigm," he explained. "The new idea was finding the cancer and removing tumors. Then we could treat the lymph nodes around them."

"So your clinic's gone over to that thinking? You, too?" Merrit asked. "A minimal incision?"

"Well, hardly any surgery's minimal, but a lesser intrusion. Of course, some daring theorists argued for treating the cancer only with needles and drugs and radio therapy, no incisions. They argued for placing needles in the breast and near lymph nodes. Me, I believe in ridding the body of its ailment."

"Like you said."

"We believe in science."

For some reason Flo's thoughts flashed back to her maternal grandmother Millie Fowler and her long, slow descent into old age. Ancient black-and-white polaroids of Millie showed her as a winsome young woman, who surely caught men's eyes. No cancer came into her life, but kidney stones and bladder problems laid her low in middle age, so Flo's memory was of a decrepit lady too soon old using a cane to limp from room to room in a dreary senior citizens' home, where her roommates kept her awake with coughing attacks or hellacious nightmares, not to mention lamentations about real or imagined slings and arrows dealt them, or, as could happen, tales of repeated visits from ambulatory but whiskey-slick spouses, themselves locked in a desperate struggle with death.

"More prisoner than patient," Millie had once told Flo. "It's horrible to want to die and not be able to."

Millie died indeed, more it seemed, from weakness than any noticeable illness. But Flo wanted to live. She wondered if breast cancer would weaken her and leave her, like Millie, suffering various corollary diseases, unable to lift even the lightest garments or reach up to shelves in her kitchen cupboard.

"Will you remove all my breast?" she asked Dr. Corale, thinking about the effects an operation might have on her appearance.

The surgeon studied Flo as she bit her lip and sat up straight. She intended that stance to show determination but a chilling anticipation of pain and suffering sent another shiver down her spine. She braced herself and fingered the latch on her purse until she hoisted its strap over a shoulder and rose up as if to stride out of the room.

"I know what you're thinking," Dr. Corale answered. "Better to respond frankly and quickly than hide your anger."

She turned his way, afraid of what he'd say next but intrigued by his wording. She adjusted the purse strap on her shoulder.

"Yes, tell me."

"Nothing always works," he continued. "Radically going for all the cancer cells might not be the end-all. Removing only part of the breast can maybe be just as good. It's experimental."

"Like you said," Flo uttered. She felt pale and wondered if a person's bad feelings showed in weak colors, like the dull gray and drab brown swirling madly in her confused mind. A stupid idea, she was telling herself when Dr. Corale spoke again.

"To repeat, nothing's foolproof, but I'm confident of success."

"So what'll it be, whole breast or part?" she dared ask.

The surgeon glanced from Flo to Merrit once more, though she was sure he felt more comfortable with her. Women were his patients and allies. Flo knew he preferred the scalpel. Surely, she thought, he'll take the minimalist approach because he understands me.

"Part," he said at last, with a reassuring smile. "Store away whatever newfangled dress you bought for post-op. It'll take time. You'll see a difference, but it'll heal over. My scheduling assistant will be in to see you."

9

Flo felt numb, or more like stupefied. She sat back down and had only reawakened to the dullness of the white rectangular room, with Merrit beside her, when Dr. Corale's nurse opened the door.

"Can I get you anything else?" she asked while straightening a chair the surgeon had moved at an angle to create a more private feeling between him and the Maxwells. Flo saw Merrit nod absently at the nurse while she herself shook the cobwebs from her head after hearing her worst fears confirmed. There would be an operation. Even after the nurse tidied up the doctor's office, which had never lost its antiseptic flavor, Flo and Merrit were still motionless. The scheduling secretary came in finally and gave them a list of suggested times for Flo's surgery. Merrit took the papers from Flo's nearly limp hand before leafing through them. He marked days he was free from work. He read the dates out loud, but she only nodded. She felt certain they'd reached the end of something together, but she only wondered what.

Without knowing why, she stood up at last and touched Dr. Corale's chair back. Then she gave it a quick swipe with her right hand and fastened the hand to her chest as if surrendering her fate to his skilled surgery and also gently incorporating him in the suffering every woman feared and many experienced. She saw Merrit look at her curiously as she performed the act and watched the chair back swivel round and round. She knew her husband understood her worry and fright, but after other impersonal and straight-to-the point interviews unlike today's, with other medical men, only

Anthony Corale had come close in Flo's presence to internalizing his female patients' primal fear, which tended to strike in silence. Dr. Corale somehow found a balance between the professional and the personal. His learned reticence went deeper than Merrit's empathy. But in his way Merrit was not lacking in feeling either. When her husband felt emotion, he verbalized it.

"Don't worry, good times are just beginning, you'll see," Merrit uttered sincerely and put an arm around her shoulder.

"Beginning implies an end. What's ending?" she asked, mostly to herself, and stopped the chair back from swirling.

When Merrit didn't reply, she faced him beseechingly. He stood his ground and waited for an answer.

"My life? My womanhood?" she whispered. On one hand she felt engulfed by her question's personal scope. What had her life been about, besides marrying Merrit and rearing Ronny and his sister. Had it added to human understanding? What had she accomplished? Other women forcefully made their mark in a society managed by men, while she remained a devoted homemaker seldom experiencing any newness outside Salina.

She remembered her youthful dreams of a modeling career, which never came true because of Salina's limited exposure to the world of fashion. As a teenager and newlywed she'd posed long hours before the bedroom mirror vainly admiring her svelte figure and firm bust line. She blushed but never doubted it when others remarked how local fellows stopped in public and admired her stylish figure as she passed along Main Street in Salina. Pregnancy suited her well also. When she was carrying Ronny's sister, now grown and married, Flo felt fulfilled. As those days passed, she feared becoming matronly. That uncomfortable feeling could move her to tears on a bad day, and her visit to Dr. Corale reinforced the melancholy.

Merrit held up a meaty hand to stop her from crying. Then he caressed her cheek with his fingertips, which were soft in contrast to his palms. His understanding smile brightened as Flo turned to leave. On the way out, they stopped at the receptionist's desk to sign up for surgery in early September. Flo gave the packet of instructions to Merrit, who put it under his arm and opened the door for her.

"I didn't marry you for your breasts," he said on the way to the car park.

"Anyway, I'll still have them, just a little bit less," she replied with a faint smile and wondered if she believed her own words.

"I succeed," Dr. Corale had said.

She needed to believe him.

10

Adjusting her time frame to the present, April 14, 1954, Flo stood with Ronny outside Union Station and studied travelers hurrying to and fro. She thought about events following discovery of her cancer. In the weeks after Dr. Corale's diagnosis, her mind was a' jumble with impressions and assumptions, which caused the steady flow of happenings to mix with her suddenly disappearing ability to think chronologically. If an event happened before or after another and whether it meant one thing or its opposite created a confusion that belied her normal clear-thinking approach to time and its passing.

There were days when she imagined her visits to Dr. Corale preceded her standoffs with Dr. Perdition, as Merrit started calling Radebach, who transmogrified in her husband's mind from a sadistic schemer to a rep for the criminally insane. Other times she imagined the impoverished, socially marginalized, and disenfranchised folk, mostly colored, living along Market Street as evil thieves lurking in the shadows of folks' existences to rob them blind, or they appeared to her in night-time dreams as kind-spirited beings semi-freed from slavery but gracefully bearing the world little or none of the ill will it deserved.

In short, her thoughts wandered to wild extremes she would never have recognized in herself before. Naming happenings one by one was no problem, but she struggled to remember them in order and sometimes wondered if they were real or imagined.

Above all, fearing death dominated her emotional life. She imagined pain and then a slow loss of sensitivity until both faded from her all-too-palpable everyday life. The new feeling seemed a tangible nothingness unbearable in its dark monotony. Concealed in those feelings was her need to love Merrit and their children and be loved by them while she pretended she was the same lovable lady of old, who laughed and cried with equal abandon at the world's foibles.

It became habit to carry on like normal while bearing suffering in the back of her mind. Living so was a token of her frailty. Such mannered traits only began disappearing at the intriguing moment the tugboat *Huckleberry* chugged into view and unmuddied her mind with its dodgeball maneuvers through the Mississippi's relentless flotsam.

Seen now from the hustle and bustle of Union Station, her former excruciating task of preparing for surgery, treading the uncertain waters of post-op rehab, and imagining how she'd bid farewell to her loved ones if need be, all that seemed a muddle. Now she felt her surgery and its aftermath as the stuff of clearer thought. Going to hear Dr. Corale's pronouncement about her fate would be something she'd meet as part of taking life like it was. What's meant to be will be, she decided in a moment of clarity.

Like the indomitable tugboat, she'd take life's hard hits. Afterward it was a matter of keeping the right order of events. First the mass in her breast. Next Dr. Sawbones. Repeated visits to Barnes' Oncology Staff. Then Dr. Corale. Finally, the surgery Dr. Corale performed. Her later exams and physical therapy followed. And now she was appearing for what was surely her last visit in the big city hospital. There was nothing for it but to face the worst, if it appeared.

She wondered what narrative a skilled author might create from her cancer episodes? For two years it'd seemed a wildly spinning stream of consciousness. Deep down inside she recognized only one steady thread. That was Ronny. He alone had gone along on her visits to Barnes. Outside the hospital he'd seen and studied the city streets with her. She thought of those things again and evaluated what led the Market Street neighborhood to its dilapidated state, but she reached no definite conclusion. Instead she took

Ronny under the arm and marched resolutely away from both the River and Union Station.

"Mom, what's up now?" her son asked. He pulled himself loose and strode ahead. "I know my own way."

"That's it! We're going there now," she announced and felt herself stomp the pavement with a clang that caused passersby to glance her way.

"Where's there?" Ronny wondered out loud as he matched her pace to the nearest bus stop.

"Barnes now," she explained as she sprang ahead, holding Ronny's hand like a child's.

"What the devil's up?" he asked.

Flo bounded onto the bus like a school girl. "To my doctor!"

She guided him to a bus seat and plopped down next to him. In jumping aboard, she'd reacted instinctively for the first time since finding The Lump. In plopping down beside Ronny, she continued just as impulsively.

"It's like the good doc said," she told him.

"Yeah," the boy answered. He glanced up to see her smiling and Flo understood he read her thoughts. "You know, it's like Dad tells me, there's nothing to fear but fear itself."

Flo nudged him and replied in mock anger. "Who are you anyway, quoting your own dad like he was FDR, the great man?"

She led him into Barnes with an even more resolute look and a greater spring in her step than she started the morning with.

11

D
r. Corale was in no hurry. Either it was he himself acting slowly by choice or finishing a delayed appointment with another patient, something kept Flo waiting past her appointed time with him. The surgeon greeted her without smiling or apologizing for the delay. Like before, he spun the office chair with a swoosh, though he acted laconically. When the seat spun around his way, he sat down and studied her as if she were the only part of the room he recognized. Flo felt eager to break the ice, but she didn't dare speak out of turn.

He held out a calming hand and said directly, "Good news, you're clear!"

Flo felt immense elation sweep through her like a mellow electric jolt beginning in her toes and shooting upward. Yet it wasn't the same jubilation she'd wished for during the months previous. A sense of liberation was something she'd spent this day preparing herself for, so in a sense she was already set free by the time she and Ronny got on the bus to Barnes. Fears ceased being her master. You've got no reason to quake in your boots, she reasoned with herself like an ever-patient FDR.

"I stopped fearing my own fear," she told the surgeon.

Whether he sensed that change and wanted to move on or was simply tired, Dr. Corale produced a case report and went through her papers in a professional manner. *Amelioration*, *abatement of symptoms*, and *restoration of health* were understandable enough, or at best the expressions sounded tamely joyless, even though they showed the result she so fervently longed for.

"You're saying the cancer's gone? It hasn't spread?"

"No, we got it all, like we said, no symptoms now," he reassured her.

As she smiled, his shoulders drooped and he assumed yet another guise. It hinted at a lessening of his professional stance, so she waited and listened.

"Been on the phone," he said with no inflection. Hearing him begin with such a trivial comment, she guessed he felt exhausted after a day of fixing failed bodies, and then meeting other, recovering owners, who he'd send home, so they'd slog through a few more years of fading energy. No, his job must have its sobering moments, of that she was aware. A perpetual downside, she guessed.

Or was that too mean of me? Flo wondered. She herself felt spry and thought back to the long mental and physical struggle that brought her where she was now. She asked herself what personal battles the good doctor could've faced in the War and at Veterans Hospitals. Or was the affluence his operating room skills now afforded him insufficient to hold off the work place bugaboos and life frustrations he faced like the rest of humanity? Were professional and material successes buffer enough?

My visit here's for me, Flo reminded herself, yet she saw the surgeon absorbed in his own thoughts. It wasn't the usual behavior in wrapping up a successful visit to Barnes Hospital, yet her good news was a bounty she thanked the surgeon for. Or was it his science she should say thanks to and regard him only as its implementer? Was he the dancer or only an able choreographer?

"A strange job this," Dr. Corale said. He glanced at her before assessing the bare ceiling with a roll of his eyes. The room wasn't his private office, so he showed no need to familiarize himself with it. So was he summoning the courage to give her a hunk of belated bad news, which she thought she'd banished from her mind? Flo directed an edgy smile his way, which his apparent nonchalance deflected.

"Strange?" Flo asked.

"You see, I just got off the phone with my aged father," the doctor commenced. "He reminded me, there's an everyday world out there. I'm an oncologist and here I'm giving advice to him, who has no cancer and knows it. He's smarter than this. Smarter than me, if he'd remember."

Flo nodded, more out of confusion than encouragement. *My results? Anything more?* she wished to scream at him. "Cancer specialist," she said feigning disinterest. The surgeon's off-the-cuff manner hardly seemed the right prelude to his announcing whatever he might be keeping from her. As Dr. Corale reclined in his chair, Flo sat up.

"It's this way," Dr. Carole resumed. "My father. He fell off a curb, hurt a hip, and is on a walker. The therapist says it's been 12 weeks, give that contraption up, or he'll become a cripple. The walker broke and Dad's family doc refuses to order a new one. Dad wants me to give him one. I say I'll send him to physical therapy instead."

The surgeon sighed again. Flo saw that a thought occurred to him. He sat up and turned her way. "Can you imagine? Me the son being father to the man, my own father. Cancer specialist as orthopedist?"

He turned Flo's way showing awakened awareness of her. She thought that unusual. Has he never really seen me before?

"If only my father had those guys' gumption," the doctor continued. "You know, what your sister saw in GIs at Long Beach. How they struggled."

Indeed Flo's sister had tried telling their family touching tales from Veterans' Hospital, but the suffering she saw in the wards only deflected her into describing SoCal as an escapist paradise. Flo peered at her surgeon to try and judge if his comments were leading in a similar direction.

"Or your own bravery and strength," the doctor continued. The hint of a smile brightened his countenance. His gaze struck a linear path her way.

"You and our science," he said. "Amazing."

12

Flo likened her cancer-related events beginning two years previous to a wintry darkness no sensible adult would tolerate, much less make sense of. Yet in seeing Dr. Corale's varied approach on this day, which she likened to a mix of shifting seasons, she realized the most constant thread in her experience was Ronny, like she already knew and couldn't help thinking about. No, not any adults, who would've found her travails an unneeded interruption in their schedules. As she reminded herself, the boy alone followed on all her visits to Barnes. Together they decided whites and colored people could live only blocks away from each other but worlds apart in habits and assumptions. The determined white commuters dashing in and out of stations and bus stops contrasted to the Negroes living their city street life in no more apparent discontent than the harried nine-to-fivers. Yet *apparent* could be tricky. As her taxi driver of two years ago had said, suffering could cut through many layers of wealth and reduce us all to an equal footing. Where we take it from there depends on group willpower and individual persistence.

Flo was wondering what conclusions to draw from those impressions of city life when Dr. Corale smiled wryly. "Looks fine. Like I said."

A new burst of joy filled her as he sat up straight and tightened his tie. She leaned forward and considered, in her fantasy, whether to complete his report for him, or loosen his tie so it matched the relaxed tone of his voice, but she found no words or fitting action to show her merriment.

"You ..." she began.

His expression brightened only a smidgin.

"We got it all," he repeated with a nod. "Like I said, no sign of it spreading. Home free."

"So your intuition was right?"

"Our science," he corrected her mildly. "Yes, it was right. I told you that."

He showed her the x-rays, as his attitude turned sprightly. He nodded and faced her to show that he understood her sense of relief.

Upon seeing different signs of the incision and the strange sight of her flesh broken open in the film, she nodded at him. Her inner parts seemed a foreign realm in black-and-white, which she'd carried as a guarded secret. Now the X-ray turned those parts out for the medical world to view. She was shocked by the strangeness of herself, but guessed Ronny would've gazed upon the x-rays, boy though he was, with the detached clinician's view. He had more of the scientist in him. Feeling her thoughts meandering in a butterfly-like rapture, Flo threw caution to the wind and uttered a muffled barbaric yawp.

Dr. Carole had surely heard greater outbursts, so she placed a hand over her mouth to stifle the now disappearing yawp.

"You'll have that scar, but will notice it less, as I predicted before," he continued. "Or you'll learn to feel it part of you."

Flo fingered the collar on her blouse as a reminder that indeed she bore a mark from his scalpel but could wear it with pride. In herself. At the same time she experienced a reawakening of herself as a woman still in the prime of life.

"Get on with it," Dr. Corale encouraged her. "I'll see you in six months. Regular checkup."

She looked for the lobby. Somewhere in this labyrinthine maze her son would be serenely observing the staff's and patients' comings and goings.

"My nurse will schedule you" the surgeon had explained.

Flo felt sure he'd said that, so she looked for Ronny while imagining the doctor receding to his former weariness. She realized he was his brilliant self in the operating room but had begun showing the signs of all flesh since his first meeting with her and Merrit two years earlier. She thought of the suffering and uncertainty he must've witnessed and wondered how many other medical men had his degree of empathy. Or humane concern. Think though she would and by her nature must, her strongest urge was to be gone from this somber clinical realm and greet life anew.

13

"Or is it the last step before burnout?" Flo asked.

She wandered the halls of Barnes Hospital till she spotted Ronny sipping a chocolate malt in the coffee shop she'd left him at. She realized her consultation with Dr. Corale had taken only a fraction of the eternity it felt like.

She paused and watched him from the entrance. He'd grown and lost his lanky appearance the past year, so she imagined him one day being a powerful man like Merrit, though never as brawny. Not much escaped the boy's notice, including Miss Jordan. True, she was his teacher and ten years older, but she'd set a stamp on him for the better. She wakened his school pursuits and posed questions he brought home to discuss at dinner. If the two were the same age, maybe there'd be a spark.

What was Miss Jordan like? Flo found that question hard to answer since the two women knew so little about each other. Kristine Jordan's faculty photo from Ronny's high school yearbook showed a pretty, blond young lady of just-above-average height and a serious, though not stern, expression. Whether she was dedicated to her studies as a profession or was pursuing societal revolution remained an open question. Whatever, Flo thought, she's a newer generation than mine.

"You're okay?" Ronny asked and broke Flo's train of thought when she approached.

She sat down, told him about her visit with Dr. Corale, and smiled. "I'm free! And so what now? Your choice."

She moved closer and used his straw to taste the malt. He looked unsurprised at her cheerful mood and offered another sip.

"Clean bill of health, huh?" he asked in a pleasing but offhand way. The comment was in line with Ronny's thoughtfulness, indifferent though it sounded.

"On a good day, yes, that's both of us," she replied and saw him frown. She wondered herself what she meant, if anything at all, beyond a gentle jest.

"Burnout?" he asked with a quizzical look. "What's that?"

"You wouldn't know, not yet," she replied. "I meant my doc. He looks tired, is all. A good day for me."

After he sucked the straw dry and disposed of it, she watched him gulp down the rest of his malt until only a trace of the chocolate remained. She gave him a paper napkin and made sure he wiped off the ice cream.

"You're too young to get it. Burnout, I mean. Bodies get old and wear out. Like an ancient lawn mower or used cars."

"Use gets to you, huh?" Ronny asked with a casual shrug.

"Like I said, what's next?"

He shrugged again.

Flo showed him the way out of Barnes. She felt the stress desert her as quickly as it'd mounted on the way in, so she slowed her pace and took the long way around, just like the Yellow Cab taxi driver from two years ago had driven the long route because he said it was faster. While the cabbie showed Merrit, Ronny, and her the sights, she realized the fare mounted, but she learned new things on that route. She decided she and Ronny would see more going a different way this time too.

Strolling the hospital grounds, she talked about what they'd seen in the city so far. Pumping the boy with endless questions was her time-tested way of dragging info from him. One answer for every ten questions was par for the course. Or she could test him with short phrases to see how quick-witted he was.

"Crossing the Mississippi?" Flo suggested.

"Entering the State of Misery," Ronny retorted. "This city I like. The countryside in the state, no."

"On the Hill?"

"Where Yogi lived."

"Incendiary ball team?"

"Gas House Gang," he replied.

"Gateway to the West?"

Ronny stopped looking puzzled. "No clue," he admitted. "Maybe where Lewis and Clark left from, exploring?"

"Yes, that's what we did, too, crossing the Mississippi," she agreed. "Forest Park Zoo?"

"Next up," he said with a quick smile.

"Okay, let's do it."

14

Flo paused by the Carnivore Exhibit of Forest Park Zoo and waited. Ronny had nixed the roundabout stroll to get away from Barnes in a leisurely fashion, so the two hastened to Forest Park to see the tiger and ape exhibits, which he'd heard about from Miss Jordan in school. The Zoo would've come in a close second to his cherished baseball if there'd been a game. Flo showed less craving for carnivores than her son did, so she leaned against a guard rail until he came from the big cat building. He was excited to talk about the animals, and she settled into a contemplative, increasingly mellow mood. She'd wondered how workers in the medical profession dealt with patients that complained of boring ailments in a never ending stream, only to realize she herself had spent two cancer-ridden years with thoughts riveted on herself.

"I'm as human as anyone," she explained.

"You're burned out?" Ronny asked, seeing her dreamy appearance.

She acknowledged his joke but made no attempt to explain her mood.

He kept a quizzical expression while she studied Zoo visitors. When several Negro families passed her way, Flo fixed her gaze on them, especially the children, young and well behaved.

"Their kids are cute," she commented. "Easy to see their moms care for their hair and clothing. They're obedient."

"Meaning what?" Ronny asked with keen interest, though he usually seemed distracted at similar comments. "I don't obey you? That what you mean?"

"It's nothing," she replied. "I like studying folks, like where they come from, why they're the way they are. Different folks, different ..."

"Burnout. I like that word," he interrupted her. "Burnout? But I still don't get it."

"Like I said, never mind. Your time will come," she said and decided his comments were only a cry for attention. Visiting the Zoo was her subtle reward to Ronny for keeping her company in the city while Merrit went to work and the Cardinals played on the road. So she quit talking about herself and got insights his words were an invitation for her to turn an interested ear his way. Yet she had trouble staying totally silent.

"Wanna hear?" he asked.

"Tell me," she agreed.

"It's like Miss Jordan. She came to the Zoo because she studied animals herself. In college."

"Zoology, I'd guess. And?"

"She loves them but not what she saw done to them here. She says Forest Park treats 'em bad, the way some people treat other people. Maybe worse."

"Even worse? Like who?" Flo answered. She was interested in hearing more but wondered about his ideas. "They teach that stuff in our schools? Or you make it up?"

"Miss Jordan was here, at the Zoo, like I told you. She saw polar bears in tiny tanks and monkeys and apes got it terrible. No space and they're too smart for their keepers. They got brains like us."

"Brains like humans? What humans? And which humans does she mean that we treat like animals? Who treats who that way?"

"I never said she said that ... well, maybe she did, but listen ... she quoted the famous philosopher."

"What philosopher?" Flo asked.

"Rousseau. It's like he said, *Man is born free and everywhere he is in chains.* See?"

"No, tell me."

"Look around, you wanna see who we treat bad. You yourself like their kids."

"Who?"

"The people we just passed. With cute kids."

Flo wakened from her mellow mood and realized Ronny maybe knew what he was talking about. Could be he's right we don't reckon other folk as people. There aren't any in Salina, so does non-present mean non-existent? Do I need to meet them in person to know them? Or vice versa?

"She being Miss Jordan, again? That you heard this from?" Flo asked.

Ronny nodded yes and acted irritated. "I have a mind of my own."

"Ok, as she was saying?" Flo asked, pretending to ignore him.

"Miss Jordan went to the Chimp Show, here, and saw how it is. They got chimpanzees that perform. Ride bikes, play in an orchestra, swing on a trapeze. They do it coordinated-like. Play trombones even. Cavort. That's what Miss Jordan calls it, they cavort on stage."

"Meaning they're trained?"

"Yeah, to perform, a whole troupe. With trainers in tuxes running 'em through routines."

"Through the hoops, they say. They have real hoops? Hula hoops?"

"Maybe. Crowds laugh and clap. That's what I hear."

"What's so bad about that? You're leading up to something," Flo responded.

"Nobody asks the chimps if they like it. No people would do it, least not smart ones. They'd revolt. Unless they're football cheerleaders."

"And what answer would the chimps give if you asked them? They're apes. They'd understand what you ask?"

"They're thinking individuals, held captive."

Flo strolled along rethinking Ronny's words, probably suggested to him by a teacher, Miss Jordan. Much of what the boy said sounded like teenage enthusiasm gone overboard. Yet she could accept his logic. After all, she'd just been liberated herself from a dread disease that held her in its sway. She'd often thought the mental stress worse than the ailment itself. How indeed might nimble and resourceful beasts respond if trained robot-like to pedal trikes around in endless circles or blast away without harmony on trumpets and trombones?

"Why would they like it any better than we do?" he asked.

"I see. Just like I was held prisoner to my own fears," Flo reasoned.

She remembered Oscar, an aging draft horse and his owner. She'd met both of them while visiting her County Fair years earlier. The horse's owner ran the County Concessions and used the nag to pull carriages of sightseers until the horse grew too slow to manage the load for a full day. The concessions man did the humane thing and put the horse out to pasture only to discover life in retirement sent Oscar into deep depression. He was bred for work and without it lost his will to eat. Flo learned from the Concessions man that returning Oscar to part-time draft work restored his vitality. He showed a renewed friskiness and desire. In horse's logic, he felt free doing what he was bred for.

"So we feel imprisoned doing what we don't want?" Flo asked.

Her reflections seemed to anticipate where he was headed. He looked straight ahead but had her in mind anyway. "Know what Miss Jordan told us?"

She thought, oh, her again? Are there no other teachers in that school? She turned toward him anyway and answered with a frown.

"Tell me, what?"

"When she was here, a strange thing happened. Two male chimps, Sailor and Sinner, were chained to poles while others performed. These two male chimps were heads of the pack. At a planned moment, their shackles were removed and they were to climb up on a scaffold and jump down on a pony and ride him around the stage. This time things went wrong."

15

"My goodness, aren't those dangerous animals? Chimps?" Flo asked in a hush.

"Males, yes, but no more than their keepers. When the head trainer came over to loosen their chains, the chimps revolted. They swung the big, heavy chains and made a mad dash to escape. At the last second a guard shut the gate shut and workers tranquilized the runaways with darts. The chimps knew they wanted out and went for it."

"Yes, so would we, I guess, there you see. Wanna know about burnout? You just described it," Flo added. "Forced to do too much of the same thing, for too long. Boring."

Ronny stared past her like he could see the burnout concept hanging before him, but had nothing to say until he asked, "Like if I had to sit in a dull study hall for the next hundred years with no interesting homework?"

"Yes, or doing the same old homework each day for a century or two, or jumping down on ponies' backs year after year with no reward for it. Who wouldn't need a breath of fresh air."

Maybe, Flo reconsidered, chimpanzees were of a higher order than horses, which meant endless repetition of senseless tasks was sure to stunt them, where the horses would trot on and on till they lasted no longer, or so she'd heard.

"But still, where in the world …" Flo thought to continue, but Ronny cut her off.

"You mean where does my ticha get all her ideas?"

Not to be outdone by her cheeky son, Flo interrupted him.

"Yes, where in the world?"

"That's my point. She was there. She saw the anger in those chimps' eyes and recognized their fury toward the trainers."

"So, she was here and saw them, huh? Smarter than their keepers?"

"Madder anyway. They knew when enough's enough."

"Understanding what words mean, like captive and freedom?"

"You can be something without knowing the word for it, can't you?"

Flo nodded in agreement, more or less. She'd read about chimpanzees recognizing themselves in a mirror. Grown orangutans matched human toddlers in mental development, it was said, but she wondered about the truth in those things. Somewhere there had to be a line separating animals and humans.

"We're not the same species, but we're equal, chimps and us?" she asked.

"Whatever," Ronny answered. "Miss Jordan says this zoo's a prison for primates."

Hearing those words, Flo switched topics.

"So big cats, what're they like?" she asked.

"Waldemar and Kalista," he began. "Two tigers from the Northern wilderness."

"Tigers at the Arctic circle?" she asked in astonishment.

"Well, they're warm, they wear fur coats, you should see 'em," Ronny joked. "A natural place for 'em, the Arctic."

Thinking things hot enough as they were, though the April day still hadn't warmed up to suit her, Flo moved her son along the pathway toward the real object of interest, which she shared with him. That was Hominid House, where sure enough a troupe of chimpanzees performed tricks, like riding bikes and turning somersaults. Ronny told Flo about our nearest cousins being forced to act more like human children than adult apes. Flo wished for Ronny to act more like a child himself, rather than talking on and on about killing-machine predators from deep, dark forests or apes who, given an electric typewriter, learned writing on their own, though he admitted it wasn't real script.

16

"Waldemar and Kalista are Amur tigers I saw," Ronny said once in the house of predators. "Not many left in the wild."

Flo heard his enthusiasm and glanced at the outdoor enclosure, where furry felines lay in far recesses under bare branches of scattered bushes, unmoving and unperturbed. A few visitors crowded by the railings. Flo wondered if the tigers' blank yet penetrating stare sent the same chill down others' spines as it did hers. *Tiger, tiger burning bright in the forests of the night,* she remembered from some school textbook of her youth. What author wrote that line or what context it fit was a puzzle that flitted around in her mind. She knew only the rhythm of the line reverberated in her soul. She gazed at the majestic felines, while Ronny, too, peered at them.

"We saw this exhibit on a slide show in class. We read how people living in forests believe animals like Waldemar and Kalista protect people and stand for power and courage," he explained.

"You mean fighting against dragons?" she jested. "Fairy tale stuff?"

"Yeah, the tiger spirit caused rain during famines and delivered babies to women that wanted kids."

Flo flashed glances at Ronny and then at the lounging tigers. She thought of a movie short. Anatomists had studied the cadavers of a dead tiger and a dead lion and determined they had the same anatomy, except for their fur, and were programmed to the same degree by nature, even if not totally in the same way. They were instinctive killing machines, Flo learned, but that never stopped her from wondering what the beasts were thinking behind their placid stares. They had no existential qualms, she was sure. Only us humans can question our own motives and alter our ways.

"Change or perish," she said, mimicking a thinker she'd heard on the radio. "Are we really the only beings who can change?" she asked Ronny without giving a foretaste of her thoughts.

He glanced up with the comprehending smile he used for adults meaning he anticipated the question even if he lacked an answer.

"I know," he said, "but I got stranded. I mean ..."

"Like this," Flo said. "Can something like a ferocious tiger from Amur, wherever that is?" She stopped and waited for Ronny until she saw he had no idea either. "No clue," he said, so she returned the favor to show him sympathy. "Not even a king among beasts can change his stripes and become another version of himself? A new man, so to speak?"

"Man?" he replied. "Me?"

Flo knew he was thinking 'Boy!' so she paused. The two locked in a congenial staring match, both pretty sure what the other was thinking but needing to remind themselves what stage of development each was in. Precocious son. Observant mother.

"Okay, man or boy," Flo admitted at last. "All the same, you and your dad are more alike than different."

As Flo strolled the pathway, Ronny tried hurrying her on to Hominid House. He humored her as she stopped to look back at the Amur predators. Their look connected with hers, so she imagined an interlocking fellow feel between the tigers and her. Only Ronny's jostling roused Flo, so she followed him toward his reward for the day's excursion.

"House of chimps," he said.

17

"Primate Prison, so that's what Miss Jordan calls this?" Flo said, as they entered Hominid House. "Not Carnivore Cave like where the cats live?"

A few howler monkeys lazed on limbs near them, but a towering tropical forest extended toward the ceiling, which Flo craned her neck to peer up at. In the canopy, a mixed troupe of brown and black gibbons swung from branch to branch, impervious to danger. She watched them in awe of their long arms and sure-handed antics.

"Some are lesser apes, not great ones," Ronny explained. He acted casual.

"You read about them?"

"No, heard about 'em. In class."

"C'mon, kid, what else? Your belly's too full of milk shake?"

"Malt. It was a malt."

"Sorry, but your mind. It's somewhere else."

They continued walking through the building until Ronny stopped. He seemed to freeze in place, unable to unlock his thoughts and move on.

"Chaining them to a pole, with no freedom? You call that caring?" he asked her with a slight sneer. "It's just to keep the zoo audience happy?"

"Exactly," Flo agreed. "To entertain us, you and me."

Flo stepped back. Partly she needed to check the time. They'd have to get a move on to catch the last Flier home, and there were City buses waiting to take them to Union Station. Mostly she observed her son, still a youngster but in a few years, what then, she wondered? In her mind she saw him in a mental tug-of-war with two sides struggling for his attention. One was Salina's concealed but ever-present exploitive side and another the concerned humanism of a Miss Jordan. There came moments of truth in everyone's life and this would be Ronny's. In years to come, he'd have to figure his path in or out of Salina.

"Let's go, Mister," she finally said to him in rough jest. "Our ride's waiting."

"No, I wanna know," Ronny insisted, digging in for a standoff with the chimpanzee trainers of the world. "What'll happen?"

"Where or what? And to who?"

Flo watched Ronny, a teenager ready to face down the tuxedoed trainers and security-clad Zoo people of the world. She was considering a quick exit from the spot when a softer voice spoke within her.

"To who? Those two? Sailor and Sinner?" she asked echoing a hunch her inner voice suggested.

"Yes," he said but avoided her inquiring look.

"The facility'll reintroduce them in a couple days. It's only sensible."

Ronny didn't respond.

Along a straight, narrow walkway, a row of lamps lit the way to a waiting city bus marked *Union Station*. They started in that direction, but Flo stopped when Ronny pulled himself away to stare back at the receding shadows of Forest Park Zoo.

"Thanks," he whispered as though speaking to a shade. "I learned a lot."

They walked on.

"*Some* spring." Flo whispered that remark apropos nothing, as they got on the bus. "Home by dark, if we make the last train."

18

Despite everything, Flo would've bet on real spring soon. Yet nothing was certain and so what if warm weather took its time, delays had made a patient philosopher of her the past two years, even if her ideas were homespun. She'd waited for Dr. Corale to tell her she was cancer-free and she'd come to realize even that judgment could be a misnomer. Her malady was like alcoholism maybe. Once you're addicted to the bottle that's what you are for life, no matter how long on the wagon. Cancer surely worked that way, too. She'd had it and abided by it. Now she needed to live with its facts. Nothing lasts forever. Is that how it worked? Freedom even? She felt herself learning to reserve judgment.

That felt like the gist of this weekday. Watching, listening, keeping judgments on the back burner. She'd found freedom from fear and an awareness of how others fought against their confinements. In addition to her own dilemma, she realized life's drama, as it played out in Forest Park, extended from the confined to their confiners. Maybe the afternoon's problems exemplified how we feel the effects of our experiences but struggle to identify their causes, in those cases when we bother to search for them in the first place. What's the price we pay for not searching? What Ronny would face in his lifetime Flo had no guess, but she saw his social side flourishing. He was joining the human conversation.

From the Zoo they reached Union Station early and plopped down on a bench, famished. While Flo luxuriated in her own sweet silent thoughts, Ronny complained of his stomach growling. Next to him sat a colored child about half his age, his mother by him. The kid had two cartons of Cracker Jacks. He opened one.

"Want some?" he asked Ronny.

"Cameron, that's a nice boy," the mother praised him.

"Love some, sure," Ronny answered and cupped his hands for an ample helping.

"Share and share alike," Flo said to Cameron's mother. "I like that."

"Our boys aren't shy, mine and yours," the mother said.

"Peas in a pod," Flo agreed.

After that, Flo watched the youngsters in a Cracker Jack feeding frenzy. She herself sipped at a take-out decaf, now cold, that she'd carried around since earlier. Sitting in the chill did nothing to warm her. So she stood up and walked the length of the platform. She heard a sound from the evening's last Flier. It glided in as smoothly as the A. M. Special had left Salina. The late evening run was a streamliner's version of old-fashioned mail trains.

"Ronny, time to go," Flo said.

"No, Mom, we got another hour," came her son's reply.

"Oh, yes, I read the schedule wrong."

Flo leaned back to imagine Merrit meeting them in Salina. She was relishing that thought when the small boy's mother spoke up.

"Where are you heading?" she asked Ronny.

He accepted another handful of Cracker Jacks.

"Back home."

Ronny spoke while munching the last of his Cracker Jacks.

At first Flo said no to a share of them, but then took a few and thanked Cameron.

"My mom saw the doctor here. At Barnes," Ronny continued. He nodded toward Flo, to include her in the conversation.

"I'm Clara," the lady said.

Ronny didn't answer, but Flo tossed her empty decaf cup in a trash bin and watched Clara, Cameron, and Ronny finish off their treat. Flo realized Clara had spoken to her.

"Your name?"

"Oh, I'm Flo," she responded.

"The doc, you were to see?" Clara asked with a soft and deep voice remindful of Merrit's. "Who might that be?"

Flo came out of her self-absorbed state to tell her medical history, or as much of it as she felt comfortable cramming in while keeping an eye on the station's overhead clock. Clara acknowledged her anxiety, but talked on indistinctly.

Of a sudden Clara stood up and strode toward the exit, drawing Cameron and Ronny with her. Intrigued, Flo followed after. Anything to fight the tedium.

"You all, come with me," Clara said.

She led them outside to an open plaza with fountains. As often as Flo passed Union Station, she'd never noticed the profusion of flowing fountains. As they got closer, Flo saw the center of the plaza was a watery theme park featuring two sculpted and stylized human-like figures, male and female.

"This is what we learned when we moved here," Clara told them.

"What's that?" Ronny asked. His tone showed he realized his mother had something else on her mind.

19

Flo heard the impatience in Ronny's voice, but she was amazed at the elegance of the sculpture and her failure ever to know about it.

"It's like something from ancient Greece," Clara explained. "If not Greece, somewhere Classical. My man and I read about it when we moved here."

"About what?" Flo wondered embarrassed to ask what she'd missed.

"The sculpture. It's by a modern guy, Carl Milles, called *Meeting of the Waters.*"

"And so?"

"See," Clara said. "It's about the rivers. This guy here." She pointed to the sculpted male figure. "He's on a rock and stands for the Mississippi. The woman's on a sea shell, the Missouri River. It's how the rivers are wed, that is, their rush to join together as one and flow down to St. Louis."

"Two as one," Flo said.

"And these littler statues, 14 of them. Water sprites and mermaids? They're small rivers that flow into the big two."

Flo and Clara studied the fountains and the joyous image they created. They faced Union Station while their sons splashed in the water, each leaving the other sopping wet. Seeing their light-heartedness, Flo thought this city wasn't as uncertain as first impressions made her feel.

"Like I was saying, me and my man came here from way far away and this was the first we saw."

"You liked it?" Flo asked.

"At first, until we saw the fountain closer up. See?"

"Show me," Flo responded. She peered at the fountain.

"Here we were, two Africans seeing these figures are copies of white folks. We've never forgotten that. We get along in this city, but without feeling we fit in. They been redlining us. Crowding us out."

The two women turned and strolled back toward the station entrance. As they moseyed along, the talk turned to health issues.

"You're younger than me," Clara said. "Cameron here is my grandson. I'm 50 and been lucky, no medical costs, don't need insurance. You have that, Dear? Health insurance?"

Flo nodded and wished to have her discarded decaf back. Again in the station, she looked blankly into the distance and at the resting express train. While Ronny played games with Cameron on the passengers' platform, Flo sensed Clara wished to talk more.

"Everybody's got their story," the African woman said. "Most unfinished."

Flo felt the silence broken, though not shattered given Clara's even tempo. Flo saw a sparkle from the lady's eyes, mixed with weariness.

"We came here from Cameroon, my man Youssef and me and our three kids, all grown, and Youssef's sister, Sasha. Cameroon. Cameron. Get it? Only one *o* in his name. We're from the English side of Cameroon."

Thinking this info between total strangers an overload at a train station bench, Flo lacked the energy to straighten up and listen properly.

"Cameroon?" Flo finally asked while trying to place the country on a mental map. "Where d'you live here?"

"We're in Hazelwood," Clara answered. "Youssef is a teacher at a college here. In African history. We've been at the hospital today, just like you folks."

"You look so healthy," Flo said to Clara.

"Not me and Cameron. We're not sick, but Sasha."

Flo caught sight of the Flier's coach lights going on. She stood up.

"Going our way?" Clara joked. "We take your train far as Hazelwood."

To Flo, what was upcoming, meaning a long hospital tale from Clara about Sasha, felt way too overwhelming. Still, Flo smiled sympathetically at Clara and the two women gathered their wayward sons off the platform.

20

What followed worked surprisingly well. Clara and Cameron sat across from Flo and Ronny. Clara told of Sasha, who'd come to America and joined her Youssef's family, but after a couple months developed an ear infection, or brought the ailment with her, nobody knew, not even the American docs. Sasha saw a local healer.

"That was some fellow practicing voodoo or whatever they do."

"What happened?" Flo asked. She squirmed hoping Ronny wouldn't hear anything gruesome. Luckily, he was nodding off.

"Why, she came down with such a pain we whisked her off to ER," Clara explained. "And there she is still. Her life in the balance."

The Flier started slowing and Clara gathered up her purse. She took Cameron by the hand. Hearing the ending of Sasha's tale would have to wait, most likely forever.

"Why, here we are, Hazelwood already," Clara said. "You folks have a safe ride."

Clara and Cameron exited along with folks from other coaches. All spoke in muffled tones, or so it seemed to Flo, who judged their modulation to be strange, even if she didn't know why, maybe because of her own sudden weariness. From the platform, Clara and Cameron waved back at Flo before meeting up with a stately gentleman, likely Youssef. The coach was nearly empty and Ronny fell asleep.

Dusk was falling when Flo saw the Mississippi below her again. The dock housed tugboats, but *Huckleberry* had moved on. Next came the *S* towns in Illinois and she made a few stray associations as they passed each one. A kid she dated in high school had once ditched her at a barn dance in Shiloh. Salem was the hometown of a long-ago politician, famous for only one line: *You shall not crucify mankind on a cross of gold.* His name was largely lost to present-day area inhabitants, including Flo.

Thoughts fought for her attention. The day had started with fear and confinement, a phrase she made up herself in a bored word play. Evening settled now into *Sweet silent thought*, a saying that stuck in her mind. Along with it came the memory of Dr. Corale with his unusual switch of conversation topics. She also recalled the chimps that dashed for freedom and almost made it. Now at the tail end came a fleeting mental image of Sasha clinging to life at Barnes. That lady's struggle would go on in Flo's mind, like a stage play with no curtain. "Unfinished," Flo said to herself. Ronny stirred and mumbled.

What Flo remembered longest about the day was shortest. In the harried pedestrian traffic near Union Station had come a quick jolt, which tore her from her self-absorbed medical worries. She remembered a colored woman's penetrating glance. They smiled as though recognizing the magic of an all-seeing eye, which spotted them in the bustling crowd and led them to each other. Flo's sudden sensation of meeting a kindred spirit remained.

"Companions, for one supreme second," Flo whispered to Ronny, but he didn't hear.

She sat then through a quiet hour reconstructing what she felt about life and people and where they were heading.

"If only..." she whispered as the Flier slowed.

At Salina, a few lights lit the evening. They flickered strongest from the Starr Hotel, whose neon insistently flashed gaudy red, white, and blue. To some that mixed symbol of European grace and American flag-waving could suggest sophisticated taste, but Flo was sure most Salina people, given access to any piece of Old World elegance, would shrug and wear it like a loose, ill-fitting garment.

Yet a sedate image of Old Europe stayed in Flo's mind. She'd once seen a painting called *Bourgeois Brussels*. It showed staid

Belgians strolling through a pristine city park. One gentleman wore a suit and top hat. His wife led a tiny Pekinese. Flo wondered how people so staidly complacent lived their lives. At the station she'd ask Merrit. He met traveling folk and knew their minds.

As for Flo, she'd need to reinvent herself in the bright cancer-free world she entered anew. She couldn't pretend she'd never been away.

BOOK IV

Home Forever

1

The evening Flier from St. Louis glided into Salina and waited while the Starr Hotel's massive sign glared down at it. *European Style,* here we go again, Flo Maxwell thought with a sigh. She and Ronny watched while a handful of freight conductors and switchmen rushed to tend the train. Flo was disappointed not to see her husband on the platform, where he had waved them off early that morning. Figuring him a puzzling no-show, she waited behind other passengers and went down the Pullman steps after them. The others hurried along the walkway toward Station Parking. Flo followed.

"There's Dad," Ronny said calmly after a while.

As if emerging from a mist, Merrit waved excitedly. The multi-colored neon lit up his broad shoulders as he looked eagerly at Flo. She nodded yes to his unspoken question, you're home and well? and they hugged. She felt his warm embrace and smelled the metallic filings and oil from the railroad roundhouse where he serviced locomotives when not overseeing his section gang.

"Yes, I'm fine! Cancer-free, that's me!" she said and they shared a joyous yippee.

"I knew it," he replied. "I had a feeling and it came true."

Merrit reached out to embrace his son with his free arm. Ronny woke up quickly in the night air and slipped away from his father's hold. He walked ahead toward the nearly empty parking lot where the family's rusty but reliable '48 Chevy was to be waiting. Merrit let the boy go so he could hear Flo tell about their day.

"Terribly nervous, that was me," she said. "Well, I mean I knew deep down in my bones I was okay, but it felt too good to be true, it was like putting a hex on myself to believe the obvious. But then Dr. Corale sat me down in his office and gave me, gave us, the good word. He asked about you."

"You don't mean it. So simple?" Merrit asked in astonishment.

Flo nodded yes, knowing he couldn't see her nod in the darkness but confident he assumed she was doing so.

"And now for you," Merrit said with a smile Flo knew would light up the night sky. Her husband seldom showed such joy, but when he did those around him felt the glow.

Flo paid scant attention to exactly where they were heading, but she wondered about the 'something' he had. Soon she saw Ronny standing dumfounded in the parking lot. He turned abruptly to his father. "Where's our car? We're taking a cab home?"

"You'll see," Merrit assured him.

"See what?" the boy asked in mock cynicism.

"Or we're walking home? Oh, that's just like you," Flo chided her husband.

Merrit pointed out at the parking lot, only partly illuminated by a few dim bulbs on wooden poles.

"Where's our Chevy?" Ronny asked in growing frustration.

"Look!" Merrit said. He produced a silvery car key and strode over to a Ford Fairlane parked under one of the few bright lights. The key shone in the light as he handed it to Flo, who saw immediately the car was robin-egg blue and sparkling clean.

"A new car!"

"Yes, I got it for you, I had to go all the way out-of-town to for it."

"But why?"

"To celebrate. I planned this. For you!"

Flo gave him a huge hug. He loosened her grasp and gave a joyous laugh.

"You know better," she continued. "Still, I see now, you didn't stay home to protect your seniority at work."

"Well, yes and no. I took this morning off to get the car, then worked overtime this evening."

Suddenly Ronny couldn't contain himself. He grabbed the car key from his mother, so all three hustled to inspect the vehicle. Ronny hopped in the passenger seat, while Merrit insisted Flo drive. She refused with a happy giggle and crawled in back. Merrit took the wheel instead.

"Have we ever had a new car before?" Ronny asked.

Merrit grinned. "You kidding? Used is cheaper than new, Son."

"You two've been talking about this forever?"

Merrit whispered like he thought someone was lurking outside the car. "A cool million it cost."

"No, don't you joke about that," Flo admonished him. "Money doesn't grow on trees. I can tell you, I saw lots today."

Flo could tell Merrit let her words sink in. She was tempted to continue about the urban poor, but she thought it best to save words. She leaned forward and asked cajolingly, "C'mon on now, how much for this lovely crate?"

"I put it on my charge account. Month by month and it'll cost fourteen."

"Fourteen thou?" Ronny burst out.

"No, of course not, hundreds," Flo corrected him. "Fourteen hundred smackeroos?"

"Yeah, I gotta admit it," Merrit said. "Got it by trading in the old crate, but you're gonna like it, Congrats again! How'd she do, kiddo? In that clinic today?"

Merrit was talking to Ronny but noticed the teenager had dozed off. Flo saw they were alone, so she wrapped her arms around Merrit's neck from behind and massaged his forehead as he drove.

"I know it's kinda low-key, this gift," he said in response to her tenderness. "I wanted you to have something for what you've been through."

"You've been with me on Barnes jaunts and know how calm, cool, and collected I appeared, which impressed nurses. This woman will come through it with flying colors, they said. Me, keeping my cool and passing for super brave. It was all playing theater. This time, though, I was a nervous wreck, filled with certainty I'd be all right, but scared to death anyway."

She talked on and on, being what any outsider would've taken for her usual manic self when that was in fact the furthest thing from the real Flo. Merrit let her talk as seriously as she wanted or jabber as she wished. He relaxed under her soothing massage.

"Forest Park. You remember that taxi ride we had once with a cabbie that knew so much?" she asked.

"Hmmm," he replied, as if that were a word.

"Our first trip there," she said.

As Merrit adjusted to the Ford's special quirks, Flo watched the road, realizing she'd also be its driver. She braced for a couple of potholes, only to feel how the Fairlane's shock absorbers took them smoothly and sped ahead. At last her talk faded to silence. Only as Merrit pulled into their driveway did she speak again.

"Wow, going off in a '48 jalopy and coming home in a near limo," she said. She uttered a subtle sucking-in sound like she was inhaling all that'd transpired in the day to let it become a part of her.

Somehow in the moment of parking and getting out of the car and smelling its splendid new-vehicle aroma and feeling its solidity and remembering the all-so human smell of her husband hugging her at the station, a working man straight from his shop, she felt this was the culmination of a day incorporating a lifetime of knowledge and empathy. In one day's swoop of train rides from here to there and back again she'd gained insights to a different way of being. While getting her things together and walking to their front door, she wondered, is our cultural blindness of our own making or a result of our narrow surroundings?

As she placed her house key in the front door lock, Merrit's voice crowded in on her thoughts.

"What else did you and Ronny do today?"

Despite her husband's pleasant tone, she felt interrupted, as if her cheerful world lost its color and contour. She thought of Ronny's teacher, Miss Jordan, who introduced new ideas to her son.

Like a flashing light, the young woman's ideas seemed simple yet profound. They brought to light a different order of values, that is, how all beings have an equal right to freedom and fulfillment, to be released from their chains.

That idea struck her as one many in Salina, herself included, would agree with in principle but be quick to reject if faced with the task of remedying injustices. In other words, after all Flo had seen and heard today, subjects Miss Jordan taught Ronny began to make sense.

"Home, sweet home," she said when she finally stepped in the house.

"True," Merrit agreed. "You've had a long, hard time of it. Now we can move on."

Marvelous, she thought, the kind of man I have, that comes straight from a roundhouse repair shop and apologizes to me like a gentleman. Yet not even he would grasp the question of presenting new ideas in a town like ours.

"Never mind, honey. I'll tell you about it when we're alone," she promised. She smiled to herself as Merrit hung her sweater in the clothes closet.

"To think I once thought," she began.

"Thought what?" he asked.

"That I'd never reach up to that hanger again."

2

With Ronny in his own teenage world, Flo and Merrit lounged in their easy chairs and talked about their day. Merrit had left the station early in the morning and rushed to neighboring Salem to pick up the new Fairlane from a dealer. In fact he almost beat Flo's train to that town. He traded in their old car. The drive home felt heavenly compared with the morning rush.

"I thought about you," he said. "My thoughts got jumbled wondering about your appointment and how we'd afford $1,900 for a car, but they were both necessary, your health and our transport. And it ended up being only $1,400."

"For sure, but it'd been grand if you were along. So much to see and do," she replied. "Sweet of you to think of me."

She described the city, aware Merrit knew more about it than her. "The faces of people and the languages we heard and exotic places. Like Cameroon. Ever heard of it?"

Merrit shook his head no. Flo guessed he was disappointed she seemed more interested in a sick woman named Sasha from an unknown land in Africa than the new Ford.

"The Zoo, then. You saw it?" he asked.

Flo didn't fully understand what she'd seen at Forest Park but was excited by the chimps anyway. "Two tried running away," she exclaimed.

"And Ronny?"

"He's only been away a day," Flo joked.

Merrit pulled her close to him. They kissed. Longer than in ages. They melted into each other so she remembered their time as newlyweds. Yet slowly she pulled away and delivered yet a quick kiss before speaking again.

"My own son knows more than me," she assured Merrit. "He's like his dad. The boy'll amount to something."

Flattered by her praise of Ronny, Merrit cracked a smile, which made him appear as imposing in happiness as he looked in anger at Doctor Sawbones. She wondered what gave him the power to impress people equally strongly in either mood.

"What impressed me most was Ronny's teacher, even if I never met her, only heard him talk about her," Flo said and hesitated. "Miss something-or-other Jordan."

"You don't remember her name?"

"Yes. Miss Jordan. I'm jealous of her maybe. She knows science. And believes in it."

"Such as?"

"The rights of all things."

"Rights?"

"Yes, to live their lives."

"So what's your question?" Merrit asked.

Flo wondered herself. She remembered thinking weighty thoughts on the train rides. Doubts and new insights popped up as the train sped from city to country. But those abstract matters faded into a palpable wonderment.

"Big city," she started in hesitation.

"You bet, lotsa people."

"I mean *new* people. Art and architecture. Fresh ideas."

"Like I said, such as?"

" Meeting of the Waters. Plus Miss Jordan's newness to the big city herself… Be on top of things, she says."

"But we're not school kids. We've got everyday worries."

"It struck me for the first time today, a whole world to explore."

Merrit studied her with a disinterested expression. He was willing to hear her out.

"Maybe that's why I got the Fairlane?" he asked. "So we could be out and about and see more? Things to touch and feel."

"Fair enough, Dear," Flo agreed. She understood her own feeling as incompletely as Merrit did, but she was encouraged they could talk about it and not argue.

"I wondered, though." She thought back on happenings that suddenly felt so far distant, as though she'd covered vast stretches of mental time in a single day. "If what I was seeing and hearing was like Dr. Corale treating battle-scarred GIs back from overseas or folks from Cameroon facing the New World. Emerging in a new presence, so to speak."

"I get it. Needing to adjust," Merrit added. "To something their experience hadn't prepared them for."

"More than that. A new way of being."

"We're all in it together. Life, I mean."

"There's differences. Guys coming back from war with both legs missing or being plopped down before a fountainhead in St. Louis, straight from the wilds of Africa. A whole new order," Flo explained. "What if somebody brought completely new values to Salina and preached them as permanent truths. If you told folks, accept them or else."

"Change or perish, is that it?"

"Something like," she said.

"We'd see what happens," Merrit said.

He stifled a yawn and turned back from where he'd been headed, unclear in his fatigue where that was. He took Flo by the hand to retire for the night.

Flo realized she was too clearheaded to abandon the day. She loosened her hand from his and remembered leaving Salina in the early morning. Now she was back home staring out at a murky midnight. Insistently, the Starr Hotel flashed its neon brightness in her mind. Unable to blink the colors away or fathom if they were real, she decided to follow Merrit after all.

3

Daily life moved ahead in Salina, or stood still. That's what Flo was uncertain about, whether her town was going somewhere or stagnating. Business and commerce set their schedules by the rhythm of farm markets and the cash flow from nearby oil fields. According to Merrit, a number of monied gentlemen even invested in the grain and cattle exchange at Kansas City. A few followed Wall Street markets and had late model Cadillacs to show for it. Even for ordinary working folks, the post-war years were boom times. The few factories in town manufactured items like automobile accessories, ladies undies, and workingmen's boots. In pre-war years those work places had been sweat shops, but the GI bill gave returning veterans the chance to educate themselves for trades, attend college, and buy homes. It became possible to earn a living wage from honest work.

Yet other facets of Salina living followed lockstep patterns, which Flo could look askance at and keep her distance from. Spread across town were taverns and fraternal clubs for military veterans. Occasionally Merrit went to a few of them with local railroaders. Flo knew he talked politics, hunting, and fishing with the boys, but he seldom came home with more than the faintest beer breath on him. From Merrit, Flo caught wind of the older vets still talking about Truman's decision to drop nuclear bombs on Hiroshima and Nagasaki years after it all happened, while the youngest had been in Korea and complained about the relentless winters, not to mention hordes of Chinese pouring across the Korean border.

"Young guys talk about meaningless orders they got to attack hills and take them from Communists," Merrit explained to Flo, who listened with interest but had trouble deciding who her husband's words came from. Merrit had been in the military during World War II, but he served at a Naval Air Station near Lake Michigan. Stateside, that is, so he couldn't have known much about combat. "Then the next day they'd retreat from that hill, but be ordered to take it again next day. The troops thought it was stupid."

The men of Salina seemed easily to get mired in repetitious jobs, so she could imagine them taking orders to run up a hill and then down it again, over and over till kingdom come. Of course, there were no literal hills on the Illinois prairie around Salina, but some men were predictable. They'd do what they were told, run headlong into an immovable barrier of any sort, or languish in its vicinity, and then complain forever about its existence.

Flo had seen Salina's religious life stand still as well. Methodists, Baptists, and Catholics had their stately church buildings. Folks flocked to those sanctuaries. Clergy sent out cries for donations, which flowed in for upkeep of buildings and grounds. She felt no sentiment among the congregations for supporting social issues and secular causes across America.

"We send our most promising youths off to college and they come back to forswear the faith," she heard a pastor lament at her and Merrit's First Methodist Church. Only those youth that attended the Christian Service Seminary in far-off Cincinnati and later accepted calls in Methodist churches received the Salina clergyman's approval.

Flo remembered when she first heard and read of social protest. The Chicago and St. Louis newspapers ran reports on a black family in the Midwest that was suing their local board of education to allow their daughter to integrate a public school in Kansas. Or was it Missouri? Flo didn't rightly recall, but Brown v. Board of Education became a major thrust toward civil rights.

"Those people are not like us," Flo's pastor declared. "They're different and don't want to live by us. It's not us whites rejecting them. It was not ordained by Our Lord to allow our inferiors a place at the table, and those folks realize it. They and the Catholics are not worthy." There weren't any colored people in Salina and no religious groups preaching non-Christian beliefs. So why the insistence on separation? Was there something inborn with humans that made anything different feel like a natural threat, even if it, meaning integration, was proven beneficial?

Flo had only been left with lingering questions. So she'd never examined assumptions taken for granted in her home area. Rule by the rich, as happened in Salina, or segregation by skin color and religious belief, as was the rule in society at large, was what she knew from growing up and marrying in Salina. At least she'd never heard anybody argue against community practice. Still, Flo wondered, if everybody in Salina looked, thought, and worshipped the same, why the strict insistence on separation? Among Salina's residents, a majority had surely never met or exchanged a single word with a colored person, let alone brushed shoulders with one.

Back in Salina, Flo remembered Sailor and Sinner. Ronny's words about them and Miss Jordan's ideas stuck with her. So one day she passed by the City Library and looked for Rousseau's book. She thought the line Kristine quoted to Ronny was in *Confessions*, but she located it in *The Social Contract*. In a hurry, she leafed through the book but read only the first sentence. *Man is born free, and everywhere he is in chains.*

Someday, she thought, maybe I'll read it, it looked like heavy going. Who was to say?

4

Few Salina residents were aware of her trip to St. Louis with Ronny. Flo celebrated Dr. Corale's declaration of her cancer-free status in the company of those near and dear to her. A small group of co-workers and relatives shared a bottle of champagne. She promised to make the most of what might come. In the months following Flo returned to her millinery work.

"Spring has sprung," a neighbor of Flo's said one day in May. He was Mike, recently retired from the postal service. He'd done most of his work sorting mail on postal cars running from Kentucky to Chicago. "It was 35 in the Windy City and pushing 70 by the time our train chugged into the last Illini station down south," he told Flo.

Mike's knowledge of meteorological differences was hard to miss, and the spike in temps hit with a wallop with May underway. Nobody could avoid it. Salina residents proceeded with commerce and work. Many eked out the barest of livings only ten or more years from the Depression. News seeping in on local media reported troubles elsewhere as well. Bus boycotts across the South caused backlash, and talk of integration of public schools led lawmakers to seek legal methods for maintaining racial segregation.

On the way home from the millinery shop one blazing hot afternoon, Flo ducked in Carnegie library, one of the few well-ventilated public buildings in Salina. She looked for *The Social Contract* on the shelves where she'd found it before.

"I'm sorry, checked out," said Sylvia, a friendly librarian and one-time school chum of hers. "Rousseau's pretty heavy stuff," Sylvia explained. She asked Flo how she was.

"How I am?"

"Oh, just you look so hot. Burning sun?"

"Even worse before I came here. Nice ceiling fans."

Flo wondered how Sylvia would know so much about a writer of philosophy. As a school girl, Sylvia ranked high on the social circle popularity charts, but showed little interest in studying. Maybe four years at college changed her. Flo had heard other ladies in town comment about Sylvia that way. Everybody has to grow up and make discoveries.

"I thought about it once," Flo continued. "*The Social Contract*, you know, that first line."

"Yes, that's about as far as most people get. Where I stopped reading, too, in college. Never got farther. It's famous for one line."

Flo wondered if Miss Jordan was another former college student that got Rousseau as a class assignment, read the beginning of *Social Contract*, and then chucked it. An easy thing, Flo thought, but a striking sentence for sure. Worth thinking about.

"Try his *Confessions* instead," Sylvia suggested and stuck a copy in Flo's hands. "Hot off the shelf."

Sylvia eyed Flo mischievously. Flo peered at the book she held and ignored Sylvia. She dived into the Intro immediately. Finally she gave in and tackled a bit of the first part. She emerged from the volume with thoughts of the author losing his mother at his birth and later being turned over by his father to live with an uncle. She also skimmed various episodes from Rousseau's childhood, such as his once peeing in a cooking pot in his home and another time framing a servant girl for the theft of a minor item Rousseau had pilfered himself. After only an hour, Flo tired of the narrative, already forgetting specific details. She put the book aside only to hear Sylvia's voice.

"Hot?" the librarian asked.

Flo nodded with a frown, as if to indicate she'd had enough. "I see where he's headed, sort of," she said.

"Yes, there he tells his story," Sylvia said. "The women he had and their kids. Out of wedlock. He took some poor woman in, had kids with her, but farmed them out. He said the woman who had his kids and her mother, too, were too uncouth to raise *his* children."

"If the women were couth enough for Rousseau, why not for his kids, too?" Flo asked.

Sylvia shrugged. "Some of his ideas got me thinking, though. How later Rousseau tried retracing his son to the adoptive parents but never found him."

Flo picked up *Confessions* again. "Like," she said in a whisper so no others would hear. "Like, I'm an honest woman. I'd never leave my son. He's my life."

Sylvia backed off a step, embarrassed. "If you're interested in the author."

"Thanks," Flo replied, as Sylvia moved on to other patrons.

Left holding Rousseau's book, Flo was unable to decide whether to re-shelve it or give it a read. *Man is born free.* So Rousseau really wrote that line, she realized. It's not something Ronny or Miss Jordan made up. She struggled for words to describe her feeling that all she'd experienced since the beginning of her cancer was vaguely constructed and open to interpretation. It seemed the world around her had become increasingly, well, abstruse, that is, full of vagueness. The environment opening up before her seemed filled with what Clara from Cameroon called unfinished stories, which lacked a cut-and-dried way of interpreting them.

At the same time there were those attempting, seemingly against the odds, to create new paths by insistent pounding at the deaf door of suppression. She couldn't escape a gnawing dislike of those who chained wild animals in the Forest Park Zoo and explained their actions as a step to preserving species or others who constructed urban neighborhoods with intentions of planned obsolescence. Or, what was worse, communities that built walls to keep minorities in or out. Those leaders struck her as confusing an *is* for an *ought to be*, an expression she heard making the rounds lately.

Flo began to understand devotion to a strict set of ideas could lead to entrapment, but if her realization of that fact was an awakening, as some thinkers called it, then awakening from what to what? She knew of no circumstances so clear-cut she could emerge from them as a new person. Despite all she'd seen and heard, she lacked a totally enlightened set of beliefs and a definite goal.

Motionless before the library shelves, she at last laid the book on a table and went to the newspaper rack. Among the mainstream Chicago and St. Louis papers, she was surprised to find the *Kansas City Call*, a Negro publication. She picked it up distractedly and leafed through the pages. Spotting an article about Roy Wilkins, a prominent Civil Rights leader, she remembered news about his work, as reported by the St. Louis *Post Dispatch*. Ardent civil rights champions, she knew, had criticized Wilkins as being too middle-of-the-road in his demands, but Flo reflected that colored workers and activists like Wilkins shared a drive to get something done. They stood for direct action.

Suddenly there appeared a headline from May 17. It too reported the U. S. Supreme Court's decision in favor of Brown over the Board of Education in that family's suit to erase school segregation. Since that issue was so in the news, Flo tried to imagine how far the decision could go in promoting equality. Unable to get her mind around possible problems, she got up to leave. She picked Rousseau off the table and put it back on the shelf. Sylvia saw her pass the circulation desk.

"Don't forget *Confessions*," she said. "It's all true, Flo."

"True confessions, huh? Thanks for the tip. Maybe I'll try it next time."

Flo returned Sylvia's friendly nod and continued out.

What is true? Flo asked herself.

5

"Did you hear?" Flo asked Merrit while they relaxed before supper. She opened a bottle of lager beer, not Merrit's usual bock, and poured half in each of their glasses. He took a swallow and let out a sigh of satisfaction. He waited for her to continue.

It was early June and summer appeared ready to burst out with a flurry of heat waves. This was the time of year that set her husband back on his heels. Rail repairs would soon be needed, which meant longer days on the section crew. The hard labor made him less communicative. Stories abounded about crews frying lunch-time eggs on blistering rails and birds dropping dead in mid-air air from sun stroke. Before crews could firmly lay railroad ties, spikes melted into black fudge and dripped on the gravel underneath.

Old-timers hanging around in the depot canteen spun tales of old-fashioned locomotives. As heat rose from them, steam roiled up till it covered the roundhouse and men were covered in it, boiled to bare bones, then laid out to dry in a merciless sun. Or those who'd been scalded by the billowy vapor grew weak and lost work hours. They littered the alleyways behind Salina's taverns thirsting for life-giving liquids the infernal heat stole from them. You could tell the sufferers by their reddish hue from where skin had boiled and then healed but never got its natural oils back. Those men were like boiled birds, never to be themselves again.

Of course, Merrit would have no truck with those vapid myths. In fact, his skepticism increased. He'd heard enough scuttlebutt in the military and it continued on the rails, so his patience wore thin.

That's where he got the nerve to blare out at Old Dr. Sawbones his thoughts about Flo's first cancer diagnosis. His nerves shattered, Merrit stood over the bungling doc, ready to take him down and pummel him for his mindless declarations. "You coulda ended up in jail for that outburst," Flo said to Merrit. Once he calmed down, her husband agreed. He spoke out of turn that time, but he was slow to learn his lesson so well that he'd never repeat it. We all make lots of mistakes again, he argued.

"Hear what?" Merrit finally asked Flo while savoring his beer and munching on a pre-meal tidbit of carrots and broccoli. The sauce covering them cooled him. Besides, this was different. The temps weren't really that trying yet, so he was ready to listen. Merrit rushed to judgment only when others spoke nonsense and pretended to know more than they did.

"About the Supreme Court decision," Flo announced. "Brown, you know."

Merrit's contorted reaction let her know she assumed wrong about his laidback mood. He was in a testier mood than she judged.

"They voted for the plaintiff," she said. "Negroes have the same rights as all other Americans. Schools can't practice racial segregation."

"So you're saying Caucasians and Negroes will be allowed to sit next to each other in classrooms and eat together in cafs?" he burst out.

Flo nodded yes. Judging from his puzzled look, she guessed his emotions ruled. Ideas seemed to knock about inside his head. She knew him so well it was clear Merrit needed for the jumble to settle so he could speak in a calm voice. She waited.

"Didn't know this would cause you such a stir. I just thought it was interesting," she tried explaining. "It won't affect Salina schools. Plus Ronny graduated."

Merrit went back to finishing his snack. He nibbled at the cauliflower and broccoli. His small beer seemed to calm him even more. He let out a sigh after the last swig. Considering his family background, Flo had no expectation he'd approve of the Court decision.

Merrit came from a dour Presbyterian clan that left Scotland for the Tidewater region in the 1700s. Once settled in the Midwest, the Maxwells lost track of where the spot called Tidewater exactly was, but a sketchy genealogy they patched together hinted at Maryland or Virginia, both of which places seemed as mysterious as the lowlands of Scotland.

What little info filtered down to them told a vague tale of how Tidewater folk sided with England during the American Revolution. To the Maxwells, formal education and history were foreign concepts. That was especially true of Merrit's parents, now deceased. Flo remembered them as conservative in every way. That started with living most of the winter months in semi-darkness to save on electric bills and extended to their insistence that America was a white man's world.

Following their Red Coat disappointment, the Maxwells' story was vague, though Flo helped Merrit trace their journey west-ward. Eventually the men latched onto railroad jobs in Illinois. The Maxwell women were quiet homemakers, but the men settled into a pattern of wildly contrasting habits. They could be forceful and combative but also ready to flee at a moment's notice. Jedediah, one of Merrit's great-grandfathers, fought for Union forces in the Civil War, but boasted in a few preserved letters of capturing runaway slaves and returning them to their owners. Merrit found another of Jedediah's letters in his family bureau. There he admitted to secret pride when Union officers reviled him as a Copperhead.

Other men in Merrit's family touched mellower chords. On their first dates as youngsters, Merrit told Flo tales of his aged great uncle, Joe Ben, a lifelong bachelor. Joe Ben never spoke directly about the he-manly railroad work that Merrit and his father Manfred followed. The military braggadocio of other men in his clan, who fought with what they themselves described as great brav-ery in World War I, was in striking contrast to Joe Ben's fearfulness.

Flo met Joe Ben a few times shortly before his death. As an innocent younger woman and newlywed, she listened to him tell without shame of fearing lightning and thunder storms. While plowing, he'd been known to abandon horses in the fields and flee to the nearest barn.

Joe Ben was the only one in Merrit's family to show an aptitude for book learning. His parents sent him off to the University of Illinois before the U. S. entered World War I. There he excelled at geology and Ag Science, but after two years he joined the US Army's field artillery units. Joe Ben showed symptoms of battle fatigue before seeing combat. In an act of mercy, a commanding officer got him transferred to the Ambulance Corps in France, but artillery barrages on the front reduced him to panic. Merrit's soft-spoken uncle returned home on a troop ship laden with soldiers suffering bodily injuries. Back at his farm, Joe Ben resumed his solitary life.

In his own right Merrit did military service dutifully and was an outgoing leader on the railroad. Given his family history, Flo was little surprised Merrit hesitated to applaud the Court's Brown v. Board of Education decision. Yet he had enough of his uncle Joe Ben's gentleness to sympathize with those who disagreed with him. On their trips to Barnes Hospital, he listened carefully to St. Louisans' stories about their city. During Flo's cancer ordeal her husband stood by her when others might have failed.

"I don't know what to say about your news report," Merrit started in after considering Flo's cautious interest in school desegregation.

His reaction to her reaction was iffy but not unexpected. Racial matters had never interested her because she'd never known anybody from another race. No Negroes or Spanish speakers lived in Salina. To her, they existed in another realm, which she saw from a distance but seldom wondered about. She had no way of knowing how they thought or what their dreams were. Perhaps Merrit was smart to be standoffish about others. He studied individuals before warming to them.

6

"I figure those people," Merrit began slowly.

Suddenly it struck Flo he spoke the same white folks' lingo as her. They echoed each other, just as her friends in Salina seemed mirror images of one another. Negroes, Mexicans, and foreigners were *the other* or *those people*, classifiable in bunches.

"Yes," Flo urged Merrit on. "What about 'em?"

"They have their own ways, they don't want to be like us," he said.

"And you know this how?" she asked. Flo knew Merrit by the habits he had from Salina, but he'd been other places, too, before they met. Like always, she assumed he knew stuff she didn't. "From the military?"

"Among other places, yes," he replied. "The colored near our base got civilian jobs there, but they never mixed with us guys in uniform. We were stationed near Chicago, but they lived separate from us. It was way up North but like deep down South, too, Alabama or someplace. They had their own foods, never went to our dances."

"But did you ever go to them?" she wondered. "They always went to you?"

Merrit stopped nibbling on his treats. He shook his head no, and would've taken a last gulp of beer, but it was gone. He looked thoughtfully away or maybe was only drifting blankly from the railroad. He rued management's lack of feedback about the work he oversaw.

'We were friendly on both sides, but never got to know each other. Not really, with exceptions."

"Such as?"

"There was Frank, a short easygoing guy." Merrit smiled to himself, drifting off into his own world. "Frank sang songs by some Negro crooners, The Ink Spots. Know of 'em?"

"Yes, you hear 'em on the radio. Least I do," Flo answered.

"Well, Frank looked nothing like a man of melody. Like I said, he was short and overweight. Was a janitor at the naval facility and had part-time work as a handyman. Taught us lots of stuff."

"Like I said," Flo interrupted. "Such as?"

"How to handle a spade. Keep your hands apart on the handle. Shoveling with both hands together'll give you back trouble from lifting."

"And?"

"Stuff like that. Practical. Believe it or not, we had young rich guys whose folks taught 'em to drive automatic transmissions. Frank showed them how to shift gears on the old pickup trucks we had on base. Military issue."

"So Frank could sing, too?"

"Not really. Thought he could. He couldn't believe us white guy's'd never heard of The Ink Spots. *If I didn't care,* he sang all the time. *Would I feel this way?*"

"*Would my every prayer begin and end with just your name?* Yes, I know that one. What I feel about you, too," Flo said to Merrit, hoping to get a romantic rise out of him. He responded with a wink, but she saw his thoughts were on what he'd seen of the great wide world in the 1940s.

"Frank sang that song over and over," Merrit continued. "He told me once about his life in Corpus Christi. He grew up in Texas near the Mexican border and had a real Mexican name, though he was black, Francisco, which was Frank in English. That's how they anointed him, but he only spoke English. He came all the way up to the Lake Michigan area to live with an uncle, got married, stayed here. That's his story. Loved those songs."

"*Would I be sure that this is love beyond compare,*" Flo sang from The Ink Spots. Once again she saw Merrit wasn't responding.

Despite claiming he hadn't known many minority workers, Merrit sure seemed to remember lots, which came as a surprise. Flo had heard former GIs seldom told their wartime experiences to folks who remained civilians for the duration. Yet here was Merrit reciting stories he'd kept to himself. He went on talking about the colored folks he remembered. They'd left an indelible imprint on him, no mistaking it. He remembered the women as charming and talented cooks in the enlisted men's caf. "Some of the dishes they prepared were pure South," he began. "Hominy grits came in more ways than we imagined. One meal was more delicious than the one before it. Only the real racists, and we had some, rejected any of it and not because of the taste. Because people they abhorred were preparing dishes for them. Like they were afraid."

7

Flo studied her husband a few minutes. They needed dinner. Ronny was due home any time, famished as any guy in his late teens. The appetizer plates and the empty beer glasses needed removing and she'd promised to scrape together something they'd like. When Ronny showed up, he strolled over to where they were sitting and looked from the one to the other.

"Hey, folks, what's up?" he asked cheerfully. When neither Flo nor Merrit said anything, he got quiet like his mother. Seeing a stalemate, Flo got up to clear the table and act like she knew what was for dinner. She rattled a few pots and pans, while Merrit began talking again.

"The guy nobody ever forgot was this pugilist from Birmingham," he was saying when Ronny stopped him.

"Hey, wait a minute, what's this about anyway," the boy wanted to know. "A boxer from Birmingham? Geez, you two. That's the stuff you talk about when I'm not home?"

Merrit gazed around the room some more, not ignoring his son's pretended cynicism but only half honoring it. Flo was surprised Merrit's stories had stayed with him. Most military vets were reluctant to dredge up stories about comrades who'd been forced on them and maybe died, or so she imagined.

"He had the strangest name, Magyar. He told even stranger stories, said he grew up with boxing champs and even fought with them. Sparred, know what I mean? This Magyar's ma was single, with eight kids and he was the oldest."

"What happened to his dad?" Ronny asked. Flo heard his stomach rumbling, but noticed the boy's father grabbed his attention. As usual, tales about wildlife or people of different stripes caught Ronny's attention.

"His pa got Shanghaied, not by men like you'd expect but by booze and disappeared. Wandered away. Magyar wasn't very sure himself about his old man. But he said his ma raised her brood as a washerwoman. He himself started work at the gym downtown."

"Doing what?" Ronny asked.

"Mop and broom. Cleaning up, helping support his six brothers and little sister. But pretty soon the guy running boxing noticed he was strong and quick and put gloves on him. He got to be a Golden Gloves fighter, boxed all over."

"And was real good, I suppose. That's your point?" Flo added on a guess.

"No, not really. Magyar got tired of it fast. Win some, lose some, he said. Not so much fun when you're on the receiving end, or the other guy runs circles around you. He always said three minutes in a ring can feel like three hundred if you're not trained good.

The ring's where you meet some real characters. That's where he ran into this thin kid named Joe, only about 17. That's all they called him, Joe. A real stud. Went by his ma's last name because his dad disappeared even earlier than Magyar's. The kid was only two when the old man lit out. His ma got married to another guy and this Joe took that guy's name, Louis. Joe Louis it was. Or maybe he just made that name up and used it as his signature. Yeah, that's how it was. They were in St. Louis for a Golden Gloves and Joe needed to sign his full name, so he figured Louis sounded good as anything.

"Anyway, Magyar started traveling with Joe Louis, was his sparring partner, part-time, when Joe turned pro. Magyar saw how shady people came outa the woodwork to get a piece of Joe when he started winning. First all the girls tailing after him, which Joe didn't mind, he got married at 19 or something, and there was talk about how he was the next big heavyweight challenger.

"That's when New York bigshots came after him with offers, sharks out to use him. So a group of Negro investors stepped in and set Joe up real nice and protected from the mobsters who woulda dumped him with nothin' to show for it. That's when Magyar fell by the wayside, he told us that at the Naval Base, which was just as well. He went home to get a real job and help his ma and brothers and sister."

"This Magyar, you believed what he told you?" Flo asked. She hoped to calm Merrit from any racy stories about loose women and the saucy world of gangland guys she'd read about in women's magazines.

"I wondered myself," Merrit said. "But after a while I believed him. I checked some of his stories with what I heard other colored guys say about life in their neighborhoods, like what we saw in St. Louis. Remember?"

"Do I ever. Are you kidding?"

"I know. You're still living with that. Aren't we all three?" Merrit agreed, looking at Ronny also, who nodded but said nothing.

"Anyhow, like I said, I believed this Magyar. Why would he be lying when he wasn't trying to build himself up in our eyes? 'I'm just an ordinary slob,' he reminded us.

"Magyar's career as a hanger-on after Joe Louis wasn't gonna get him anywhere. But he said it wasn't Joe, people thought Joe was dumb, but he was really pretty sharp and spoke up for people when he could. His business manager knew there were other colored champs before Joe that gave their race a bad name in folks' eyes. Like the old-time champ Jack Johnson, that beat all the challengers in the ring and then married a white woman to boot. No, that wouldn't work. No Negro was ever gonna get a title fight with that reputation. So the manager gave Joe the nickname The Bronx Bomber, and he fought Max Schmeling, from Hitler's Germany and knocked him out in the eighth round. That made Joe a hero in some whites' eyes. A gent who could beat up on Nazi boxers in the ring. Get it?

"Of course, Magyar was back home by then and here was Joe Louis, his ex-best buddy, a world's champ beating challenger after challenger. What they had in common was being around the military after the war started. Like Joe Louis the soft-spoken champ dodging controversy, Magyar never expressed any opinions around us. He told stories. Every time Joe had a bout, folks sat outside in the summer nights and listened on radio. There was one old lady down the street whose hero was any boxer that could beat Joe Louis, which was the same as nobody. Magyar never saw her, just heard her yelling out in the summer heat. 'Kill him! Murder that damned bum!'"

Merrit looked a bit embarrassed for using foul language before his son, so he paused, more wound up in Magyar's use of words than Flo's or their son's reaction. Merrit seemed to be looking in on himself or back at his Naval Station workmate.

"Magyar laughed as he told that story, like it was a fond memory or a joke on a kind old lady, but of course she was nothing of the sort, only hate-filled. Magyar took the woman's insults, sent out semi-anonymously in the sultry night air, with an air of humility that hid the jolt levied against his manhood."

"I understand," Flo replied. "Imagine how many times during a lifetime a person like him bears such insults."

"No clue," Merrit answered with a shake of his head.

"Have you ever been talked to, behind your back?" she asked her son.

Ronny bowed his head sadly.

Flo thought of the mixed mindsets of the two males she shared her life with. She loved a sensitive man born to a family who wouldn't curse a champion like Joe Louis or wish him ill, at least not directly, but never consider him their equal either. Magyar and Joe Louis belonged among *those people*, an attitude that sometimes clouded over Merrit's humane instincts. On the other hand, Ronny showed signs of heading in another direction. He'd learned science and believed truth mattered.

Flo drifted away from Merrit's story and tried to reconstruct, in her mind, the broader human community they lived in. Her thoughts went no further than Merrit's Naval Base, with its US Navy crew and staff of kitchen workers and maintenance men.

Abruptly she awoke from that image. She got up, gathered the family plates, and went to the kitchen. She felt no desire to make dinner.

"Okay, my men," she said kiddingly. She realized her son stood as tall as his father.

They looked up at her, wondering.

"Let's take my Ford and go for dinner."

Her men liked the idea.

8

"Like a dream, huh?" Ronny said with a teasing smile.

He was driving the Ford Fairlane, but Flo wondered if he was asking about the car or his driving. He'd passed Driver's Ed, but hadn't gotten a license yet. When Merrit asked him when he intended to, Ronny cast a quick look back at him.

"Soon as Mom gives me this buggy," he said.

"Watch the road and quit swerving," she warned him in jest. In truth, she felt more comfortable with him driving than herself, but she chose to stay silent until he took his driving test.

Though famished, Ronny kept driving. All three were content with a carefree spin before deciding on a place. As they tired, Flo suggested each name a restaurant. When none did, Ronny tooled up and down the main drag from east to west, until he turned at a wye on the west end and headed north, then back south again. They passed the public swimming pool with a snack bar and some mom and pop cafés. Then came the local country club, whose restaurant featured prime rib and steaks. Ronny drove on as teenagers did by habit.

Observing her town from the passenger's angle, Flo remembered how important her family had been in founding this community. At the same time, she admitted her family origins were as vague to her as their names. What she knew with certainty was that her forebears came from the vast steppes of Ukraine in the 1880s. But not to farm. They were town people from a bigger place called Cherkasy, but loyal to their home village, which legend said was saved from armed nomads by a girl named Smilya guiding local militia through a dangerous swamp.

After her village name was changed to Smila, a statue of Smilya with outstretched arms was erected. Emigrants pledged to carry her tradition out into the world. Whatever the whole truth was about Smila, Flo knew her predecessors were hardworking laborers, who defied the odds. Husband and wife Mykhaylo and Zenaida Vasylenko packed a small bag and followed oxcarts from Smila to Bremen, then sailed to New York. The promise of factory jobs turned to hell in Gotham's sweat shops, with summer temps over a hundred.

Undaunted, they packed up again and traipsed off to the coal mines of Pennsylvania, where they lasted "not so long," as Flo's maternal grandmother gloried in telling her relatives. By some unknown process, the wayward Ukrainians ended up following the Ohio River to Illinois, where for unknown reasons they got off the boat at a god-forsaken hole named Cave-in-Rock. There they settled in as the sole Ukrainians. Cave-in-Rock nestled between the riverbank and farmlands above. Their isolation had the advantage of making them change names to Michael and Zena Wallace and learn English.

Cave-in-Rock was perfect for river rats. It was also the home of a new puddle jumper to the north. Michael caught on as a steamfitter on locomotives. On one run he smuggled Zena aboard the passenger coach. The two hopped off at an uninhabited spot in the farmland of south-central Illinois, set up a shanty, and stayed put. When an east-west line intersected with the puddle jumper, a settlement sprouted up. The only problem was it had no name.

For years the settlement continued nameless. Yet it had two rail lines crisscrossing and a smattering of ever richer farmers. Among those was Michael and Zena's brood of Wallaces, three girls and three boys. Eventually the community got a post office, which meant it had to be called something for mail to be dropped off. And that's what puddle jumpers were, post offices on wheels. Passengers rode in one coach and postmen in another.

Eventually the oldest Wallace boy, Yure, meaning farmer, which he wasn't, won a place naming contest. He labeled the town Smila to honor his own family. From then on, Smila's people got letters from far and wide.

As far as Flo knew, that was the settlement's story. It was named after a country and a peasant village in a distant land the average Yankee hadn't ever heard of. So the community evolved to its forever name Salina. Whatever personal history Mykhaylo and Zenaida left behind on the steppes was a mystery to Flo. Theirs was a journey lost in time. The enormity of that stupendous move a quarter of the way around the globe was, in truth, something Flo never understood on even a basic level, unless the two original immigrants to America were starving at home and had no choice but to leave.

Most amazing was that the barely literate emigrants set out on a voyage and survived it. It wasn't clear either how Michael and Zena lived their lives as new-minted Americans or at what point their tongues grew rusty using Ukrainian. Flo suspected their trials and tribulations in America were legion, maybe unspeakable. She could only guess that being them in America was like her lying in agony with cancer or those chimps suffering entrapment at the Forest Park Zoo. What she wondered was: Did immigrating to a new land make you feel your soul was ripped in two? And death the only way out? Or if not death, what was the necessary way to carry on when days grew darkest? Equally mysterious was how the unobtrusive village of Smila transfigured to Salina.

Nobody in Flo's family was ever likely to understand how Smilya got to be pronounced as Salina. Likewise Flo wondered about her long-lost kin in Ukraine and their broken ties to the American relatives. Aside from tidbits of genealogy she recollected, Flo felt like a woman without a history. Never had she heard a word of Ukrainian spoken or heard aged kinfolk reminisce about the Old World. Less than four decades passed and the descendants of Michael and Zena Vasylenko knew next to nothing of their homeland and only bits and pieces about the Vasylenkos. For the generations with Ukrainian blood in Flo's part of Illinois, the prevailing culture became a layer of English mannerisms and

Anglo history watered down to standard American size. Vasylenko became Wallace in less than a lifetime.

Those thoughts floated untethered in Flo's mind for more than an hour, but the minutes also gave her time to reflect that she'd now been a Maxwell nearly half her forty-something years. Time moved on and maybe that's how Michael and Zena experienced their move to America. Why hang on to a life 5,000 miles away in small-town Cherkasy county? They left it. Now it was gone.

"We're getting older," Flo said. The suddenness of her declaration took her by surprise more than it did her husband or son, who stared ahead, hearing only the growling of their stomachs.

"If you're not aging, you're dead," Merrit replied.

"Yeah, like me with no dinner," Ronny chimed in.

Flo glanced at Ronny with a combination of irritation and understanding. She spoke up to Merrit after turning slightly his way. "More true than you know, come to think of it. Michael and Zena were alone here. Their family stayed at home, so my living relatives, if I have any, are in Ukraine."

She paused to think, but about what she couldn't decide. Was it the past that had its hold on her? Or the present and what would follow?

"How old was I when we met?" she asked Merrit at last. "Twenty-five? I typed copy at the newspaper office after high school and then came homemaking and this thing here after his sister." She poked Ronny in the ribs, so he snickered good-naturedly while pretending to lose control of the steering wheel. "It's been the milliner's for ages."

"Old ladies and their dresses?" Ronny said with a shrug. His movement was like the words he uttered, "Who cares?"

"And indeed who does?" Flo agreed in a way her son surely didn't understand. "It's a living anyway. What I earn, I mean."

"Gee, Mom, back at the pass. Our relations on your side are distant cousins," Ronny added.

"Have you every stopped to examine that, your relatives on my side?" Flo asked him. "What language they speak and where they live? Under the thumb of Russia?" Hers was one of those questions that answers itself. She waited anyway.

"You mean that the only ones I know in person are on Dad's side?"

"It's easy sometimes," she said.

"What?"

"To feel on the outside looking in. Not knowing if you're part of the whole, or if you count," Flo said with a nod.

Silence met her. So she hesitated, thought to speak, waited some more. Late afternoon was on them.

"You ever felt that way?" she asked again.

They didn't answer.

9

Ronny was still tooling around Salina, when Merrit put his foot down.

"Darnit, boy, I'm hungry!" he announced.

Ronny smiled at his father. The problem was where to calm him. They'd already nixed every hamburger joint, hash house, and pretentious supper club in town. And so came the question again.

"Tell me," Flo urged her men. "Where do *you* want to have dinner?"

Flo guessed Merrit might settle for another quick brew with saltines and Velveeta at the Eagles Club, but Ronny wasn't of age. Ronny would've had his heart set on the Victory Café, where the teenage waitresses wore short skirts. Flo suggested Matt's Malt Shop, which Ronny relished but Merrit hated. Giaconda was a spaghetti place, whose wine she loved. She didn't trust their food, cuisine they called it. A friend at work hinted at rat meat in the pizza.

"A dumb joke, but it fried me," Flo said. "Leaves the Starr," Flo said.

"So blasted stodgy," Merrit moaned.

Ronny had never been there. "Old people."

In the heyday of passenger trains, the Starr was Salina's swanky spot. It attracted traveling salesmen heading east and west. They relaxed in their Pullman cars on the way and planned sales pitches from the hotel. Businesses flourished. Next to the Starr stood a large restaurant called Forever Home. There traveling men took their meals on weekdays and staid families dined in perfect propriety of a Sunday.

The idyllic picture faded as automobile traffic grew. Traveling men increasingly drove company cars, and rail traffic slumped little by little. The numbers of Fliers passing through Salina sank from eight daily. Soon, it was rumored, there'd be hardly any. As Ronny drove toward the Starr, Flo turned to Merrit and asked, "How many trains a day now, east and west? Five, right?"

Merrit didn't answer, so Flo realized she hit a sore point.

"Four," he grumbled.

That number surprised Flo, but it seemed about right. The fewer paying passengers, the less service. Rail employees had gotten surlier.

Flo looked at her Ford Fairlane admiringly. The car ran smoothly. Before she knew it, Ronny had parked and the three were at Home Forever.

"Bachelor Hotel and eatery, for sure," Merrit said as they stepped inside.

Flo took a step back to study the vestibule and then followed Merrit past the reception desk. The hallway carpet was a fine dark green and gold, but it showed wear. Threads were exposed around the edges. Some damage was less visible because the ceiling lamps shone with uneven strength. Against the wall leading to a second-floor stairway slouched a few older men in 1930s-style easy chairs or at small card tables. Those seated at tables rolled dice or played cards, but the others looked blankly into space.

"What's that?" Ronny asked his father. "Bachelor what?"

"Flop house they call it in the city. Some real bachelors live there one guy per room, no family. Others on their last leg."

"Hanging on, you mean?" Ronny added.

"The whole locale can't be that much a downer," Flo assured Ronny. "C'mon."

Her spirits sank seeing the hotel lobby for the first time since her younger days, when it indeed sparkled and maybe did have a European touch. She'd never seen Europe and had no true idea. Nevertheless she led the way through a large portal to Home Forever, where an older blue-haired lady in a low-cut dark dress and a pearl necklace welcomed them.

"Maxwell, party of three," she said. "Near the window?"

They followed the receptionist to a table with a slick cover and three chairs. Through the window they saw neon signs advertising items from car parts to ladies' garments, the most prominent being Ollie's Styles, which Flo's millinery shop did work for. Lording it above the others was Starr's gaudy reminder of service *European Style.*

A young waitress, who Ronny said "Hi" to, gave them menus. They were typed but dog-eared and lightly smudged.

"What'll it be?" Merrit asked.

Ronny shook his head. "Dunno."

"You know her?" Flo asked Ronny and nodded toward the retreating waitress.

"Name's Katie, she's in Miss Jordan's class with me."

"And likes her?"

"I guess, but hates this place. Why I didn't wanna come here. She describes it to us."

"What does she say?" Merrit asked.

Ronny smiled. "Nothing that meets the eye."

"Then why's she work here?" Merrit wondered.

Flo smiled back at Ronny to show her understanding for his not wanting to answer. The boy smirked. "Like Miss Jordan says, it's a small town."

"Meaning?"

"Dough, if you gotta know. For college," Ronny responded, his irritation showing. "She doesn't wanna be a housewife. If I gotta spell it out."

Flo guessed he didn't want the waitress to hear and think he was speaking out of turn.

"And?" Flo asked to urge him on.

"Miss Jordan. She thinks girls get the short end."

Flo looked up at Merrit. Her husband was listening, like things young Miss Jordan said, or was reported to have said, were new to him and interesting, but not wholly clear. Somewhere, Flo recognized dimly, there was a line from a poem she read in school days, about the child being father to the man. That phrase seemed vague but meaningful, too, like so much in life, somehow you could make it mean what you wanted. Like *ambiguous*, a word she kept coming back to. But where would uncertainty get you? Surely lots of things could be understood in more than one way. And maybe Miss Jordan planted ideas in the heads of kids she knew would think them through, that is, if Flo knew what she was dialoguing with herself about. Was ambiguous a word, she wondered again? If so where'd it pop into her head from?

"Different strokes for different folks," Merrit said with a dismissive wave. Flo felt he wanted to move on from the young schoolmarm's ideas, but couldn't quite bring himself to it. Flo understood the impatience. It was intriguing that Merrit picked up by intuition the very thing Flo was thinking but didn't say out loud. What was there in being committed to anything or anyone, that made it open to question? Some new approach the young generation latched onto?

"What is there in it?" Flo said out loud. "Why keep this place open as the times pass it by? Conflicting emotions. Shut down or stay afloat?"

"Keeping folks going," Merrit answered. "Give them a place, a chance to earn some money or spend it. There're always different ways and means."

"But sometimes only *one* way?" Flo asked. "Don't we get in the habit of thinking just having something in existence means it ought to be there?"

"You mean the same as Forever Home?" Ronny asked with a tone of disdain for the place mixed with a sympathetic glance around. He made a gesture at the dining area that left Flo wondering if he disapproved or enjoyed observing it.

Flo also understood Ronny might have been doing neither, but beckoning Katie to take their order. Whether he was or wasn't, the girl soon appeared. The three agreed on hamburger steak for dinner, mainly because the other dishes seemed too fatty or too salty to satisfy Flo's dietician at Barnes Health Clinic.

10

The Maxwells dined in silence, as though they'd talked themselves out. Hamburger steak was far from a delicacy. They'd had it at home only once. Forever Home's serving wasn't half bad, though. They relished it nearly, along with the assorted steamed vegetables. If that enjoyment was due to their hunger Flo didn't consider. Between sips of her Royal Crown soda, she studied the other diners. Most were lone older salesmen, who still followed their trade by train. A familiar town and a different aging hotel each night until a long haul home on Friday evening. Those men sat hunched over their stale fare glancing at evening newspapers. Most sipped at lager beer or cheap wine.

"Strange," Flo commented. "They must all know each other, but sit alone."

"Maybe competing for the same territory or similar products," Merrit suggested. "They arrive on the 5 o'clock trains. The ones that come in late are the guys with loosened ties and five o'clock shadow."

"Five o'clock? Meaning?" Ronny asked.

"Needing a shave. Railroaders talk about them. Their traveling salesmen's adventures in the past. Some drink. Some had driver's licenses but lost 'em. Others mind their own business and call the wife each night, if they have one."

"A woman in every port? That stuff?" Ronny said out of the blue. His parents looked up in semi-surprise. "I read about it. In novels."

"Could be," Merrit agreed with an ironic smile. "They can be secretive, so you never know, about their younger days, or during the war."

A child's shriek came from a larger round table near the back, where a couple of families had finished dinner. The parents sat and talked while the small kids romped around or played tag under the table. As Katie went around giving diners their checks, the families thanked her. In turn, the traveling men looked up and spoke politely in receiving their bills. As they left, the men rolled out a few dollar bills and left tips for Katie.

Glaring neon invaded the dining room, when the Maxwells rose to leave. Katie had forgotten them, so Ronny motioned to her. The only other diner left was a strikingly attractive, stylishly coiffed woman in her late twenties, who'd sat unnoticed, or so it seemed, among the older gentlemen. After looking up from a book she'd been buried in, the woman stood up on high-heels, took her bill, and hastened to the cashier. Katie said she came to town every so often selling class rings and taking orders in jewelry stores and bridal shops. She lived a few towns over.

"Strange thing, though," Katie remarked. "Never seen a woman come here alone. She has dinner, then leaves. Must stay somewhere else, or have a car. It's bachelors, remember?"

"How are the rooms?" Flo asked.

Katie turned to go. With a quick look back, she said in a huff, "*I* wouldn't know!"

Home Forever lamps dimmed even more with the darkness, indicating closing time, but as the Maxwells made their way out, new lights came on. They lit up a corner of the restaurant, where rotating beer signs shed multi-colored hues on the shiny bar top and reflected off a huge mirror. In that guise, the bar stood out against the wall and a darkened window to the street. As if on cue, a group of husky younger guys wearing VFW t-shirts came in and grabbed a table.

"Round of brews. On me," one said in a resounding voice. He nodded at Merrit.

"Gotcha," said the bartender, who Flo realized had been there all the while, near the traveling men. He carried a copy of *Racing Gazette*. "Brews, Butch, the usual."

Butch nodded, but didn't need to reply.

11

Once outside, Maxwells realized how far their afternoon had stretched into evening. Merrit waited for Ronny to fish the car key out of his pocket, so he could drive. To stretch out her legs, Flo took a back seat. The Fairlane was idling smoothly when Ronny got in the passenger side. He'd taken a while and was looking up from the car when he spoke, like out into the night air.

"*European Style.* What's that mean anyway?"

No one answered.

"I always wonder," the boy said.

"Makes two of us. Ask the brain of the family. He knows everything," Flo joked.

Merrit took his hands from the steering wheel and turned, first toward Ronny, then back at Flo. He formed his lips in a smile meaning no secret, but common knowledge.

"*Whites only.*"

Flo felt aghast. So simple. But it wasn't. Only a hundred miles away in St. Louis races mixed or lived close by. A shorter distance away a few small towns had Negroes that played football and basketball with whites. But not in Salina?

"Aw, c'mon, Pa!" Ronny ribbed him. "Cut it out."

The uncertain tone of Ronny's voice made it clear he didn't know what should be cut out.

Speechless, Flo glanced at the Starr neon. She couldn't tell if the blinking was intended or the light was burning out. She also watched Merrit. He let his hands fall to his lap and stared ahead out the window. The car's headlights faintly illuminated dark bushes.

"I thought everybody knew."

"Knew what?"

"Salina's Sundown."

"Sundown?" Ronny asked. His frustration grew, like he felt left out of an adult conversation. Something had passed him by and that smidgin stranded him between adolescence and adulthood. Flo felt equally left out. She'd seen the Starr sign all her life and understand it only now.

"Sundown means any colored passing through Salina have to be outside the city limits before sunset," Merrit explained patiently.

"And if they aren't?" Ronny insisted on knowing. "Jail?"

"No choice. Staying's against the law."

As Merrit drove home, Flo stayed quiet. With no street lights turned on, only the Fairlane's headlights showed the way.

"Strange, this is how things felt during cancer, too, wishing for light in the dark," Flo said.

Salina settled for the night, like under a stolid fogginess.

12

In the weeks that followed, Flo tried her best to penetrate her mental fog.

"I'd never have dreamed! All the things around me," she said to Merrit after their dinner at the Starr. It didn't matter how hard she tried to understand the community. Many things had happened, yet she had so little awareness of them.

"Salina's where you and I lived the American Dream," she continued telling Merrit. "Now I wonder who that dream's intended for."

He gazed at her uncomprehendingly. "We do our best," he offered.

"Here's what I mean," Flo hoped to explain. "Why do only men stay at the Starr? There must be women equally hard off. What if their man beats them?"

Merit was slow to catch on. The puzzling gap between them remained for over a week. They'd been together continually since her cancer diagnosis, so he ought to track her thoughts as well as she did. Only when a news item about the St. Louis Zoo came on the radio one evening did she understand.

"What's this?" Merit wondered. "They're changing the chimp show at Forest Park?"

"Yes, didn't you hear what happened?" Flo asked.

Merit pursed his lips. "No, well, maybe yes," he said. "Too busy at work, I guess."

Flo realized her day in St. Louis with Ronny meant something important to her. Her cancer was banished, yet other quandaries existed. Flo regretted not seeing them before. First was the glaring problem that females were discouraged from dining alone in the depot's hotel restaurant until a brave young traveling saleswoman took it on herself to challenge the unspoken rule. Her action looked straightforward at first. No one stopped her from taking a table for herself. Restaurant management took no warning measures against her, but the more closely Flo considered the young woman's behavior the more it appeared a purposeful protest to male control. Flo wondered if similar actions took place in other towns along the salesmen's routes. If so, she stood ready to applaud them.

When Flo asked her co-workers at the millinery shop about the young traveling woman, she learned restaurants in other towns took no out-and-out steps to ban unwelcome guests. Instead they served them tough, grizzly meat and uncooked vegetables, which the outsiders were sure to leave uneaten on their plates. The owners also jacked prices sky high as an unspoken statement that newcomers weren't welcome back. Such treatment smacked of non-violent abuse.

The banning of Negroes from the Starr Hotel and the city council's Sundown ordinances also came as a shock to Flo. She felt like a Rip Van Winkle waking from a decades-long slumber. She'd always known, of course, that Salina had no Negro inhabitants. She berated herself for being ignorant of the cause. Or that she'd never even heard of Sundown towns, though born and raised in one.

Thinking back on her St. Louis visits, Flo tried to imagine how it must feel to be colored in America. Banned from a town like Salina surely felt like being shut out from home. Just as she felt an outsider in parts of segregated St. Louis, so Minorities must know their native country as a foreign land. All that despite the recent court ruling that separate but equal no longer was legal.

Equally strange for us women, she thought. We're mothers and daughters of all the men in Salina, yet we must be guarded from entering a half rundown restaurant in the middle of town? Guarded from what?

Those were questions Flo came to struggle with. Where, she wondered, were the answers?

13

Ronny fell into a late adolescent slump. He was ready for college but hesitated. He'd had it with Salina but clung to routine. He'd become competent behind the steering wheel, yet hesitated to take his driver's test. That tendency puzzled Flo, so she went for more rides with him, as a patient passenger. She let him drive the Ford Fairlane like its owner, a man who mattered.

On one drive he swung out of town and cruised through the city park. It had a long lake dug by the WPA to give working men jobs in the depths of the Depression. Merrit had worked on it. His job station had been down below a steep cliff Ronny was driving on at the moment.

"Your dad earned a dollar a day here," Flo reminded Ronny. "Hauling mud out of the bottoms below us now."

"A buck a day?" Ronny asked.

"Yes, don't be a wise guy. That bought lots of food," she explained. "You'd never know how poor people were. Some still are. Look how we've recovered. Salina's got new stores, its own radio station, and a new highway planned."

Ronny shifted down thoughtfully. Sure, this was his hometown. Yet it didn't measure up. He wanted more and better.

"This place stinks," he said with a smirk he couldn't conceal or maybe didn't want to.

Flo could've admitted to her own doubts. She was establishing a list of problems that needed tackling. They concerned her own level of awareness more than the town's. She was deciding how to live with her conscience in the face of the prejudice and inequality she'd taken for granted. Dealing with her son's new-found cocksure stance, she found herself defending things she doubted herself.

"Our town's got only one movie theater left, but tons of Bible camps and Boy Scout hangouts," Ronny continued. "All for book-worms and do-gooders. Not the place I'd send my little brother to, if I had one. And old farts running the places. I know, the Boy Scout leaders tricked me and my buddies into attending a join-up meeting when we were little. 'Just take a peek, see what fun,' they said, but they were gonna shanghai us. Me and Eddie Slaughter beat that pop stand. We clambered down some rickety backstairs where winos were peeing and swigging Mogen David, then we headed for Paddy's Pool Hall. We hid out in that joint. Salina's just as bad as every town with an *S*."

"You been there, done that, huh?" Flo asked in a teasing tone. "Man about town?"

He gave her a sly smile. "Yeah, seen it all."

"Not," she replied. She wasn't in any mood to talk to her son about what he did or didn't do. There wasn't much doubt about some stuff, though. He heard off-color jabber from local roustabouts and read between the lines. He knew what they did, or said they did. Tons of hijinks no sensible adult longed to hear about. Luckily, some teens were smart enough to close their minds to trash.

"Lots of holes in the head that think they're something special, all right. Down the way's our sister city, so-called, Salem. That's short for the earthly paradise," Flo said to change topics, at least partly, "but we all know our Salem in Illinois. About all it has is a ratty train stop. Full of chippies and loiterers."

She saw Ronny hesitate at her words. She realized she'd said those things before, so she felt embarrassed at herself. Unsure what she meant, he mouthed *loiterer* in distaste. He kinda swished the word around like mouth wash but swallowed it at last with a frown.

"You coulda spat it out," she said with a chuckle.

"Chippies are what, girls?" he asked instead.

Flo nodded. She was about to whisk the word away from him like a regrettable dust ball, when Ronny beat her to it.

"Never heard that one in the boys' locker room at school. Old-fashioned? Like outa date kinda? ... what folks said back in your day, huh, Ma?" he tried asking in jest.

"Yes, but don't say it," she warned him. "Hush!"

He screwed up his mouth to stop from breaking out in laughter at her outburst.

"The names of other towns down the road from us are from Scriptures we sigh over in Sunday school, Bible Belt stuff," she said in a mock sibilant tone to hide her mild cynicism. Flo had trouble admitting to herself that she lived among some of her state's loudest Bible Bangers, but facts were facts. In addition, she felt desperate to avoid describing to her son what certain guys did with girls in railroad station bathrooms on the sly or right out in the shameless open air. She wasn't sure what she heard whispered about here and there was even utterable in polite company. She feared how blithely Ronny might use synonyms for chippie among his buddies, given a dare in those ill-famed boys' locker rooms at school.

"How some people will carry on," Flo said to herself in imitation of tongue-clucking sewing circle women. About folks carrying on and being up to no good, the gossipy ladies and Ronny were right. Salina wasn't any better than Salem and Shiloh and Sardis or any town with a major highway running through it. She heard plenty about smut in Salina, and Ronny surely ran into some shady sides on his teenage rambles. By contrast, she knew the town's well-to-do areas had a country club aura, with prim and proper landscaping and blossoming gardens, but even there suspect stuff lay hidden behind the scenes.

Flo passed swanky areas on her way to work as a seamstress for the local millinery shop. She trimmed headdresses for Mayor Miller's wife, Dolly, and the pretty fiancée of the town's Methodist pastor, Mr. Willard. Those ladies' morals were above reproach and Flo knew their husbands or betrothed to be movers and shakers of a genteel stamp. Yet she'd heard of stag parties and rowdy sprees among members of fraternal lodges off on duck hunting trips. Traffic pileups on the way to those lodges were common and Sheriff's deputies could be slow to bother about them so the gentlemen involved got good time to clear out before sirens blared.

14

"Salina's the City of Flowers," Flo continued, though she judged by the ever slower speed Ronny drove that her prattle was boring him to death. "Our town enjoys a sterling reputation. Son, we live in a city of believers. Our preacher Reverend McElroy writes poetry and quotes his own verse from the pulpit. He says the First Christian Church spires 'send celestial sounds sailing to the skies.' A master of sounds our preacher's called. He writes lines you remember forever."

Flo thought briefly about her own words and wondered if she believed them, and if so why or how strongly, but she felt a need to guide Ronny along the straight and narrow, so she relaxed and talked on. Knowing only the workings of a couple congregations, she chose them.

"First Christian calls itself a New Testament church. What's that mean?" Ronny asked. Flo heard his confusion. She understood his suspicion about church-going grownups, an attitude inherited from his father, who gave up on Sunday services long ago but thought it a good idea their son get a chance to decide himself.

"It means our congregation follows what Jesus taught and how he lived, like in the Sermon on the Mount."

"Love thy neighbor? That stuff?"

"Yes, do unto others. That's how our town folks are."

She paused and let the fine sounding sentiments float freely around her, like verse from Reverend McElroy, until she felt ashamed for fibbing. Increasingly rich and smug burghers had recently decided by unanimous proclamation to dub Salina a city of love, not flowers, but she'd seen how bigwigs and common workers alike lived their greedy lives with more reason to fear a Heavenly Father's wrath than love Him. She wondered if God cherished the likes of her and her fellow townspeople for clutching after selfish needs and shutting others out.

At the same time she remembered her own parents, Henry and Alice Wallace. Born and raised in Salina, they were humble and hardworking. Henry was the one in her family who got away from home, at least for a while. He went off to state college but struggled with the Greek-laden campus and came home almost every weekend. Henry toughed out four years and graduated with a geology major. Flo knew him as more dedicated to classifying objects than winning new friends. So he found work as a field geologist for an oil company near home and flourished among the derricks and slush pits of their prairie home. Her mother Alice assumed the role of homemaker well enough to raise three kids, of whom Flo was the youngest. Remembering Alice made Flo feel sentimental in the years after both her parents passed away.

Flo was certain her father and mother never clutched after selfish needs or pursued questionable desires. She was uncertain how they viewed the shadier truths of local life. In specific she would now give anything to confront them and ask about the Starr's flashy neon sign. They lived long lives in the shadow of the discrimination the sign spoke of. Were her parents even aware of the sign's message, which any passing Negro traveler would have recognized immediately because they faced the bitter facts of it daily? Now, she knew, it was forever too late to ask them or others of their generation to explain where they stood on issues of race and civil rights.

While Flo considered whether she should let Ronny venture out and discover truths about their world for himself or try telling him about them heart-to-heart, she saw him grow sulky. She felt he guessed her thoughts and wanted to avoid them. He glanced her way like her play on the *S*'s in *savior* and *citizen* sounded as stupid as the town names themselves. Even so, he preferred talking about dumb stuff like sibilant sounds over the grave concerns in his mother's mind. He gave her a kind glance. For the time being his countenance said he was happy driving with a learner's permit. Facing life's serious traffic would come soon enough. Flo watched him as he switched between frowns and smiles.

"Saints and sinners, huh?" Ronny finally muttered with a wink as if testing the sounds for his own enjoyment.

His wink flattered Flo, who pretended to be angry anyway. She tried guessing his next words. "Cease your simmering," he said and laughed out loud. He also sped up.

BOOK V

West on East Main

1

"Life plays us strange tricks," MayBelle grew fond of saying. "Here I like staying put in one place but send others off to Timbuktu." That wasn't far from true either. First it was Carlos that said he was going east for home but headed west. Then MayBelle talked about her own family long ago moving up to St. Louis, though she sent both her sons back South to Mississippi. Now Charles had packed a surplus Army backpack and marched off. To where or why? Nobody knew.

That left Eddie at home with Charlene and two kids in 1954. Bonnie was six now and her little sister Helena going on four. Life was "pretty danged good," as MayBelle described Eddie and Charlene's existence. He was the head Poli Sci teacher now and Charlene directed the choir at Sumner. They carried a mortgage on a house in the Heights and drove a rundown beater, though they still commuted to work by city bus. Whether Eddie's flat feet were truly bad or an invention of Edna at the Selective Service to keep at least one of the Washington boys at home, well, that was never clear. At any rate, his feet didn't stop Eddie from dabbling at golf. He and other teachers at Sumner found a few public courses open to Negroes; so he swung away to his heart's content, always aware he lacked Charles's supreme athleticism, but happy to be accepted by colleagues and administrators alike. All in the spirit of fun. Brotherhood, some called it.

As a one-woman music department, Charlene kept the school choir singing, while also raising her daughters. She remained her level-headed self. She kept the Sumner singers and her own kids in line and generally out of mischief. Eddie, for one, had trouble keeping track of post-War time. Among non-combatants, World War II seemed like a long ago and drawn-out conflict in which one major front after another had fallen but with agonizing slowness and unpredictability. In retrospect the battles over Tobruk, Leningrad, and Berlin seemed cut-and-dried pieces in an inevitable march to victory, but at the moment of conflict the process had hung in a delicate balance. Ex GIs who'd seen combat remembered territory being torn from the enemy inch by bitter inch.

By contrast, the late 1940s and early '50s were a frenzy of social and financial success for the movers and shakers across America. Eddie found himself losing track of sequences. Events? Yes. It was easy to recall big happenings. The Berlin Air Lift, a police action in Korea, and 1948, when Truman pulled a Presidential election victory out of the hat and somebody other than the Yankees won a World Series. The order of events? Barely memorable. Mainly that the first half hundred years of the 1900s saw two world wars. In addition, Eddie's sports minded buddies in the teachers' room at school could recite the years-in-a-row when the Bronx Bombers were World champs. 1949-1953. That felt like a tedious and never ending line of Yankee triumphs. Still, the team failed to field a single colored player, a fact MayBelle in particular never forgave.

2

As for his mother, Eddie sensed uncertainty creeping in when Charles didn't come home. His brother shouldering an Army backpack and traipsing off with not much more than a word or two of farewell seemed pretty unremarkable when it happened. Now five or six years had passed. War and its aftermath had weighed on Charles's mind the same as on other ex-GIs. He wrote his newspaper articles but never landed a permanent job, not even at the prestigious *St. Louis Argus*, which he applied to over and over. The memory of Clarys stayed with him, too.

"Missing her hounded him for sure," MayBelle told Eddie and Charlene after Charles left. She seemed somehow content with the thought he'd gone off to find his dream. "After all, other men've done the same and started with less," MayBelle repeated. She wore a happy smile, which broadened as she looked out in the distance and imagined her older son reaching goals he dreamed of but never mentioned, which made him mysterious to some relatives and a glory to his mother.

"Your Ma acts delusional," Charlene told Eddie when the two heard MayBelle speak in those tones. Eddie thought better of answering Charlene. He'd tried his whole life to understand his brother fully. Clarys had seemed to remain in Charles's head hauntingly. Others had also stayed in Charles's mind, principally his military buddies, now long gone, in many cases dead. After the War, Charles missed them, even grieved for them, but in their cases he'd accepted that they were part of an irretrievable past.

Only Clarys lingered in his thoughts as a wartime experience still waiting to be reclaimed, like MayBelle somehow hoped? Even if renewing their affair was possible from a romantic standpoint, how would he affect such a reunion with his paltry resources? It was, of course, impracticable for a lone and virtually penniless man to set off from the Midwest on foot, pay passage on the Atlantic, and reclaim his lost love. Yet hardly impossible.

Time was the grand culprit. It stole one's youth, altered memories, and dulled reality. Eddie had to remind himself of time. He remembered clearly the day Charles walked away, but what year he did so began to slip from Eddie's memory. Was it the late forties? Yes, but, darn it, what year specifically? Eddie didn't recall. Surely MayBelle did.

At first he and his mother expected Charles' s separation from them to be a short-lived jaunt into some other phase of his existence. Whatever wild venture that could be, it wouldn't be permanent. Surely he'd come back. How could he not do so, given he returned from War?

MayBelle looked eagerly each day for Charles to stroll back, with his gallant sportsman's gait. When that didn't happen, she began checking the mail box for a letter or a card. Lacking word from Charles, MayBelle's moods changed from eager to anxious and then, slowly, they settled into disappointment and even despair, which only the presence of her grandchildren assuaged.

That desperation next led MayBelle to imagine Charles had gone off to find Carlos. His father abandoned the family, yet he must still be out there. Somewhere. Back in Santo Domingo? Or holed up in some dubious Spanish-speaking community? Some place. No word ever arrived to say that's what Charles was seeking, his father. Or if he sought anything at all. Therein lay the worst seed of doubt. What if he was deranged and aimlessly wandering? Eddie persuaded Dr. Russell at Sumner High to request the police put a trace on Charles. The principal did so at last. To him it seemed unlikely the police would bother looking for a lone Negro wandering the roads of outstate Missouri or farther afield.

The only report came from an Illinois state trooper. He vaguely remembered a lone colored man walking along a state highway near a small town in the Prairie State. The man had heavy Army surplus boots. Wearing a backpack and carrying a sack of fast food from a Piggly Wiggly, the man claimed he set his sights on Kansas City but, strangely enough, was heading the opposite direction. The trooper took him to a newer highway and bought him a soda. That sole lead dated from years ago.

"A miracle the trooper even recalled," Principal Russell told Eddie and MayBelle. "The trooper judged it was part of a crazy hike the man was on. He showed no hurry,"

3

Yes, 1954. No matter what year Charles walked away or why, the years would mount up. Eddie and Charlene carried on, with a workaday approach to life in Richmond Heights and Sumner High. They did, in other words, as they must. They dutifully worked and attended to their daughters, whose growth was a reminder of time. Gray streaks became more obvious in MayBelle's hair and a few wrinkles appeared around her eyes. Bonnie and her little sister Helena, or Belle for beautiful, as they called themselves together, brightened MayBelle's visage; she had a new generation she could convince to stay close by home.

Word also spread among colored communities, items of chatter that never made the white controlled media. Gossip popped up in human interest columns. Other talk filtered by word of mouth, much the way MayBelle said news spread among traveling folk about the Tulsa riots and other killings of the past. One person whispered to another across the back fence at home or someone else mumbled to a stranger over the bar of a local tavern. Most talk faded away, but some stuck in folks' minds. Gradually Eddie caught bits and pieces of a tale he whispered to MayBelle. Eddie had no idea why he spoke so. Maybe it felt like an open secret.

"You know, Ma," he said softly.

"No, what, Son?" she urged him with an eager smile and an ear tilted his way and so closeup he saw the white roots in her hair before him.

"There's talk in these parts of a miracle, kinda," Eddie continued. "They say there's this black dude. That's what he calls himself,

Black Dude, a Santo Domingo guy, that's emerged down in Fort Worth, in Texas, as a deputy sheriff and the official consult for the Dominican Republic."

"Consult? Meaning?" MayBelle asked in confusion. Eddie saw he'd caught her ear and real good, too, though she feigned a so-what attitude.

"If it's true, it's Dad," Eddie responded. "Plus, don't you see, they never let folks like us in jobs like that. He musta improved his English a blasted lot, and they use him to process Spanish speakers' requests for visas and stuff. He'd have to know both lingos real good."

"But why him? Carlos?"

"Maybe they got nobody else there from Santo Domingo. He popped up out of nowhere before. Like how'd he ever get to Tennessee and meet you?"

"Yes, Lord. What does he call himself down that way anyhow?"

"Who knows? It's only rumor. Others say there's a guy like that in Kansas City, too. Something about this old guy, who got this job, the dark man that spoke Spanish and came from who knows where."

"So my Carlos made a name for himself? I don't believe it. No, not my man," MayBelle argued.

Eddie wondered why MayBelle refused to believe the story about Carlos when she could hold onto other unlikely beliefs about his wanderings. Or was she, in truth, convinced, deep down, that both her husband and son had met their end in deep, dark mysterious ways?

"Well, whatever," Eddie concluded with a shrug.

"Yes, for sure," added Charlene, who joined them. "If Charles went looking for his dad, we have a puzzle. Makes no sense."

Eddie scratched his head. That's how it always is with those two, he thought. He turned to MayBelle.

"Like I always figured about Dad and Charles," he explained. "Where they're concerned, never the twain shall meet."

"And they loved each other so much," Charlene agreed with a gentle but resigned shake of her head.

"But will we ever find them?" MayBelle asked, her despair showing as openly as her hope once had.

"Or they us?" Eddie asked in equal bewilderment. Even as he spoke, he guessed it would someday fall on him to find the answer.

4

A nd so it was. Years of wondering about his long-gone big
brother led Eddie to trade in his old beater and buy a new
orange and black Ford Fairlane with his ma's cash and drive
it himself.

Naturally Eddie felt uncomfortable explaining why MayBelle
paid for a car that fancy but didn't know how to drive it or plan
to learn. The matter boiled down to the simple soul of Eddie
Washington, who felt excitement equaled big adventures on the
open road.

Reason told him temptations like that led to trouble, but his
passion for cars left rationality in the dust. Eddie saw guys in the
movies with personality flaws, like chasing ladies. Temptresses they
were called, who the gentlemen knew were out of their class and
surefire jezebels, but the men couldn't lay off. Eddie's temptress was
flashy cars. Charlene kidded him and MayBelle wagged a warning
finger any time the motorized jezebel from Jackson came up in talk.

Eddie couldn't live down that bad rep or resist MayBelle's
Fairlane, which he drove like his own. Being in the Fairlane made
him wonder about the mystery that wouldn't vanish, Charles. Once
he and Charlene piled Belle in the backseat with MayBelle and
drove out to Fort Leonard Wood. Another time they took a shorter
route to Jefferson Barracks. Both places had been short stops on
Charles's military journey.

A third time, Eddie talked a couple of fellow Sumner teachers
into a quick dash southward. They drove overnight to New Orleans
for Mardi Gras, hanging out for an entire night on Bourbon Street.

Eddie remembered a similar jaunt during his college days. He and a gang of dorm mates took buses to The Big Easy. The music intrigued him more than the visual attractions of New Orleans. On their return trip, the three took it slower and saw the flatlands and cotton fields of the Mississippi Delta. Eddie remembered his mother's tales of life on the Mississippi River banks, which he saw she described pretty darned good considering she'd never been there.

Yet those trips got the Washingtons no closer to Charles in the mid-1950s. What events meant to that gent was anybody's guess. He shone brilliantly in some things but flopped at others, in the world's eyes anyhow. In time Eddie saw his own shortcomings. He became aware he and Charlene had spent all their recent energy on raising two daughters and marginalizing other concerns. Even Eddie's love of nice vehicles took second place in a pinch to teaching and staying close to home.

"You all know this old lady'll enter her sixtieth year pretty soon," MayBelle announced one spring day. Indeed both had watched MayBelle show her age. Only after his mother made that comment was it clear time was wasting. Eddie decided to go out and find Charles as a gesture to his aging parent.

He talked with Charlene by candlelight one night, all for privacy. The result was a plan. Plain and simple, MayBelle could babysit the girls, which she loved doing anyway, and Eddie and Charlene would go looking for Charles. They'd head east. They figured out, with MayBelle's help, that it was seven years since Charles disappeared. If they found him, it'd be the happy result of Eddie's own vain and foolish fancy, done for his mother's sake and a sense of closure as well.

And so one day in late summer 1954 Eddie and Charlene hopped in the Fairlane and went off looking for that brother of his. Who's to say, Eddie thought, me driving off like this, as nuts as my father and big brother before me. At least I have wheels. Hopefully all my marbles, too.

5

"Look at her," Eddie bragged to an attendant at the local Mobil station. "Colorful body. White wall tires. Snappy chrome stripping, too. V-8 engine. Let's go, huh?"

The attendant, a grinning kid, studied the Ford and nodded. "I see that." He hesitated. "Mr. Washington, sir. Albert, that's me. I was in your class one year."

"Yeah, sure," Eddie said.

"Not many new crates in this neighborhood," Albert said.

"There's a story here, my older brother," Eddie said and Albert nodded, like he didn't know the story but understood it was a big day.

"Not many tichas stoppin' here," he said, chuckling.

"My big brother, he did his duty. Came back from the last war," Eddie explained. "Then one day he set off, on foot."

"Where to?" Albert asked, partly out of a newfound interest but also in confusion about what his high school instructor was rambling on about.

"Who knows. London maybe. That's what me and the wife gonna find out."

Perplexed, Albert gazed blankly at the Fairlane. He kept his gaze on the car as much to avoid Eddie as admire the vehicle. Finally the boy flubbed out a laugh he couldn't stop. He glanced merrily at Charlene.

"On foot he say? Across the ocean? A whole ocean?"

Albert waited for an answer. When none came, he flipped the rag he'd used to check oil on the Fairlane at Eddie, like he was aiming for some buddy's rump in the boys' locker room at school.

"Believe it when ya see it," Albert said at last. "Pay inside, man."

Eddie got back in the car and rolled down the window. "Take it easy," he said to Albert and began backing out of the station.

"Good kid, huh?" Charlene asked him.

"Has a sense of humor."

"Yes, especially when you didn't even recognize him."

"You're kinda right, but there wasn't too much to remember."

"Why not? A slow starter?"

"I never had him in class. But it started coming back to me when he said his name. I only got to know him by the sound of the marbles he used to roll down the aisles in 8th hour study hall. I wouldn't ever've got to know him but for reporting him to the principal's office."

"Guess the marbles were a way of begging for attention?"

"Most likely. He ended up telling me about this brother of his that kept threatening to go downtown and jump off some insurance building tower."

"And did he?"

"What?"

"Jump."

"Doubt it. I used to see him around town before I ever knew Albert. Hanging out."

"Looking for himself maybe? Like Charles, a younger version?"

Eddie shrugged. He knew only some aspects about Albert and his brother. The older boy was the more troubled, while Albert rolled with the punches and saw the droll sides of life. He knew how to talk in a relaxed way with an older person and even flip a greasy gas station rag at him.

As Eddie drove off eastward toward the Illinois side, he thought much the same about Charles and himself. As everybody who knew them agreed, Eddie lacked his brother's all-around gifts. Yet in the eyes of relatives and community, he was the one that succeeded at work and starting a family.

"I wonder where he is?" Charlene asked out of the blue.

"My brother?"

"Yes, is this a wild goose chase?"

"A fool's errand maybe," Eddie responded honestly.

"I know why," Charlene comforted him by softly patting his hand that rested on the gear shift. "Why you're doing this, I mean."

"And then?"

"For your ma, to end her longing," Charlene said calmly. "Yours, too, maybe."

6

As Eddie guided the Fairlane onto U S Highway 50, he assumed a calm mien. Traffic was heavy in downtown St. Louis, but he steered through it smoothly. He thought more about his mother and brother. The cadre of distant aunts and uncles and their many kids were a loose fitting outer garment. They sheltered MayBelle from too big a dose of the outside world. He remembered a summer day in childhood at the house of Rudy, one of his distant cousins, a teenager then. Eddie was on the lawn while Rudy, a husky and loud mouthed youth, played rubber gun tag with his buddies.

"The idea was to shoot your enemy with thick rubber bands wrapped tight around a wooden toy pistol. The rubber band had to be stretched real tight around the revolver and shot off at a high speed. It really stung if a guy got hit by a bull's eye. Rudy was in big trouble. His pistol went unloaded and this other guy was chasing him around an old shed," Eddie told Charlene.

"Rudy threw me the pistol and a rubber band and told me to 'load the darned thing!' while he circled the shed. Those guys kept running round and round. Rudy trying to get away and the other guy wanting to unload and splatter him real good but never getting close. Every time Rudy ran past me, he shouted at me to load the darned thing, but I was weak. I got more frantic every time they rounded the shed, but I never got it taut enough to fit the pistol. Rudy yelled at me like mad. 'Dammit, Eddie, load the pistol, he's gonna get me!'

"And eventually the guy got him, put a red mark on his forehead with the rubber band, and there I was, this little weakling sitting in the grass, a failure, and Rudy fuming at me. 'All your fault!' he shouted. 'If only you were Charles!'"

"So how'd that turn out?" Charlene asked. She welcomed a chance to forget the traffic noise.

"Nothing turned out," Eddie answered. "The guys wandered off. Rudy tossed a broken rubber band at me. It was still there when I moved on."

"And, dear, what am I to understand?"

"You know. The others were bigger than me."

"And that impressed you?"

"Like any little kid, I wanted to tag along but couldn't keep up. Not making it, but trying."

"Other times, too, then?"

"Yeah, I wasn't learning to swim, but big brother could. So once Ma told him to teach me. He hated it."

"Sounds scary to you, even now. Why?"

"Because Charles learned the hard way. Carlos took him to a river and threw him in. That's how he learned. Toss 'em in."

"So that's how your dad had it, too, growing up? Sink or swim?"

"Maybe," Eddie answered with a shrug. "Lucky for Charles. When Pa threw him in, he hurtled through the air, Ma said, but he took to water like a fish. So there you have it, suddenly he was a swimmer."

7

As Eddie spoke, traffic was thinning. He gripped the steering wheel hard with both hands and grew quiet, which surprised Charlene. She obviously expected him to lean back and tell her even more. Instead he concentrated on the road. After a while he realized he was dreaming of those days when his brother behaved like a boy in his teens acting snotty. In letting his mind drift, Eddie lost the thread of his own story.

"So your brother tossed you in a river?" Charlene asked and yanked him back to the present.

"No, he didn't chuck me in. He walked me to the deep part, decided I wasn't gonna learn, and swam back to the bank. A buddy of his brought me in and they took off."

"So he wanted to escape little brother. I get it. So how'd you learn?"

"Never did. Not very great anyway. Tried at college, was required to get a Phy ed credit. They passed me without ever checking if I knew how. Lifeguards laughed while I splashed and tried not to drown."

Charlene dropped the thread and sat as still as her husband while a long stretch of highway lengthened out then led to a bridge. Eddie drove out on it and the Mississippi appeared below them.

"Eads," was Eddie's only word.

"Eads Bridge?" she asked.

He glanced her way and said, "My point was how everything I did with Charles left me in second place. He had the talent. But we get along."

"Get?"

"Get. Got," Eddie said with a shrug.

"So you figure we'll never locate him?"

Charlene gazed down at the broad River and shuddered.

"After all these years? Looking is our idea, not my ma's. Glad we're together, you and me."

"Why so pessimistic?" Charlene asked.

"I know my brother."

They were nearly across the bridge when Eddie made a sweeping gesture at the water with his free right hand.

"Don't fall in," he kidded Charlene. "It's deep and dangerous. I can't save you."

Charlene nodded at his dark joke. She looked out at the Illinois side.

"East St. Louis?"

Eddie nodded yes, while thinking how to describe it to Charlene. "I'll show you," he said instead.

8

"For finding Charles we have a plan," Eddie had told MayBelle before they set out from Richmond Heights. "Sort of."

In truth, he barely knew. The Bureau of Missing Persons wasn't about to waste time searching for a shell-shocked colored man. Moreover Eddie himself knew little about the flatlands north and east of St. Louis and Charlene even less. To rely on they had the past report about a state trooper meeting a Negro wanderer on Highway 50, a road guide called *The Green Book,* and their own inventiveness in prying info from strangers, who may or may not have good memories.

Driving into East St. Louis, Eddie came to terms with a silent funk he'd fallen into while crossing Eads. On the bridge he felt in two states, which in fact he was geographically, Missouri and Illinois. Once in Illinois he couldn't rid himself of that divided sensation. He'd talked so much about Charles he began confusing himself for his brother. After pretending for nearly a decade his brother would return on his own, Eddie forced himself to believe he had to find Charles and convince him to come home. The challenge now felt impossible. He'd try for their mother's sake. Tugging at Eddie's heart strings was also a burning desire to drive the Fairlane and show it off. He explained that selfish lust to Charlene.

She listened patiently while gazing around at the ramshackle town they'd entered. It seemed an extension of St. Louis but more down at the mouth. Homeless peopled the streets.

"Yes, I see that," she said to confirm she was listening. "Are you sure that deep down what you really want isn't to show the white world you're worthy of them?"

Charlene sounded sensible. It felt natural a man had a sense of self and desired to show it even in a base and worldly way.

"Henry Ford was as big and haughty an Anglo as any other," Charlene continued. "Why emulate him by driving his auto? A Ford? Not many of his kind are around in this neighborhood far as I see." She nodded toward the streets of East St. Louis.

Despite her words, Eddie relaxed behind the wheel, the way he'd tried in highway traffic. He reminded himself the plan was to search for Charles. Once he decided against letting MayBelle spend the rest of her life pining for two men in her life, who disappeared, he'd sat long nights and brainstormed, not very ingeniously, about how to solve the problem.

In fact, Eddie, Charlene, and MayBelle had no true idea how to conduct a search on their own. Neither did they have the cash for a private eye. What they knew "for certain, sure," as MayBelle put it, was that Charles wandered off to the eastward wearing Army boots and carrying a duffel bag, which she thought was Army surplus but couldn't swear to. What Charles had hoped to find anywhere east of St. Louis was a mystery not even his own mother could do anything but shake her head at. A wild plan, which only a guy who survived Normandy could think up?

To rehash. Eddie decided he and Charlene would leave the kids with MayBelle in Richmond Heights, which is exactly what they did. They'd cross the Mississippi taking the straightest shot east, meeting people and asking what they remembered of a solitary colored man with athletic build and military backpack, well-spoken, never thumbing rides.

"Who's to remember that far back?" MayBelle asked.

"We'll see," Eddie answered. "Do our best."

9

What he and Charlene saw before them now was down-town East St. Louis, which he'd passed a few times in his youth. Eddie pulled off at the base of Eads Bridge and tooled slowly around town. Places of business stood shuttered and abandoned as far as the eye could see. Several buildings, which must once have been stately office complexes, were hollow and blackened shells. Who could say if that was the work of arsonists or faulty wiring.

While Eddie looked for a gas station or any open forum to ask people about his lost brother, Charlene studied the garbage-strewn streets and a railroad crossing overgrown with weeds. At a corner, occupied mainly by a few loitering youth, stood a food market bearing a once imaginatively painted sign picturing smoked sausages, cold cuts, and ravioli. The word *Charcuterie* was written in fancy italics, now faded and peeling off the wall. Judging by the garbage out back, Charlene and Eddie guessed the business had only been a convenience store used in a last-ditch effort to rescue the neighborhood from visual decay. Scavenging dogs emerged from behind the building and rummaged through refuse left by the absent owners.

"You know," Charlene said. "Once in college our prof had us read some text or other."

"Yeah? What about it?" Eddie asked while gazing out at the ruin around them and searching in vain for a place to pull in. "What text?"

"I think it was DuBois. They were at the riot here your ma talks about, East St. Louis race killings."

"Yes, 1917," Eddie said. "I remember her talking about that. Dr. Russell mentioned him, remember?""

"Let's say it was DuBois. He described this as Urban Hell."

"That's what it is."

"I never realized."

Eddie drove on down streets nearly deserted and lacking the vibrance he knew across the River. Parts of St. Louis could look bad, but lacked the collapse of the place where he was now. Eddie slowed even more to check their exact location. Broadway and Fourth. He continued onward until he spotted more stray dogs crossing a street. He slowed and then sped up. Other dogs were lazing at the edge of a thicket. They were sleek with short black fur and an alert appearance, which meant well-fed. He guessed there were ample dumps to forage at, but lord knew what health the mutts were in. A veterinarian would likely blanche.

"There must be some businesses open," Eddie mused. He spoke as Charlene pointed at a small shop advertising groceries, money orders, and gas *for cheap*, whatever that could mean. Eddie remembered Charles once telling him those stop 'n shop stores often offered cheap white bread and chips plus soft drinks. No nutrition, but they made their dough on drug sales in the back room.

"The breakdown of City government cuts the police force, so drug deals go down under the authorities' eyes," Eddie remembered Charles explaining. It was the same in Jackson, Eddie later learned from guys that roamed the streets in Mississippi.

With those thoughts in mind, Eddie turned into the store lot and parked. He decided if he was going to buy anything useful it might as well be gas.

"For cheap," he reminded Charlene with a humorous glint in his eye.

He let Charlene out and filled the tank himself. When he went in to pay, he found her talking to a white-haired man, who was standing near the door to the back room but retreated to the cash register when Eddie got ready to pay. He handed over change to Eddie but kept talking to Charlene. Eddie understood she'd already asked the man about his town's past and he knew it inside out.

After a while the clerk looked at Eddie studiously. The intelligent sparkle in his eyes contrasted to the several days of white stubble on his face and the faded, poorly patched bib overalls he wore over a yellow-and-blue t-shirt.

"Yessir, Layney Comber. At your service. As your lady was asking about, 1917? Yes, ma'am, I been here ever since then. An early teen in those days."

"You weren't hurt in the riot? Whadda you remember?" Charlene asked persistently so Eddie understood she repeated an earlier question.

"Right there on Broadway and Fourth, that you'uns just drove past. There were hundreds shot, clubbed, and burned to death. In plain sight. Layney, spelled with a *y*, that's me, I was a schoolboy and me and my pals run all the way downtown to see what the commotion was. There was fightin' all over. Soon as we seen it, we hightailed outa there. They's setting fire to people's houses in broad daylight and them inside screamed for their lives."

Eddie saw Charlene listening closely while he worried about their Fairlane left by the gas pump. "But what caused all that?" she asked.

"Messes of businesses were goin' full-blast in those times, day and night, three shifts, seven days a week. Then we entered World War I. White guys got drafted and sent off to France. Companies here brought in whites from other countries to fill their places," Layney was explaining when somebody honked for Eddie to move his car. He rushed out to pull the Fairlane off to the side. Charlene stayed to listen.

10

Convinced Layney would be far into his story by the time he returned, Eddie was surprised to find the older man still on the same point. "Those factories was sweat shops but they paid good, my pa always said. He oughta know, he worked there. A fella could buy lotsa booze with a day's wages, but not him, he slaved away but ruined his back," he explained.

"What about the shifts?" Eddie asked eagerly. "What happened there?"

"Got real complicated. Newcomers, the immigrants, I mean those new from other countries, took over jobs the regulars left when they went to war. The new guys wanted more money, so they went on strike, but most couldn't speak English. Bosses refused to pay more. So whadda you think Whitey did next?"

Layney looked at Charlene and Eddie like he expected an answer. Like what did they expect one group, the tight-fisted owners, to do against another gang, the unwashed immigrants, with no English, rising up and demanding money?

Eddie hesitated.

"Scabs!" Charlene spoke up quickly. "Companies brought 'em in."

"You got it, Sister," Layney answered. "Striking newcomers hated coloreds for taking jobs they left to go on strike. Added to that was some of the ordinary whiteys started coming back from fighting in France and wanted their jobs back, but they found poor white immigrants or lowly black men at work on jobs the returning white men said was theirs. All three groups went at it, roaming the streets with blood curdling cries.

"You shoulda seen 'em, stabbing and raping and killing innocent ladies just for the color of their skin. They threw screaming
babies in the fire. The rioters ran over men in the streets with their
tractors. Locked families in their houses and barricaded the doors.
Set fire to buildings.

"Me and my buddies hid in the ditches and watched. They said
40 coloreds was killed and nine whites, but it was worse. Hundreds
murdered. A killing rampage. Savage grunts in foreign tongues. One
down-and-out race murdering another looking for their rights, and
cold-blooded."

As a youth, Eddie heard MayBelle tell of that massacre, but he
kept in mind his own gnawing suspicion, *My ma wasn't there, what
can she know? All hearsay on her part.* Now here Eddie was listening
to a gentleman, who *was* there and knew what he saw. Layney's
thin fibrous body lent a deep tenor to his voice and he rolled his
eyes at the lasting image of one subjugated group butchering
another for a few added coins. He gained an added emotional tone
in describing the boys in his group lying in a sewer and ducking
under the water as hordes of knife and club wielding workers ran
by killing other kids.

Layney described three mad workers pulling one of his school-
mates out of the ditch, clubbing him, and then dunking him in
sewer water. *Yes, he was there. He saw the murders, smelled the burning
or putrefying bodies.* Eddie imagined Layney placed—by what force,
fate?—at this very spot all these years later as a teller of real tales
clarifying what outrages took place against his fellows.

Once again Eddie felt torn between opposing forces. One said
stay and hear more. The other said, *Ask him about Charles!* If any
man was in downtown East St. Louis and saw Charles hiking down
off Eads Bridge and maybe along this very street, it was surely
Layney Comber. He, who seemed to know about everyone passing
this way. So in spite of the info Layney gave out about 1917, Eddie
kept looking to ask him about any lone wanderer passing by here a
few years earlier.

"Yet, you folks got something else on your mind, I can tell" Layney suggested at last. "Looking for something? I can always tell."

Charlene glanced down in pleased embarrassment at Eddie's clumsy attempt to ease his way in. "My husband wonders how to ask you without coming out of the clear blue."

"Ah, yes, like that, huh?" Layney said with an understanding of the male wish to seem in control. "Oh, yes, fellows looking for something long lost, or never found?"

Knowing himself cut off at the pass, Eddie blurted out, "My brother, long gone! Gotta find him."

Graciously Layney sat them down in his half-dingy store, or at least the one he managed for better or worse, and asked about their search.

"We started across the River, came here. Any lone wanderer?" Eddie asked.

"You came to the right place for that. Yesterday or today?"

"A few yesterdays."

"How many you mean?"

"Closer to the end of the War than to now. My big brother Charles. A timeless guy. Was at Normandy. He walked away, the same way our dad did farther back."

"Runs in the family, huh?" Layney asked.

"No, not him he's staying home, with me," Charlene answered moving closer to Eddie to show their ties. "I roped him in."

"My brother, he walked away from home. Pretty much the way he left for the War, but he came home from that."

"But not home now?" Layney asked with a nod to show he already knew the answer.

11

A brief silence followed. The three looked down like mourners for the fallen dead, but Layney quickly spoke up. "He's in delayed reaction. Guys go a long time like normal. Then it hits 'em. Like mutts. I found a stray dog once and raised him. Doolittle, his name. A good boy, strong, street smart. Ran circles around mutts raised in homes, but after a couple years this Doolittle started bitin', especially fat guys wearing warmup jackets. I figured whoever beat him musta looked like that, fat and outa shape. The vet said dogs has been abused as pups can act like that, obedient till about three. Then the bad they experienced comes out. No way you stop it or control it."

"So war vets?" Eddie asked.

Layney nodded. "Dogs are never the same again."

"Men?"

"Some normal. Some like dogs, you can never say."

"Say what?" Charlene wondered.

"What's wrong with 'em."

Layney's sympathetic mien faded to a sad face, which said been there, done that. Whether the experience meant military combat for Layney or 1917, who was to know. After a bit he nodded toward the street and made a jerky motion with one hand.

"Seen lotsa souls wandering. East or west. Some back and forth. Others following the River. Up and down."

"What about a tall, lanky fellow with Army boots? 'Bout like you, lots younger," Eddie added.

"Looking for?"

Eddie shrugged. Charlene raised her eyebrows.

"Dunno," Eddie answered for them both. "Finding our pa. Or a girl. Two girls maybe. You know, that the war stole."

Layney sensed he'd coaxed what he could out of his visitors. He ran a hand through his thick gray beard. "There was a gent came by here. Talked about out West. He sounded educated but confused. Better yet, undecided."

"About what?"

"Didn't say. He camped out hereabouts. Needed something. Somewhere. Didn't stay long."

"Why not?"

"Stay here?" Layney asked with a new smile as he waved dismissively at the city outside. "You kidding?"

Like others leaving East St. Louis and shaking off the dust behind them, Eddie also would've left town. Then. At that moment, except Charlene shook her head no.

"Remember," she said. "*The Green-Book?*"

Out of her purse, she produced a tiny paperback. "*The Negro Motorist Green-Book, 1940,*" she read to him in full. "I ordered it as a surprise."

While Layney patiently looked on, Eddie cooled his heels. He put his eagerness for testing the Fairlane on hold while Charlene leafed through the pages. "This copy's over ten years old and doesn't say much about this state, outside of Chicago. See, only 48 pages."

"But a gold mine of info," Layney added. "You can't go wrong with it. It was put together in the 1930s when colored folk started getting enough dough to buy autos. They needed safe places to bed down where white folks refused them."

So much for Layney. Charlene did the rest by showing her husband the book.

"We're not wanting a place to stay," Eddie explained. "Just ask."

"Yes, and that's what we'll do," Charlene insisted. "But we gotta sleep. This Mr. Green lists places that'll put us up. Look, page 11. A hotel and three tourist homes listed in East St. Louis. Imagine, if Charles stopped at one of them?"

"Sure enough," Eddie admitted. "You got it!"

"Wanna try?" she asked.

"Let's go," he said.

Charlene stopped him.

"Whoa," she said loudly. "We gotta figure out where to. See where I marked. Board Street. Two places."

Eddie took the book. "What page?"

"You know that street?" she asked Layney.

He nodded yes.

"Heddy Charteusse at 1484 and Maggie Mann at 1509?"

"Know them well," Laynie replied. "Splendid."

Pen and paper in hand, the aging store manager wrote out directions to the boarding houses.

12

Charlene nudged Eddie out the door. Happy behind the wheel, he carefully maneuvered one empty street after another until Charlene spotted Board Street, which had several blocks of white frame houses. All were apparently former company homes for some giant corporation that fled town leaving only crumbling brick walls of a once-thriving plant. Whether the present residents of Board Street were former employees or recent move-ins to the low-rent neighborhood was hard to say. Their homes were well-kept but aging.

"Heddy Charteusse?" Charlene asked when a middle-aged woman with a skeptical expression answered her knock. Charlene knew her own short-sleeved summer dress spoke of a lady with a steady income.

"Who wants to know?" the woman asked.

Eddie stepped forward so he and Charlene explained what brought them to her house. The woman listened, but shook her head no.

"I'm Hedwig. Heddy was my ma. She passed away last year. Just me and my man here now. And our boys."

"We thought it could be that someone remembered my brother. A tall lanky guy?"

"Maybe my ma, but she gone now. We not been rentin' out since she passed. You folks be well."

A block farther along stood another house, this one bigger but not white. It had yellow Depression era siding. This time Eddie knocked. Two elderly women opened, one tall and erect, the other shorter and stooped. The short woman held the door open.

"Mrs. Mann?"

"Miss Mann," she corrected him.

Charlene stepped up to introduce herself and Eddie.

"I'm Maggie. My sister's Mildred," the woman at the door said nodding toward the other in the background. "Won't you come in?"

Eddie and Charlene found a comfortable living room cooled by a table top fan. Maggie and Mildred sat in its coolness and heard Eddie's tale.

"Of a prodigal son," Mildred spoke up first. "Like my boy Algene. He went off to the Army. Making a career of it. Sends us cash, like for this fan."

"We get lotsa visitors," her sister added to keep the conversation on track.

"Yes, I know," Mildred agreed.

"It's this gentleman's brother they're askin' about," Maggie reminded her sister. "I been here longest. Mildred only moved in when her man died. A pity that."

The crux of the matter was that folks stopping were motorists, of a genteel sort with a destination in mind and heading straight for it, no wayward wanderers, as the sisters explained, folks with an appreciation for a cooling drink and fine music on the Victrola.

"Like The Ink Spots?" Eddie asked.

Maggie looked up at him in surprise but answered only in brief.

"Not many wanderers on foot," she said with a touch of philosophy in her voice. "Men of that sort act and sound lost."

Eddie's spirits sank, but they rose when Mildred left the room and came back with coffee. In silence the four sipped at their cups. Eddie had trouble deciding which was slower going, the clock or the coffee. He took his time finishing the huge cup of light brew. He was nearly ready to say so long, when Maggie spoke up.

"There was a fellow once. Sort of walked in off the street. Took a room and sat here just like you two. Spoke like he had some schooling, but didn't say much. Never entered my mind till you mentioned Ink Spots. He hummed one of their songs. I heard it from his room. Upstairs."

"What song was that?" Charlene asked.

"You know music, dear?" Maggie asked.

"She teaches music in school," Eddie replied. "The choir."

"I asked him. *Whispering Grass,* he said."

"I know it," Charlene agreed speaking more to Eddie than Maggie. "I heard it from him, too, at MayBelle's house, remember, honey? *Why tell them all the old things?*"

"Yes, that's it. *They're buried under the snow,*" Maggie said and sang a line.

The sisters listened with interest to Eddie after that, but it finally came time for Maggie to ask. "I see you young souls don't need a room for the night?"

Eddie thanked them so much and rose. "Any idea where this brother of mine was heading?"

"No, heavens, so long ago, just said he was from across the River. Not likely to walk back where he just came from."

Maggie followed their guests to the front step. "*Don't Get Around Much Any More* was another tune," she said. "*Might've gone but what for?* he sang as he left."

Driving away from Board Street, Eddie looked at Charlene. "I remember that one, *Awfully different without you. Don't get around much anymore.*"

Charlene pressed his hand in affection. "That's Charles, all right."

"Where next?" Eddie asked. He felt nostalgic.

13

"I have a feeling this urban hell won't last long," Charlene said. "We'll be drowning in cornfields. A taste of The Prairie State?"

"Leaving one no-man's land for another," Eddie said as they headed back onto U. S. 50.

"I feel it already," she said with a sigh.

Eddie took that response as a sign his wife longed for a place to rest their weary heads, but not only that. She was also looking for a phone to call MayBelle from and talk to her girls. That worried Eddie, who saw *The Green-Book* listed no colored accommodations east of where they were. It struck him their venture might end quickly. Downstate Illinois was Copperhead country. A former slave house from before the Civil War still stood on the north bank of the Ohio River and had once contributed heftily to the state treasury. Even if it no longer served a practical purpose, the building's continued existence was a reminder of past realities.

Upcoming villages offered no colored hostelries. Sardis had a small convenience market. Eddie pulled in there to get gas, which gave him a chance to ask about any old-timers whose memories might stretch back a number of years. The customers were all jostling teenagers interested in illegally buying cigarettes. Most had long scraggly hair and beginning beards. Their blue jeans narrowed at the ankles and had patches at the knees.

The cashier who took Eddie's gas payment was a talkative guy about 60, but he himself had a smoke dangling from his lips, which made his chatter hard to understand. Eddie deciphered from him that there was no hope of finding a City Hall that might have information. Sardis and nearby Shiloh were incorporated into one administrative unit now, so no use to ask about Charles in Sardis, try Shiloh instead. Neither did the store have any public pay phone, the cashier added. Eddie didn't bother to ask whether he meant no phone or no access to it.

"I'd let you if I could," the cashier mumbled.

"Sorry, boy," one of the teenagers said. He was bright-looking but a slightly built kid with close-cropped blond hair and jeans-clad like the others. He studied Eddie closely and smiled showing a row of straight white teeth that gave him an intelligent look, kinda like a movie star, Eddie thought. Soon the boy leaned back against a pinball machine where he used a pencil stub to sketch on loose drawing paper. An unlit cigarette dangled from the lips of his nearest pal, who peeked over the sketcher's shoulder.

"Whatcha doon?" the pal asked him.

The blond kid shrugged but held up his sketch and nonchalantly handed it to Eddie, who saw it showed a Negro man with a knife in his back and blood dripping down. "Don't come back," the kid slurred.

Eddie folded the paper and stuck it in a shirt pocket. He drove away with nothing to say. Salazar was the next stop, ten miles away. Charlene said the town name was Spanish, but they spied out no migrant workers or Latino neighborhood. Another highway intersected with U. S. 50, so they spotted numerous motels and guest houses on Salazar's outskirts. Charlene ignored checking for accommodations in *The Green-Book*.

Eddie pulled into the largest and best lighted motel, The Landlighter. "A new word. Whatever it means," he muttered.

Asking for a room, they met a friendly young woman at the reception desk. "I'm Joy," she announced pointing to her name tag. She listened patiently. Charlene spoke politely but Eddie wondered if his man's voice would carry more weight.

"I'm sorry, but the management doesn't accept coloreds. Not my policy. I'd help you if I could. Anything else?"

"A pay phone?"

Eddie stood up straight, refusing to beg. In the young woman's manner he saw a spark of understanding, which encouraged him to talk more.

"Very helpful. Is this a full-time position for you?"

"No, it's part-time. I go to a college down the way. This job pays for me at school."

"Can you suggest another hotel or boarding house for us? Near here?" Charlene asked.

"I'm sorry, would if I could. I don't know this area. I'm from up north. The college gave me a great scholarship, luckily. The motel manager's nice, Mr. Jorsalafar, but Landlighter's in a corporation. Mr. Jorsalafar follows directives."

"Which are what?" Eddie asked.

"Salazar's Sundown, you know. Has been since back in 1893. Folks say they intended it that way. They tell the story like this. Two Negro carpenters came here then hired on to construct an apartment building, but they had to be rescued from a white mob by the building contractor that paid them but wasn't from here. He got them out of town in a rush."

"Wow. Sixty-one years ago then, and nothing's changed?" Eddie said with a sardonic smile. He and Charlene turned to go.

"Nothing new," Eddie said.

"Under the sun," Charlene whispered.

"So, we're told to say, no coloreds. Nothing against you folks."

Eddie and Charlene were nearly out the door, when the receptionist spoke up again.

"But, ma'am, yes, you can use our business phone," she said. "Right over there. I'll tell the manager, so he knows."

Eddie said a thankful prayer for Charlene's sake. She'd get to make her call.

"It's to our daughters," he told the young woman. "You know? Mothers fret."

The receptionist smiled at Charlene, who was fumbling with coins in her purse.

"No charge, it's the company line," Joy offered.

Charlene took her up on the offer and smiled. "Nice name, Joy," she said to the girl.

14

"Wanna try one more day of looking?" Charlene asked.

Sitting in a super new crate with nowhere to go. Or anywhere to sleep. Those were Eddie's thoughts as the idling Fairlane showed signs of being impatient to hit the road again.

"Why not? Just let's do it, tomorrow," he agreed. There weren't any other words. Eddie spun the car around so sparks glistened and rocks flew in Landlighter's gravel drive. Giving MayBelle's car a chance to show its stuff for real, Eddie got himself and Charlene back to Maggie Mann's tourist home before darkness fully fell on East St. Louis. True, he broke a few speed limits, which the state troopers missed, and only narrowly avoided head-ons with a couple of semis. Maggie and Mildred were still up and hardly surprised to see them.

"We saved you a room," Maggie said calmly. "Right this way."

"We couldn't find any other place," Eddie admitted with an embarrassed smile.

"Yes, we know," Mildred said.

Their upstairs room was spacious and the double bed creaky but comfy. Not exactly a bed and breakfast. The next morning Maggie served them a cup of coffee each and a single banana, unpeeled.

"You're the only guests from last night," Mildred said. "That's unusual. My Maggie's a lifesaver. If only you knew."

Charlene nodded the two ladies' way. Otherwise the four sipped their coffee with a few pleasantries. Eddie and Charlene took their banana with them. "One for the road," Eddie said offering a toast with the souvenir cup he bought from them. Mildred said a brief farewell, and Maggie watched them depart with an understanding but sad smile.

"Very humble," Charlene said once she and Eddie were alone again.

"Yes, I wonder what stories they could tell," Eddie mused.

Back on the road, they retraced yesterday's route. Eddie let the Fairlane whiz past Sardis and Shiloh until soon they were on the open road again, which gave him a sense of freedom. The landscape had a dull flatness to it, but along the creeks a few wooded hills added a touch of scenic loveliness. Just east of Salazar he spotted a man-made lake, which looked good for fishing. He remembered reading how the area was a known and protected flyway for migrating waterfowl.

Hiking along this route, where traffic was light and steep hills few, Charles could well have made it a long way in a few short weeks if people treated him decently. More importantly came the questions: Where was he heading? Somewhere or nowhere? Where is he now? Of course, after East St. Louis he might have left this eastbound route and headed almost anywhere. Could be he found a bus station or signed on with a migrant work crew.

"You know," Eddie said, "we're doing this for my ma. I mean, to set her mind at rest or ease, don't know which. Like I've thought before, it's occurred to both of us this may be a wild goose chase?"

"Or something, like we said before," Charlene added. "I wondered last night. Ugh, those creeps in Sardis. Glad they didn't have guns."

"Or did they?"

They grew silent again while Eddie let the car sail along at the speed it wished, never a glitch in this straight-as-a-string road. Once again a sense of release filled him. Next came Salem. Highway 50 ran through the business district. They passed a county museum dedicated to William C. Bryant, a prominent politician of the past. Eddie knew little about him, but noticed the town's railroad station. The depot stood out. It was dilapidated with weeds growing out of cracks in the platform concrete. As in Sardis, a gang of high school boys was milling around the vending machines. Eddie paid them no further notice.

In another half hour a roadside sign appeared. *Salina Population 7,806.* The road sloped downward and then went into an S-curve. Eddie expected a river valley but none was evident, and the landscape reverted to a lovely flat green stretch of flower-bedecked roadside businesses. Farther along lay a nine-hole golf course with another sign saying *Welcome! Edgar Jones Memorial Park.* Fronting the park was an extensive athletic field with baseball diamonds and tennis courts.

Inside the city limits was less impressive. The U. S. highway widened briefly to four lanes allowing for access to the railroad station and its work sheds. As in Salem, the depot was in need of fixing, while several signs outside the station's attached hotel looked in disrepair. Charlene squinted to read the lettering. She glanced up to read the biggest sign.

"*European Style?*" she asked in a puzzled tone. "Hard to figure what that means. They're that stylish hereabouts? A place for us, maybe?"

"Don't think so," Eddie answered with a sarcastic smirk meant for the hand that created such self-praise, not his wife. "The sign means Sundown."

15

Charlene hushed, but studied Salina as Eddie tooled around in it. They carefully avoided attracting attention but were curious about the community, which helped him quickly locate a City Library, the Town Hall, and Salina County's sheriff's office. Those city offices gathered around the town's central park.

"What first?" Eddie asked.

Charlene guessed Carnegie Library. They walked in together and found it nearly empty on a weekday. It was an older brick building, dating from 1916, if the sign above its entrance could be trusted. The ceilings were high and the bare wooden floors creaked, but the shelves and stacks were orderly and well-marked. A shelf of *Classic Fiction* caught Eddie's eye. One middle-aged librarian stood at the circulation desk, while an older woman pecked at a typewriter in the back room. The head librarian was helpful. She introduced herself as Sylvia, but hesitated. Eddie judged she was unsure of herself because she intoned every statement like a question. On first impression Sylvia seemed more like an uncertain first-time client than the person in charge.

After Charlene explained they were looking for Eddie's lost brother, the woman smiled in relief. "Certainly, we'll see what we can find in our files, but please understand it's not everyday folks like you come here."

"Like never, I'd guess?" Charlene asked.

"Right. I mean with queries like yours." The librarian smiled sympathetically.

"I understand. I'm from the South, but my folks sent me to music camp at Interlachen," Charlene said. She stopped to judge Sylvia's uncertain reaction. "That's in Michigan."

"Sorry, I didn't know that."

"Upper Peninsula. My roommate was from South Dakota. Native American. We were the first of our ethnic types we'd ever met. We made music together. That's what I mean by understanding. Meeting different people."

"Well, welcome, about all we have is old newspapers from those days you're referring to. You know the year? More or less?"

Eddie and Charlene agreed they did and plowed through a file of Salina *Daily Records*. No news popped up about Charles. If he passed that way, the local press ignored him.

Sylvia told them there were other unusual stories that would've caught the public's attention. Families of gypsies crisscrossed the area sharpening knives and saws for farmers and camping on their land, with permission. "And stealing anything they get their hands on, or so people say. Women're warned to never leave their babies outside in cribs, those wanderers are fond of blond-haired, blue-eyed babies. Sell them at county fairs. Or so folks used to say. I never believed it," she explained.

Sylvia said stories like that went around, crazy, weird stuff, yet they tantalized people.

"Every couple of years Harley Moat, the Goat Man, tramped through town with his wife and goats, whose milk he peddled on city streets. The goats' milk, I mean, not his wife's," Sylvia giggled, at last loosening up in her visitors' presence. "A lot of folks think the Goat Man's only a wild myth, but we have photos of him in our files and my own parents remember him from their days on the family farm. How he herded the animals on foot all the way from Indiana to Missouri with our state in the middle. They followed highways, pulling a cart behind. It was said his wife left for her folks' home in Arkansas after four or five years on the road and sleeping in sheep shit." She chuckled at the wording. "Folks forgot Harley had goats."

Sylvia was whispering in excitement when she finished, which caught Eddie's attention. Surely, he thought, this lady knows lots about her county. The three paused to think over their next step. What about Charles?

"You know there was one fellow the oldsters talk about," Sylvia continued. "He wandered into town way, way back. Named Jimbo, lived in a shack outside town and racked balls at the pool hall. Claimed he pitched ball for the Browns in St. Louis and struck out Babe Ruth seven times in a row. We did find a newspaper report about him, but I don't think he was a full Negro, got drunk one night and a semi ran over him on the highway."

"So you're saying if something out of the way happened, it'd get reported on? Like, nothing escaped notice?" Charlene guessed.

"That's right," Sylvia agreed. "Lots of noses for news, if you get my drift. I seriously doubt your brother passed this way. The police woulda checked him out. No mysterious dead men in ditches. None of that. Local lore wouldn't let it pass."

Eddie and Charlene nosed around in the library's other records and even chatted with the typist in the back room, only to discover she was making out bills to subscribers. As they exited, Sylvia rejoined them. She wore a warm smile.

"You could always check at City Hall. The ladies there are helpful. Or see Sheriff Thornbuckle. Not sure if he's there or will let you folks in. Ask for Grubby. He knows lots."

"Thanks," Eddie answered.

"But be careful, my friends," Sylvia said in a gentle tone. "His name matches his moods."

16

After Carnegie Library, Eddie felt undecided. Not Charlene. Quick to take Sylvia's advice, she got Eddie back in the Fairlane driver's seat but took control herself. She told him to leave their metered spot and move to parallel parking away from the library. After he did so, they sat peacefully under the shade of a large sugar maple. She unfolded their state road map.

"We could go on like this, farther east," she suggested, "but every town between here and there…well, wherever there is, there's no there there."

"I get it, a continuity of nothingness," Eddie murmured.

"And this is what your brother struck out to explore?"

"Seems so."

"Let's have a look ourselves."

"And forget Grubby?" Eddie asked, not surprised at her thumbs down.

Happy to see they were in agreement, Charlene sat back and enjoyed the sights while Eddie glided from gear to gear around Salina. It took only a while to discover the way from Carnegie Library to the County Court House led along Main Street. Driving straight ahead from the main drag, they were on North Main, and by turning around to head the opposite direction they were on South Main. At Salina's only traffic light, they stopped for red. When it turned green, Eddie hung a left and found, to their surprise, they were on East Main.

"Which means Highway 50 back to East St. Louis is West Main?" Charlene asked in astonishment. "This town has two different Main Streets?"

"Weird, all right," Eddie agreed. "There's one way to find out if it's true."

He drove east for a few blocks passing a large gray school building and a row of stately private homes. Marring the residents' view in the back of those homes was an oil industry chemical treatment plant and an Express train track. An Express sped by with its warning signals blaring. At the eastern city limits, the street curved and disappeared up an overhead bridge above the railroad tracks. Realizing it led on westward and they hadn't yet decided to continue that way, Eddie hung a sharp right. He drove across the tracks and followed a long street parallel to the tracks named Indianapolis Avenue and guessed it once, in the mists of time, marked the main highway to Indiana.

Eddie followed that Avenue past a large brick building. He saw a sign for Salina Township High School and turned once more, this time to the right and then back left again.

"So intriguing a tour, my dear," Charlene joked. "This puts us back on East Main heading West."

"Yes, irony of ironies," Eddie said with a soft laugh as the traffic light turned green. "I'm just wondering where we're headed ..."

He didn't finish. Instead he slammed on the brakes with all his might, too late. He felt a panicking and bone wracking shock as a speeding Dodge slammed into MayBelle's Fairlane. It broadsided the Fairlane on Charlene's side and sent it swirling at a 45-degree angle toward the curb with a horrendous screeching of tires and skidding. Window glass shattered and skidded across the street in splinters.

The world went black around Eddie. He didn't know how long he was out, only that he woke up to find his wife gone and a large man wearing a sheriff's hat looking in, at, and down on him. Eddie realized he was sitting in a police car, not his own.

"Thornbuckle here," the officer said. "Ambulance done took your lady to Emergency. We reckon you're all right, boy."

Gazing around, Eddie saw a sheriff's cruiser flashing bright red and blue. He knew where he was and remembered the shock, but felt strange. His world, formerly so sharp in focus, swirled in uncertain circles. They were in a mess of his making.

Eddie fumbled for the door handle. Looking at the faces whirling around him, he felt a desperate need to locate Charlene. Just as much, he needed a phone. He had no clue where to find either one.

His patience wearing thin, Thornbuckle rattled his keys and handcuffs while barking out orders, first to the officers directing traffic and then to Eddie.

"C'mon, boy, get a move on now! Think I got all day?" Grubby commanded. He spat out a wad of Old Copenhagen and angrily ground it down with the heel of a heavy boot.

BOOK VI

Family Four

1

Flo's moods were mixed as the summer of '54 moved on. The coolish spring weather lasted into early June, when it gave way to stretches of August-like heat. Both extremes made her feel fickle and in need of a steady presence, like Merrit gave her.

Her joy in being cancer free went sky high. Knowing she'd won the battle with a dread disease continued giving her immense exuberance. She strode to work everyday never needing a brand new Ford Fairlane to buoy her confidence. She felt self-motivated. She left it as Merrit's thing to show off the energetic new car among co-workers at the roundhouse or Ronny to tell pretty girls from high school about the delicious car rides he'd treat them to.

Flo strode off from home in the sunlight and fearlessly challenged the heftiest cloudbursts at night. In former times she would've felt unladylike arriving at the millinery shop with her hair in relative disarray, but at times she did so now perfectly convinced she was stronger than any bodily ailment or whatever cautious glances co-workers or customers might give her. At the same time, doubt crept up on her now and again. Tripping on a crack in the sidewalk, feeling an unexpected jab of pain or a minor lump from an insect bite, losing her train of thought with a shop customer, those small glitches were troublesome. Having random distractions pop up could plunge her into fearful reminders requiring a gentle nudge or a kind word from Merrit or Ronny to set things straight again.

After returning from her decisive visit with Dr. Corale at Barnes, she came home feeling death was the most mundane of things, not the monstrous master people made it out to be. One day you fall ill and the next you're no more, just as a rock tumbles down a hill or a bird falls from the air, but the now healthy Flo came to see life from a broader perspective. Hers became a struggle to grasp that no healthy organism desires to die. Realizing that fact made her once more extra intent on maintaining a sense of wellbeing. The intensity caused a delicate balance between the joy of the moment and a healthful awareness of her own frailty. Existing within that awareness and cultivating it carefully would be her steadying motivation.

With those thoughts in mind, she lived a selfish life. Not shrewish or demanding. Her daily living with Merrit and Ronny was, if anything, more loving than ever. The wife and mother of old was back in her men's arms, both literally and spiritually. No, selfish in the sense she was consumed with her own sense of self. By late summer Flo was ready to alter the imbalance between her and her community. Balance yourself and make it healthy, she told herself.

First she looked at Salina. There she spied in miniature the social injustices she saw writ large in her family's repeated visits to the huge city across Eads Bridge. The Salina poor were white, but they toiled for low wages at the same back-breaking jobs as colored folk in the cities. She thought of the Krutzes, a swarthy and unwashed family from the wrong side of the tracks in Salina. The father Jacob and his husky grown sons canvased the town collecting trash in an exhaust-spewing flatbed truck.

At an even lower social level came Charlie Polka Dot, an aging loner stuck in Frog Island, a mosquito infested bog on the south end of Salina. The inhabitants of that slum were folks who'd suffered most from the Depression two decades earlier. Even in the 1950s, a few still lacked electricity and a single City hydrant supplied families with fresh water. Charlie Polka Dot was their sewage controller. With his faithful mule Zeek and a trusty Dalmatian dog, he patrolled Frog Island's alleyways, emptying outhouses for those who lacked indoor plumbing. In fright, children ran from him and the stench preceding him, but he did his job dutifully. Whether that was with or without support from the City of Salina seemed anyone's guess. No one talked about it.

In their early married days Flo and Merrit had joined the First Presbyterian Church on North Main. There for Sunday services sat the entire Krutz clan, with Jacob at the fore, all dressed in dark suits and white shirts but looking no more bathed or combed than on their weekday flatbed tours. In church they were relegated, notably and without fail, to pews against the far back wall. Sharing their row of benches invariably was Charlie Polka Dot, also decked out in a white suit coat. Flo wondered how he kept it clean.

The Maxwells had long ago quit the Presbyterian congregation. Not for any social cause but due to their general disenchantment with the pastor's hell and damnation sermons. Yet the economic makeup of the folks who attended the services left its imprint on Flo. Why people of "that lower sort," as the congregation referred to them, hadn't pulled themselves out of their dire living conditions was a question the pre-cancer Flo never asked herself. Now she did. The more she considered the question the more she realized those closest to the bottom of the economic barrel were often women. She remembered the young traveling lady at the Starr hotel's Home Forever. Looking back on her recent dinner there with Merrit and Ronny, Flo understood how probable it was that the young woman's choice of a table in the midst of professional salesmen was an unspoken demand for fair treatment of lone or abandoned women.

Considering the church experience, Flo realized that her congregation's leadership was in its way a bystander to repressed needs. Those issues of subjugation fit under an umbrella-like call for equality that cut across society's unwritten strictures about the treatment of all who weren't properly presentable, by which Flo meant either physically or socially accepted, and preferably male. Where in small-town Salina could she find a clarion call for change? Were there folks of solid household economy and community standing, who understood and spoke out about the social disparities Flo saw around her?

2

"Compassion, truth, and meaning," the student said in a mild tone carrying a feeling of sincerity and concern. "We all need to be educators and activists."

Flo glanced at the tiny gathering seated around her, mostly women. She had popped in a few minutes after the opening comments. So she listened closely, while also feeling she was there under a misunderstanding being easily the oldest person attending the informal gathering. She'd seen a note in the *The Salina Sentinel* about a newly formed women's group wishing to study Unitarian teachings, with the intent of starting a congregation. Much of what the speaker said sounded fine but it seemed quoted from some written source. "Dignity of each and every person" was followed up by the phrase about a "free and responsible search for truth and meaning."

Learning to understand those phrases felt like an impossible task to Flo, but they put an emphasis on people taking responsibility and avoided reference to any all-knowing deities, as in other congregations. The slavish reliance on supreme powers was the very tendency that led Flo and Merrit to leave their former congregation and look for another way. She didn't know how to explain why they hadn't found one. Maybe they didn't look hard enough, or maybe Salina was just too small to tolerate that much diverse thought. So she listened to the group discussion, which led into comments she eventually recognized as Unitarian in spirit.

"And can we conclude with a story for all ages?" the speaker asked to conclude her presentation.

When no one volunteered, the woman delivered a brief tale of her own. "It's about a student of mine," she began. In an instant Flo saw that, of course, the speaker was a grown woman, mid to late 20s, and a teacher in her own right, not a super young college student. Her tale told of a boy who listened to her classroom lectures on evolution and the cognitive powers of higher apes. This student took that knowledge with him to the zoo and witnessed a pair of chimpanzees attempting to escape from their dreadful life in captivity. Of course, Flo recognized the story and figured who the presenter was.

On the way out, she stopped and waited. "I appreciated your introduction," she said to the speaker. "I'm Flo."

The other woman said a few grateful pleasantries, which led the two into a string of expressions of mutual appreciation. That gave them a moment to study each other, as if figuring who and what the other was there for.

"I'm ashamed to say it, but I felt old as Methuselah when I got here," Flo said.

"Why's that?"

"You look young enough to be a student yourself. Then you told about your own student's experience. Eye-opening, for me anyway."

The women stood longer testing the waters. Flo felt she knew the speaker as well as possible without laying eyes on her before. In the other's eyes a faint glimmer of recognition shone.

"I'm Kristine," the younger woman said at last.

"Yes, of course. I know you as Miss Jordan."

"And so, you're?"

"Yes, Ronny's mother. I've heard so much about you."

Flo and Kristine Jordan stood momentarily in silence with each other, the younger woman seeing in Flo her son's likeness; Flo recognizing in Kristine the empathy and intellectual keenness her son found attractive and irresistible.

"Will you come to our next meeting?" Kristine asked.

"Knock and it shall be opened?" Flo asked.

"We'd welcome you, always," Kristine answered.

"Maybe," Flo answered weighing whether to speak the truth or fudge on explaining her intentions. "Don't know if I'm all that enthused about Unitarianism."

"Me neither," Kristine replied. "But we must start somewhere, if we're to get anything rolling in Salina. This all seems enough like religion to make it intriguing. To begin with."

"And so begins, I hope, something to shake things up," Flo offered. "Don't know what. Action on some social level?"

"Coffee then?"

"Yes, sometime," Flo said. "I've heard so much about you."

They shook hands. And said goodbye. For now.

On her way home Flo remembered once more the young traveling woman she, Merrit, and Ronny saw sharing a crowded hotel dining room with road-weary salesmen. The confident way she carried herself physically when leaving and paying her bill made Flo feel there was a connection between her and Kristine. Women with a strong belief in themselves were needed. Flo imagined a new spirit awakening in Salina.

3

"We're stretching out a hand," Kristine stated as Flo hurried into the Sovereign Grounds coffee shop. Just like at last month's pseudo-Unitarian confab, Flo showed up late for their agreed-on time. Ethel's Millinery let her off work early, but it was a long hike to Sovereign Grounds. In a rush she took a seat across from Kristine without greeting her. "A helping hand to the needy is what we need," Kristine continued with a wink to acknowledge her own small play on words.

While the waitress served each a first cup of coffee, Kristine's white and Flo's black, the two smiled at each other. Flo recognized in the younger woman the same thing as at their other meeting. She had a pleasant manner and resonant voice that spoke of confidence and leadership. The young woman was aware others listened when she talked.

"And who are they, the needy, and what do they need?" Flo replied. "Is that what you're asking?"

"Not asking, just saying," Kristine answered. "Lots of people are hurting, more than the big shots admit. We're just a few souls wanting to help them. We're very few in number."

"Hurting." Flo didn't know if she meant that word as a question or a statement. She saw in Kristine's expression that both were puzzled by the frankness of the expression.

"Let's put it this way. We're just a handful of souls looking to make things better," Kristine stated.

"And last month's meeting, you got started there?" Flo asked.

"We tried. I thought you'd come back to the next meeting. Missed you there."

"I was interested but busy."

Flo detected how the young teacher guided their conversation like she was the older of the two. She tilted her head back after a sip of coffee to show she wished to hear what Flo meant by busy. Flo took the hint to reply directly.

"I'm a cancer survivor. At least I'm surviving cancer. It changes things. Been busy searching," she said.

"For what? To live less self-absorbed?"

"Maybe, or something like that. To notice other people. How they live. And act. I try to figure how you see things, for example. Or how my son says he hears you explain the things you see."

"Really? Such as?" Kristine asked.

"The Zoo. The chimps. He says you say we all oughta be free."

"I think I used the word fair. We should all be treated fair."

Fair or free seemed the same to Flo, but she gave Kristine some leeway. It's going to college that does it, she reasoned to herself, makes people split hairs that way. Or gives them the vocabulary to make endless distinctions, but no doubt about it, society didn't need to be the way it was. Better to tell things like you feel, and not let them fester inside you. There's a need to speak out, Flo was feeling it for the first time. That was certainly true about things she was beginning to understand, like figuring how whatever's unfair or unfree got to be the way it is in the first place.

"There are reasons people are hurting in a rich country like this," Flo ventured. She realized she had no fancy concepts and fumbled for words. "Poverty has causes."

"My profs called them social determinants," Miss Jordan said.

"Salina wouldn't have the Krutzes and Charlie Polka Dot if people understood that and helped them," Flo argued.

"Maybe Krutzes don't want help, least not if it feels like charity."

"Yes, people want a place where they're respected?" Flo asked.

Kristine smiled at Flo and finished off her coffee. "You don't get a good brew like this everyday," she said.

"No," Flo agreed. She could see Kristine was ready to go, but willing to chat a while longer.

"We're hardly a group at all, that's why we thought you'd fit in, don't even have a name yet for our group-that's-not-a-group, to be honest," Kristine added. "Here in Salina we're only four or five. We have a guy, Rev. McElroy, and my friend Donna."

Flo nodded with interest. "Thanks, that helps to know. "

"Donna says she saw you once, at the restaurant, Home Forever? With your husband?"

"Yes, could be. And Ronny?"

"She saw him, too. Nice young man."

"So Donna's a traveling person?"

"Yes, kinda. She's a teacher like me, but in Salem. Lives here, works there. She sells stuff on the road, as a hobby. Us girls, sometimes we plant ourselves in places like cafés and shops that mainly men are at."

"But whatever for?" Flo wondered.

Kristine smiled in slight derision, not at Flo directly but at society's unholy biases. "To get the message out. We'd like to be treated fair. To show we can go wherever men go."

There seemed no reason to argue with such an idea. Flo let it be.

"Our movement will grow," Kristine promised as she got up to leave.

4

"Movement? Did I really call it that?" Kristine asked the members of her group, Family Four. "Whadda they say? I overexaggerated? Just desperate. I saw a need and wanted people to join in. In that case, you. So I overstated myself."

She was talking to her close circle of co-helpers, who smiled at her humble words knowing that without her they wouldn't be there as they were, having dinner at a Mongolian Barbecue. Mongolian food? A previously unheard of concept in Salina and its only ethnic restaurant. Not a chain store, but a small business, run by an Asian family that moved to Salina fron the West Coast. Little more was known about them because of their reticence, which limited English reinforced. "We do what we can," their friendly cashier explained to Kristine and Flo.

"We do what we can," Flo repeated to Family Four. "There are folks in dire straits. Still don't know how we arrived at such a silly name, though. Family Four?"

"It was your suggestion, remember?" Kristine jested.

"Well, I tried to suggest a catchy name, to no avail. Like Family For meaning For Everybody. Or Family Four meaning Four of US. Actually, I blamed the name on Ronny, who happened to remember he has a sister almost old enough to be his mother."

"But you are a family of four, right?"

"Yes, and here we four sit as well, I'm happy we're here," Flo answered.

Around the table sat the group's leaders and only active members, at the moment. Kristine, from the Windy City, had started her career in pre-Law at a state college in Indiana, but graduated from the University of Chicago. She herself wasn't sure how she came to teach school in Salina, except to say she fell for a Chicago Law student. When he graduated and found work with a Salina law firm, she moved there with him. He soon fled to California.

"And here I am, embattled but not bitter," she told anyone who asked, which was quite a few people. Young women like her with brains and good looks didn't normally stay long in Salina. Or even show up there to begin with.

Her friend Donna Vazquez stayed in the area around Salina but wasn't sure why. She was an energetic Home Economics teacher with a Latina mother, who ran for and won the race for mayor of her nearby hometown, against all odds. Donna had learned from her mother not to take a back seat or be over voiced by others, a facility her English and Spanish language skills aided her in. Donna seemed unlikely to move anywhere simply because a guy lived there. Since their first group meeting, Flo had listened as Donna insisted Family Four's main charge must be aiding any and all women suffering abuse.

Many had attended Family Four's open meetings, but no one new joined. For the moment the four were sunk in their individual thoughts. Recently they'd followed Donna's ideas and worked to make life better or at least bearable for a succession of troubled women. At times it proved hard to tell if the abused were victims of wayward and violent men and organizations or equal participants in the troubles afflicting them. Other times Flo thought the best counterweight to Family Four's female, sometimes knee-jerk, reactions against domestic abuse was the fourth member of their budding group, Gene McElroy, pastor at the local First Christian Church. Flo studied him closely at their meetings and found a kindly soul.

The good reverend claimed to be a product of the Midlands, like pretty much everybody in Salina, but Flo heard him clipping consonants and shortening vowels in his speech, which made it hard to hide his Michigan origins, which he admitted to, if anyone proved curious enough to ask. While his Northern speech could shock locals in Salina, his soft touch on personal matters calmed all but the most hardened opinion makers. Reverend McElroy spoke up for marginalized people with an unflinching candor, which hid behind a mild exterior approach.

"Why is that, why you're that way, Gene?" asked Donna, who proved curious enough to wonder.

"Something in the water maybe," he mused. "As a kid, I lived in a town that had chemicals in its water. My folks got us out of there, but the prejudice against poor people rubbed me the wrong way."

Sensible talk like that impressed Flo. Gene being concerned about folks reduced to drinking polluted water in a rundown town helped her understand he favored the underdog. As a pastor, he often found himself answering rural emergency calls, and in time Flo was riding along with him.

On this day Family Four was taking it easy. Their conversation reflected as much. "We've had a quiet start," Kristine continued. "Nothing special brings us to the forefront of anyone's attention."

"And we're not licensed to step in when it's emergency stuff," Flo agreed. "Except for Pastor Gene."

She nodded his way.

"A couple of calls, though, got pretty grizzly. Couple stuck out in the country. Domestic stuff," Gene stated.

Donna looked their way. "We can imagine. What you do, Pastor, while Kristine and I work with school kids and their families. We're careful not to intrude on households but help with stuff like homework and truancy. It adds up, keeping people on track," Donna explained.

"But Gene has faced some tough situations," Flo put in. "Sure, I was there, but only observing. Tell them, Gene."

"Sorry, you know I have ethical considerations," he apologized.

After that he delicately changed the subject, but Flo let her thoughts drift away to the cases she'd ridden out on with Pastor McElroy. First was the lady who climbed out of her family's attic. That happened after a long argument with her husband. In fear, she'd tried to bundle her kids and take them to a neighbor's, but her spouse dragged her up the stairs and locked her in their hot attic from Friday till Monday morning. Nearly collapsing, she survived without food or water. Only when he left for work was she able to bang open an attic window and climb out on the roof. She jumped down into a gravelly driveway and hobbled in to her children, who the husband had left alone. A neighbor called Gene McElroy, who took Flo along to meet the abused woman. The pastor comforted her when she refused to press charges.

Another case was both horrible and tragic. A young couple in a rented farmhouse had both lost their service jobs as waitress and convenience store clerk. In an unheated farmhouse, the man grew irritated about their child's crying. He blamed the mother for ignoring the racket. When she didn't respond, he picked the child up from its bassinet and banged its head against the wall. If a nurse had not arrived to deliver medicine, the injury might never have been discovered.

Flo rode along with the pastor that time, too, and waited out-side the hospital as police took the father into custody and Gene reasoned with the stricken mother.

"The tragedy is manifold," Flo heard Pastor McElroy telling Kristine and Donna. Flo took a back seat in the conversation and realized Gene was discussing the same cases she'd been reliving in her mind, or similar ones, though he skirted naming names.

"But the most noticeable is that many of the women don't rec-ognize what they're experiencing as abusive."

"As what then?" Donna asked.

Gene shrugged. "That no one hit them, so there's no abuse. Or if he did hit her, she says she deserved it."

"What about the guy hitting the child against the wall?" Flo wondered.

"That's a tough one. She thinks it's her fault for letting the baby cry."

"So she didn't put two and two together about her baby?"

"The doctor said the child may have brain damage," he answered. "The mother didn't show any reaction, like she didn't understand what it meant. The dad was already in police hands."

The four sat in silence. Flo thought how long ago their Mongolian meal seemed and the happy light conversation they'd had when it was served. It'd be impossible to chit-chat when someone's life might be on the line. Gene seemed to intuit Flo's thoughts, so he talked on about people he served, and where he drew the line between people's spiritual needs and their secular ones.

"Secular?" Flo asked and listened to Gene's explanation.

"No, can't be easy," Kristine sympathized.

"At times I'm more social worker," he said. "Maybe that's what life prepared me for."

"Yes, hard to believe the abused can't see that's what they are," Donna added.

5

onna's comment caused the conversation to go quiet. It wasn't sure everyone thought so poorly of the abused. If they did in fact wonder about others' faulty thought processes, they might express themselves more subtly than Donna. Despite everyone's appreciation of her sentiments, no one in the group was fully comfortable with her direct approach. So Flo, Kristine, and Gene looked for other topics. Kristine glanced quickly at Gene and caught his attention.

"You write," she said.

He raised an eyebrow in surprise. It was clear he wasn't used to being asked about himself, which made his reaction more attractive.

"Yep, can't deny it," he answered. "How'd you know?"

"Saw your book of verse at a bazaar."

"I can imagine. On the dime shelf, I suppose." Gene spoke in a self-deprecating voice, which did little to hide his delight.

"*The Garden Book*. Isn't that it?" Donna asked.

"Yep, close enough," Gene acknowledged. *The Garden Book of Springtime Verse* or something like that. I'm beginning to forget the title myself." He scratched his head in confusion.

"I have it at home. I read in it from day to day, a poem daily, something like that. I'm not a poetry nut, but I recognized your name on the cover," Donna continued.

"I know, Donna," Flo added suddenly. "You were buried in the book when my Merrit and Ronny and I saw you at Home Forever."

"Yes, there I was. I planted myself at a table reading poems among a dining room of dullard men."

"Hush now, honey," Kristine quieted her friend. "You have no proof they're dull."

"I know," Donna replied without showing any special humility. "I got no proof, *Pero creo que si. Es cierto.*"

"Tell us about your verse," Kristine suggested to Gene.

Flo noticed that changing the topic was Kristine's way of calming her dear friend without admitting she didn't know Spanish. Kristine seemed sincerely interested in hearing about Gene's verse as well.

"Pretty simple stuff," he began. "I like Vivaldi, so I write about the seasons or my garden at home. Shadows and shifting colors. It's a relief from daily cares."

"Nothing about your parishioners? That'd be a lot," Donna said.

"No, way too much. Besides, they'd recognize themselves in my words. At least those that read. I don't dive into psychology."

"How would you define your poems?" Flo asked.

Gene scratched his head over the question. Not that it took him by surprise, but like he'd heard it before and always found his own descriptions trite and redundant.

"Let's say the psychology's in the feel the poem gives you," he said at last. "Kinda like a still life in words maybe? It needs to grow on you."

Kristine applauded him kindly.

"And so," Gene teased them, "let's rush out and pluck up those copies. I'll autograph 'em all."

"Do you get many readers?" Flo wondered.

"Some admirers, for sure, not many. I get letters sometimes from enthusiastic readers. One woman from Selective Service in St. Louis has sent me cards for years. Great Lady. Keeps me sane, what she writes."

"Right," Kristine agreed. "Verse calms the nerves."

"Food for thought, all right. If cancer and Barnes taught me anything at all," Flo said, "it's to see how other people can have it, too. I never thought of that." She looked at the others and shrugged. "Sometimes all you can do is listen, and hope people'll speak up."

In fact, nobody did, talk, that is. The others sat with their thoughts. Only Flo had anything else to say, for now. "I met this woman in St. Louis once, the big city. She moved there from Africa, somewhere. Liked St. Louie some. Disliked it some. She had this relative in the hospital maybe about to die, and she told me, 'Everybody's got their story, most unfinished.'"

"Interesting," Kristine reflected.

"Ronny and me were at the chimp show. That's when he told me about you and Rousseau," Flo said to Kristine.

The young woman gave a sign of recognition.

"*Man is born free and...*," Flo quoted with a friendly grin.

"Yes, that's him, Rousseau," Kristine said. She looked quizzically at Flo and waited for a reply.

"That's us all, you mean," said Donna.

Flo wondered if Kristine had read all of *The Social Contract* or only the first page, like her and most everyone.

6

"That's me, free as a bird," Ronny declared. He spoke while lounging at home with a couple of school friends. Jack and Paul were his closest buddies, but from the kitchen Flo overheard parts of what they said, which made her feel sure their ties were weakening.

The three had grown up on the same block in Salina, where neighbors knew the boys as The Three Musketeers for their youthful exploits on various playing fields. Jack was an outspoken kid, a superior athlete who by junior high had outgrown every kid in his class. At Salina Township High he became a football star and All-State candidate. Paul had also excelled on the gridiron, but lacked Jack's bulk and speed afoot.

Ronny never took to football. Flo remembered him limping home from practice one foggy October evening his freshman year. At 115 pounds, he'd tried to tackle a running back 40 pounds heavier. The ball carrier landed on his right leg. Ronny described the crunch he heard, "like a brittle soda cracker," as he later told the doctor, who encased his leg in a cast.

"A green willow break," the doctor told the boy, Flo, and Merrit. "No need to set it, let it heal."

That's what Ronny did. He hobbled around school on crutches for weeks on end. While the other boys gained strength and won games, he had little to do but sit on the sidelines. It was spring before The Three Musketeers were playing together again, on the baseball field. During the next four years they helped Salina win conference championships and tournaments on the diamond, but in football Ronny lagged behind. He was on the squad, but showed little enthusiasm. Flo and Merrit watched him avoid contact when he got into games. In essence he sabotaged the team practices when the coach turned against him. In baseball the three boys worked as a team.

Flo heard that their mutual love was still the diamond sport. They chatted on about the games they'd starred in and even chuckled over defeats that once had felt heartbreaking. Next year would be different. All three were headed for state colleges but whether Jack and Paul could make it on the gridiron or Ronny at baseball was an open question. None seemed bothered on that score, but in academics Flo heard a divide.

"Free? In what way?" Jack asked Ronny.

The silence that followed was punctuated by Ronny's shrug, or so Flo guessed. "Free to take the courses I want. Meet new people," he said at last. "Think the thoughts I want."

"What are those, the thoughts?" Paul asked.

Ronny paused and the silence seemed to hang heavy for a moment.

"So you decided on a major already?" Jack followed up with.

"I think so. It'll be a science of some sort. Bio, maybe."

"What for?" Jack asked. "I hated that in high. Studying animal parts was a big bore."

"Really? Didn't your big brother do taxidermy on birds when we were little?" Paul asked Jack.

"Yeah, he was nuts about that stuff, but I figure the only thing birds are good for is shooting 'em. Quail hunting's my favorite," Jack said.

"I had these teachers last year who're big on preserving nature. There's this new field these days, called ecology," Ronny said. "I might do that. Or History. I dunno. You, Paul?"

"Huh, I dunno either."

Paul grew quiet. Flo knew the boy had some smarts and a sense of humor. He processed info slowly, though, like his dad, who ran a lumber yard and did excellent work but added customer charges on his fingers. Flo gave Paul a break by taking the three a serving of lemonade. They said thanks, took it gladly, and sucked on the straws.

"So what'll it be, buddy?" Jack urged Paul between sips. "Your major, I mean."

"Well, stay eligible, that's what I figure."

"Eligible for what? Football?" Ronny asked.

"Yeah."

"What if you don't make the team?"

"Then just pass, I figure," Paul said. Flo saw him shrug in mock despair as she left the room. That answer brought a laugh from all three.

"I'll do the same, I hope," Jack added. "Pass and make the team, too, but where you get your ideas from anyway, pal?" he asked Ronny. "All this stuff you spout off about?"

"Hey, he doesn't spout off, he talks sense," Paul butted in with.

"I mean this about animals having natural rights, whatever that means, and Communists practicing free love in Russia. I don't get it," Jack said.

"Don't take it too serious," Ronny answered. "It's what Miss Jordan says in class. She covers lots of topics. Darned smart."

"Oh, okay, I get it. She's pretty hot, all right," Jack teased him.

Flo heard a peal of kidding laughter from Ronny's pals. It hurt her that they were making fun of him, because she knew he took Kristine Jordan's ideas seriously, even those he didn't fully understand. Flo did her best to let the three carry on. Surely this little chat wasn't far different from any other jostling they did in private, when nobody's teenage feelings were sacred.

"I thought teacher's pets was grade school stuff." Those words also came from the boys' room, but their laughter make it impossible for Flo to hear whether Jack or Paul uttered them.

The boys' laughter fell off after that statement. Flo heard them keep on talking in a softer tone. Whatever it was they discussed seemed of little importance. The only clear statement came from Ronny, who said in a neutral voice, "I don't believe in mistreating or killing animals." Flo didn't hear any reply. She judged there was none. When she went in to collect the boys' lemonade glasses, Jack was telling about his invitation to fall football practice. Flo stopped to listen.

"State relented and gave me a full scholarship," he said. "We report two weeks from now. They wanted me to go to summer school and get my grades up, but I didn't. Our high school coach wrote a letter for me and changed their minds."

Paul had a hard time beating that act, so he kept his words short. "Don't think the football coach where I'm going ever heard of me. Said I could walk-on. Guess I will."

Ronny smiled in understanding for his friends. "Baseball season's next spring. Somebody or other signed me up this fall for classes in *Human Ecology* and *Music Apprec: The Ink Spots Before and Beyond.* I can't read a note."

Neither could Jack or Paul. Strange stuff, they agreed, those college courses.

7

"By the way, what are ink spots?" Ronny asked his folks a couple days later. They were finishing lunch on their back porch. The late summer sun shone strongly enough to induce a mellow glow on their faces. Flo and Merrit were sharing a small bottle of wine, which meant each swallow made it even harder for her to concentrate.

"Ink spots?"

She would've let the words settle, but her head swirled.

"Who or what?" she asked.

"Something in that course I'm registered for," Ronny said nonchalantly. "What comes after?"

Merrit ran a finger around the rim of his wine glass, but he waited before saying anything. He seemed less likely to grow tipsy than Flo. Ronny was drinking lemonade, just like the day Jack and Paul were at their house. He kept clinking the ice cubes in his glass. Maybe, Flo thought, that's why he came up with his question; he remembered the guys started talking college when Flo brought them refreshments.

"The Ink Spots're Negro balladeers," Merrit said suddenly. "Smooth-voiced. They sing a lot about what used to be. Or never was. Colored guys in the Service listened to them. A lot. I remember ..." He paused to think, so Flo understood he, too, felt the wine's effect. His thoughts were clear but the words came slower.

"There was this one line. *Don't tell them all the old things. They're buried under the snow.*"

"Meaning what?" Ronny wondered.

"Dunno. Coloreds had a lot to remember maybe. We'll never know."

"But, why study that at college?"

"A lot's come after their music, times change."

Little more seemed worth saying on that topic, nothing at least that Flo could imagine and apparently not Merrit either. The minutes drifted by in silence.

"Change. Which reminds me," Ronny said.

"Oh, yes!" Flo looked up in sudden realization and remembered. "How could I forget?"

"College begins."

"Yes, in two weeks. You'll be getting a year older as well."

"I need supplies," Ronny reminded her.

"We'll go tomorrow. I promise."

"You'll get a grand farewell," Merrit said to Ronny. "I promise, too." Meanwhile he studied their wine bottle for its last drops, which he poured for them.

Flo emptied hers slowly in a thoughtful mood. Seeing Ronny leave home would bring her to the empty nest. Not that it was a new thought. She'd prepared for it, but losing her companion for the last two years of cancer fears and battles wouldn't be easy. Yet worse than that loomed ahead. She had it gnawing at her since her younger years. She'd never left Salina as a young woman and so never knew any youthful farewells. She lived with her parents until she left to marry Merrit and move across town. They had, in fact, never even had a honeymoon. Merrit wed her in church on a Friday and returned to the railroad on Monday. Ronny's sister was born a year after they married. She, her husband, and their two children, spaced far apart, were a stay-at-home family.

Sad to say, my break-out from home was our first trip to Barnes Clinic, Flo thought as her wine-driven thoughts flew closer to chaos and she grew sadder over the idea of Ronny leaving. The cancer clinic started me growing up to the great world outside Salina? she asked herself, but realized she needed to stir from such self-consumed thoughts.

"Let's go," she said to Ronny, only to realize he'd already gone out.

"He's on a date. Took the Ford," Merrit told her.

The two remained, aware of seeing their son starting on his own path.

"That's how it'll be," he said.

"Yes, from now on," Flo agreed.

8

Next day and summer seemed the same. The warmth held on. The millinery store demanded Flo's time, but she arranged for the afternoon off. Gene called from Family Four and talked about various troubled souls. As usual, Ronny needed school supplies. This time, though, he was leaving for college, not high school.

Flo called him from work to meet for lunch. After last night's date, he still had the Fairlane keys, so she waited. Sure enough, he swerved in outside the millinery, where they sat for minutes deciding where to go. At last he gave up on his mother's indecision and drove them to Jolly Jim's, a clean but simple café on the edge of town. Flo wasn't hungry and Ronny acted distracted, so they shared a salad and were satisfied with the usual lemonade.

"What happened?" Flo asked after a while. "Bad date? Or what?"

"No, dunno. Molly's nice, but not much to say."

"Her, you mean."

No, neither of us. High school seems like a long time ago. Already. And we're just only finished."

Flo didn't follow up on that angle. She thought, yes, that's right, life's still ahead of you. Then she remembered they were there to go shopping for his college supplies. She had a long mental list of necessities. Stuff the average college freshman guy would likely never think of. She also wondered about his dorm room. The university had sent him that info, but Ronny kept it to himself. So she asked and learned it was a square cubicle barely large enough to hold two guys, but beggars can't be choosers, he assured her.

"And your roommate?" she asked.

"Don't know. Some guy."

"But I see you got a letter from him. He introduced himself, I assume."

Ronny cleared his throat and mumbled something that sounded like forget it.

Flo didn't know what he meant or why he was in such a mood. So she let the topic of dorm rooms and roommates ride for the time being. Instead she paid their bill and piled into the Fairlane. She told him to drive to Sycamore, Salina's only shopping mart, where the staff knew everyone in town and what sizes they took, oftentimes even guessed what they were there to buy, so fast did news spread.

"The one place where dieting never works for anyone," Ronny said. "They already know how fat you are."

Knowing he was an exception to the unwritten blubber rule, Flo hushed him. Or *was* he the rule? He'd grown a whole foot and gained weight since his sophomore year. He didn't want any "old people" measuring his waist and seeing "how skinny I still am."

"Be quiet. You sound like some silly teenage girl worrying about your figure. I never heard the likes," Flo said at last, unable to hide her combination of annoyance and pride.

In the end, Ronny bought only a sweatshirt with *Tigers* on it. "My college's got the same team nickname as Salina High," he explained.

Flo added a heap of notebooks and some pens for him and hurried out to the car. She took the keys from him and sat behind the wheel. "Shopping with you is like riding the train to St. Louis in your company. How am I to know what you want?"

He didn't answer and she drove on, faster than she knew was smart, but she felt frustrated enough to let it show.

"What is it? A bad date last night with a girl you thought you liked?" she asked.

Without expecting him to answer, Flo had second thoughts about her little tirade and released her tight grip on the steering wheel. The Fairlane slowed down little by little, almost against its will.

"Don't fight it, Ma," Ronny urged. "This car is built to run. Let it go!"

9

Against her will, she listened. Thinking to herself that a man's voice is always good with advice about motors, if nothing else, she slowed even more and regretted that their final shopping trip had failed. Not anyone's fault, she knew, just a day getting off on the wrong foot. She didn't want it to stay that way.

"Things happen," Ronny said. She knew then he'd read her thoughts, like always, and she placed a hand on his to share their comfort. There'd be another day. She'd go shopping alone for him tomorrow and buy the things he needed. He couldn't wear summer gear all fall, she was thinking when she heard a siren wailing in the distance. The sound came at her in waves, falling off, then reaching a crescendo, before fading again.

"Where's that coming from?" she asked and slowed even more.

Ronny craned his neck to look behind them. "Nothing there, coming up," he said.

Suddenly Flo saw an ambulance's flashing lights and heard its siren grow more shrill as it drew even with them. It honked loudly at traffic and then sped on in the opposite direction from her and Ronny on Main Street. The blare died away in the distance.

"That's a hospital run," Ronny commented. "Wanna follow it?"

Keeping her eye on traffic around her, glancing in the rear view mirror, and wondering if she could believe her ears at Ronny's question was all Flo could manage, so she crept along.

"Good gosh, boy!" she exclaimed. "You nuts or something? Chasing ambulances?"

"Ok, just kidding. Besides, there's bound to be more where that came from," he continued. "Keep going."

"More what? Death and destruction? That's what you clamor for? Maybe that'd be a good major for you at college, never a dull moment," she joked.

Before he answered, Flo caught sight of more flashing lights at the intersection ahead.

"Accident?" Ronny asked.

Other motorists were braking in anger and swinging hard rights and lefts down side streets. Flo crept ahead, more out of frustration with Ronny than curiosity. When at last she got close to the cop cars, she saw little more than a covey of law enforcement officers huddled around two smashed vehicles. One was an old and battered orange and black Dodge. It had rammed against the passenger side of the other car knocking out the Dodge's own windshield.

"Hey, the other's a Fairlane. Late model, too. That could be ours!" Ronny said in surprise after seeing the second car, which was indeed sparkling and elegant except for its dented passenger door and right front wheel, bent out of shape.

Flo saw no one she recognized in the intersection. Her disinterest lasted only until she pulled over to the curb and Ronny hopped out. She called out to him, "Steer clear!"

When he didn't listen, she warned, "Look, don't dream of it, that could be a crime scene. What's more, who do you know out there?"

Flo made a wide sweep with one arm toward the accident, which convinced him she was right. He knew nobody there, but she did. Immediately she caught sight of a large man waving his arms while talking animatedly to the law enforcement crowd around him. He was County Sheriff Grubby Thornbuckle, and no stranger to her. Grubby and Flo were in the same graduating class at Salina High, where he made a name for himself as a self-important loud mouth. He'd failed at all the sports he tried for being too slow on his feet. In addition, he got politely dismissed from school choir for his booming voice that drowned out the other singers. During a school dance her senior year, Grubby, whose real first name Wendelin sounded too like Gwendolyn, which was why he never used it and was maybe what made him such a bully, the shame of being mistaken for a girl, that is. Well, he'd stomped on Flo's feet often enough that dance she turned him down for other dances, which had been her wish all along, though getting a word in edgewise to him and explaining her wishes was impossible.

After high school Grubby went to work for the railroad, where he met up with Merrit on a section gang repairing broken track between Salina and Salem. A few days of back-breaking labor and the two men became agreeable workmates. Grubby was known for his brawn, but as a judge of people, the socially awkward sheriff-to-be shared nearly every prejudice and bias floating around among Salina locals. That included a suspicion of welfare mothers, curses carried by white squirrels, and the pigeon-toed Negro Jackie Robinson. Those were the very traits needed to win him favor with the city council and a victory in balloting for county sheriff. Merrit, though, saw early on how it was possible to call Grubby's bluff. Well hidden inside his thick skull, Grubby Thornbuckle had a warm spot for kids. They could do no wrong. Woe befall the man who abused them in Grubby's presence. Habeas corpus wasn't needed for such evildoers.

"Seeing Grubby Thornbuckle swear and shout at work, you wouldn't believe him around youngsters. You'd sure think he was a doting grandmother," Merrit told Flo. Hearing that, Flo had understood at once why Gene McElroy discovered the young father that slung his son against the apartment wall and immediately contacted the State Police rather than the Salina County sheriff's office.

"That young father would've been smithereens for sure in Grubby's hands," Gene told Flo at the time.

Now today there were only grown men on the accident scene, and Grubby was fit to be tied for other reasons. "Crazy lunkheads! Get a friggin' move on!" he yelled at his deputies. Only when Flo caught his eye did he calm down. The sheriff sauntered her way and lifted his hat. Flo and Grubby exchanged pleasantries before he glanced Ronny's way.

"You in a fix, son?" Grubby asked. "Brought your ma along to get ya out of it? Mighty fine lady, your Flo."

"Grub, this is my son, Ronny. You wouldn't remember him, been a while. He's off to college soon."

Grubby made no apology but nodded suspiciously at Ronny before looking Flo's way again. Trying in vain to guess at her issue, he grimaced in obvious suspicion, nobody came to him unless they were in big trouble and needed it fixed above or below board or wanted the Law to pitch in at their hour of need.

"What then?" Grubby demanded to know.

"Nothing special. Just wondered, what's up here," Flo asked.

Grubby looked relieved. "Oh, nothing much. Outsiders. Couple a' oil field roughnecks up here from Texas banged into another car. Drunk, we think. Rowdy guys. Easy enough to handle them, though. Slam 'em in the clink, sleep it off a couple hours."

"The others then?" Flo wondered. "Anybody hurt?"

Grubby took off his hat and scratched his head in dismay. He peered at Flo like asking for help. Certainly that look speaks of something he doesn't like, Flo thought, like he doesn't like it at all.

"Real crazy, a fella never knows what's next these days. What to do about it."

"Do about what?" Flo asked.

"Like this. This skinny colored guy's drivin' through town with his woman an' don't have the brains to get out of town before dark and now gets stuck here. They's dumped on my lap."

Flo glanced at Ronny and both looked Grubby's way.

"Well, I tell you, I gotta do the right thing," the sheriff told them. "This is my town."

As Flo considered his claim to owning Salina or whatever he meant, the intersection crowd thinned. Onlookers strolled off and what little backed-up auto traffic there was now moved on.

"Gawkers go home, huh?" she tossed out, knowing full well Grubby's mind was elsewhere.

She was right. He was making sure a few deputies and uni-formed cops were setting up warning signs in the street.

"A little late, huh?" Ronny whispered to Flo.

"Hush," she said.

The Dodge was damaged but movable. Its drunken occupants were already in police hands. A tow truck operator was getting ready to move their car. Meanwhile a Salina police officer stood in the street writing a report on the Ford Fairlane. He bent over to check the Missouri license plates.

"I don't know what you can do," Flo said to Grubby. "By the way, what's the policeman going to do with the Ford? It's just like mine. Only a different color."

"Oh, that thing's a wreck, all right. Totalled, I guess. Or maybe a bad wheel. Belongs to the skinny boy I gotta deal with."

Flo looked at the Fairlane a while and then studied Grubby, who shifted his weight impatiently undecided whether to get back to work and pretend this never happened or stay and talk. Finally Flo took Ronny's arm and told him to go and check the damaged Fairlane's driver.

"That boy, as you'd call him," Flo snapped at Grubby. "I wanna meet him. Okay?"

Grubby eyed her suspiciously, but nodded. "Him? Whatever for?" he asked. "One a' them?"

BOOK VII

Sundown Sheriff

1

Eddie looked at the unfamiliar surroundings and tried to remember all that happened. Flashing in his mind was an orange and black monster appearing in the corner of his eye. It smashed into Charlene's passenger door and the world went blank. Now glimpses of what followed began popping up to Eddie. Someone must've pried him out of the driver's seat because he remembered an intersection. He answered questions and showed his Missouri driver's license. Next he thought of MayBelle and the girls at home in St. Louis, after which he patted the Fairlane's front fender and wondered if it was a loss.

In the police car he also remembered he was looking for Charles, but it remained a mystery what town this was or how he got there. He glanced up and saw the sheriff peering down at him again. Maybe the sheriff's grave look made him remember. The two had talked earlier and now Eddie felt something missing at his side. Charlene. Yes, how'd she get out of the car? He remembered she was in Hospital Emergency, but where and for what procedures? The sheriff leaned in and boomed out some new message or other. Eddie nodded, but it disappeared from his mind immediately. Most vital to him was reconstructing what happened in the intersection. How could he grasp what was to happen next without remembering what led up to where he was now? Remember and remember. He recalled what happened but needed to place it all together.

Appearing aggrieved at Eddie's distant gaze, the sheriff muttered to himself, then said, "Leave you to yourself."

Slowly Eddie's mind cleared, but his growing clarity only emphasized how shocked he was and how terribly alone he felt.

"Just like Charlene predicted when we crossed the River in this direction," he remarked to the sheriff, who'd returned to poke his head back in the car window but suddenly straightened up and spoke over his shoulder to someone else Eddie couldn't see.

"Yeah, Thornbuckle here. Tryin' to figure out what to do with him," he said in frustration.

Eddie guessed the other person left, but he knew he himself was the one the Law had no idea what to do with.

Thornbuckle kept talking at the inside of the car, like he was addressing it because Eddie was invisible, or if he wasn't the sheriff wished he was. Written on the sheriff's face was a single thought: Two drunken Texans blithely run a stop sign and find a colored couple blocking the intersection and ruining *my* day. "I gotta find help, but how?" Grubby said at last before turning to leave again.

Eddie heard him talking at a distance, but he didn't come back this time. Instead a middle-aged white woman opened the car door without a word and sat down beside him.

"May I?" she asked after a minute. She'd already been there for several minutes when he nodded yes. "I'm Flo," she said.

Without changing his blank expression though he was wondering about her, Eddie began to answer.

"No need for introductions," Flo said. "Grubby told me your name. I asked him."

"And?"

"I'm here to help. If you don't want it, say so."

"And what's my choice," he asked.

"Like they say, it's a free country. Do as you wish, but good luck otherwise. We're a help group, Family Four. Sometimes five, with my son."

Eddie stayed quiet, but he didn't bolt from her presence either. He nodded.

"I called ER. They said your wife hit the bottom of the dashboard with her knees. They're bruised and swollen. She's also got cuts and scratches on her arms and legs from the car door caving in on her. They're sterilizing them. She's also got chest pain. Could be internal injuries," Flo explained.

"Internal?" Eddie asked. "Meaning?"

"You name it. Broken ribs, internal organs. Or nothing. They'll need to keep her overnight. Maybe longer. The X-ray guy's off now."

"We need to move on," Eddie insisted.

"When the time comes, not before. ER's surprised the sheriff didn't take you for an exam, too. Where they been keeping you?"

Eddie shrugged. "Here, I guess."

He looked around and outside the cruiser. He shook his head. "Don't remember it all so clear. Salina?" he asked in confusion.

"Salina, that's where we are now. Our town."

"Safe here?"

"I'm safe. We're safe," she said and gestured to Ronny, who stood outside the car. "He's the son I mentioned."

Eddie fished around in his shirt pocket and took out a sheet of scratch paper. He handed it to Flo, who studied it with a frown.

"Phone number? To who?"

"MayBelle. My ma in St. Louis. Tell her where we are."

"That's where you're from? Heading back there? Or where?"

"Looking." He tried to tell her more, but stalled, as though some things were clear as a bell, others on the tip of his tongue. "Just tell her where we are, that's all."

"Will do," Flo responded.

She looked out. Eddie's car had been shunted to the curb at one of Salina's busiest intersections. Except for a few remaining law enforcement officers, the accident was a thing of the past and traffic sped by. Eddie, Flo, and the sheriff's vehicle they sat in formed an island unto itself. This is Eddie, Flo thought, a wanderer separated from his wife and stranded in an ocean of faces, uncertain who's friend or foe.

"You recognize your own car?" Flo asked.

Eddie shrugged, then pointed toward the curb.

Flo got out. "We need Grubby. I'll go find him," she promised. "Yet again."

2

"Boy, you're in a Sundown Town!" Grubby Thornbuckle announced. "Salina is law-abiding and you people ain't welcome here. We got law and order."

He stood with his legs planted apart and hands on his hips. Flo and Ronny had located him, some place or other, they didn't say where, and brought him back. Now mother and son stood beside Eddie, who'd gotten out of the car. The three stared back at the sheriff.

"We got laws. I gotta enforce 'em. Outa town by dark, so you just get in your jalopy now, boy, and move on. Pronto!"

Aware of the dilemma before them all, Eddie, Flo, and Ronny said nothing. Ronny shrugged, like what's to say?

"Where is that fancy Fairlane anyway? Where you stole it from? Just get in it and keep goin', boy," Grubby ordered.

Flo tried to explain about the City wrecker, which was news to Grubby. It'd already been there and towed Eddie's Ford to a local mechanic. Or she thought that's what had happened. The mechanic would try to fix it. Even if the car was in good shape, Eddie couldn't leave town without Charlene, who the doctor was keeping at the hospital overnight. An impossible situation of Grubb's own making and everybody knew it, except for Grubby himself.

"Forbidden by law to stay, but I can't leave?" Eddie asked.

Grubby set his jaw meaning *No Lip!* "Sundown! Law's the law!" he barked out.

"See, Mom," Ronny said. "Dad told us. It's European style. Miss Jordan figured that out on her own long time ago."

Flo grew puzzled. The men were anchored in the midst of traffic and still talking. Pedestrians and shoppers paid less and less attention to them as signs of the accident disappeared. When the last City policemen left off directing Main Street traffic, only the unusual group of four remained. She, a millinery shop woman, her son in his late teens, and a colored man were debating a ridiculous local law with an ill-informed and prejudiced sheriff, both sides convinced they were in the right. No middle ground.

They stayed in a standoff until Eddie asked, "Can I talk to my wife?"

His request made sense even to Grubby, who promised, yes, they'd see about that and then he decided to save face by telling Flo to leave as well. "I'll take this boy to the station," he said, "and you go on home to your man. He'll tell you what to do, him, Merrit, your man. He knows the score. I'll take this boy to the station and book him for vagrancy unless he gets hisself outa my town by nightfall."

Now in a hurry, Grubby put Eddie in the sheriff's car again and hustled back to speak to Flo. "You understand I'll have to book him for vagrancy if he won't leave town. It's just not safe."

"Not safe for who?" Flo asked.

"Well, good folk, a fella never knows what might happen with those people roaming loose in town. You know all we hear about what goes on. In big cities."

"You don't think the other way around? Folk here in town might do him ill?"

"That he'd be in more danger than us? Why, you don't know the things I seen in my day," Grubby said. He stood up straight so his 6' 4" inch frame seemed larger. His free hand rested on the holster of his service weapon. "Why they's guys that'd just as soon shoot ya as look at ya. And they don't need no dark alley neither."

"Oh, yeah, who's that?" Ronny mouthed off.

Grubby ignored him and turned fast. He got in his car, and drove off with Eddie, while Flo and Ronny beat a hasty retreat. She figured the next step was up for grabs. Anything could happen, but she considered the chances. Grubby might simply slap Eddie in jail and go home, leaving the captive there until the courts took over. In Grubby's mind, that would solve the task of first preventing Negro crime against Salina's town folk and second providing overnight accommodations for two coloreds in a Sundown town. One in hospital, another in the clinker.

Flo also saw the odd chance Sheriff Thornbuckle could be struck with a surge of unexpected humanity and take Eddie to visit his wife at the hospital. What would happen with Eddie's car and how the two colored strangers stranded in a sea of whites would then find their way out of town was anybody's guess. Rumor told how the Law had always by custom merely dumped previous wayward souls at the city limits or county line and washed their hands of all untidy complications as the wanderers walked off into oblivion.

"And what if the man's wife is sicker than it looks?" Ronny asked Flo.

"I thought of that," she answered, "and if he refuses to leave town and is out of jail where does he stay?"

"The two jerks that broadsided them, think the cops already released them?"

Ronny glanced over at Flo from the driver's side and smiled cynically while he maneuvered traffic and tried guessing at her answer.

"Or they weren't even questioned or charged to begin with, that's what you're suggesting?"

"Fat chance considering who they hit. Which is worse, driving while drunk or just being reckless?

"There's the irony for you," Flo continued. "Same colored cars. Both orange and black."

"Yeah, but different colored drivers," Ronny replied.

3

O nce at home, Flo saw the situation brighten, though not as Grubby expected. Merrit came from work and listened while Flo told Eddie and Charlene's story. His impulse was a rush to the Sheriff's Office, but the two husky men would only have stood chest to chest and threatened to fight it out. Merrit decided at last to lift the phone. Three tries and he had Grubby on the other end.

"Dammit, man, you always were a numbskull, use your head for once!" Merrit shouted over the line in a raucous voice Flo hadn't heard since he read the riot act to Dr. Radebach. And that, she reminded herself, happened in the Doc's own office, imagine if Merrit was meeting Grubby in person now.

"He's gotta let that man see his wife," Merrit told Flo after the call, "no two ways about it."

"And so, what'd he say?"

"He agreed."

"To what?" Flo asked. She didn't need reminding that Merrit sometimes acted as slow on the uptake as their sheriff.

"He's taking the colored guy to Holy Shepherd's and meet his wife."

Flo felt relieved at the good news, but depressed more definite decisions weren't made. "Can't we go along?" she asked.

When Merrit didn't respond, Flo said heck with words. She tugged at her husband's shirt sleeve. He said okay.

Holy Shepherd's in Salina was badly misnamed. Flo and Merrit found its front entrance cold and forbidding granite. The main corridor was dimly lit with only a few clerks carrying papers from office to office. Sensing this was not a place for merciful service, Flo had to remind herself she'd never been in the building before. Dr. Radebach's office was located in a clinic on the other side of town, and her out-of-town cancer treatments were the only serious ailments she'd ever known. Once they found the in-patient section, the staff showed another side. The nurses proved cheerful and welcoming.

"Mrs. Washington? Yes, this way, please, room 202," a receptionist said.

The direction she showed Flo and Merrit led them to a waiting room in a narrow hallway. Perched uncomfortably on a wall bench they found an armed sheriff's deputy holding handcuffs. Farther down the hall, Grubby paced back and forth. Merrit started to approach him, but Flo tugged at his sleeve and nodded toward a sign saying *Patients 202*. They entered together and saw two brown faces in a whitewashed and antiseptic looking room.

"Hello," Flo greeted Eddie, who was on a chair beside Charlene's bed. Aside from some scratches on her face and a cast on her right arm below the elbow, she appeared hearty.

"Same to you, Mrs. Maxwell," Eddie answered.

"How they treating you here?" Flo asked. "We worried about you. Merrit called the sheriff. This is my husband," she said, doubting her ability to string a few sentences together.

"My wife," Eddie interrupted.

"I thank you for helping Eddie," Charlene burst in, not as calm as the others. "Do you know, they brought him here in handcuffs to see me, his wife. And what did he do? We obeyed a traffic sign and were nearly killed and here those bozos out there got him in jail and parading him around like a criminal for all to see."

Flo calmly searched for something to say, some clever word to make everything all right but found nothing. "If only," she stuttered.

"What?" Merrit asked.

"If we just had Gene here, or Kristine and Donna," she continued. She explained to Merrit the young women were out of town.

"You need to call him, Gene," she added to Merrit. "The girls'll be back in a day or so."

He hesitated, which made Flo lose her cool. "Don't just sit there liked a darned fool, do it. Like I say!"

As Merrit left in an embarrassed rush, Flo came to her senses. She wanted to say something sensible, but Charlene beat her to the pass and showed a temper to match Flo's. "And what am I doing here? A lone lady in a room for four women? Just because not a single white woman patient will share the room and breathe the same air I do?"

"But, dear," Eddie said to calm her.

"No buts about it," Charlene cut him off with. "I heard them whispering about it in reception. 'No new patients for 202, you know, that Negro lady is in there. How can we place any other ladies in a room with her,' they said."

"Not everybody's like that..." Eddie wanted to explain.

"And why am I being kept here for two more days? Like a prisoner myself."

Eddie sat in silence with no answer to his wife. He'd been in police custody when the ER examined Charlene and was in as much doubt about his own injuries and treatment as hers. He looked at Flo for advice on medical matters and saw she had none.

"I'm not a doctor," she said. "In fact, I'm a nobody," she added, her tone of voice sinking.

"They wanna X-ray my chest, the doc says, but then this lady comes in and says, 'The X-ray is broke'. And I think, What? Or did the technician run off, all to avoid filming my innards, which are the same as everybody else's here," Charlene said. "This is criminal. I'm a regular person, like everybody else, can't they see that? The X-ray's broke, the X-ray's broke, can't they even speak English?"

Flo looked to Merrit for whatever words he might have, only to remember she'd sent him away to find a phone. Not even Ronny stood by her side because he'd gone home to pack for college. Suddenly Flo felt as alone and victimized as the two being kept there, Eddie and Charlene, who looked at each other bewildered.

4

"But they can't arrest you for getting run into, that's wicked," Flo said, at the same time she realized that's exactly what Grubby intended. "Blaming the victim."

"What else did he bring me here in handcuffs for?" Eddie asked.

Merrit came back in the room to report he'd phoned Gene, who had the time to look in on them, but Kristine and Donna weren't answering, just as expected. Seeing Merrit back on the scene, Grubby came in the patient room as well. He also motioned to his deputy to take Eddie.

"Where to?" the deputy insisted.

"Book him. This boy's soon gonna be breakin' the law if he stays in Salina and he's not outa town yet. By nightfall, you hear? Besides, he'll also be breakin' the law if he tries to run away, he was in an accident."

"Yeah, one he didn't cause," Merrit argued. "Remember?"

"But this boy's gotta go, them Texas fellers weren't botherin' anyone till they saw him," Grubby continued. In trying to explain his own reasoning, he was becoming more confused by the minute. "He's gotta be outa town by dark. If he ain't, he's breakin' the City law. So I then gotta lock him up."

"But by locking him up, you'll force him to stay in town, and that's illegal for him to do," Merrit argued. "You just decided to lock him up for the accident, which you claim he caused, but you also want him outa town by nightfall to obey the City law. By fleeing the town to avoid Sundown rules, he'll then be libel for arrest for fleeing town after causing an accident, which everybody here knows he didn't cause?"

"Yes," Flo agreed, "that was the whiskey slick drunks you let go without ever charging them for anything."

By now Grubby had his officer's hat off and began scratching his head. "Confound it all, Merrit, my old pal, you got it all twisted outa shape. The whole case is this simple. 'Cuff him up and back to jail with him. We'll settle this the right way. This is a man's town and we all know it. *I* got the say here. *I'm* the arm of the Law, that's what I'm called."

With those words, Grubby motioned to the deputy to put the handcuffs back on Eddie, who complied.

"Were you able to call my mother?" Eddie asked Flo, who shook her head no, but looked at Merrit.

"Yes, I did. She's fine, but shocked," Merrit assured Eddie. "I'll call her again soon. Don't you worry."

"All right, folks," Grubby boomed out and wanted to hustle them away.

"But what about his wife? You can't just leave her here alone," Flo lambasted Grubby. "And what're you going to charge Eddie with anyway? He didn't do anything wrong."

"Ok, let's say just a formality, people, then we can release him and get him outa town, before night. It's my sheriff's job," Grubby said.

"Get out of town? How? I don't have a car," Eddie complained.

"And his wife's got two more days here," Flo added. "Where would he go, even if he had a car? Back to St. Louis, then come back to get his wife?"

Lost by then in the flood of absurd arguments and counter comments, Charlene broke down in tears. She rang for her nurse, an outspoken young woman who reminded Flo of Donna. She straightened Charlene's pillows and saw there was nothing wrong with her but the fear of abandonment and isolation and the knowledge that such things could happen. "I'm sorry. The lady needs rest," the nurse said with the stern smile of a middle-aged matron, which she wasn't.

Himself fettered like a criminal, Eddie took a step toward Charlene's bed but Grubby stopped him.

"Whoa, wait a minute, boy!" he warned while giving his deputy a warning look.

In between the sheriff, his deputy, and Eddie stepped Merrit. He put an arm around Grubby's shoulder and suggested a word in private. The two men followed the nurse out to the hallway, from where Flo heard them talking, sometimes heatedly with a few laughs blended in. The sheriff's absence gave Eddie the chance to step toward Charlene, which the deputy failed to stop him from doing. Meanwhile a receptionist from the nurses' station down the hall peeked in the room and said, "202? Flo Maxwell. Phone."

Flo went to the station to discover Gene on the phone downstairs. He hurried up to meet the others, including Merit and Grubby, so now eight persons, mostly strangers to one another, crowded in a room meant for four bedridden patients. Nearly all eight were talking at the same time. Only Grubby insisted on speaking over the others.

"As the voice of authority, I decided to keep the prisoner in county jail to prevent him from fleeing Salina, which the law says he must do to avoid jail time, until such time as his vehicle can be repaired with a new wheel from a Ford dealer someplace so that he can leave with his wife."

"But, Sheriff, what's the sense of charging him if he didn't commit any crime?" Gene asked with a shake of his head. "As a man of the cloth, I can't countenance it. He can go or stay as he wishes, as an American citizen, I mean."

"The Law speaks its own language, not you or me, it says he has to go before sundown, it's getting late afternoon," Grubby argued. "And I'm in charge here."

"Nonsense!" Merrit announced. For once everyone else fell quiet and listened. "You and me agreed in the hallway. Why should he be kept from leaving town or fleeing, whatever you wanna call it, if nobody wants him here in the first place?"

"But that's the point. We *don't* want him here or her neither. Police radio says he was passin' white motorists all 'round town today in his Ford, and we got ordinances saying that's illegal for a colored boy, they gotta stay in their place," Grubby said pointing at Charlene. "None of those people. That's why I gotta keep him in jail, to make sure he leaves!"

"So how can he leave with no car? Hitchhike?" Flo asked. "Or should he walk to St. Louis? Alone?"

"Yes, he's got a car," Grubby insisted. "My deputy called the mechanics. We'll fix it, only the boy gotta pay hisself."

"When?" Merrit insisted.

The deputy stepped forward for the first time. "Officer Oliver Plunkett here. Mechanic says they got a wheel bearing to fix. Be a couple a' days."

"And me leave?" Eddie burst out. "Without my wife? No, no whitey's gonna separate us that way. Damned if this is any slave market."

Grubby's ire rose in an instant. "No insolent bugger gonna talk to me like that, an officer of the law. Boy, I seen enough a' your kind in the Army," he spat out. He raised a fist and made a move toward Eddie, but stopped when the deputy stepped between them, followed by Merrit, who put a hand up to stop the sheriff's rampage.

To establish calm, Gene came forward, but he ignored the four men at loggerheads. Instead he walked over to Charlene's bedside, where he put a hand on her shoulder and said mildly. "We are all the injured party. Blessed be the sick at heart, they shall find help."

Everyone heard him, but they soon turned to look at the doorway, where Kristine and Donna suddenly appeared. The two had listened to the Reverend's words and guessed at the intended fisticuffs preceding them. They strode into the room, the youngest but the least ruffled of the bunch.

If Kristine was the thinker, Donna made things happen. Against all expectations, the young Latina, as much a minority as Eddie and Charlene, needed only minutes to face Grubby.

"Take this man in cuffs off to jail, if you must, both of you," she told the sheriff, who was storming out with Merrit, Plunkett, and handcuffed Eddie, which despite Grubby's anger appeared to be exactly what he wanted, an easy way out. To lock a brown-skinned person up was considered the directest path to justice in the sheriff's world, as Donna knew from growing up with a mother like hers.

"I know you think we're created less than you, but we're not," Donna continued haranguing Grubby. "To hell with jurisprudence, or whatever they call it, that's your approach."

Watching the young woman in action gave Flo an insight that started making it clear to her how society dealt with the disadvantaged. Donna turned to Gene, Flo, and Kristine, all of whom got the message after Donna broke through the formerly unflinching veneer.

"I'm staying here with the wife," she said for once uncertain because she didn't know the name of the woman in bed.

Charlene started to say her name, but Donna stopped her. "We'll get acquainted." With that, she waved a hand at Kristine, who nodded in agreement, then herded Gene and Flo out the door behind her.

"This seems totally planned," Kristine told her companions on the way out of the hospital, "but it's only spur of the moment. My idea, but Donna's doing."

"Doing what?" Gene asked.

"Digging up the county judge," Donna said.

5

Studying at the University of Chicago and having a member of the bar as an ex-boyfriend served Kristine Jordan more than once. She'd thought up today's possible solution to the Eddie enigma in a jiffy but, as she herself admitted, left its implementation to a woman who'd learned how to stick it to puffed-up bullies. That was Donna, who had her mother to thank for what she knew. The last cog was Gene, who fit in as a pastor and soft-spoken poet.

Only Flo knew anything special about Oswaldo Winesap, the official whose door they knocked on. After studying law at Berkeley and serving as a second lieutenant at Anzio during the War, he'd been on the Salina County bench for a handful of years. Recently he bought a ramshackle house in the Maxwells' neighborhood, tore it down, and built a new rambler for his family. Passing by there, Flo had often seen Oswaldo digging out crabgrass from his yard and heard him explain they were a foreign plant not meant for Salina's environment. Flo worried if he thought the same of her and Merrit for their humble origins, but talking to him made her feel relaxed. He'd seen much of the world and viewed it with acceptance. Only when she met Dr. Corale at Barnes did she find a man of eminence with a comparable tolerance of others.

Speaking of tolerance, Flo thought. They caught him in his chambers just as he was getting ready to leave for the day. She was sure he only welcomed them in because he knew Flo from the crabgrass patches. The judge listened while Gene and Kristine talked. Try as they might to invoke reason, even as they gave a tongue-twisted story about a Negro couple forbidden to stay overnight in

Salina but prevented from leaving there, both instances governed fairly by law, at least in the view of the county sheriff, "whose animosity bulges threateningly near the surface of his thick skull."

When Kristine uttered that last passage, she sounded more like Donna than Donna herself. Flo looked up at the young woman, surprised at her sudden lapse into saying exactly what she meant.

"I see. In no uncertain terms," Judge Winesap commented. "And just what are these aforementioned souls up to? Where are they headed for?"

The question knocked Flo for a loop. She realized she knew next to nothing, so she shrugged. Kristine and Gene had only met Eddie and Charlene in her hospital room and so they knew even less.

"The man, Eddie by name," Judge Winesap said. "Who might he be?"

"A school teacher from St. Louis. He says they're driving cross country looking," Flo said in a half stuttering voice.

"Looking for what, if I may ask?"

"His brother that disappeared. And hasn't been right, I guess, since the War in Europe, years ago," Flo continued.

The judge started to ask a further question, but dropped it. He looked at each of the three before him, starting with Gene, but fixing on Kristine, as though recognizing her role as a leader or perhaps best educated of the trio, despite her youth.

"And the woman with Mr. Washington? What do you make of her?"

"His wife. I'm sure."

"And why so sure?"

"She's smarter than him, a second mother for him, his lover, but a mother, too, herself," Kristine answered.

Flo squirmed in her seat, unsure where the conversation was heading. Kristine's composure impressed her so she guessed the young woman had already considered the very aspects the judge asked her about, but why not get to the point?

"Flo here told me on our way to see you that he asked someone to call his mother in St. Louis," Kristine said.

"So you're saying Mr. Washington needs the women more than they need him."

"We're women. We're angry, he's waiting?" Kristine said.

"And they've got kids back home, too," Flo added.

"So what were they doing here?" Judge Winesap asked.

Kristine and Gene both shrugged, but Flo said simply, "Looking for a brother, a missing person, that walked away from home."

"How long ago?"

Flo said she thought a few years.

"Sounds half-hearted to me," Gene broke in. "We find lotsa lost souls, you and me, Flo."

"And Sheriff Thornbuckle says what to all this?" the judge wanted to know.

"Guilty for being different, different-skinned, and all. There were reports of them driving aimlessly around town. I checked police radio before going to the hospital. That's all," Gene reported. "The Law always talks to me, you know, I'm a pastor. Whether they tell the whole story's another question."

Glancing up at the wall clock but showing no particular hurry, the judge sat in silence a few minutes so Kristine squirmed a bit and Flo wondered what he had on his mind. She remembered Dr. Corale doing the same when he had crucial thoughts about a medical case, which memories of his own experiences intruded on. It struck her as intriguing how much important men revealed about themselves unintentionally.

"And this brother? Is he real?" the judge asked coming back to the matter at hand.

Flo looked at Kristine and Gene, fully aware they knew even less about the newcomers than her. "Might as well come clean. We don't know much," she admitted. "We just wanted…"

"To do a good deed, help out. Where it's needed. I see. Nothing wrong with that."

"It's Kristine," Gene interrupted. "She got us started doing…"

"Yes, I know what you do. Seems legal enough, though you might need a license down the line," Judge Winesap explained.

"This brother wandering the countryside a few years ago? Probably shell shock. Happened a lot after the War. I saw the causes in Italy. Europe's soft side, they called it. Nothing soft where we were."

Once again his thoughts seemed to wander away, but he stopped himself and shrugged. "I'm surrounded by dodos," he continued with a sad shake of his head.

Flo, Kristine, and Gene sat patiently waiting for the judge to follow up on his introductory question, "What can I do for you?" He seemed to have dismissed that question from his mind, so they wondered what he'd move on to.

"Not much to say. Seems innocent enough. Two schoolteachers have an accident. Doesn't matter their skin color."

The three visitors wanted to thank him, but he held up a hand to stop them. "I'll talk to Thornbuckle, but your job's only beginning."

"What job?" Gene asked.

"Finding someone who'll put this colored gentleman up for the night."

Flo saw the judge study her group's puzzlement.

"Salina's not in *The Green-Book*," he warned them.

6

"Damned traffic!" Grubby snorted. "Can't get anywhere these days." He honked and turned on his flashing lights in frustration, though only one other vehicle appeared on the street. "Who can decide what the law is about better than a law man can?" he continued.

Next to him sat Merrit, who kept a steady eye on the road fearing the sheriff might get it in his head to crash the cruiser to get back at the magistrates in City Hall, who took it on themselves and created ordinances or protocol intended solely to counteract Grubby's interpretation of law and order, in this case his treatment of Eddie Washington, the very runaway fugitive or law abiding schoolmaster now seated in the back seat of Grubby's official car.

"Just you look at what I got to put up with along with these hellacious drivers. This vagrant bum in the back seat?" Grubby waved behind him as though Merrit was clueless of Eddie and Deputy Plunkett, who sat silent and handcuffed together in the back seat. "Well, he gets hisself run over uptown and I do my duty and lock him up to teach him a lesson, for comin' here to my town and messin' stuff up for me. I did like any good officer of the peace would do, I'll remind you. You know me now, Merrit old buddy, doin' what the citizens elected me to do, law and order, but then this worn-out old judge," he continued, forgetting he was really only talking about a 29-year-old schoolteacher and a part-time peddler named Donna. "This judge comes along and orders me to take the dodo to the hospital and then bring him back here to the lockup again, where I had him to start with. And can you think it through? All this jaunting around to keep a fugitive from runnin' away, when that's pretty much all those people do anyway. Tempting our patience, seein' how far they can test us."

In the back, Eddie moved to his right to take the pressure off Officer Plunkett's right side, which was scrunched against Eddie's left shoulder, like the two were Siamese twins. When Plunkett rolled his eyes, Eddie looked at him out of the corner of his eye to see if the deputy felt more discomfort from the handcuffing or the sheriff's blathering. To try and forget all that, Eddie decided to think about something else, but all that came to mind was his two-hour stint in a county jail cell, where the concept 'a free country' took on new meaning. One in every four Negro men spend at least some time in prison, Eddie had heard, and there it was happening to him. He felt trapped like an animal in a cage and knew there was no escape.

Grubby's loose talk and Eddie's thoughts stopped on a dime when a youngster dashed out from the curb and crossed the street in front of them. Merrit yelled, *Watch it!* Grubby braked and the youth ran on, which gave the sheriff no chance of stopping him in the maze of houses he disappeared in among.

"Aw, what the heck, no bother, he's just a harmless punk, probably a good kid," Grubby chuckled.

The episode suggested a new topic to rant on about, so he launched into a tirade about kids, in this case his own. So was this a mixed message, Eddie wondered from his back seat perch?

"I got the damndest mess at home. Two twin sons," he began.

Eddie wondered if Grubby meant twin sons or two sets of twin boys, but he dismissed the thought and listened.

"Here they are 24 years old, and they act like 14. They go downtown and buy a motorcycle. Mind you, not one but one for each of 'em, and come home to me with the bills to pay for 'em. Like, I explode and say where 'n the hell do you think I'm gonna get that kinda dough, and they answer, well, you're the sheriff, set some speed traps uptown for moulah like that, that's what you do in other cases when money's needed, for raffles and sheriff's fish fries at the hunting lodge. And I'm getting even more mad, because I wonder about young people's morals any more. And so I say, yes, of course we do those extra speeding traps, but it's always for a good cause.

"My own sons start guffawing at me for me admitting they got it right about the tricks we law officers play on the public for extra income, and I give up an' let 'em have their cursed toys.

"But, now, I gotta tell ya, Merrit, my boys're the greatest athletes you ever saw on those bikes, dashing every darn way down dirt roads in the county and gravel alleys in town. Makes me so proud to watch 'em and never any need to arrest 'em either. Just watching 'em warms my heart now an' then for them creating an' me seeing the beauty of their dirt bike riding."

As Grubby talked, he made it clear what folks said. He was a mean ass with grownups but a pushover around youngsters. Eddie figured out that trait in the sheriff and immediately started jabbering about his own daughters and how much they were missing him back home with their grandmother. They were sure to be pining away, more each day. He made up new names for them, June and Joy, and told how they studied dance and the Bolshoi Ballet was after them to come to Moscow, and they sang in their mother's children's choir, which latter 'fib' was a fact, but Eddie made it sound like they were teenagers or maybe a lot younger or, at times, even older, depending on what spin he needed to put on it, and, believe it or not, now the Bolshoi was offering them money.

"Real moulah, for sure, I'd even show you a snapshot of them, but it's with Charlene, that's my wife, that you saw, poor woman, in her hospital bed at Shepherd's, and her daughters pining for her, too," he told Grubby.

The longer Eddie talked about kids, the more Grubby slowed his driving, which let Merrit catch on to Eddie's ploy. He, too, joined the conversation and rhapsodized about his clever son Ronny, who was a bit older than Grubby's twins, yet maybe a bit younger, too, who could remember? But he shared with them so many habits sure to make them all specimens of sterling youth. In the end nobody remembered how old anyone's kids were anymore, but what did it matter?

"It's just that we have our trials with them, but they all come out good in the long run," Merrit said. "Right?"

Grubby drove merrily along now, with only one hand on the wheel. "That's why I got the county to get this cruiser for me," he said looking at Merrit, "to cruise the county with."

Eddie joined in with added wonders about his girls at home until Grubby turned in his seat and spoke to him directly. "Why, boy, I surely am impressed with your daughters back in St. Louie, from what you tell me. Your stories do warm my heart."

At the turn-in for County Sheriff's Office, Grubby pulled to a soft stop and told Deputy Plunkett to help Eddie out. Grubby himself walked around the car and stopped before Eddie.

"I sure would love to see those photos of your girls at home," he said. "I bet they got the blondest curls for all the dancin' they do."

Eddie stood before the sheriff feeling every bit his equal and, in truth, a whole lot more. When Grubby took out his key chain, Eddie held up his hands and let the sheriff unlock the cuffs. His arms hung free.

"Now, boy, you're on your own," Grubby said. "Just stay outa trouble."

Eddie and Merrit looked at each other and heaved a sigh of relief. Eddie had heard men tell about worse treatment in Whitey's world.

As Grubby headed for his office, the sheriff's dispatcher met him at the door.

"Hey, boss," the dispatcher said. "You got a message here from Judge Winesap. Call him. Now. It's urgent!"

Grubby passed the guy by without a glance.

"Tell that asshole to go screw hisself," he muttered.

7

E ddie was handcuff free. He'd sat behind bars for a couple hours, but the feeling of incarceration lingered strongest from the clank of steel around his wrists. He wondered if Deputy Plunkett had the same feeling he did from their ride together in the sheriff's car. Who imprisoned who during that time?

Those thoughts ran through his mind from Charlene's bedside. Merrit had driven him to Holy Shepherd's and explained that the Negro with him was a free man. The staff accepted Merrit's assurances and let Eddie in to sit with Charlene. Though exhausted from a day at the roundhouse, Merrit quickly left to check with the mechanic fixing MayBelle's Fairlane, which Grubby had neglected to worry about.

Eddie and Charlene had room 202 to themselves, and she was asleep. The other beds were still unoccupied because no white women had yet agreed to share the room with a lady of color. So Eddie sat with his own thoughts. For the first time since the wild youths plowed into him and Charlene at the Salina intersection, he remembered Charles and wondered what villainy his brother had run into. To an unfathomable degree, this white man's world struck him as schizophrenic. Its behavior models ranged from a good hearted lady like this Flo to an unpredictable scoundrel wearing the sheriff's badge. Middle ground was Family Four.

It dawned on Eddie this trip to locate Charles, or at least to track his wandering, was only a few paltry days long and geographically brief, yet it packed a wallop in terms of showing even experienced and educated individuals how invisible they could be in the world of a man like this local sheriff. Here Eddie sat by his wife's bed at a place that called itself the Holy Shepherd and they found themselves alone in a room for six. A medical staff ministered to them but gave scant attention. Such solitude was surely Charles's fate as well if he tried hiking across these sections of mid-America. Maybe, Eddie concluded, his brother was headed somewhere special after all, like across the wide Atlantic to his lady or to find their father, somewhere in vast open stretches of America. Yet even if Charles left home with a plan, it must've blended in with some level of madness.

This trip will never get us anywhere, a fool's errand? he was thinking when Merrit strode into 202. "Get a move on, things are happening," he said and hustled Eddie out the door. "I told the nurses we'll be back."

"But when?" Eddie asked without knowing even where they were heading. He was afraid for Charlene's reaction when she woke up. Still, having seen what the sheriff should've done but didn't, he understood Merrit was acting in his and Charlene's interests.

8

They met at Gene's apartment to find a place for Eddie to spend the night, or nights, until his car was fixed and Charlene got released from Holy Shepherd's. Gene's Three Square congregation, with its illogical name, was still seemingly the only more or less logical place to start looking for kindly souls willing to take in a stranded couple. The problem was that Gene had been living single since leaving his wife in Michigan over two years ago.

"Getting hitched was a youthful mistake on both our parts," the pastor explained to Flo. "We keep pretending we'll get back together again, but we won't. The idea is I'll keep up appearances with my churchgoers, but even those with the lowest critical thinking skills are starting to catch on. No, I'd have to admit to folks Joanie won't be joining me. On top of seeming to live in sin, that is, without a woman, which makes them wonder about me, I don't dare ask anybody in the church to take in someone who's colored. Living with another man may be against the Lord's laws, but nothing would be half as bad, in a congregant's eyes, as taking in someone they commonly call by a bad name."

Gene paused to consider his words. "Pardon my language," he added. "A description of reality, not a value judgment."

After Gene ruled himself out as a possible host, Kristine and Donna announced they lived alone in small apartments. Left with a family residence were only Flo and Merrit, but Ronny's presence there made their modest house too crowded for five people, and he'd yet to leave for college.

Of course, the town's hotels accepted whites only. The hope for housing was to make calls. So Eddie and Merrit waited while the others put their heads together for a phonathon. Family Four made lists of locals presumed to have space enough in their houses and sufficient care to accommodate a pair of Midwestern schoolteachers, albeit colored ones. Gene and Flo paired off with a phone book in the pastor's room while Kristine and Donna did the same in an outer vestibule.

While Merrit checked again about repairs to the Fairlane, Eddie sat and stared at the doors the callers had disappeared behind. The time following was nearer to hell than the two hours he'd spent locked in a Salina County cell. At least there time had felt as finite as the 9' X 12' confines. Now he was waiting in an empty Three Square church building, whose members were sure to turn down the chance to house him and his wife overnight. Housing a man of a different race would prove a hellacious misdeed if it made the rounds of local gossip mills.

Eddie imagined the horror of men with skin color like his denied domicile and put out to rot in the burning streets of Tulsa and East Saint Louis or his brother's Army buddies thrown in jail cells and left to fester as living corpses on the muddy floors of men's dungeons. Or women raped. Such infernal torture, he saw in his mind, was worse than any gruesome dream. It was a reality visited on people of his race for the merciless slavery they endured for four hundred years, as his mother MayBelle never quit reminding those around her.

When at last Gene and Flo came out from his office, they told a tale, not of courage but cowardice. They gathered a list of community leaders hailed for their leadership skills and had called them for help. To start with Gene appealed to businessmen who might donate cash for the repair of the Washingtons' damaged Ford. His very first such call went to Mercury Motors, the local Ford dealership, but he received a blank no from the chief financial officer, Dick Derelec, who also told Gene that the firm's owner, Mr. Mercury himself, was out of town or indisposed.

"Actually he hemmed and hawed for a long time unable to say whether out of town and indisposed also meant unreachable," Gene told Flo. "After I pushed him for a definite answer, Derelec informed me Mr. Mercury had been on the Salina City Council for years and spearheaded the drafting of our sundown laws."

"So that's that for Ford motors?" Flo muttered in disgust. "So the ordinances are meant to stick, huh? The folks I called mostly pretended they didn't know me or they realized who my husband is and changed tunes in a rush. 'We're business owners, don't you know?' was the common response."

"Which means what?" Gene asked.

"It means they are indeed owners of companies or friends of business owners, which means they also know my Merrit is a railroad foreman and a local Labor Union member," Flo explained. "Like they say, next thing we know unions'll be in our work force, too, taking jobs from honest men."

Still, they kept calling. Same message. Same responses. Flo understood that Gene, as a pastor, was used to locals with some education evading sensitive issues or taking neutral stances. Most were not about to admit they were agnostics or doubted religion. If nothing else, folks respected his pastor's collar. By the same token, some refused to say their opinion on racial matters, but claimed they lived in too cramped houses, had poor finances, or just quite simply couldn't associate with "those people."

"What will our neighbors say if we did take them in?" Flo reported as the most common excuse.

Kristine and Donna called folks of humbler means and more outspoken views. After a couple of hours they emerged from the vestibule with news just as negative as Gene's. Donna volunteered with the Salina Red Cross blood donor program, but she was careful not to mention donors unless it was necessary.

"Some townies knew me and my mom that way, all around the area," Donna explained. "Some are so poor they donate blood for cash. So soon as I mentioned a car accident they assumed we wanted them to give blood. But not even for pay would they donate here, they said. 'Don't give me none a' that save them people stuff,' one guy ranted at me."

"And human blood is just human blood," Kristine added.

"Yeah, blood type doesn't know any skin color, I tried to tell them that, but all I got was swear words in return. 'No bloody fill-in-the-blanks in my house,' several folks added."

"You know, I heard some swear words just now that're new to me," Kristine said in dismay. "And just imagine, these are churchgoers."

Thinking they'd heard enough, Flo and Gene could only bow their heads. Returning to Eddie, Flo saw him shake his head no, showing he anticipated their sad thoughts. So the five of them sat in the anteroom to Gene's office, reflecting on the injustice of how any of them might fall on hard times and be denied housing, but only one, Eddie, could feel the pain of brutal deprivation. Family Four knew they failed.

9

Merrit's knock reverberated through the open doorway. His expression showed he came bearing good news and was surprised only Flo looked his way.

"Got anything good to say, dear?" she asked.

"I do," he replied and waited for them to listen up, which they finally did. "Eddie's car's being repaired. The mechanic'll replace the wheel, rim and tire. The mechanic did a double take when he saw two Fairlanes at his shop at once. Ronny brought ours. He's in the car now, outside."

"And how long?"

"They're waiting, you mean? There's car parts to pay and Eddie's got no insurance. Him and me called his ma. She's on her way now."

"Here? Now?" Flo asked. She found that hard to believe but said nothing else to avoid raised eyebrows.

"Yeah, she'll pay the bill, all right," Eddie admitted in a low voice. "My ma always does."

Merrit stood before them with his arms folded like a discouraged prophet saying he caught on to the impossible task Family Four failed at, but the struggle remained.

"Folks'll change their mind and step up?" he asked in a demanding voice. "Dream on."

"Like, what else's new?" Donna asked. She alone showed a raging anger.

"Look, there's no reason to sulk," Merrit insisted.

"Not sulking, just pissed," Donna shot back at him. "Their blood's too good to share?"

"It's just all the … I dunno … Men with no sense that think they're superior, superior to what?" Kristine said bitterly. "I never heard dirty words like the ones today."

"You don't need to be colored to get the short end of the stick," Merrit said in a heftier tone. "There are many targets. Other people's religion or wealth or politics. But there's good, too. Grubby went home, so I called Holy Shepherd's. They'll do Charlene's X-ray tomorrow. And she can see the doctor. Good service."

Oh, yes, Flo thought, seeing the doctor, that's where this whole story began for me, too. Seeing a doctor and getting the horrible word.

"You have to move on," Merrit urged. "Plus there's still a problem to solve."

"Yeah, a plenty big one, if you ask me," Kristine agreed. "Where does Eddie spend the night? The townies here won't have him, Donna and I are single, Gene's church won't use its parsonage, and Flo's house is full. We've wracked our brains."

"Yes," Donna agreed. "I tried my mom, but she lives a fair hike from here. She says nothing. We got no solution."

"I have one," a voice rang out so it echoed off the church choir loft. Flo recognized it immediately as Ronny's. "I'll leave and he can have my room at home."

"Leave for college?" Flo asked. "But when?"

"First-year orientation starts a week from now. I'll go there now. I can always hang out for a few days. He can have my room at home. My buddies'll pick me up tonight."

Flo studied her son in astonishment. His growing independence, as shown on their repeated trips to Barnes Hospital, was blossoming. In addition, him turning away from adolescent hijinks with his school chums was making itself felt. She'd cherished the thought of having him at home another week or two before relinquishing her grasp to the university. Must the last vestiges of his childhood end so soon, she couldn't help asking herself?

That thought flashed through her mind as Ronny looked at his mother the way she recalled him doing on their last trip to St.

Louis, that time the last ice resisted melting. It was then she'd realized they could reach each other in a wordless dialogue. That day at Forest Park Zoo the son guided his mother through the minds of captive creatures, who managed in a world of thought but lacked words. From then on, she'd begun to understand the minds of all those in need but deprived of a voice.

Flo observed her son making his manlike decision.

"But, Ronny, your room. It's yours. You'll need it," Flo insisted praying she didn't sound like a wimp.

Ronny came back and gave her a hug.

"Call ya later, Mom. Bye, Dad."

He turned, was gone, and Eddie had a room.

"Eddie, your mother then, what're her needs?" Flo asked drying her unseen tears.

"A noble act, by your son, giving up his room for me," Eddie answered. "My ma? A tough lady. Can we meet her at the bus station? We'll see if they let her off it," he joked. "Or maybe they'll pile me on it and get us both out of town."

"I know what," Donna suggested. "MayBelle, that's her name?"

Eddie nodded yes.

"She can stay at my apartment. She'll have it all to herself. That is, if Kristine'll put me up for a night at her place?"

"A night or two maybe," Kristine answered. Her smile was a friendly invitation.

10

Flo and Merrit's house dated back to the early twentieth century. In their first married days they'd lived in a series of apartments in Salina. Most were shabby but low-rent. Their decision to buy a house came after living a year above Derby Dan's Roller Rink. Through the building's flimsy walls, that apartment offered unending tunes, so-called, from a calliope and the steady whir of roller skaters. Merrit nearly bit the dust for lack of sleep given his need to get up every morning and hit the rails for Pan Pacific. Upon learning that Flo was pregnant with Ronny's sister, their first child, Merrit said yes to moving when a bachelor uncle of his retired to a nursing home and offered the present house for a song.

Merrit and Flo took the house, knowing it wasn't problem free. The location was a genteel but somewhat rundown East Fifth Street. The house's original owner, Fordyce Fuller, had been a land surveyor, whose prime pastime was leading a free church group that foreswore organized religious services and worshipped in Fordyce's front bedroom. That room had blue, red, and yellow stained glass windows facing the street and carried exotic incense odors from the Far East. The followers held sacred a species of viper known, it was rumored, to inhabit tall grassy meadows, so they never mowed Fordyce's lawn, preferring instead to spend their time doing seances on a Ouija board, which was said to conjure up images of their dead ancestors and enormous serpents.

Once Fordyce was dead and buried, Merrit's uncle moved in and forswore the cult. He kept the stained glass, though, and grew too old to cut the grass. Merrit spent a month of his section gang salary replacing the unsightly windows, whereupon he set about hacking and mowing the lawn, which had grown to the height of the region's fabled prairie grass of pre-European settlement days. Merrit never found any vipers. They were, he knew, imagined and never real. Yet he swore he'd remember for life his two solid weeks of tall-grass removal. Since those early and hectic days of conjugal bushwhacking, an activity Merrit knew to be very real, not at all imagined, the Maxwells had lived in Salina-like peace and quiet.

On the evening of the incredible day of frantic phoning, Flo and Merrit were at home again, hosting Kristine, Donna, Gene, Eddie, and MayBelle, who against all expectations had just arrived from St. Louis after a hundred mile Expresss bus ride. Flo put together a meal of veggies and baked salmon, which the group dined on with relish. As Flo watched them at their meal, she thought she saw something resembling a happy ending taking place, even if it took a form wholly unexpected. The surprising part was that Eddie's mother proved not at all the talkative lady Eddie's few comments about her indicated. To Flo, she seemed smart but subdued.

"So nice to have you all," Flo said.

"Eddie and especially his mother," Merrit added.

"You're welcome here, but what brought you to us intrigues me most, the whole story?" Gene asked partly in jest, since he knew the bare outlines of Eddie and Charlene's mishap in town.

Eddie looked up from his plate, but he hesitated to launch into his tale with great gusto, partly because he'd have preferred hearing MayBelle speak. "First, I wanted to thank your son," he began.

Flo smiled in appreciation, but Gene spoke up on her behalf. "Yes, Ronny's grown up before our eyes. Thanks to his great folks here and a special teacher, too, I suspect." He nodded toward Kristine. "That's the word from his mother anyway."

Eddie took in the interplay among his Salina hosts and understood better than before that their goodwill was real. So with a nod toward his mother he began telling their family story up to the day Charles mysteriously walked away from home and didn't come back. Eddie's tale, including the part about Heights Homers' losing softball game, lasted into a late evening hour. Flo had already served coffee and two rounds of a shortcake dessert by the time the last dramatic out of the game happened, in Eddie's retelling.

"The game's already entered local lore," Eddie explained. "At least if you read the Negro press."

"So Eddie and his wife decided at last to go off and find your older son, is that right?" Donna asked MayBelle in a quiet voice unlike her usual boisterous one. "I find that *so* admirable."

"I believe he's out there," MayBelle responded, sounding as subdued as Donna. "My boy Charles."

"But do you think he's findable?" Gene wanted to know. "It's been a long while."

"I don't know," Eddie answered. "We set off to look, Charlene and me, for my mother's sake. Now Ma's here herself, paying our car repair bill."

"For *my* car don't forget. And you gotta have transport, my boy," MayBelle said and laughed for the first time.

MayBelle finding her voice lightened the atmosphere. So Gene scooted his chair closer to the table and looked closely at Eddie.

"Tell me," the pastor asked. "Is that true, that you can't outrun the ball?"

"It's an established fact," Eddie assured him.

"But did Charles know that?"

"Of course. He preached it in the dugout."

"But did he believe it?"

Eddie had an answer to Gene's question, but he gave way to MayBelle.

"Ma understands my brother best of all," Eddie said.

Flo realized that was right. Etched on MayBelle's face was pride mixed with sorrow.

"The last thing my boy Charles told me was, 'Sometimes you outrun the ball and still lose the game,'" MayBelle said. "He thought he was safe at first, but he knew the rules."

"I see. So he realized that," Gene said.

The group understood Gene's utterance as a statement, not a question. So silence fell over the room, mainly, Flo guessed, because none of the Salina people knew Charles and so were reluctant to hazard a guess about what motivated him. Surely each person around the table was more engrossed in their own thoughts and life dilemmas, to the extent they had any of pressing importance at the moment. In short, a man like Charles ten years removed from combat but still suffering from it, in whatever strange form, who's able to function normally in society and write acclaimed syndicated columns for the press, one day walks off into the sea of humanity across an immense continent, leaving as a measure of himself only blurbs of info he utters about an obscure ball game on a dusty diamond in a Midwestern city. And he's never seen again?

As Flo considered the disparate grouping gathered around her table, she guessed each was thinking, what if it happened to me? She herself wandered back in thought to the brave tugboat she'd seen from the Pan Pacific Flier on her and Ronny's last visit to Barnes Hospital. The small craft had battled stubbornly to make its dock when giving up to the River would've been an easier option. Why couldn't Charles have been tougher? Or luckier? Or less brilliant?

"We'll never know for sure, I suppose," MayBelle said at last in a half whisper. "Seven souls, all of us cast adrift on life. Like I say, family. Share and share alike."

"A hate-inspired Sundown law, which we don't even believe in, brought us together around the Maxwells' table," Gene commented.

The others smiled graciously at the hosts, and Flo thanked them. In doing so she caught Eddie's and Kristine's eye and guessed they, like her, found Gene's words a bit too churchy.

In turn, Eddie glanced at Merrit and spoke up thoughtfully. "You know," he began, "it never occurred to me, but this is my first time ever in a white man's house."

Eddie didn't know where those words came from. Or if they needed a reply. "Come to think of it, I've never had a conversation with a white man," he continued. "Till now."

Eddie realized he'd encapsulated a feeling without spelling it out. An essence. "We're not only separate but unequal, too," he added at last.

"Amen," Gene whispered and waited.

"Men?" Kristine asked. She too waited. "As in a-men?'

With those words, the mood grew solemn until Eddie opened up with a chuckle, "Except for traffic cops, I guess. Those men and me. We talk a lot."

Light laughter spread around the table, which led MayBelle to raise her voice.

"Yes, my boy, I should know. I be the one paid for all your speeding tickets."

"Ah, well, now you're talking," Kristine explained to Eddie. "Won't be the last time."

"No, not just man-to-man either," Donna said. "We're here, to stay." She pointed to the other ladies.

That comment ended the evening. Flo thought of the young people. Ronny, going off to college. Kristine, the spark plug, taking in Donna. And Donna, the go-getter, loaning MayBelle her place.

MayBelle hugged Eddie.

"Another first," she said.

"Meaning, Ma?"

"Now tonight you'll sleep in a white boy's bed."

11

Strange how an impossibly jampacked trip to a neighboring state could feel so long. It left Eddie weary and shaken, so the next morning he was thankful for Ronny's room. That was Family Four's favor to him. After coffee in Flo's tidy kitchen, Merrit drove Eddie to Holy Shepherd's to see Charlene. Her X-rays showed no internal damage, so she checked out. She was happy to feel good despite a cast on her right arm and a few bruises. The fellows told her MayBelle arrived.

"Think her and Flo have much to say alone together?" she joked.

In truth the ladies talked at length. They said the usual, as Flo always recalled, but the memories lasted. To start, MayBelle accepted an ample serving of Dogwood coffee, which Flo just happened to have on hand. Both agreed it was the best brew anywhere but, well, yes, way costly. "Dogwood's brewed for its full body. I find it at a shop in the next town over," Flo said. "Small shop, big prices."

"Yes, but sometimes worth it," MayBelle said with a nod. "Like us today, or me paying for my boys' college."

After that, MayBelle talked of the Delta, where she claimed it was so special to grow up, like no place anywhere. "You gotta open your heart, dear, that's what they teach," she said, and she told about the streets of St. Louis, with the mementos she peddled and the good folks she met there and the stories and events she heard tell of, plus the People's Finance bank account she had. Not to forget Carlos, the love of her life, that all the women in her clan reviled for coming and going till at last he just was gone and how he never could figure out the past tense of 'go' was 'went' but someday he'd go back to her, the way they talked English in his world, and about Charles and that Clarys, such a pity. And how MayBelle had Eddie and Charlene, her chauffeurs.

"That's what I mean about paying my boys' way to college. It gave me a brand new Ford Fairlane," she said with a chuckle.

Flo had crossed the River to St. Louis as well, and seen the Zoo, which once had chimps, Sailor and Sinner, and met Clara and Cameron from Cameroon, wherever that was, but they now lived in Hazelwood, and she learned about a sculptor, the guy from Sweden, wherever that was, too, and his homage to the Meeting of the Waters, Missouri and Mississippi. She saw how folks lived there in the City and worked, and she learned to love urban life even with its troubles, with crime and such-like, and folks who moved in here and there over and over again and got run out just as often by big spenders, for a new ballpark or shopping emporium, but never lost their spirit and their men built churches with their own hands that lasted. And how she shed a tear now and then for poor Ronny who missed out on Natalie Wood and also now and then a sob for Dr. Corale, who saved her life only to lose his own so early, only 50-something, but her Merrit, there weren't enough good words for him.

About all those topics the ladies were in accord. Most likely they agreed on other things as well that didn't come to mind. Like one spring that wasn't, which some people had already forgotten about, that is, when it'd been so beastly cold and ice lingered on the Mississippi even to Easter and Flo brought Ronny to the city, bless his soul, and she made that super mistake of wearing a summer dress. Ronny was then reaching the age when he couldn't keep his crushes straight. The latest was Kristine, the teacher that saw the world and the creatures in it through a different lens than most folks and made youngsters think about what they saw around them. It was just Miss Jordan's charisma, that's all.

"That's the last time I saw Dr. Corale, that spring," Flo had said. "That spring it was so chilly coming to Barnes, like I said, and now that surgeon, a good man, passed away. So young."

"We had a World's Fair," MayBelle rhapsodized. That happened way before her time, but she wouldn't admit it.

"Yes, *Meet Me in St. Louee, Louee*," Flo joined in and they'd sung together like Judy Garland.

"Then my time in Tennessee …," MayBelle continued and grew teary-eyed.

"Okay, Ma, enough of that," Eddie interrupted her. "Pa'll come back. Someday."

Eddie and Charlene themselves had made it back with Merrit a while earlier. Charlene hugged her mother-in-law, and she waited for the older ladies to finish their chat. When an end to the chatting didn't seem upcoming, Eddie made up his mind. "It's time," he repeated.

"One last sip of this Dogwood," MayBelle agreed as Flo gave her the final refill.

After that they had "not much to do but wait," as MayBelle said. The Sheriff's Office promised to return the Washingtons' Fairlane from whatever mechanic's garage had it. Eddie and Charlene called their girls at an aunt's house in Florissant, where MayBelle had dropped them off. All this happened while Flo waited for Ronny to call, which he'd promised but failed to do.

Only at long last did the sheriff's cruiser glide up to Maxwells' house, followed by the Fairlane. Deputy Plunkett drove the official car and Grubby was behind the wheel of MayBelle's vehicle. The sheriff wedged his way out of the Ford making it unclear which was worse, the car's cramped seats or his girth. Either way he looked sour as he lumbered to the door, but brightened when Merrit answered.

"Got your key here," Grubby said.

"Mine? Not mine," Merrit answered.

"Car's fixed anyway," Grubby commented with assurance. He craned his neck to see past Merrit inside the house. "Tell your boy repair's on me. County footed the bill, that is. I made 'em. And he's to take care a' his young girls. Family, you know."

From the bay window where he stood, Eddie saw a combination of child-like curiosity and affected superiority in the sheriff as he spoke and made conversation.

Indoors Flo was busy. She helped MayBelle and Charlene put together what meager baggage they'd brought or salvaged from the collision. After Merrit gave their key back, the five of them stood on the curb around MayBelle's Ford, the one thing she owned but couldn't control. They chatted about this and that. Flo would've delved deeper, but she sensed their energy fading.

"Well, here we are," Charlene said.

"Or almost all," Eddie added.

MayBelle had no words. Then Flo remembered, there was no Charles.

"Got your road map?" Merrit asked at last.

"No need," Eddie answered. "I learned what to avoid."

"Not what you expected."

"Ever changing landscape," Eddie replied but gave no explanation.

Instead he got in and drove off, slowly for once. Charlene up front. MayBelle in back. Charles still missing. Flo and Merrit behind watching them depart. They all knew how far it was to St. Louis, so nobody asked how long the drive would take.

"Strange, no hugs," Flo said. "I would've expected it. From them."

"Couple hours, maybe more," said railroader Merrit, unable to resist telling the schedule like it was. "Nothing in their way now."

BOOK VIII

The Right Way

1

"The dust settles," Merrit said with a sigh. He could kid like that, in a brusque tone. Flo remembered him acting that way with the St. Louis taxi drivers and other service oriented workers they ran into here and there. Or maybe distant relatives and new acquaintances, who thought him dismissive, when he was only reflecting on small happenings or new people worthy of note but unlikely ever to pop up again. This time Merrit was referring to the Washingtons. They drove off, minus dust, or maybe shaking it off without looking back, like someone or other in the Bible. On their way home.

Merrit had aided them gladly as needed, but without gaining any life changing insights. At least nothing Flo recognized. For her husband, it wasn't worth the effort, thinking how it could feel being a minority in America. It's true, Eddie showed Flo the sketch of him with a knife in his back and dripping blood that the teenage kid in Sardis made, and Flo relayed the story to Merrit, who shrugged at it.

"No worry, a teenage prank."

"I could have Eddie show it to you someday. How would you like seeing a knife poking out of your ribs?" she persisted.

"Like I said, you know," Merrit comforted her, or so he likely thought he was doing. "You imagine something else?"

"Yes, whatever. What we learn … Love? Hate? Prejudice?" Flo asked.

"The Washington family needs to get back home again, like anyone else would, move on with their lives. That's all."

Flo floundered. She had something vital to say and wished for Donna's or Kristine's way with words. "Colored folks face this hatred every single day of their lives in this country, do you not hear that from them, read between the lines?"

"You heard it from MayBelle, the family thing," Merrit replied. "That's the biggie for them."

"So that pencil drawing, you figure any hate there? Any at all?" she asked.

"Nope, not where there's none intended," he answered.

Flo stood dumbfounded and wondered if it was Merrit speaking. She knew it was.

2

Cleaning up after last night's dinner and today's coffee, Flo found no fault with her husband, she'd never found any meanness in him. Sometimes he sounded callow and unfeeling. She already knew that about him, but what if it had been Ronny playing pranks in Sardis? Was it no more than that? A prank? No way, not with their Ronny. We're good people, she thought. We'll carry on looking for the right path. I'll be cancer free. Merrit a picture of manhood. Ronny a good college student. We won't ever know want. But what if it *was* Ronny? Imagine, a sharp knife in another man's back?

She knew that would never happen, not *her* son. But stranger things happened. Flo felt flummoxed as she put the silverware away and straightened her and MayBelle's chairs at table.

"Open your heart, dear," she remembered the large lady with the big voice repeating. Her words felt rich and full like the aroma from the Dogwood they splurged on.

Flo hoped the lessons of their past would be worth the price. She thought of her own forebears, who ventured away from distant Ukraine leaving all behind. Flo heard stories of Ukrainians who wed themselves to the flatlands of America, but kept their Ukrainian spirit. They seemed not so unlike the African slaves of the past, except that the Ukrainians chose America. The Africans were ripped from home and nurtured their souls in longing.

Flo would never know a cataclysm like enslavement or mass emigration. Even World War II had affected her little. Merrit was in uniform, but he served with the Coast Guard and could tell only of occasional brushes with Nazi submarines. Flo had worked throughout the war and moved on to the 1950s without a deep awareness of social strife in the US.

"What do you think speaks loudest about how oblivious we were?" Flo asked Merrit one evening when the nest felt emptiest.

"Oblivious?" he replied. She wondered if it was the word itself he failed to grasp or the concept it stood for.

"Just wondered," she said.

"How so?"

"I mean *European Style*. The sign. Which is worse? That I've spent my whole life ignorant of what it means? Or that you never cared enough to tell me?"

"Never thought it mattered," he answered.

"You know, when I saw Eddie at the scene of his wreck, he wondered what caused it. He said he and his wife talked a lot about cause and effect in their life."

"Like I said, and so?"

"I mean, is that sign on the Starr Hotel to say there are no coloreds in town? Or are there no coloreds here because that sign's on the wall?"

"It is what it is," Merrit replied.

"Yes, you could argue that, but I think of it like my cancer."

"The cause and effect? Be happy it's gone."

"Yes, but no, too. The Lump could've killed me. Yet it gave me a new life. I think of all I was unaware of, and what I am now."

"Which is?"

"New. An older version of Kristine and Donna. Or even a new man of sorts, if you wanna say it that way. Gene's poetry, I understand where he's coming from."

"I know," Merrit insisted. "We got you the new Fairlane."

"Yes, you stood by me. Through it all."

She folded her arms like in a huge hug and he smiled back lovingly. Flo could remember that, a moment when she recognized how cancer, in its cruel mode, claimed her long enough to start her on the path to awareness. Above all, she intended to stay in touch with the Washingtons, Eddie and Charlene and their dear MayBelle, who made her wishes heard.

"I'll write them or call and we'll meet a lot," she told Merrit. "I feel it."

3

Getting out of Salina proved harder for Eddie than getting in. He felt discombobulated again when he had to use East North Main to find the westbound highway. Then Charlene nodded off on his shoulder. Before long he put an arm around her shoulder and drove one-handed. He saw no sense milling around in other small towns like the ones they passed, so he hit the road for home.

"You think any ofay gonna stop me for driving with a wife under my arm?" he asked MayBelle. "Ofay, that's what my students call cops. Whitey with a badge."

Still hearing no answer, he glanced back and saw his mother's head bobbing like a cork. She fought the weariness before also falling asleep. So Eddie drove ahead in the fading light.

"Awake alone," he said to himself.

The highway snaked ahead as he came up out of a river bottom he had a dim recollection of seeing on the way in. It was a place where nighttime lured weary travelers, so Eddie stayed alert. He imagined his brother treading this very path years ago and how it could've felt to him, longing for a night's sleep but destined to lose out in a Sundown town.

Yet Charles must've known that feeling before when crossing the Pacific. Eddie remembered his words, *You give up hope and then one day there's light on the shore and there you are, back where you left off.* No matter how far the path, you always end up where you started out from. Figuring Charles's way in life presented Eddie with puzzles. Was his big brother somehow the odd man out because of his many talents or despite them? Whichever way Eddie looked, he met the impenetrable problem of inherited psyche and learned experience. No doubt Charles had their father's blood, but he'd also stumbled on society's taboos by being a colored man smarter than those in Whitey's world. The more sensitive the soul the harder the fall.

"Throw in landing on Normandy Beach, witnessing senseless killings, and you get a man that walks off into the night back home?" Eddie asked out loud while urging his mother's Fairlane up a steep incline.

Eddie reached the flat, fertile Illinois prairie before MayBelle spoke. "Why, when my boy was just a tyke he came down with scarlet fever. We went with him to the docs. Some thought it was the rheumatic stuff, but our doc said no. Anyway, he got to be big and ran like the wind, so we never knew what the matter was. You saw it when he got older, those jerky movements."

"Yes, I recollect."

Sunk in thought, they drove on.

"Strange," Eddie said at last. "We set out as two Washingtons, hoping to return three strong and so we are."

"Yes," said Charlene, who came back to life and stretched her arms so her cast nearly struck Eddie by accident. "A glorious triumvirate."

They chuckled at much but not about Eddie in jail, which only a day before felt like a nightmare. The minutes passed.

"Grubby!" MayBelle squealed. "Some name, all right. Why, I never!"

The more Eddie weighed what happened the more profound its bitter absurdity, as though 400 years of brutality and hate were reduced to "a one-D Salina sitcom. Played out at society's expense on its most mundane street corners."

"But none the less murderous," Charlene commented. "Consider its reverse side. From farce to tragedy."

"I always wonder, why Charles was the one seeing so many bad things and not me?" Eddie wondered.

"You see, the fever caught him early," MayBelle explained.

"So simple is it?" Charlene questioned.

"Simple?" MayBelle asked with a shrug. "I'd tell you simple, girl. Livin' in the Delta'd shiver your timbers. Big-time."

"D'ya think we'll find him?" Eddie asked after chuckling at his mother's dark humor.

He slowed down on the lonely road skirting Salem and looked back at his mother. Her eyes shone, so her sad veil of longing for Charles lifted at last. Like in clairvoyance, he experienced a transfer of feeling from her to him and then out onto the world, where her patient indulgence could prosper.

"No, we'll wait," she uttered.

"Wait for what?" he asked.

"Him to find us."

Eddie agreed. "If he wants to be found?"

"You know, that burgh, Salina, I thunk it done me good," MayBelle dared to say.

Not a word more. Eddie drove on thinking through the past few moments and wishing his mother were at the wheel, where she belonged, guiding the family. To her way of thinking, fate, if you believe in it, is like the Delta, a creature of our own invention. We are how we shape it in our psyche.

Maneuvering on auto-pilot, MayBelle's Fairlane cruised smoothly along Highway 50 through what turned into a starry night. Trees on the right-of-way cast clear shadows while the flat green farm fields seemed verdant even in the silvery moonlight.

"Or is that my imagining?" Eddie asked himself out loud.

When neither lady said anything, he realized they'd dozed off again. Passing the three wanderers next were the other out-of-the-way burghs Eddie and Charlene stopped at before. It now seemed eons ago they kidded themselves into believing Charles or some trace of him would pop up and reunite MayBelle's family. So it wasn't only Salem. For miles thereafter MayBelle's and Charlene's light breathing competed with the sound of Ford tires on the rough asphalt beneath. At last Eddie started up Eads Bridge. Spying the lights from St. Louis, he felt at home. Delivered, as he phrased the feeling to himself.

"Ma?" Eddie and Charlene said at the same time.

"Are we almost home?" MayBelle asked.

Her voice rang out like a small child's, so Eddie thought of their two Belles at home.

"Getting there," he said with a tenderness he hoped would glow in the darkness.

4

Eddie found the relatives' place in Florissant and picked up their girls. Together the grandmother, son, and daughter-in-law, as well as both granddaughters made it back to Richmond Heights before midnight. Both girls were happy to see them but fell asleep crossing the city. The grownups had intended to buy them presents, but unexpected events nixed that plan. Charlene promised the girls a special treat soon.

"Oh, boy, and what will that be?" Bonnie asked in excitement.

Charlene toyed with her joyously, suggesting first this and then that. "The Magic House? Children's Theater?" were the first ideas she came up with.

The girls voted yes, but went wildest for the Botanical Garden, since both were outdoors kids. Charlene wrote BG on the tabs and put her daughters to bed. Soon she and Eddie were slumbering as well. MayBelle stayed the night with them.

So ended the search for Charles. Waiting continued, but it settled in under the hustle and bustle of everyday. MayBelle kept on peddling doodads, souvenirs, and baseball cards, especially those for Jackie Robinson. At summer's end she bought a wheeled cart and was hawking her wares from a kiosk between Union Station and the Meeting of the Waters.

Eddie and Charlene went back to the classroom. Pretty soon and it'd be a decade-and-a-half since they started at Sumner. In the post-war years younger, better educated teachers joined them. Desegregated schools grew in number, but Sumner remained all-Negro. Charlene took evening classes and summer courses from the University and earned a Masters in Music Ed. Her choir grew and sang Negro spirituals and German *lieder* for churches or television. Eddie thought of starting a Ph. d. program but thought better of it. He liked it where he was.

"It still doesn't pay to be uppity in Whitey's America," MayBelle declared.

"Maybe, maybe not," Eddie answered. "It is what it is. You remember what Flo wrote about Merrit's opinion on whatever comes up."

"You believe that?" Charlene interjected. "If something is, then it surely is what it is. Whadda they call that, a tautology?"

"Dunno," Eddie answered with a shrug. "Unless it can be something other than what it is. But I see why Merrit believes it. Anyone ever challenge *him*? On anything?"

And so it came to pass. Flo and MayBelle *did* write to each other, often actually, and even called now and then during the months after MayBelle, Eddie, and Charlene returned from Salina. Taking place, as it did, across a stretch of country and the racial divide, their correspondence felt like a friendly and welcome tie between lovely ladies.

"Smooth sailing on calm waters," Charlene remarked.

Eddie nodded yes.

5

The first ripple on those calm waters came one lazy week-day. Charlene showed a letter. It came from Salina and had an official looking return: *W. Thornbuckle. Salina County Office Building.*

Shocked at seeing the sheriff's name, Eddie handed it back.

"You open it."

Charlene removed a card and read, *Dear Traveler: Happy to serve you. We know you enjoyed our lovely city.*

"What do you make of that?"

"Dunno. Is what it is," he joked.

"Your ma says you always did judge a man by his deeds."

"How do you figure? File it away?" Eddie wondered.

"Yes, for future reference," Charlene agreed.

Watching her put the card away, Eddie remembered MayBelle doing something like that, too, the last time Carlos wrote, long, long ago. She'd muttered something like, "Life'll knock you for a loop sometimes, give it half a chance."

Eddie was just a kid in those days and wondered what she meant.

EPILOGUE

1

He returned, all right, like MayBelle figured he would. Carlos, that is. On a spring day in the 1960s, MayBelle came home from peddling her wares near Meeting of the Waters and found her man leaning in the yard, on a cane. He had white hair and a graying beard. She didn't say hello, but motioned him to the door. He limped toward it.

"It's not locked, you know that, never is," she said at last. "I told you how it was down home. Never a stranger. Open your heart."

They went in. The bungalow was theirs again, after 23 years in limbo. Or maybe more. Neither said exactly how long, didn't remember maybe. Carlos looked around before spotting an easy chair. MayBelle made coffee and served him.

"Dogwood from outstate," she said.

He smacked his lips in satisfaction.

Not long afterward Eddie stopped by and found his parents at home. Carlos tried to get up but faltered. Holding his cane upright, he extended the other arm and Eddie helped him. They shook. Awkwardly. Standing face to face. Charlene looked in later, which meant more cups and fresh brew.

"We never met," Charlene said in greeting.

Carlos smiled broadly and uttered something in Spanish, but no one understood.

MayBelle flashed a joyous smile. "Like my man never been away."

But he had, of course. Carlos took his time saying why, most likely because he didn't know himself. Not fully anyway. His words didn't come gushing out in Spanglish like before, but he spoke pretty good English. If nothing else, he laid rumor to rest. No, no Santo Domingo consul's job in Texas and whatever folks said he did in KC, it was, you know, *tonterías*. He'd never been there.

What Carlos seemed to have done was hit the jackpot on a horse bet, for once. Years ago. Next he skedaddled to Albuquerque with a blonde, blue-eyed floozy named Reg, short for Regina. There they lived as man and wife before getting hitched. When his race track winnings ran out, they landed in the calaboose for vagrancy and bigamy, but Carlos so impressed the Law some discerning judge, who wanted to keep him underfoot and out of trouble, appointed him probation officer in a *barrio obrero*. Carlos lived in peace and quiet, but never forgot MayBelle, he swore. "Quarter of a century," he said and gnashed his teeth over the mistake of deserting her, until Reg drove her drunken car into a tree trunk one dark New Mexico night, probably on purpose. She killed herself and smashed Carlos's hip. He limped home again.

"To make things right," Eddie heard his father repeat, sometimes even to the Belles—Bonnie and Helena—when they came home from college. Yes, they were that big now and could smile, or smirk, when hearing fact mix with fiction. Yet Charlene wondered if her girls listened too much, despite themselves. With sheepskins in hand, the sisters did what the Washingtons, MayBelle's forebears, long ago didn't do. The young women headed off for jobs in the Golden State. "Exchanging one fable for another," their mother said with a sad but not displeased sigh.

2

After 1954 Dogwood became a constant. Flo sent new packages of its mellow brew to MayBelle and attached notes. She was still cancer free. Likely to remain so. Family Four now functioned as a woman's shelter. Gene McElroy went back to Michigan and kept an eye out for a new wife. Kristine and Donna moved on to bigger towns and better jobs, probably to be with their guys, who they insisted they had absolutely no need for. Ronny stayed at college and studied Psych. "A perfect shrink-to-be," Flo wrote.

Grubby hung on as sheriff. "How's that skinny boy in St. Louis, the one that loves his daughters so much?"

That's what Grubby must've wondered a lot, for some strange reason. Anyway, Flo quoted him asking Merrit the same question every time the two men met in town. Eddie saw in Flo's handwriting how she thought twice about using the n-word and crossed it out for boy. "The sheriff's always wearing an interested expression on his face, any time he asks his question," Flo concluded. "Grubby's just our Grubby."

For Merrit work went on. Diesel replaced steam. Passenger trains disappeared one after another. With them went the Starr Hotel. *European Style* tumbled down with the hotel bricks. Dust and smoke rose from the pavement, then drifted away with the wind.

"Youngsters leave, and don't come back," Flo complained about Salina.

MayBelle, who'd had Eddie read Charles's letters to her in wartime, looked through Flo's messages and penned a few herself.

Once she commented on the Forest Park Zoo. It was closing down the chimp show for good after reviving it a while. A new age. Many protests.

Then one day it was Carlos. Crossing a grocery store lot, he dropped a bag of oranges and papayas. He looked quizzically at the rolling fruit, then stood up straight and keeled over on his back. He made snoring sounds before passing.

"See it a lot in this heat," the ambulance paramedic said. "Sorry, folks."

MayBelle cried over him. On the hot asphalt. "Four hundred years you been pickin' cotton, silly man." A lesson in life, never learned.

Then there was Charles, never forgotten. Some people asked about him, too, and more than once. A few never let MayBelle lose hope, even if most folks shook their heads in private and guessed he was gone forever. MayBelle herself never wavered. "Wait some more, like me," she answered her kin and reminded them Charles was nothing if not his father's son.

Pasted to MayBelle's kitchen fridge was Charles's simple note, "Shall return."

"The men always do," MayBelle declared, with a shake of her head.

Slowly it boiled down to only Merrit and Flo in Salina, the farm town her kin had built, sort of. And MayBelle, Eddie, and Charlene in St.Louis, a Southern city just far enough North to be a little of both. The families wrote back and forth, then sent cards, till at last nothing. *Nada*, as Carlos would've said. They struggled on, black and white separate as always and unequal still, like Eddie once had stated, a nation seeking peace but at war with itself.

Eddie kept the Sardis teenager's penciled sketch for awhile, then tossed it out. His daughters never saw it.

3

Sylvia was happy to see Flo at the Carnegie Library one day. They chatted. About this and that. Flo had quit the millinery shop. Or maybe it quit her. No need to quibble, business had flagged for a while now. Flo admitted that with a shrug.

"I just wanted …," she started to say.

"Yes, I know. *The Social Contract*," Sylvia offered.

"No, something else … tunes I heard about."

The librarian waited while Flo hesitated.

"I thought Rousseau," Sylvia stuttered. "Well, to be honest I never read it all myself, that Frenchman's tough sledding, but we held it for you, the longest time, back then."

"Yes, but I thought of something kinda different."

"Like?"

"Phonograph records? The Ink Spots. Ever heard of 'em?"

Sylvia brightened. "My gosh, yes! Love 'em, gal, this way."

Carnegie's vinyl was in a high-ceilinged backroom. Lint covered most of the records, but Flo spent the hours winding and rewinding an ancient Victrola and listening to four suave colored crooners in the prime of their lives during the 1930s and 40s. The Ink Spots. Now nearly forgotten, they sang melancholy tunes about fond treasures and lingering losses. She wondered if the songwriters themselves experienced what they wrote about.

It touched Flo to look back. For her, the War years had felt too hectic to pause and imagine anyone else's darkest longings, like she heard in these lines. *Why tell them all your secrets? Who kissed here long ago. Whispering Grass, don't tell the trees, 'Cause the trees don't need to know.* Flo could imagine thousands of World War II GIs in fox holes overseas and their girls or mothers waiting back home. Longing. It was clear a sensitive man like Charles Washington might march off one day long after all that was over and be lost to his dear ones. Maybe lost from himself as well.

If I didn't care, would it be the same? Would my every prayer begin and end with just your name? There among the stray shellac 78 rpms, another glimpse of the past appeared. Flo saw MayBelle, who held steadfast to all around her, fearing what those who left might lose. *I'll never smile again, Until I smile at you. I'll never laugh again, What good would it do?* Flo remembered the talkative colored lady she'd learned to love so well smiling *and* laughing. Despite her troubles, MayBelle could dream of other worlds, where souls that wandered away always came back again.

With that soft mood over her, Flo saw a vision of her own, which had a way of coming back, always without warning. While enduring dull interludes of small-town living or the hurley-burley of rushing to and fro, she could stop and stand up straight as an arrow, as if transfixed. There before her appeared a frozen image of the smiling colored lady outside Union Station. Scores of people passed by during that day so long ago, but only one left a trace on Flo's psyche. This dark lady broke through her shield of privacy and fears of cancer and spoke to her heart. With a visceral tug Flo now wished the two of them to touch hands, join in spirit, and confirm their sisterhood or whatever undefinable need they both had.

Yet the vision grew faint, like a melody played on ancient, scratchy vinyl. Left alone with her imaginings, Flo picked up a stray 78 to file away and asked herself in quiet wonderment what their meeting might have led to in a more perfect world. She sighed and guessed she'd never know.

Acknowledgements

My HOMETOWN WAS QUIET, BUT MARKED by a Sundown ordinance. Mixed emotions about this measure reached a head on an evening in the late 1940s when our county judge answered a knock at his front door. Before him stood an African American in military uniform, who explained he was passing through town with his family and suffered an automobile accident. The traveler's wife was in the local hospital and their car needed repairs. Police had informed the man it was illegal for him to stay in town after sunset. With his wife in the hospital and he without transportation, the traveler had no way to leave town, but he would break the law if he stayed. Local hotels housed whites only. The African American was directed to the judge for a common sense solution.

I've never learned what decision the judge made. *If I Didn't Care* is my imaginative depiction of a similar situation as it might have played out during that same period, from 1941 (Pearl Harbor) to 1954 (Brown v. Board of Education). Was that era's sensibility about race different from ours? Was change truly possible?

Various individuals encouraged me to pursue these questions in fictional form. First was my father Jack McKnight. After his death, I recovered his collection of 78 rpm records by The Ink Spots. They were African-American songsters most popular during World War II. In post-war years my father had played all their songs for me. The Ink Spots recorded the ballad *If I Didn't Care* in January of 1939, suggesting humane caring for others under the threat of wartime ill will. By 1945 the recording sold 19,000,000 copies.

While writing *If I Didn't Care,* I received invaluable help from several other individuals. First was Jana Rankin, from my Illinois hometown, now living in Wyoming. She gave me information about the role her father played in seeking blood donors for the African American's injured wife after the 1940s accident. Mr. Rankin headed the local blood plasma unit and placed calls for blood donors for the injured African-American lady. He had little success. Many citizens reportedly feared they would contract a disease by donating to a colored person. Callers were said to have explained in vain that donors could only get a disease by receiving blood.

Then came literary editor Tomek Dzido, of London UK, who urged me to create my novel along present-day race-related lines suggested by events in Minneapolis's George Floyd killing from 2020. I appreciated Tomek's encouragement to keep the narrative as contemporary as possible, but I chose to base my story instead on the real-life problem in my hometown from an earlier era.

Most helpful of all has been Michael Mirolla, general editor at Guernica World Editions. I owe Michael a debt of gratitude. I queried him online about my manuscript on a Sunday morning in mid-July, 2022. That very day he invited me to submit the manuscript, but in a shorter version. I promised to try. He waited patiently, and perhaps skeptically, while I shortened the manuscript by 20,000 words. I greatly appreciate his forbearance in the face of my many subsequent questions about preparing the text.

During the editing process Guernica editor Gary Clairman has suggested important considerations. Gary asked, for example, if the word *awakening* was used as long ago as the 1930s to describe changes in public opinion about civil rights, as my text asserted. The discussion led us to consider Kate Chopin's novel *The Awakening*, which openly used the term in that context as early as 1899.

During the latest editing phase, Jacob Helton, of GTS at Gustavus Adolphus College, never failed to offer a helping hand in facilitating my work on the manuscript in its various stages. My colleague Larry Potts also generously read *If I Didn't Care* and offered valuable insights about its characters and themes. Most patient of all has been my wife Barb Zust, who has read the manuscript repeatedly, with agreements about its sentiments. Thanks to you all.

About the Author

A NATIVE OF ILLINOIS, ROGER McKNIGHT has studied English and Scandinavian Studies at Southern Illinois University and the University of Minnesota. He has worked in Chicago, Sweden, Puerto Rico, and Minnesota as a teacher of language and literature. In addition, he has worked with the mentally challenged in Sweden. Those experiences have defined his attitudes toward class, race, and civil rights. Besides pieces of short fiction in literary journals, Roger has published one novel, a book of creative nonfiction, and a social history of Scandinavian immigrant culture in America. His short story collection *Hopeful Monsters* (2019) traces the transformation of Minnesota between 1968 and 2018 from a homogeneous northern European ethnic enclave to a multi-national American state. His novel *If I Didn't Care* (2024) is a fictional reflection of growing up in the south Midlands of the United States during the debate over Brown v. Board of Education. Roger now lives in Minnesota.

Printed by Imprimerie Gauvin
Gatineau, Québec